T0271525

Carly Reagon lives in the countryside in South Wales with her husband, three young children and accident-prone greyhound. She works as a senior lecturer at Cardiff University, is a keen runner, singer and vegan cook. Her number one passion, other than writing, is wandering around historical sites and getting lost in the past.

Also by Carly Reagon

The Toll House

HEAR HIM CALLING

CARLY REAGON

SPHERE

SPHERE

First published in Great Britain in 2024 by Sphere

1 3 5 7 9 10 8 6 4 2

Copyright © Carly Reagon 2024

The moral right of the author has been asserted.

*All characters and events in this publication, other than those
clearly in the public domain, are fictitious and any resemblance
to real persons, living or dead, is purely coincidental.*

All rights reserved.
No part of this publication may be reproduced, stored in a
retrieval system, or transmitted, in any form or by any means, without
the prior permission in writing of the publisher, nor be otherwise circulated
in any form of binding or cover other than that in which it is published
and without a similar condition including this condition being
imposed on the subsequent purchaser.

A CIP catalogue record for this book
is available from the British Library.

ISBN 978-1-4087-2646-4

Typeset in Garamond Three by M Rules
Printed and bound in Great Britain by
Clays Ltd, Elcograf S.p.A.

Papers used by Sphere are from well-managed forests
and other responsible sources.

Sphere
An imprint of
Little, Brown Book Group
Carmelite House
50 Victoria Embankment
London EC4Y 0DZ

An Hachette UK Company
www.hachette.co.uk

www.littlebrown.co.uk

For my parents

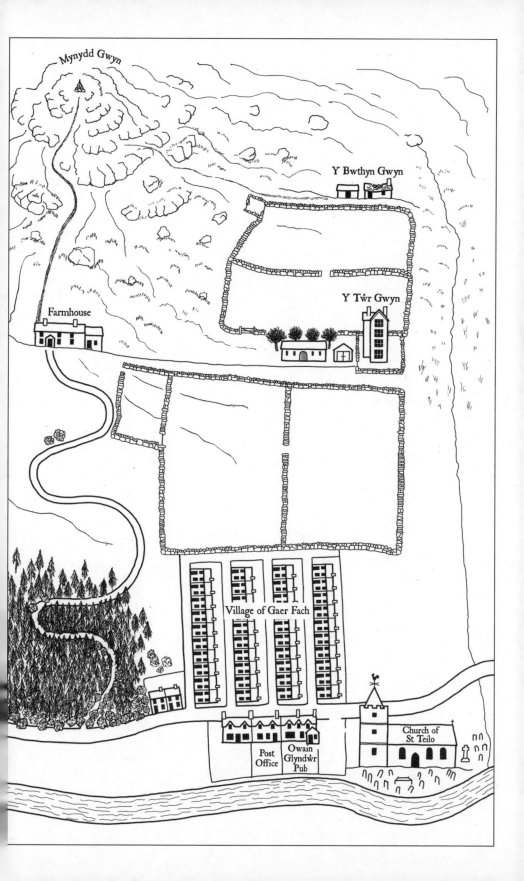

The boy looks up at the summit, at the white rocks and the concrete marker. He's lived in Gaer Fach all his life, but he's never been up there. Most days, he doesn't even notice the mountain range, or the startling clarity of the river as it rushes over stones and weeds, or the lush green fields. But today – maybe it's the heat, maybe it's the fact his parents are out and won't be back until teatime – he feels restless.

Across the yard, Cerys sits on an upturned crate, whittling sticks. She's wearing a dress the colour of the sun but it's streaked with dirt.

'Dwi eisiau ddringo i'r awyr,' he says. *I want to climb to the sky.*

Cerys pulls a face, her cheeks marked with the same dusty lines as her dress. 'Wyt ti'n crazy?'

He stares up at the concrete marker, what the grown-ups call the trig point. Is it really that crazy? All their lives they've been told to keep away from the mountain. They've been told it's dangerous. But it's the smallest mountain in the range. How dangerous can it be?

'Scaredy cat,' he pokes fun at his sister though she looks anything but, slicing a stick with the penknife – *his* penknife – alarmingly close to her thumb.

She puts the knife down. She's younger than him but just as fierce. 'What did you say?'

He smirks and wipes his hands on his shorts.

She stands up, scattering flecks of stick to the ground. 'All right then,' she says. 'Beat you to the summit.'

They run through the village, past the church and the pub, then take the mountain road that winds through a farmyard onto the footpath. The boy strips off his T-shirt and tucks it into his shorts, his white chest gleaming.

'Hey,' he calls, panting as Cerys scrambles ahead. 'Let's take this other path.' It's a copout, but he's tired. The mountain is harder than it looks, and they've been running for what seems like for ever. To his relief, Cerys doesn't argue, just follows him along the level track to the right, a sheep track rather than a real path. Looking down at the valley, they see their street, their house, their neighbours' cars like multicoloured beetles. Beneath them, about halfway up the mountain, is the place they call Y Twr Gwyn, *The White Tower*, that doesn't fit with everything else.

Eventually, the track ends in a cobbled yard.

He whistles. He's never seen this before, obscured as it is from the village by the tower. 'Look at this!'

In front of them is a rough stone cottage, no doors, no windows, just empty holes. They find sticks nearby and poke about inside, prodding at shadows, flicking the carcass of a dead bird in the fireplace. Cerys peers into a large box-like compartment at the back, while he sits in an old chair and pulls a packet of cigarettes from his pocket.

She turns. 'How did you get those? Mam will skin you alive.'

'No she won't. Not unless you tell her.' One, two, three strikes of the match. It flares in his hands, making him feel like a man, and the smoke flits upwards. A moment later, a crow screeches at them from the rafters, flapping its wings, fleeing into the daylight. He laughs to mask how startled he'd been, and makes shooting noises, aiming his fingers.

Then, everything changes. The sky darkens. A breeze tickles the nape of his neck.

He drops the cigarette and it burns a hole through his shorts, searing his skin. He jumps to standing, spins around. There's a figure in the doorway, a black silhouette against the afternoon sun. There's something about that figure. Something that makes the hairs on his head stand up on end. Maybe it's the way the figure is staring. Staring with such hate, with eyes that seem to leap from its body. Cat's eyes in the dark. Or maybe it's the glinting chain in its hand, one end wrapped around its wrist, the other end snaking to the floor.

'Rheda!' Cerys shouts from behind him. *Run!*

He takes his chance. There's a crack of light between the figure and the door frame, the gap just small enough for a boy like himself.

He darts into the sunshine and runs across the cobbles, onto the sheep track, his feet catching on the smaller rocks, not turning back until he reaches the mountain path. His thoughts gallop over each other. What is it he saw? What on earth is up there? And where is Cerys? He'd thought she'd followed him. He'd thought she was right behind. A cloud passes over, raising goosebumps along his arms. A buzzard sweeps overhead. And then he hears a ringing in the air. A sharp call of warning.

Somewhere on the mountain, Cerys is screaming.

1

FIFTY YEARS LATER

Whichever way Lydia turns, the view is stunning, the same images she's seen on Google only bigger and better: the proportions, the expanse, the sheer brutality of the rocks. They're 250 metres up, standing on a ridge in the shadow of the tower, the mountain a mere mound compared to the rest in the range. Next to her, Kyle gapes down at the valley, seemingly as awestruck as she is.

She thinks of the address on the paperwork, tries and fails to sound the words in her head. 'I'm sorry,' she turns to the housekeeper, a woman in her mid-thirties with big curly hair, 'but what did you say the mountain was called again?'

Eleri beams down at Jamie on Lydia's chest, strapped in his carrier, facing inwards. She holds out a hand and encourages him to grip her finger. 'Mynydd Gwyn. It means White Mountain in English, though some would say it's not actually a mountain, just a big hill.'

'But why is it white?' Kyle leans over and fusses with Jamie's socks, pulling them up.

Eleri shrugs. 'The rocks, I suppose. And the old tale about the dragons. You know the one I mean? The white dragon and the red.'

Lydia runs a hand through Jamie's fine hair, hiding her ignorance. Her knowledge of Welsh myths is even worse than her Welsh pronunciation. She looks back at the way they walked earlier: a rough country track to their left all the way to the top. From the trig point, they'd had a good view of the house, a tower of white pebbledash with a grey slate roof. It had been Kyle's idea to climb the mountain first, before meeting Eleri – get a feel for the area, he'd said – and she'd enjoyed the shared challenge of carrying Jamie to the top. On the other side, they'd seen another valley, another sweep of mountains. Not a house in sight.

'I suppose you already know about the history of the tower?' Eleri sorts through a bunch of keys.

'Not really.' Kyle shakes his head, looking slightly embarrassed, like he *should* know the history of the place he's inherited. But the truth is, from what Lydia can gather, he barely knew his grandfather.

'It was originally meant as a viewing tower. An Englishman named Barker had it built in the 1930s, but he didn't keep it for long. He sold it to an artist who turned it into a retreat, added the kitchen and bathrooms, but it didn't take off. There's been a succession of owners since then, as well as periods where it's sat empty. I believe Mr Jeffreys, your grandfather, was the sixth person to live here.'

'I like it,' says Kyle, looking upwards to the roof. There are a couple of slipped tiles, which make Lydia uneasy, but she supposes it's inevitable with the place so exposed. 'At least, it's unusual.'

'Not really the place for a family,' Eleri says. 'Have you any idea what you'll do with it?'

Kyle reaches for Lydia's hand and gives it a squeeze. It was a surprise receiving the solicitor's letter. They'd not even known his grandfather had moved to Wales, let alone to a tower. As far as they'd known, he'd lived in Suffolk all his life. 'Not yet.' He smiles.

Lydia traces the route of their descent – from the summit down a track, through a farm and then a right-angle along another, rougher track to the place they're standing. She understands now why the mountain's called Mynydd Gwyn. The slopes are a patchwork of stone and purple heather and, from here, with the sun brushing the summit, the rock at the top *does* look white. From this angle, it seems impossible that they were standing there an hour ago, sunning themselves and taking selfies. It's too craggy, too difficult. The phrase flits through her mind: *too dangerous.*

'Shall we go inside?' Eleri fits a key into the door at the side of the house and swings it open. There's a smell of damp that immediately takes Lydia back to her student days. *I think I've seen enough already*, she wants to say, but Kyle is pulling her in, bending his head though the doorway is higher than he is. She supposes it's the darkness of the place. The feeling that they're entering a cave deep underground.

'Light switch is somewhere. I haven't been here for a while. Aha, here it is.'

A chill runs up Lydia's arms and Jamie whimpers, pulling

back from her chest. 'It's okay, little fellow.' Outside, it's baking hot, but in here it's like standing in the depths of winter. She cradles Jamie through the baby carrier as she makes out an L-shaped kitchen with dirty yellow units. There's a microwave that looks like an early model, an electric cooker encrusted with dirt and rust, and a fridge with its door wide open. The stumpy tail of the L is dominated by a sink and, above it, there's a small square window.

'I cleaned everything after your grandfather fell ill,' Eleri says, though it's hard to believe. She pulls back a curtain in the interior wall and steps through an archway into the next room. Then she folds back the shutters. Sunlight floods in, pooling on a coffee table and a couple of tatty armchairs.

'From London, did you say?'

'That's right,' says Kyle.

'I bet there aren't many views like this in London.'

Lydia lingers in the kitchen, running her fingers over one of the worktops, gathering dust. 'Strange they only put big windows at the front of the house. Why make the kitchen window so tiny? It doesn't make any sense.' She thinks of the building from the outside. The south side, facing the summit, is completely devoid of windows bar this one. 'Why would you build a viewing tower with only half a view?'

She leans over the sink and presses her hands against the pane. She can see the top of the mountain and the cloudless sky, but it's as if she's holding a postcard rather than viewing the real thing.

Eleri's still fussing with the shutters on the other side of the archway. 'All I know is that Barker ran out of money. Or lost interest in the project. Or maybe both. It was quicker to finish the tower this way. Mr Jeffreys did some research, told me bits and pieces, and that's how I know. I think he was lonely. I used to clean up here once a week. It was about all the company he had.'

There's a heavy silence and Lydia imagines Kyle thinking about the side of his family he doesn't really know.

'Do you want to see the rest?' Eleri opens a door into a hallway and ushers them through, up a flight of stairs. The rooms are stacked one on top of the other, following the same stumpy L-shape as the ground floor. 'It's a strange design,' Eleri admits, 'but then, I'm no architect. This was Mr Jeffreys' bedroom here, with the en suite bathroom.'

There's an oppressive smell of old clothes and damp linen but Kyle doesn't seem to notice, testing the floorboards, whistling at the view. Lydia wonders if he's imagining his grandfather waking up in the old-fashioned bed, shuffling on the slippers that are still tucked beneath it. She glimpses the bathroom behind, filling the small protruding space above the kitchen window – the bath and overhead shower, the extractor fan, the faded baby-blue mat.

'And then, if you follow me up the next flight of stairs, there's a spare bedroom here with another en suite bathroom.' They peer into a space that mimics the one below but without the furniture. 'And then, on the third floor, which also has a washroom, is the room Mr Jeffreys used to paint in.'

They follow her up the last flight of steps.

'Wow!' Kyle catches Lydia around the waist as they enter the painting studio and stare dizzily at the wide sweep of valley. Instantly, she forgets her reservations. With the extra height, the view through the window is mesmerising.

'You can see Cadair Idris if you look far enough to the left. Snowdon's a little further around. That's the village of Gaer

Fach below us, the one you drove through to get here. I run the village shop with my husband, Jon. It's a nice little community. Pub and a shop and not much else. It's very quiet. Did you say you're a sculptor?' Eleri looks at Lydia.

'That's right.'

'No doubt busy in London?'

Lydia smiles. Truth is, not busy enough.

Eleri fills the gap. 'I'm sorry about what happened. I found Mr Jeffreys on the doorstep downstairs. Heart attack, as I'm sure you know.'

'It's okay. We weren't close.' Kyle speaks to the window.

'Still, family's family.'

'Is it?' He turns towards Eleri, taking in the stacked canvases and paint-splattered easel. The paintings are traditional, country scenes: moonlight through the forest; a sleepy canal. 'Did you say there was a cellar?'

Lydia shivers. The last thing she wants is to explore underground. 'I think I'll take Jamie outside instead if that's okay?' She needs the warmth of the sun on her face, not another musty room. 'We'll wait for you in the garden.'

She leaves Kyle to nose around the house some more and takes the three flights of stairs to the ground floor. Jamie's fallen asleep, his head snug against the inside of the carrier. She spends a few moments ensuring he's comfortable, then steps outside. There's not much of a garden: a small patch of lawn that's knee high, an oil tank and a drystone wall bordering the steep rise to the summit. Adjacent to a garage, there's a barn that's padlocked shut. She stands on tiptoes and peers through a cobwebbed window at the space inside. It's bigger than she'd expected and she feels a quiver of excitement. This place would make a perfect studio. She imagines her workbench against the far wall, her tools laid out, her stones covering the floor, her favourite pieces on shelves and plinths. The idea of a space to herself thrills her. A space that she wouldn't have to pay rent on, or share with other people. A space with enough room to make a safe area for Jamie, where she can keep an eye on him as she works.

She steps back onto the lawn and lifts her gaze to the summit. There's something up there, halfway between the house and the ridge at the top. An outcrop of rocks or another building? In front of it, a man is waving down at the tower. No, not the tower. He's waving at *her*. She can feel it, just as she can feel the breeze in her hair and a chill on her neck.

She's about to wave back when Jamie cries out in his sleep. She leans over and rearranges the muslin cloth behind his head. At the same time, the house door creaks open.

Kyle appears, blinking in the sunlight.

'God, you gave me a fright!' She looks back to where the man was standing. Nothing there. Just a trick of the light, the hazy summer sun.

Kyle rubs her bare shoulders, sliding his fingers beneath the straps of the baby carrier. 'Here. Let me take that. You've been carrying him for ages.'

She shakes her head. 'He's asleep. Leave him be.'

'You all right? You've got goosebumps.'

'Just a breeze.' She hesitates. 'You're not seriously thinking about moving here, are you?'

Kyle sweeps flecks of dust from his hair. 'It's not that stupid, is it? Haven't we always dreamed of the country? Getting away from it all? Bringing up our family somewhere safe?'

She looks down at the crown of Jamie's head, then across to the valley. The same thrill as when she looked inside the barn.

The possibility of escape, of getting away from London, from the crowds and the traffic, the feeling of being hemmed in, the panic attacks. And then, there's the potential of this place. She thinks of the view from the front of the house, the same view she's looking at now, the way it transforms the space inside.

'Think about it,' he says. 'Out here we'd have no rent. No mortgage. All this space for J-J to grow up in. All this healthy fresh air.'

'I thought I saw someone on the mountain,' she says, turning in the opposite direction, glancing up at the trig point and the jagged rocks. 'A man waving down at me.'

'A hillwalker, probably. Or a shepherd. Remember that farm we walked through earlier?'

'It freaked me out,' she says, though she knows it's stupid. 'Someone watching me like that. Watching Jamie.'

'There's bound to be tourists.' He grins and she knows he's right. *Of course* there are tourists. 'Come on. There's something else I want to show you.' He finds her hand and pulls her further into the garden.

'What is it?'

He doesn't answer, just leads her through the long grass, past the kitchen window and the rusted oil tank. A sheep bleats from the fields. A buzzard circles overhead, so close she swears she can hear the beating of its wings. 'It's on the other side of the tower. Something that makes this whole thing perfect.'

2

Three months later, Kyle brings the kettle to a rumble and fishes teabags from a plastic carrier bag. The kettle's ancient, a grimy white, marked with indiscriminate splodges of food. Since arriving in Gaer Fach two days ago, he hasn't unpacked. He likes the idea he could grab his stuff and leave at any moment if he needs to. Not that he *will* need to. It's just that the house – his grandfather's brick tower – isn't quite as he'd remembered it from the time in the summer. He'd not realised it was quite so damp and cold. He'd forgotten just how isolated it was, or rather he'd thought only about the view and not the fact the village was miles away. This is going to take some getting used to, he thinks. Living in a tower in the middle of nowhere.

He scrapes paint from his arms as he waits for his tea to brew. There's a patch of dry skin on his elbow that's irritating him, that wasn't there before. Maybe it's the mountain air or something in the paint. Something that's making him itch like mad. He makes a determined effort not to scratch, takes one of his grandfather's spoons, and squeezes his teabag against the side of the cup. Then, he turns to the lounge and views the scrappy paintwork through the archway. He'd offered to come up ahead and start decorating the place as a favour to Liddy, but progress is slow. The paint doesn't want to stick to the walls, and it's so bloody cold, he can barely move his hands. On top of all this, he's got a permanent headache, made worse when he thinks about Liddy and J-J, his desire to make this perfect for them both.

If he's honest, it's not just Liddy who's scared about the move. Every night since he's been here, he's woken to utter blackness, wondering what the hell they've done. He thinks of their tiny flat in London, the one Liddy is packing up ready for their official move on Monday, and wishes he was there, breathing in the scent of her, hearing J-J snuffling in his cot. In the light of day, he knows it's just change. Change always messes with you, regardless of the reasons behind it. Even if it's for the best. And this *is* for the best. Liddy gets so panicked in London, and he needs the change too, desperately so. His career as a web developer is taking off and he wants to make a real go of it, escape from the gang of mates he hangs out with, old mates from university, headed by his best friend Charlie. Of course, he likes his friends, but he doesn't have rich parents like they do. He can't afford to hop from one job to another, partying all weekend, sometimes into the week as well.

He takes his tea into the lounge, hugs it tight in an attempt to warm up. The lounge is still dotted with his grandfather's furniture. The paintings on the walls are all originals, landscapes signed by Edward Jeffreys. Not for the first time, he has a sense he's trespassing in someone else's house. Searching his mind for memories of his grandfather, there's not much there: bumpy car rides to the house in Suffolk, a dark hallway, a narrow-mouthed lady who must have been his grandmother, a game of toy soldiers laid out ready for him on a rug. He's already found the old set. A box shoved under the bed upstairs, an army of plastic soldiers. And something else: a wooden soldier-doll with tattered khaki clothing. Had he remembered this as a child? Before his grandfather stopped speaking to his mum altogether? There'd been a chime of something, but then it was gone and he'd shoved the doll back in the box with the rest.

Now, he takes the paintings down and stacks them in a corner, humming to himself, wishing he had a radio for company. The internet signal is intermittent at best – something that *definitely* needs sorting, and which hadn't seemed a problem when he'd checked the coverage – and he's not used to feeling so disconnected. Then, he thinks of that other thing that impressed him so much in the summer, spied from the upstairs window: the stream. He's going to divert it into a forebay, run pipes to a generator, feed electricity directly into the house. He'd shown it to Liddy on that very first day, though she hadn't quite grasped its significance. She'd been freaked by something she'd seen on the mountain, and though he'd tried to take her mind off it, telling her his plans, he'd had a feeling she was only half-listening.

He climbs to the top of the stepladder, leans sideways, dripping paint on the floor. He's dying to get going with the stream – it's mind-blowing just thinking about powering the entire house off that tiny flow of water – but his plans will have to wait. For Liddy's sake, he needs to make these aesthetic changes first.

A noise startles him from somewhere in the building. He stands stock still, paintbrush raised. There it is again. A sound in the kitchen. He breathes audibly, gritting his teeth, then clambers down again, inadvertently knocking over his cup of tea.

He picks up the mug and listens. Just the wind buffeting the tower. Y Twr Gwyn the house is called. *The White Tower.* Except he doesn't like that. He wants to call it something light, cheerful, like Mountain View or Sunny Hill. He'll suggest it to Liddy.

He tiptoes through the archway into the kitchen. Still nothing. He scans the knackered worktops, the mismatch of crockery he's pulled from the cupboard. Nothing there that could have made a sound like that, like a chain being dragged across the stone paving. He laughs out loud to stem his fear. That's bloody ridiculous. Probably rats. Or maybe a bird flew into the kitchen window and made a strange sound as it slipped down the glass. They do that sometimes, don't they, looking for shelter?

He looks down and realises he's scratching his arm again, scratching so hard he's drawn bubbles of blood. He pulls his fingers away. He needs to get used to it, that's all. The sounds of the countryside. The sounds of an old house.

3

Lydia stands on the mountain with the tower behind her, watching the mover's van bump back down the track then turn left down the road to the village. The difference between London and Wales is stark. The mountains are silver against the evening sky and, though it's only September, the air is sharp. She scans the wood further down, the footpaths crisscrossing the fields, the scar of an old quarry on the far left. She revels in the idea of exploring, buying an OS map, filling a flask with tea and wandering for hours. Now that Jamie's bigger, she could carry him in the baby backpack; she'll take Kyle too when he isn't working. This is going to be the making of them, she just needs to believe it.

'Don't be long,' Kyle had said when she'd left for her walk. 'I've missed you, you know.' He'd jogged Jamie up and down in his arms and she'd marvelled at the similarity between them. Mini-Me, Kyle sometimes calls Jamie. But today Mini-Me had scowled back at his father, stubby hands reaching for the barely there beard he's grown in a week. The beard makes Kyle look strange, not quite like her husband, but she hasn't mentioned it yet.

'I've missed you too. I just need to stretch my legs.'

He'd smiled. 'And I've got a little surprise for later, okay?'

She walks fast along the track to the farm buildings, half a mile to the right, the wind buffeting her coat. There's no one about, just a tractor with mud-clogged tyres and an ancient Land Rover with a dented bumper. The windows of the farmhouse are hung with sun-bleached curtains and, through the nearest one, she can make out a sink and a bottle of washing-up liquid.

She's just about to turn up the path that leads from the farm to the summit when a dog appears, barking. A one-eyed border collie with muck-encrusted fur. She jumps backwards, landing in a puddle, telling herself to act calm. The dog won't hurt her unless she makes a fuss.

'Hey, little dog.' She holds out the back of her hand. 'That's right. Don't growl. Shall we be friends?'

The dog sniffs her fingers, then crouches low as if about to pounce.

She tucks her hand back inside her sleeve. 'Okay, maybe not.' She walks fast but not *too* fast, back the way she's come, not wanting to risk crossing the farmyard or giving the dog an excuse to chase. Instead, she focuses on the tower at the far end of the track, trying to conjure a sense of safety, of home. *Home.* The word doesn't sit right. This isn't her home, not yet, despite Kyle's efforts to make it friendly, painting the interior walls, changing the name to Sunny Hill. He's even hung a sign with the new name on the gate. She glances back at the farm – thank God the dog has stopped at the boundary – and breaks into a run.

She finds Kyle and Jamie in the lounge. Jamie's in his bouncy chair still warily eyeing his father, and Kyle's crouched next to the fireplace, stacking kindling.

'There's a dog with one eye at the farm,' she gabbles.

Kyle sits back on his heels and surveys his handiwork. 'I know. She's got puppies. We're going over tomorrow to choose one.'

'What?'

Kyle grins. 'I said I had a surprise.'

'But, a dog? A puppy?' The idea sounds like madness. 'Haven't we got enough on our plates already?' She takes Jamie from his bouncy chair and holds him tight. He's warm and milky, nuzzling into her.

'Actually, the farmer was insistent. Jumped in front of the car to flag me down. Said we must have a dog for protection.'

'For protection?' She laughs. 'Against what? There's nothing out here.'

He takes matches from a tin box inside the fender and looks serious. 'That's the point. We're isolated. It makes us vulnerable.'

'I suppose.' She crouches beside him. 'What are you doing?'

'Seeing if the chimney's clear.'

The kindling won't light. Kyle blows on it gently until it sparks, darts of yellow streaking up the wisps of wood. The smell reminds her of winter evenings, bonfires and hot chocolate. She huddles into him, watching the fire expectantly, but the smoke makes her eyes sting. A minute later, it's billowing into the room. Kyle jumps up, hand to his mouth, glancing anxiously at Jamie wriggling in her arms. 'Shit.'

They run outside, gulping the fresh air, looking up at the chimney. In the semi-darkness, Lydia sees a trickle of smoke.

'It's blocked,' Kyle says like he's been dealing with chimneys all his life. 'There should be more of it than that.'

'What do we do now?' The last of the sunlight is filtering through the clouds, casting them in a pale, almost eerie light.

'Stay here until the smoke clears, I suppose. I'll get our coats and a blanket for J-J.'

She waits while Kyle goes indoors, pacing the garden to keep herself warm. The house from the back is bleak, just that one tiny window looking into the kitchen. Hard to believe they own a house like this. *Live* in a house like this. The name, Sunny Hill, is a joke; she'd rather the Welsh name Y Twr Gwyn, which is descriptive at least. She thinks of the tatty furniture, the stacks of crockery that aren't theirs, the musty smell of the wardrobe and linen cupboard. Kyle's made a start at clearing out his grandfather's stuff, heaping it in the garage for sorting later. But she's a feeling it's not going to be that easy, sweeping one life out, replacing it with another, transforming the house into the one she's designed in her mind. Maybe she'd feel better if she knew more about him, what sort of person Edward Jeffreys was.

Holding Jamie in one arm, she traces a finger over the thick wooden frame at the bottom of the kitchen window, lingering over the grooves carved in the middle. There's a cross like the Christian symbol deep in the wood, and something more intricate, a circle with interlinking lines. She's seen it before, or something like it, in books about the area. It's a Celtic cross. Above it, nestling right against the glass, is a line of small red berries. She rolls one between her fingers and glances across the garden, to the tree behind the barn. A tree with yellowing leaves and brilliant clusters of red berries, the same sort of tree she's seen growing near the farm. A rowan tree.

'Oh, there you are.' Kyle comes back, lumbered with coats and blankets. Then he swings out a carrier bag. 'Surprise number two. A little celebration. Our new house. Our *first* house. J-J's first proper home. I was saving it until later, but hey.'

He pulls items from the bag: champagne, two mugs, a bottle of milk for Jamie. He takes the champagne to the wall at the front, uncorks the bottle and fills the mugs. 'Sorry, it's not exactly glamorous. I couldn't find any wine glasses, let alone flutes.'

She tucks Jamie inside the blanket and takes one of the mugs. They sit on the wall, drinking in silence, looking down at the village. It seems so far away, tiny like a toy village, two miles following the road from the farm, much less than that trespassing through the fields. She feels she could reach down and flick it all away. And then there'd be nothing. Nobody.

4

She gets up early, unable to sleep. She has a sense of everything being different: the creaky old bed, the new mattress she'd insisted on, the draught from the stairway, the pervasive smell of damp. She creeps across the bedroom, trying not to wake Kyle, feeling for her cardigan on the floor beside the cot. Then she bends down and listens to the reassuring sound of Jamie. Last night, she'd thought she would never get him to sleep – he'd slept too much on the journey and he was understandably unsettled – but now, although he'd woken twice in the night, crying for milk, he's dead to the world. She shudders at the phrase and peers behind the curtains. It's still dark, only four-thirty, but she knows she won't sleep again, despite the weariness she feels in her mind and body.

Downstairs, she scrapes the remains of last night's dinner into the bin. None of them had been hungry, too wired from the move, even Jamie had spat out his favourite yogurt and refused to finish his milk. She washes the plates they'd retrieved from the packing boxes and sterilises a couple of baby bottles in the microwave for later. Although she hates the kitchen, hates the old worksurfaces, she's a vague sense of satisfaction as she cleans, imagining how the room will look in a few days' time: the new workstations in oak and white marble snug against the walls, the Belfast sink, the kitchen island in the middle of the flagstones. It's their one big expense, one they can't afford, piled onto credit cards. Then, there's the view from the other side of the tower, the way the sunlight floods in when the shutters are drawn. She can't wait to get started on the transformation, choosing soft furnishings to complement the valley through the windows, creating a space that's practical and homely and stylish all at once. After that, she'll attack the garden, erecting decking for barbeques and leisurely summer evenings. Making it theirs.

She finds a bottle of cleaning fluid beneath the sink and pulls on an old pair of plastic gloves, then gets to work again. It's four days until the workmen are due to arrive and she can't bear the thought of living like this until then. She wipes the chipped Formica, scrapes the inside of cupboards, polishes the old-fashioned taps. A stain on the worksurface opposite the sink refuses to budge. It looks like a coffee stain, but it seems to sprawl with her efforts, seems to darken. She finds a fresh cloth and goes over it again, squirting more cleaning fluid, scrubbing harder, faster. Irritation grows inside her. How could Kyle have stood being out here like this for a week by himself?

Defeated, she wrings the cloth out over the sink and looks up.

There's a light beyond the garden, drawing her attention. A light high up on the mountain, orange like a flame, moving one way and then the other, a few yards back and forth. She's a feeling it's looking for something, searching between the rocks and the tufts of heather. She wipes the condensation from the window, then watches, mesmerised, wondering who would be on the mountain so early in the morning.

Martha.

She spins at the word, expecting to see Kyle behind her, but there's no one there. Kyle has pulled down the old red curtain separating the kitchen from the lounge, wanting the light to flood through the archway from the bay window out front. But the shutters on the front windows are closed and even if they *were* open, there's no sunlight yet, just fields and fields of darkness.

'Kyle?' she calls, her voice small and hesitant. No response. She rubs her face. God, she's seriously sleep deprived and stressed from the move. It must have been the wind or something in the house, some unseen mechanism, making a noise that sounded like a human voice.

Martha.

She pivots back to the window, pulse racing. This time it was clearer, coming from beyond the window. A man's voice. She steadies herself against the sink, knowing she didn't imagine it. The light has disappeared from the mountainside and she's staring at her own reflection in the window, ghost-like against the dark. She can't see the garden, let alone the summit. There could be anything out there, a stranger at the door, a fox near the barn, a predator either human or animal, and she wouldn't know it. She wipes the window again, the cold condensation dribbling down her fingers.

She pictures a fox, the russet of its fur, its watchful eyes. That's all it is, she tells herself: a wild animal. And the light was a shepherd with a torch on the higher slopes.

She brings her fingers away and dries them on her cardigan. Impossibly, the darkness seems to deepen. She's too scared to look up again. Too scared to catch her reflection in the window, just in case. *Just in case it's not me.*

She tells herself not to be stupid. There's nothing there. Just the garden and the fields and fresh air. Still, she wishes there was a curtain to shut it all out. She glances upwards, averting her eyes from the window. There isn't even a rail or a runner. Why would anyone have a window like this, even a small one, gaping into utter blackness? It's the first thing she'll do when it's light, go through the boxes in the garage, find something, anything, to cover the square.

5

She goes back to bed and tries desperately to doze – Kyle and Jamie are still peacefully sleeping – but all she can think about is that voice, that sound. She tosses and turns, seeing the light on the mountain in her mind. It's like it's calling to her, begging her to investigate. When she can't ignore it any longer, she grabs her running kit from the pile of clothes on the floor and goes out. As she runs along the track, she focuses on the view: the valley carved between the mountains, the sun rising on the horizon in a watercolour of purple and pink. It's thrilling but she can't quite believe it's theirs. It's all too surreal and she still feels unsettled. If only she could find the source of the light, at least that would be something.

She slows when she reaches the farm, but the collie bitch fails to appear. Instead, an older dog pads disinterestedly through a group of chickens. The farmhouse curtains are drawn but there's no sign of anyone about, just a bucket abandoned in the middle of the yard.

She retraces their footsteps from the summer, taking the path that runs from the yard through the line of rowan trees all the way to the summit, slowing to a fast walk. She'd forgotten how deceptively steep it is, how the mountain seems to take over her entire body. Her thighs ache, her throat hurts with each lungful of breath, her ears throb with the morning cold. The path breaks into a series of muddy gullies between the rock and she tries her best to select the driest. Three-quarters of the way up, she stops and scans the countryside to her right, looking for signs of life, anything to explain the light. But the only thing of note is a sheep track running parallel to the tower's own track. She follows it as it weaves between the rocks. Suddenly, she's sliding, her trainers slipping through bog, unable to get a grip. She hits the ground with a thump, landing on rock, and lies dazed for a second, looking down, seeing the cascade of smaller rocks beneath her. A few feet more and she would have gone tumbling over.

She pulls herself up, shaking the mud from her trainers, scanning the way ahead. The path, which had been clear to begin with, is a suggestion rather than a definite line, pitted with darker patches of bog. At the end of it, directly above the tower, there's a shadowy lump, which looks like another farm building.

But after the fall, she's no longer in the mood for exploring. She has a sudden impulse to get back to the tower. She imagines Jamie waking up, calling out for her, his little cries echoing through the baby monitor into the lounge, through the archway to the kitchen, bouncing off the window. She's only recently given up breastfeeding and the physical bond is still there, still strong.

'You smell of fresh air,' Kyle beams at her when she steps into the cocoon of coffee and toast smells. The kitchen has transformed in the time she's been out. Kyle has laid Jamie's playmat on the floor, padding it with a blanket beneath, and Jamie's smiling up at her. 'Where did you go?'

'The mountain,' she says. 'Or rather, further *up* the mountain. I found a footpath beneath the summit. If I'd carried on, I would have seen down our chimneys.' She feels awake, clearheaded, no longer the neurotic woman who woke at four-thirty to clean, who imagined – it hardly seems plausible now – a disembodied voice.

Kyle hands her a mug of coffee and surveys her sodden trainers and mud-splattered leggings. 'Talking of chimneys, I found rods in the cellar.' He nods at the sheet of plastic and various poles and brushes through the archway. 'You see,' he says, just as Jamie begins to bawl. He picks him up and hands him over so that she's juggling both her son and her coffee. 'I'm on a mission to make this place work.'

Two hours later, they walk to the farm, Jamie in the baby backpack for the first time, seeming too small, too vulnerable within the bulky frame. Lydia keeps checking him, fiddling with the straps over Kyle's shoulders, ensuring he's comfortable. Jamie gurgles back at her, blowing spit-bubbles. Satisfied, she looks down at Gaer Fach, the path of the river snaking behind the church, the main road and the four parallel streets shooting off from it that, from here, look like tines of a fork. She counts the number of identical workers' cottages.

'Forty,' she says. 'Give or take a couple.'

Kyle lifts his head from the track. She knows his mind is on other things, all his plans for the tower, his schemes to make them self-sufficient. Over breakfast, he'd taken a pen and paper, drawn out his ideas and made calculations about the generator. 'What did you say?'

'The cottages. There are forty cottages.'

'What?'

'In the village. There are forty cottages in the village. Though it looks too small for that. Too cramped. Little Fort, that's what the name means. I looked it up. Gaer Fach means Little Fort.' She smiles to herself. She's determined to learn Welsh, one way or another. But, as they near the farm, the one-eyed collie runs into the yard, tail twitching, growling into the frigid air, sullying her mood. She thinks of Jamie, how fragile he is, and wonders if they're about to make a massive mistake.

'Blodwen!' A man appears from the farmhouse. A big-boned man in his mid-fifties, wearing a boiler suit and dirty black boots. He drags the dog by its collar, shooing it inside, then scowls at the visitors. 'Beth da chi eisiau?'

Lydia shakes her head. 'I'm sorry. We're English.'

The man grunts and, momentarily, she wonders if he only speaks Welsh. Then he clear his throat, 'I said, what do you want?'

'We've come to look at the puppies. I'm Lydia. I believe you've already met Kyle?'

Kyle shakes his head. 'It was another man I met. But, pleased to meet you.'

The man nods his acknowledgement, then steps into the yard. 'Follow me.' He strides towards a barn on the other side, pulls wide a metal door and herds them through. 'There were six in the litter, but we've only four left. You can take your pick.'

The puppies are penned in the far corner of the barn. They paw over each other to get their attention, licking Lydia's hand as she leans in, sniffing her sleeves. Their little bodies are fat and ungainly, all paws and stomach, and already she feels herself melting.

Kyle crouches next to her, looking as smitten as she is. 'This is your call. Go on. Pick whichever one you like.'

She looks across at Jamie fallen asleep in the backpack. 'You're sure this is a good idea?'

'Country living and all that. It will be good for us. Good for J-J. Trust me.'

'That one!' The smallest at the back, tail wagging, desperate but unable to get over the others. 'It looks intelligent.'

Kyle laughs and she wishes the man wasn't there, standing over them. 'Is it a boy or a girl?'

The man fishes a packet of cigarettes from his pocket. 'That one's no good.'

'No good?'

'It's the runt.'

She thinks of Jamie. He's never been around animals, not close up anyway, but the puppy looks harmless. 'We'll take it,' she says.

'I said, it's no good.' The man almost shouts the words, before lighting a cigarette.

Kyle lays a hand on Lydia's arm. 'I think my wife would prefer something small.'

The man says nothing, just draws on his cigarette. She thinks he's going to resist, going to say something more, but eventually he leans over and lifts the puppy by the scruff of its neck. 'It's a bitch,' he says dismissively. 'Forty quid.'

Soft paws fight the air to get close to Lydia, landing with a flurry of tail and tongue and pink puppy tummy on her shoulder. 'I'm afraid we haven't anything,' she says. 'A basket or lead or food or whatever else a puppy might need. We should come back later.'

The man pulls the puppy away and dumps it back in the pen. 'There's stuff in the house you can have. Follow me.'

They traipse back across the yard to the farmhouse. It looks dirtier from this angle with its mud-streaked walls and grey slate roof, an eyesore framed against the valley on the other side. The man leads them into a cramped kitchen and rummages beneath the sink.

Lydia clears her throat. 'I'm sorry, I didn't catch your name?'

'Emlyn.' The man flings items onto the table, already piled high with newspapers and packets of food. In the middle of it all, balancing on the boxes of cereal, is a shotgun. 'Dad – Mr Jones – is the farmer.'

He hands them a cardboard box with a few items: lead, food, bowl. 'Must be the runt's lucky day,' he says. 'I was going to drown it this afternoon.'

The mood from the kitchen follows them as they walk back up the track, carrying the puppy in the cardboard box. The puppy seems unsettled, pawing the cardboard, chewing one of the flaps.

'We should put it on the lead,' Kyle says, kicking stones with his boots.

'Not it. *Her.*'

'Okay, *her*.' He smiles, softening. 'You've changed your tune, I thought you weren't keen.'

'I wasn't. But, well, just look at her. She's almost as cute as Jamie.'

He laughs. 'Now I know you're kidding. So, what are we going to call her?'

She looks at the puppy's white paws. 'What about Snowy?'

Kyle pulls a face. 'I was thinking of Irene.'

'You can't call a puppy Irene.'

'Why not? I had a cat called Irene when I was little. She was cute.'

She sets the box down on the track and attaches the lead given them by Emlyn, a heavy-duty choke chain that seems completely unsuitable for the task. The puppy pulls on the end of it, oblivious to the choke mechanism, seeming eager to get to the tower, to find shelter from the wind.

At Sunny Hill, they lay Jamie down in his cot, then set the puppy loose in the kitchen and allow her to roam, exploring with her nose. Lydia puts a bowl of water on the floor and dishes out a handful of biscuits.

'I think she likes it here,' she says.

Kyle smiles back at her, then bends down and ruffles the puppy's fur. 'Welcome to the family.'

They make sandwiches and sit on the sofa together, the one that had looked good in their London flat, but here seems too small, squashed between the two formal armchairs. Already, she's decided which one was Edward Jeffreys'. Which one he liked to sit in to read the newspaper, to drink his tea. The one with the sagging cushions and faded armrests. She wants to ask

Kyle to move it to the garage, but it doesn't seem right, clearing someone out so entirely.

The puppy sniffs at their feet, then pisses on the floorboards.

Kyle jumps up. 'Martha! No! Bad dog!'

Lydia dumps her sandwich on the plate. 'What did you say?'

'I said, bad dog. She pissed on the floor. Didn't you see it?' There's anger in his eyes and she realises she's never really observed him around animals.

'It was you!'

'What?'

'Earlier. It was you saying that word. I thought it was me. I thought I was going crazy.'

'What word?'

'Martha.'

Kyle starts manically mopping the floor with one of Jamie's muslin cloths. 'I only just thought of it. It just sort of came to me. Like it was ...' he crumples his brow, 'like it was meant to be.'

'It freaked me out. I thought someone else was in the house.'

'Seriously. I've never known any Marthas before in my life. It's just that she *looks* like a Martha. Or ... I don't know. Hey! Martha?' The puppy runs towards him and rolls over. He tickles her tummy, apparently no longer mad at her. 'You see?'

Lydia rubs her temples. Kyle's right, Martha seems to suit her, and weirdly she seems to respond to the name. But she doesn't like it. Doesn't like the fact they both thought it or dreamed it. 'It must have been you,' she says at last. 'There's no other explanation. You must have shouted it in your sleep.'

6

Kyle sits by himself in the cellar. He likes it down here, though it's freezing cold. Down here, he can begin to untangle his thoughts. Things out here are . . . well . . . what's the word? *Weird.* All this space. All this emptiness. This bloody strange tower. If anything, it's worse now Liddy and J-J have arrived, since this morning when they bought the puppy. The puppy's cute, he'll give her that, but there's something about her that's deeply unsettling. That name: Martha.

He swears he doesn't know a Martha. He wasn't even thinking about the name when he said it. It just sort of sprung to his lips. That's what's so confusing. Why would he think up a name he's never thought about before, just like that? It's almost as if it wasn't him that said it, but someone else, someone nearby, whispering the name in his ear.

He rubs his hands together, relieving the chill from the tips of his fingers. It's early days. Things can only get better. This settling-in period was bound to be strange. He thinks of his plans for the stream – he's been making notes, ordered wood for the generator shed, watched countless YouTube videos on hydroelectric systems, Pelton wheels and penstocks and forebays, whenever he's managed to get a decent signal – then picks up a cardboard box from the floor and pretends to sort through it. It's stuff he's brought down from the room on the top floor where his grandfather used to paint: bills and receipts, a couple of damp notebooks. He doesn't really look at it, but it gives him purpose, something for his fingers to do as he thinks about Liddy.

Sometimes she gets freaked – panic attacks, she calls them. All started at university, though he didn't know her back then. It's the main reason she agreed to move out here, to escape the crowds, the claustrophobia of the city. But now that they're here, the responsibility of looking after her weighs on his mind. He's seen her frowning when she thinks he's not watching; the way she anxiously glances at the summit through the kitchen window. In London, it was easy to provide her with reassurance. Whenever she was having a bad day, whenever the thought of the crowds made her sick with anxiety, he'd accompany her on the tube to her studio, then meet her after work and escort her home again. But out here, he's not sure what it means to protect her.

There's nothing here to protect her from.

They'd met at a mutual friend's birthday party, got talking while the others were in the kitchen sorting food. She'd seemed shy at first, but she'd soon opened up, and before he knew it, she was sharing his cab. 'I don't usually do this,' she'd said when they'd landed back at his place. If it was any other girl, he wouldn't have believed her, but Liddy seemed different. There was a genuineness about her that was refreshing. She'd put her coffee cup down on the table and leaned into him drunkenly. She was wearing an all-in-one, sexy without seeming to realise it, but that's Liddy all over. 'I haven't done this for a long time,' she'd giggled. 'And I don't usually say that to boys either.' They'd kissed. He remembers reaching for her top button and feeling her pull away. 'We don't have to do this,' he'd reassured her, though he'd desperately wanted to. 'We don't have to do anything. We can just hug if you like? Or drink coffee?'

'I'm nervous,' she'd said. 'That's all.' She'd lifted his hand back to the button and it had seemed symbolic, an act of faith.

He picks up a notebook and flicks through the pages. A few weeks into their relationship, Liddy had ditched her anti-depressants, ditched her yoga and relaxation CDs. Things had seemed to get better although she still had the panic attacks, still had the dizzy spells. She'd needed him, at times, to remind her to breathe.

But what if I can't protect her any more?

He thinks about how he said that name earlier, Martha. He's been out here just over a week and it's not the first time he's questioned himself. He's had blank spots. Whole periods of time when he can't remember what's happened: cooking dinner, taking showers, painting walls. Like time is moving in strange leaps. His chest feels tight just thinking about it. Yesterday, he put J-J down on the sofa to make himself a cup of tea, then couldn't remember where he'd left him. Couldn't remember where he'd left his own son! He'd looked everywhere apart from the obvious; even marched upstairs to his cot, but then J-J had rolled over and fallen on the floor. He'd bolted down those stairs again, grabbed his screaming son, soothed his bruised skin, slapped arnica on his forehead, feeling guilty and ashamed and bloody grateful all at once that Liddy was out walking.

But he's just distracted. His mind's working overtime, that's why he's forgetting stuff. He's so intent on making this work, this crazy move to a tower on a mountain, he's not thinking straight. He pictures Liddy upstairs, fussing over the new puppy, hair piled on top of her head, legs sculpted in their skinny jeans. Liddy doesn't like her body much, she thinks her torso's too short and her legs are too gangly, and her belly isn't flat enough after the baby. She doesn't listen to him when he tells her she's beautiful, but she's always had a twisted relationship with her body. Before J-J, she'd kept a notebook, not unlike the one in his hand, tucked beneath her pillow, charting her cycle. She'd known exactly when she'd ovulate, when was the best time in the month to have sex. It had been exhausting and, if he's honest, a real turn-off. Each month when it didn't happen, she'd pulled on her running shoes and pounded the pavements like a punishment. And then, when it did, after she'd jubilantly waved the positive pregnancy test at him, she'd been irrationally petrified of doing something wrong.

He looks down at the notebook in his hand, page after page of jobs to be done.

Clear the gutters. Buy bread and milk. Doctor's appointment at 10.00 a.m.

God, his grandfather's life had been mundane. He turns another page. There's nothing else of note, just a shopping list covering the next two pages and a final page with the word

Jeffreys

written over and over. Why had the old man been practising his signature?

He closes the book and buries it between the faded bills. Through the floorboards and joists, he can hear Liddy playing with the puppy, sounding happy as far as he can tell. He thinks of the space upstairs, the cold rooms, the blocked fireplace, the walls he still hasn't painted, and stands up, scratching the patch of dried skin through his jumper sleeve.

7

A few days later, Lydia looks up from what she's doing, sketching some ideas for her work. Kyle's sitting opposite her, at the Formica table, and she can sense his impatience. He's got Jamie in his arms and he's leafing through an old volume of the *Yellow Pages*. 'We need a four by four,' he says, stabbing the book with his index finger.

She looks back down at her page, barely touched. In the weeks after Jamie was born, she hadn't felt like sculpting, but recently, at least in London, she's been itching to get back. She's got so many new ideas, things to do with nature, the fragility of the seasons. When she was still breastfeeding, she'd lie with Jamie on her chest, imaging it all. But now. Well. She'd thought she would be inspired here, she'd thought it would be the thing that would transform her as an artist, all this dazzling countryside, but instead she feels the opposite, a sort of deadness, which is unnerving. She thinks of mentioning it to Kyle, but he's got his own frustrations, and she knows she just needs to do it, force herself to work if she can't be inspired. Money doesn't grow on trees. Maybe sketching will help?

Kyle leans over and grabs her pencil, then circles a couple of ads.

She sighs. 'What's wrong with the Audi?'

He runs his finger down the page, circles something else. 'It's running on its spare tyre for a start. I busted it last week, before you arrived. The roads up here are lethal.'

She looks across at Jamie in his arms, remembers quite how little he is. This morning, there was frost on the fields. Soon, they'll have to turn on the central heating, though they can't afford it, not until Kyle starts working again. That's the other problem: the phone and internet connection has been intermittent since they arrived, infuriating Kyle who needs it for his work. Earlier, a man came to check the wiring but couldn't find the fault. According to Kyle, he was fobbing them off when he said he'd send out someone else to help. After he'd gone, Kyle had found a message on his mobile phone: the kitchen workmen were stuck in traffic on the M4.

The minutes come and go. Kyle puts Jamie on his playmat then goes upstairs to the room at the top – the only room either of them can get a reliable signal – and phones the kitchen company again. Lydia scrubs the old worksurfaces, dismayed at the thought of having to put up with them for even a few more hours. She's never normally like this. Never normally cleans obsessively. Maybe it's all the stuff they're still living around, the furniture they haven't yet cleared, the paintings still stacked in the top-floor room, the piles of old clothes – jumpers and dressing gowns and threadbare trousers – rotting in the wardrobes. The stain on the worksurface reappears at intervals. Just when she thinks she's got rid of it, it comes back again. If anything, it's getting tougher to remove each time. She pours out all her frustration into the scrubbing, going over and over the stain.

Eventually, she pauses and lifts her gaze to the window, resting her eyes on the grey smudge where she'd seen the man all those months ago. She wonders whether it's the same place she'd spied along the path, what she'd thought might be a farm building.

'They've given up,' Kyle says, reappearing through the archway.

'Who?'

'The kitchen company. We should have paid more, gone with a reputable firm. They're on their way back to London. Fucking amateurs.' He grabs the cloth from her hand. 'Here, let me have a go at that. Must be a drip from the ceiling or something.' They both look up. Kyle's paintwork only extends as far as the coving. Beyond it, the ceiling is a patchwork of dirty white, but there's nothing obvious there, nothing that looks like a leak. 'We should get someone to look at the pipes.'

She tugs down the blind he's fitted at the window, casting them in shadow. She knows it's stupid, but she doesn't want the mountain watching them, seeing how the house is affecting their mood.

Later, she takes Martha for a walk in the drizzle. She hopes the exercise will lift her spirits, but the rain is more penetrating than it seemed from the window and she's soon soaked through. She returns to the house, shivering as she enters the kitchen.

Inside, it's as dark as dusk. She feels for the light switch, illuminating the old workstations, the rickety cooker, the archway into the lounge. Kyle's on the other side of the archway, crouched in front of the fireplace. Next to him are the chimney rods and a scattering of sticks that must have fallen down the flue. His arms are black with grime, there are smudges of soot on his cheeks, and he's completely transfixed by the thing in his hands. A pointed beak. White bones. Holes where there should be eyes. Black feathers.

'What is it?' she says.

He looks up, frowning, hair falling into his eyes. Something crosses his face, a shadow like someone passing the window. 'A crow, I think.'

'It's horrible. Hideous.'

'I'll get rid of it.'

He's through the lounge and halfway across the kitchen when Martha pulls towards him. She drops the lead and watches as the puppy paws his jeans and snatches the bird, tossing it between her teeth. Wings tear. Bones snap like twigs. A black feather leaps upwards and lands on her hand.

She screams, 'Martha, don't!' then shakes off the feather, hearing the crush of bone beneath her feet.

Outside, there's a roll of thunder followed by an immediate and heavy downpour. Fat drops of rain pelt against the window, filling the room with a loud hollow sound. Through it, Jamie cries from his cot upstairs, howling through the baby monitor.

She stumbles, slamming into the wall behind. It's all too much: the weather, the noise, the dead bird. 'Please, Kyle,' she says, her voice tremulous. 'I don't like it. I don't like that thing. That bird. Please, take it out of here.'

8

She waits until the storm's cleared before going to the shop. She feels a sense of lightness as she drives away from the tower, like shrugging off a cloud that's been following her for days. In the village, she parks beside the church, and unlocks her phone. A stream of emails bombards her screen as it picks up a signal: her mother asking how they are and imploring her to phone, an invoice from the gallery in Clapham, an offer of work from a private client. The offer intrigues her. It rarely happens just like that, someone contacting her out of the blue. The man's name is Stanley Harris. He's admired her sculptures in the gallery and is requesting work for his private collection: three related pieces celebrating the female form. She re-reads the email several times. No other instructions, no indication of size or specifics. She scrolls to the bottom of the page and sees the four-figure sum he's offering as an advance. She swallows hard, sparks of excitement igniting in her belly. She can't remember the last time she felt like this, like her work might really matter. Could this be her big break?

She responds to the email then hurries along the narrow road, past the pub to the shop, warmed by the thought of getting back to work, stuck into a new project, earning a decent wage for a change. She can't wait to tell Kyle, but first she needs supplies and that bottle of bleach.

The shop doubles up as a post office and general stores. Behind the counter, Mr Jeffreys' housekeeper, Eleri, is scrolling through her iPhone.

'Hello. Bore da.' Lydia tests out the Welsh she's been learning from the book Kyle gave her: *Welsh Made Easy*.

'Bore da.' Eleri smiles warmly. 'It's Lydia, isn't it? We met in the summer.' They shake hands. 'So, how's it all going?'

'Good, thanks.' Lydia thinks of the rooms she's barely made a start on, the vision of their dream home that is still just that: an image in her mind. 'Or rather, it's taking some getting used to.'

'I bet. Can't be easy, relocating from London. As different as you can get without moving to the Outer Hebrides. Come on, I'll make us coffee.'

Lydia hesitates. She wants to tell Kyle about the commission, but it would be good to linger, to make a friend. Besides, there's no one else in the shop, no browsing customers, no one out on the street either. She wonders how the shop makes money.

Eleri clears a space at the bakery counter, heaping a pile of toys and school books to one side. Then she brings mugs of instant coffee from the back of the shop, and indicates for Lydia to sit on one of the barstools. 'I saw Kyle the other day. He came in to buy things for the house. Said he was getting the place ready for you and Jamie.'

'I was still in London, packing up the old place.' *The old place.*
Already it feels like it belongs to a different life. She thinks of
the flat they used to rent, the park opposite, the primary school
at the end of the road. The school she'd imagined taking Jamie
to in a few years' time. 'Have you always lived here?'

'All my life. My husband too. We've two children. Mair's
eight and Iwan's six. And then, there's Pwtsyn.'

'Put-sin?'

'Our dog, a mongrel. What about you? Any pets?'

'A puppy from the farm. We've called her Martha.'

There's a flicker of something unreadable in Eleri's eyes. She
opens a packet of digestive biscuits and pushes them towards
Lydia. 'So, were you born in London?'

'Norwich. My parents moved to London when I was at
university and then I moved there too, for my work. Kyle was
born in Cambridge, though his dad's German. Kyle's a web
developer. Freelance.'

'I've only been to London once. Buckingham Palace on a
school trip. Crazy, isn't it?'

Lydia grins. 'Well, until this year, I'd never been to Wales.
It's all very different. The language. The scenery. The pace of
life.' She takes a digestive. 'Actually, there was something I
wanted to ask you.'

'Oh yes?'

'When we met you in the summer, you mentioned a legend
about the dragons. The red dragon and the white. You linked
it to the mountain, but I'm afraid I don't know the old tales.'

'Oh, that.' Eleri turns to the stack of school books, selects
one entitled *Stories of Wales*, and flicks through it. 'Ah, here we
are.' She turns the page around so that Lydia can see it clearly:
a picture of two dragons wrapped around each other, their

claws outstretched. 'It's an old Welsh myth. The red dragon of Wales, the white dragon of the Saxons. The dragons were fighting beneath a castle that wouldn't stand. Eventually, the red dragon won. The mountain has a bit of a reputation among the locals. It should be red, you see, not white. Red for Wales. Then there's the tower.'

'The tower?'

'Mr Jeffreys found the original plans. I remember him showing me. They were shoved in a box in the cellar along with a few letters written from the original owner to the architect. The tower – *your* tower – was intended to be much grander than it was. A viewing platform at the top. Windows looking out from every angle. Then somewhere along the line, Barker, the owner, changed his mind. He rushed the job. Seems he couldn't wait to get it finished. And then, he tried to change the name.'

'*Tried* to change the name?'

'According to the letters, he thought Y Twr Gwyn, or The White Tower as it's known in English, was bad luck. He was obsessed with the myths. With signs. Omens. I suppose he was worried the Welsh would somehow undo him.'

'But why?'

Eleri shrugs. 'It was the 1930s. There was widespread depression. I suspect an Englishman erecting a tower on the mountain wasn't exactly popular with the locals. Anyway, regardless of what he wanted, the name, The White Tower, stuck.'

Lydia swallows a lump of dry biscuit. 'We've changed the name now anyway. We've called it Sunny Hill.'

'I know.'

'You don't mind?'

Eleri laughs. 'Why should I? It's not my tower.'

They finish their coffee. Lydia buys a few groceries, bleach for the stain, a retractable dog lead, a six-pack of beer.

'Thanks for the coffee. I really appreciate it.'

'Any time.' Eleri glances out the window, at the grey streaks of rain. She shivers and rubs her hands together, though it isn't cold, in fact quite the opposite: the overhead heater is blasting hot air. 'I mean it. The village can feel a bit lonely. There's a folk night at the pub on Friday, if you and Kyle fancy it? I can introduce you to some of the neighbours?'

'We've got Jamie—'

'Bring him with you. Mair and Iwan will be there, some of the other local kids too.' Eleri glances out the window again. 'I don't want you to feel isolated. I don't want you to feel . . . well . . . cut off up there. It's *important*.' She stands up, gathers the mugs. 'Sorry about the coffee. You're probably used to better stuff.'

'It was great. Thank you. And it's nice to talk.' She wants to say more. She wants to tell Eleri it's unusual for her to relax like this, but she doesn't. Of course she doesn't. Instead, she says goodbye, then runs through the rain to the car. She's drenched in seconds, the rain slashing against the windscreen as she drives up the mountain road. Halfway to the farm, the car clunks into a pothole. She slams the gear into first and revs the engine. The car rolls forwards an inch before rolling back again, crunching as it grinds against the loose tarmac. She presses the accelerator, gently at first, then furiously, hearing the wheel spin in the rut. She turns off the engine and stares at the snake of road ahead, distorting through the rain, seeming longer, greyer, then checks her phone – no signal. She unbuckles her seatbelt, knowing she'll have to walk, then leans down into the passenger-side footwell for an umbrella.

Someone taps the windscreen.

She jerks upwards and finds herself face to face with a man peering through the glass, rain bouncing off his shoulders and dripping from his hat. She turns the ignition key and fumbles for the window switch. Immediately, rain sprays the inside door.

The man walks around to the side and leans in. An older, slighter version of Emlyn Jones. 'Wyt ti eisio help?'

She shakes her head. 'Sorry. English.'

He grunts. 'Shall I give you a push?'

The rain drills on the car roof. The wind tugs at the man's hat. 'Thank you. If it's not too much trouble.'

'Dim problem o gwbl.'

She wonders whether the man's up to it – he's in his seventies at least, his face deeply lined, his hair, from what she can make out beneath the hat, a silvery grey – but already he's walking around to the back, shouting instructions. 'Put her in first.'

The car growls as she revs the engine.

'That's it. Put your foot down.'

She tries again. A few false starts then the car finds its grip and rolls onto the flat.

'Thank you so much,' she says when he reappears at the window.

'You won't get far in a car like that.'

'We've been thinking about changing it. Can I give you a lift to the farm? Mr Jones, isn't it? Emlyn's father? I don't think we've met. I'm Lydia.'

He hesitates, then climbs into the passenger seat, wiping rain and sweat from his forehead, the smell of his wax jacket filling the car. 'Bloody weather,' he says, fixing his attention on the road ahead.

'Yes, we're not used to all this rain.'

He wipes his sleeve across his brow. 'You bought the puppy?'

'That's right. Your son was very kind, gave us some things.'

'Fools!'

'Sorry?' She wonders if she misheard him. She *must* have misheard him.

'You chose the bloody runt, didn't you? You should have picked one of the stronger ones. A dog to rely on. To keep watch for you.'

She thinks of Martha sniffing around Jamie as if she knows instinctively she needs to be gentle. 'She's perfect,' she begins, then bites her lip, sensing there isn't any point explaining it to the farmer.

Mr Jones snorts, then flings himself forward in a fit of coughing.

'Are you okay?'

He waves a hand dismissively. 'As I said, it's this bloody weather.'

They sit in silence until they reach the farmyard, then Mr Jones clambers out. 'Remember,' he says, lifting the rim of his hat, looking her straight in the eye. *Fools*, she thinks he's going to say again, like he's tapping into something she already knows. But he merely shakes his head as if she's something to pity. 'Remember what I said about the car.'

9

She runs from the garage, the rain seeping beneath her coat, through her jumper and jeans. The tower looks stark and ominous, framed against the pale-grey sky, the pebble-dash cracked in places. Glancing at the mountain behind, she thinks she sees something high up through the rain. Something moving, something trying to attract her attention. But when she wipes the rain from her eyes, there's nothing there.

Reaching the gate, she sees the house sign, the slate one Kyle had had engraved with the name 'Sunny Hill', smashed in two halves on the ground. It's a clean break, the nails pulled neatly from the gate. She picks them up and sets them to one side in the grass. It was the wind, she tells herself, pushing away the uncomfortable thought it was more than that. Then she opens the door to the house. A smell of cigarette smoke hits the back of her throat. Is someone else here? Has Emlyn Jones paid them a visit? Does that somehow explain the broken sign? Unease twists in her belly, but then, just like the movement outside, the smell is gone, and she's left wondering whether she imagined it. Neither of them smoke. Perhaps it's another remnant of Kyle's grandfather, the smell lingering deep in the walls.

She calls out for Kyle but he doesn't respond, and when she peeks upstairs, Jamie's asleep in his cot. When she climbs to the next floor where Kyle's set up his study, he barely acknowledges her. He's picked up a signal at last, is busy at his computer and suggests she goes out for a run before J-J awakes. She looks out the window, about to protest, but, as abruptly as it began, the rain has settled to a drizzle.

She leaves Kyle to it and takes Martha outside, attaching the new lead to her collar. The puppy strains at the end of it, sniffing the wet earth. A short distance along the track, she tugs back in the direction of Sunny Hill. Lydia lets her in and pats the rain from her paws. She's not sure at what age a puppy is capable of running, but Martha seems too young for anything more than a short walk. She ruffles the puppy's fur, promises she won't be long, then steps out alone.

This time she starts in the garden, jumping over the drystone wall at the back of the property and half-running, half-walking through the field beyond. But the rise is too steep. She stops to catch her breath. There's another field and another drystone wall ahead of her, but after that, the mountain becomes uninhabitable, just shrubs and purple moor grass and ferns between the rock. She scans the area where she thinks she saw movement, her eyes resting on the spot of grey against the green. From here, it's clear: a building lies directly above her. She looks back at the house, surprised to see Kyle framed in the square of the kitchen window, playing with the blind. She waves at him, but he doesn't see her.

She scales the next wall and lands in bog, then tries various routes upwards. There's a spring ebbing between patches of coarse heather, which she tries to cross, but sinks in knee-deep, pulling at clods of grass to lever herself up. After a few minutes, she admits defeat and climbs back into the garden, sodden and shivering but not ready to give up yet. She jogs along the track to the farm, slowing as she reaches the yard, wondering how to avoid the collie with one eye. Too late. The dog's outside the chicken shed, ears pricked, teeth bared.

'Blodwen!' Emlyn appears from nowhere, yanking the dog by its collar, booting its flank. The collie yelps. 'Cael y ffwc i ffwrdd o ma.'

Lydia stops, breathless, thinking she should say something but not sure what. Blodwen is whimpering, obviously hurt; whatever she thinks about the dog, it doesn't deserve that. Emlyn grins at her as if to prove a point, then climbs into the tractor and shuffles the gears. He's a huge man: heavy shoulders, square jaw, narrow eyes.

'Excuse me,' she says, feeling small and awkward. 'Is there another way to the summit?'

The grin dissolves into a scowl.

'Only I've seen another footpath, halfway up on the right. I wondered where it came out?'

Emlyn starts the engine and shouts above the rumble. 'You're to stick to the main path. It's not safe up there. We only keep sheep on the lower fields.'

'But someone *does* go up there, don't they? I've seen a light.'

The tyres crunch forwards. Unperturbed by the telling off,

Blodwen springs across the yard and jumps into the footwell. 'I said, you're not to go there. Do you hear me?'

The tractor rattles onto the road, muck and water spraying from its tyres. She watches until it's just a dot, then leaves the farm and heads upwards. Ignoring Emlyn's warning, or maybe because of it, she takes the footpath veering right, the one running parallel to their own track, figuring she'll be all right if she sticks to the path, if she takes greater care with her footing. She perseveres through the boggy patches, past the place she fell before, catching sight of the building she'd seen from the field.

She slows to a walk, breathless from the climb. It's hard going, trudging through the mud. She's run three sides of the rectangle from the house and below her, a hundred or so metres down the inaccessible fourth side, is Sunny Hill. Only here, it's not sunny at all, just a dirty grey tower, a blot on the landscape, so different from when they'd seen it in the summer.

In front of her, a few metres down the path, is a gate. She walks towards it, stomach clenching, thinking of Emlyn's warning. *It's not safe.* What had he meant? The path? The mountain? The building? She remembers the man standing on the mountain all those months ago in the summer, waving down at her. It was here, she thinks. The man was standing right here.

The gate hangs off a shallow stone wall and makes no sound as it opens, brushed by the wind. She steps inside, as if invited. A few paces ahead, across a cobbled yard, there's a cottage the size of the garage at Sunny Hill, built from white stone. The door is missing. The windows are blank rectangles. Remnants of paint flake from the outside walls, white against white. There's a stone trough filled with murky rainwater and, in front of it, a dead buzzard, its guts spilling onto the cobbles. Behind the trough is a stone shed, almost the same size as the cottage, but rougher and windowless.

She wants to run – there's something not right about this place, though she can't think what – but she can't, she's drawn. She stands on the threshold of the cottage, looking in: a single room with a fireplace that takes up the entire left wall and, to the right, darkness. She should go. She *knows* she should go. The place is probably dangerous, the roof is caving in, and it's so remote, anything could happen up here, but she can't drag herself away.

She steps inside, startled by the rustle of her running jacket and the squeak of her trainers. A feeling of entering somewhere private, a place that doesn't belong to her, though it's obviously uninhabited. By the look of things, it hasn't been lived in for a very long time.

Martha.

She stumbles forwards, reaching out, her hand landing on something in front of her. A wooden chair with a spindle back, sitting alongside the fireplace. Was she imagining it? Someone calling that name again? Her eyes adjust to the dark and she makes out other things: a row of shelves; a wooden platform high up, partially obscuring the roof.

Martha, Martha, Martha.

The name shouts down the chimney, riding on the wind. She presses her hands to her ears and staggers backwards, back onto the cobbles, her heart racing. Images she doesn't understand flash through her mind: a tin mug, a pair of boots, a rusted chain.

The wind tosses her ponytail. Dead leaves circle her feet. A buzzard flies overhead, uncaring of its mate spreadeagled on the cobbles. She sees the tower below her, the patchwork of broken slates on the roof, the chimneys. She needs to get the hell away from this place; she needs to get home. She focuses on the gate, on reaching beyond the perimeter, but her feet have the heavy drugged feeling of feet in a dream, like wading through mud.

Another bird – a crow this time – breaks the spell, flying low and cawing.

She propels herself forwards, swinging the gate wide, finding the patchy footpath between the rocks. Then, difficult though it is with all the bog, she breaks into a run.

10

K yle pushes his way to the bar. He doesn't want to be here. He'd rather be back at Sunny Hill, putting his plans into action. Earlier, he'd picked up the wood from the DIY store in town, great sheets of pine that need knocking together for the generator shed. Still, he consoles himself with the fact it's dark outside. Not much he could do, even if he was at the tower. He orders a glass of wine for Liddy and a Coke for himself. The Owain Glyn Dŵr is a shithole, the type of place he thought had died out with the last century. Slot machines line the walls, there's a pool table rimmed with beer stains and a jukebox that belts out tunes from the 1990s. In the centre of it all, a band sets up amidst a hive of locals, girls in strappy tops who don't look old enough to drink, and men and boys wearing the same ubiquitous Welsh rugby shirt.

He feels Liddy pressing into him from behind, clutching J-J, and knows she's regretting it too, coming out here tonight. This isn't exactly the cosy country inn they'd envisioned, but it's the only pub around here for miles.

'On holiday?' A man with peppered grey hair leans over from his stool at the bar.

Kyle's about to answer, set the man straight, when he feels himself being pushed forwards by the queue. Pushed one way, whereas Liddy and J-J are pushed the other, closer to the man.

'No,' he hears her say, visibly tightening her grip on their son. 'We've just moved in. Sunny Hill, up near the farm.'

The man frowns.

'Y Twr Gwyn,' she explains. Her Welsh pronunciation sounds off, even to Kyle.

The man swirls his beer. 'The tower?'

'That's right.'

The man chuckles and turns to his mates. 'Hear that, boys? These people have bought Y Twr Gwyn.' The name sounds completely different when he says it. The huddle of middle-aged men looks up.

Kyle smiles at Liddy. He knows how uncomfortable she feels in her casual clothes and barely there make-up. The fact she's in a different league from the other women in the room is completely lost on her. He sees them looking her up and down and knows they're marking her out as different. But fuck them. Fuck this pub. They don't need to win the locals' approval.

'How long did the last one last?' says the man.

The men debate among themselves, and Kyle guesses they're talking about his grandfather. Even though he never really knew the man, even though he was mean to his mum, he feels his hackles rise.

'Four years,' someone offers.

The man splutters. 'Four years! What's that they say about mad dogs and Englishmen? How long do you reckon these two will last? I give them four months.'

The men murmur their agreement.

'Why?' Kyle hears the tremor in Liddy's voice and wishes he was next to her. He knows how much courage it's taken her to ask that one simple question: *Why?*

'You should take more care in buying a house,' the man says, narrowing his eyes. 'It's a big decision. Worth spending the time on getting it right. Getting to know the neighbourhood. Getting to know who, or rather what, lives nearby.'

Kyle sees Liddy hesitate and wonders if she's about to point out he inherited the property. But she doesn't and he's relieved. He doesn't know why, but he guesses it would be worse if the man knew he was related to Edward Jeffreys.

'You all right?' he says when she fights her way back to him, J-J nestled close to her chest.

'Fine. Just, those men.'

'They're knobheads.' He watches the man who'd spoken, the ringleader of the group, leaning over the bar, laughing with the landlady. His nose is misshapen like he's seen a fair number of fights and the physical threat makes him feel uncomfortable. Not that he's going to let on to Liddy he's afraid. 'Come on,' he says, 'let's find somewhere to sit.'

People stare at them as they pass, pausing in their conversations. The benches are packed and – is he just imagining it? – the villagers seem to spread themselves out, filling every available space. He tightens his grip on Liddy's shoulder, wanting to impart to her that everything's all right. Everything's under his control.

'Over there,' he points. Eleri, the short curly-haired lady

who owns the village shop, who used to be his grandfather's housekeeper, is waving at them from a table near the band. He's chatted to her a few times now and she seems nice enough.

'Eleri,' Liddy says, quickening her step. 'Come on. Let's join her.'

They squeeze onto the table and the shop lady makes introductions: her husband Jon, their children, a couple of friends who live across the street. Kyle smiles and says all the right things, but the Coke he ordered doesn't quite hit the mark, and he's acutely aware of how Liddy's feeling. Usually, in London, it's him who goes out and Liddy who stays in, except for the occasional dinner with her studio friends. He tunes into the conversation near the bar, finding its way to them across the crowded room, catching one of the few Welsh words he's learned over the last few weeks: Saesneg. *English*.

When the band breaks for an interval, Liddy mumbles an excuse about it being too crowded for J-J and stands up to leave. He's relieved, helping her with her coat, fishing his own from where it's dropped behind the bench.

'That's a shame,' says Eleri. 'But I remember what it's like, everything's so much harder when they're little.' She gives Liddy a hug and smooths J-J's hair.

They make their way back through the crowd, past the people getting up for drinks and spilling around the slot machines.

'Not good enough for you?' the man calls after them.

Kyle swings around. His head is buzzing though he's completely sober. Coming out tonight was a mistake, he thinks. A big mistake. He feels Liddy's fingers digging into his sleeve, holding J-J in one arm, pulling him away with the other. But he won't let this man get the better of them. He breaks away from her, arms rigid, feeling the muscles tense in his neck.

The man drains his pint. 'Now, now, city boy. Don't cause a scene. Don't cause more trouble than you have already.'

'Trouble? What trouble?' Kyle folds his arms in an attempt to look calm, but really he's fuming. He's weighing up the man in his mind; he's muscular and tall, but definitely overweight, whereas Kyle's still honed from the gym back in London. 'I just came in here with my wife and child to have a drink. Presumably there's no rule against that around here? Some ancient Welsh law?'

The man laughs and orders another pint from the landlady. 'No law. Just having a bit of fun, that's all.'

'Kyle, let's go.' Liddy drags him through the crowd, out into the cold. He's grateful for the dark, the wind, the hush of leaves against the kerb, but part of him wants to go back in, have it out with the man. Settle their differences once and for all.

'Who the hell was that?' He hunts for his car keys, still raging inside.

'A local drunk.'

'I heard him talking to you, talking about the house.'

'Well, maybe he has a point.'

'*What?*' He climbs into the car and waits for Liddy to secure J-J in his baby seat. How can she even think the man has a point? 'He was talking nonsense.'

When she's sitting next to him, he starts the ignition then ambles the car through the village. Liddy is silent, staring at the half-lit tarmac as he turns up the mountain road.

'We'll be all right here, won't we?' she says eventually, not for the first time.

'Of course we will.' He reaches out his hand and rests it on her thigh, pushing aside the gnawing doubt. 'You've been here less than a fortnight. Give it a couple of months, let people get used to us. Jon and Eleri are nice. They can't be the only ones.'

'How about we invite them for dinner?'

'No.' He shifts into second gear as they near a bend. 'I've a better idea. Let's invite the whole bloody village. A house-warming. Invitations through every door.'

'I'm not sure—'

'Why not? Show them we're nice.' He changes down into first, pushing hard on the accelerator. 'Not stuck-up English prigs or whatever they think of us.'

She sinks back against the cracked leather seat. 'I'm just not sure it would work.'

They bump the rest of the way home in silence. Half-shapes – trees, walls, boulders – leap out at them in the headlights and he tries to regain the air of calm he somehow mustered in the pub. He's in control. Or rather, he needs Liddy to *think* he's in control. At the end of the track, they stumble out into the night, into the chill wind and impossible darkness. He can't even see his own hand. Instead, he fishes for the torch on his phone, lighting their way to the door, trying to think of something useful to say, but failing miserably. Martha greets them as soon as he opens up, proudly bearing wadding from a cushion she's chewed, then peeing on the flagstones.

He groans.

'I'll take her for a walk,' Liddy says more charitably, handing J-J over. 'We shouldn't have left her on her own.'

He straps J-J into his bouncy chair, then wipes up the mess with reams of kitchen towel. Next, he boils the kettle and searches for Liddy's favourite mug in the mound of washing-up. He turns to the cupboards, trying to think where she might have put the teabags, flinging wide drawers, rummaging between tins. *Really, Liddy, you need some sort of system!* The kettle screeches from the hob. He runs across the flagstones, lifting it to the worksurface, slipping on a dribble of pee he must have missed.

Hot water splashes on his fingers and the sleeve of his shirt, stinging the raw skin that's slowly migrating from his elbow down his left forearm. 'Fuck.'

At the same time, J-J starts wailing and Liddy appears at the door with Martha, red-faced from the cold. 'It's out there again,' she says, grabbing his sleeve and pulling him towards the window.

'What?'

'The light on the mountain.'

'At this time of night?' He peers into the starless sky. 'There's nothing there.'

The cold leaks from her clothing. 'It's gone. But I swear . . . I thought . . . ' Her shoulders dip and she rubs her brow. 'It's like there's someone out there watching us. Or playing tricks on us. I told you about Emlyn and the cottage I found.'

He shakes his head. He's been there himself, along the winding sheep track to the cottage at the far end. But there's nothing there of note, just a chair, an old loft, a cupboard of some sort. It's creepy, he supposes, but in the same way that all old buildings are creepy.

He glances at Jamie in his bouncy chair, so small and defenceless, then wraps his arms around Liddy and pulls down the blind.

11

That night the nightmares begin.

In the first dream, Lydia's downstairs in the lounge, staring at a grey-haired man in the armchair, the one with the saggy cushions and faded armrests. The man is talking to himself, *arguing* with himself, as he picks his skin beneath the sleeve of his T-shirt. She catches the odd word – *bastard, whore, vicar* – but, for the most part, she can't make out what he's saying. It's more the look of him – the depth of the disturbance in his eyes, the ferocity with which he picks his skin – that haunts her.

She wakes up unsettled and reaches for her glass of water beside the bed. The water tastes stale though she'd filled it up in the bathroom just before she went to sleep. She plumps her pillow and slides back beneath the duvet.

In the next dream, she's standing on the first-floor landing, looking down. The stairwell is dark and the tower feels different, musty and unlived in. She starts to descend, hand on the banister. Halfway down, she halts. A woman is standing in front of her on the stairs, swimming through the darkness, her head bent low so that her hair falls over most of her face, and all she can see are the half-moons of her eyes and the spots of blood on her forehead. She wants to speak, she wants to ask the woman what she's doing in her house, but the words won't form. Her head feels woolly, her lips sting as if cracked by the cold. *What are you doing here?* she asks with her eyes instead. But everything about this woman is wrong. She couldn't answer even if she wanted to. The woman is fading . . . fading . . . fading . . . until there's nothing left but the silent stairwell.

She wakes, this time sweating, and drinks more of the awful water. Her clothes are damp but her head is still heavy with the need to sleep. She falls back against Edward Jeffreys' pillow that, despite the fresh cotton pillowcase from their old place, smells of damp. She'd thought she'd put all the old pillows in a heap to be thrown out, but Kyle must have resurrected this one.

She sinks back into a deep sleep. Someone's searching for her up on the mountain, following her as she runs down the footpath, away from the little cottage. She passes the farm and keeps going, through the village, onto the main road, running all the way to her room at university, the room from twelve years ago with magnolia walls and Green Day posters. She can't believe she's made it. She can't believe she's escaped! The relief feels like wings on her shoulders as she climbs into bed and pulls the bedclothes high over her head. She's drifting off to sleep, her limbs so tired and heavy from all the running, when someone raps on the door and she remembers, in her haste, she forgot to lock it. After all that, she forgot to lock the bloody door! Seconds go by, she barely breathes. Then she hears it: footsteps crossing the room towards the bed.

This time, when she wakes, her heart is racing. She pushes herself upright and drains the last of the water, staring into the blackness. She's never known nights so utterly dark as on the mountain. She can't see Kyle. She can't see the end of the bed. She can't see Jamie asleep in his cot. She can't even see the glass in her hand. In the depths of all this darkness, she recalls her nightmares, the armchair in the lounge, the bottom of the stairwell, the university halls.

She pulls Edward Jeffreys' pillow from behind her back. As a little girl, whenever she'd had a bad dream, Mum would swipe a hand across her pillow as if the nightmare was a tangible thing that could be swept away. She does that now in the house on the mountain, brushing the pillow, turning it over, sliding down and laying her cheek on the cooler side. But she can't get back to sleep, not this time. Despite her efforts, the nightmares are still with her.

She lies on her side, staring into the darkness, almost wishing Jamie would wake up, crying for milk, giving her something to do. Instead, faces of the past float before her, snatches of light like undeveloped camera film. Faces she hasn't seen in years. Faces she'd thought she'd blocked from her memory because they remind her too much of what happened.

Kess her flatmate. Danny her boyfriend. Matt her lecturer. Nameless others.

She rolls away from them, onto her other side, facing Kyle, staring at the place where his body lies curled. Grey swirls against the black as her eyes play tricks.

What if it isn't Kyle? What if it's someone else? What if it's that woman from my dream, or one of the others, one of the people from university?

She reaches out and touches him, traces the skin of his face, the light prickle of his beard, reassuring herself it's Kyle. Only Kyle. She hears the slight wheeze of his chest as she settles into him, the asthma that hasn't bothered him since he was a child, and wills herself into a sleep that's dreamless.

<h1 style="text-align:center">12</h1>

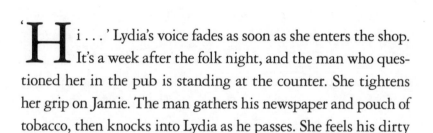

'Hi . . . ' Lydia's voice fades as soon as she enters the shop. It's a week after the folk night, and the man who questioned her in the pub is standing at the counter. She tightens her grip on Jamie. The man gathers his newspaper and pouch of tobacco, then knocks into Lydia as he passes. She feels his dirty clothes on her skin, smells the undercurrent of body odour and alcohol, and steps back in alarm.

'I'm sorry,' she says automatically, though she knows it's not her fault. She has the impression he knocked into her deliberately. Jamie opens his eyes, seeking her reassurance. 'Shush-shush. It's okay.'

The shop bell jingles as the man steps into the street and the door slams behind him.

Eleri sighs. 'Griff Davies,' she says by way of explanation. 'Don't mind him. He's got a problem, if you know what I mean.' She tilts her head at the line of spirits. 'But let's not talk about him, it's lovely to see you both. Jamie looks like he's teething with those red cheeks! Fancy a coffee?'

'I'd love a coffee.' She's not used to making friends so easily, and after seeing no one apart from Kyle and Jamie for days, this feels like a luxury. They sit in front of the bakery counter as before, Jamie on her lap, chewing his toy giraffe.

'How are you getting on with the house?' Eleri says when they've exhausted the topic of the school Halloween party. 'What did you call it? Sunny Hill?'

Lydia forces a smile. She'd rather still be chatting about Eleri's kids. But what's the big deal? It's only a house. A project, Kyle calls it. She's left him in the garden, building his shed.

'Oh, you know, slow work.' She's being deliberately vague. They'd had such big plans, decorating and buying new furniture, but Kyle spends most of his time either in the study or the cellar, dreaming up his schemes to be self-sufficient. Meanwhile, she's got her hands full with Jamie and the puppy. 'The new kitchen's eventually arrived, but we won't be doing any other serious work until the spring. Actually, I came to give you this.' She pulls a housewarming invitation from her bag. 'What do you think?'

Eleri lowers her teaspoon and takes the card in her hands. 'It's a lovely idea.'

'That's what Kyle thinks.'

'But you're not sure?'

'I don't know. I guess I'm shy.' It's not something she normally admits, but Eleri's so friendly, it's easy opening up.

Eleri twirls the card. 'The neighbours can be a bit cagey. They're not used to newcomers. A housewarming might break the ice.'

She smiles, wanting to believe it. 'What about Edward Jeffreys? How did he get on up here? I know it sounds stupid because he was Kyle's grandfather, but they weren't close, and I don't know anything about him. The house is still full of his things, and it's like,' she hesitates, bends down and scoops Jamie's giraffe from the floor for what feels like the hundredth time, 'it's like we're trespassing. Like the tower doesn't really belong to us. Like we couldn't clear it out, even if we really tried. All I know is that he had a heart attack.'

'That's right. Poor man. I found him on the doorstep, dialled nine-nine-nine. The paramedics arrived and took him to hospital, but there were complications. After the hospital, he went into a care home, stayed there until he died. He was an artist as I'm sure you know. He told me he moved to Wales for inspiration.'

Lydia thinks about her sculptures still unwrapped in the barn, the commission she hasn't made a start on. The latest email from Stanley Harris had made it clear: he wants the sculptures in stone.

'His wife died just before he moved here, I remember him telling me. I used to feel sorry for him, all alone on the mountain. It seemed strange to me that anyone would do that, buy a house in the middle of nowhere when their wife had just died. You'd have thought it would be the other way round. That he'd be craving company.'

'What was he like?'

'Difficult to say. He was unpredictable. Sometimes he was talkative, other times he barely acknowledged me. I think I told you I used to clean up at the tower? He'd drive to the village once a week to buy groceries. Friendly enough with the locals, without making friends. Grey hair, thinning on top, hands always daubed with paint. Kind eyes. I went to visit him when he was still in hospital and then, when he left, he sent me a Christmas card from St Dyfrig's Care Home. I was surprised about that. I didn't think I'd hear from him again.'

'Why not?'

'It's as I said. He was friendly, but no one really knew him, not even me. Sometimes there'd be glimpses of the person he was underneath the rather distant exterior. He'd tell a joke, or show me his research. At other times, it was like he wasn't really there. I suppose you'd call him a recluse.'

The shop bell jingles again and an older woman enters.

'Bore da, Mari.' Eleri jumps up.

'Bore da, Eleri bach. Peint o lefrith, os gwelwch yn dda.'

Lydia buttons Jamie into his coat as Eleri attends to the woman, fetching a carton of milk from the fridge. She tries to follow their conversation, picking up the odd Welsh word she can remember from her book – *diolch, glaw, mynydd* – but nothing more than that. Glancing out the window, she sees the summit hidden beneath clouds and a mist creeping down across the lower slopes, concealing the tower. She needs to get back before the mist is too thick and she can't see the road.

She's about to leave when her phone vibrates noiselessly in her pocket. She fishes it out: it's Mum calling, no doubt wanting to talk about the new house, wanting to ask if they're all okay. She hesitates, staring at the screen, thinking about answering it.

'What a sweet little child.' The older woman interrupts her. 'You're the family who's moved into the tower, aren't you?'

'That's right.' Lydia smiles politely and pushes the phone back into her pocket – she'll speak to Mum later. 'Y Twr Gwyn.' It seems natural to use the Welsh name.

Mari smooths Jamie's hair as he gums his giraffe. The skin

of her hands is papery thin and marked with age spots. 'Take care on the mountain, won't you?' she says without lifting her gaze from Jamie.

'Of course—'

'Such a precious little thing. It's such a shame.'

'A *shame?*'

'The mountain's not the place for a young family. Too wild. Too unpredictable. You'd be better off in the village.'

She unpacks her things in the barn while Jamie watches from the safety of the playpen: clay for making maquettes, hammers for working the hard materials, chisels of various sizes. She lays them on her workbench next to her aprons and turns to the pile of sculptures. Hunting through them, she pulls out her favourite pieces, displaying the smaller ones on the shelf above the bench: a horse in mesh wire; a bear made from recycled tin; a series of ceramic humans running, cycling, bathing that she'd created when she'd first rented her space in the studio in London.

She's set an intention of spending the week in here, taking turns with Kyle to look after Jamie, confronting her lethargy head on. Only, she can't get in the mood and the barn is freezing, the old storage heaters inadequate. The commission has made things worse rather than better; she's a sense of her artistic freedom slipping away. Stanley Harris has emailed again, his tone somewhat curt: in order to receive the advance, she's to produce a timeline, drawings, a written commentary on the stone pieces she's preparing. She takes a pencil and sketches her ideas on paper. *A celebration of the female form.* She tries a few ideas, but they aren't right, the angles of the faces too sharp, the contour of the bodies too round. They don't celebrate anything, she thinks, just scrawls, rubbish. She rubs out lines and goes over them again before screwing the whole lot into the bin.

She returns to the house, taking Jamie with her to the room on the third floor, past the study, past Kyle cursing at his screen. The room is even colder than the barn, a stinging winter cold though it's only October. The view through the window is completely obliterated by the mist and she's a sense of being hemmed in despite the miles and miles of countryside. She turns inwards to face the room, thinking about what Eleri said about Mr Jeffreys moving to Wales for inspiration. Apart from a bucket to catch the rainwater near the door, the lower walls are completely obscured by Edward Jeffreys' paintings, the canvases stacked one against the other. Only his easel has been taken down – one of the first things she did when they moved in – folded in the corner, a symbolic act. *He's no longer here.*

'Now,' she talks to Jamie, wrapped in her cardigan. 'What have we got here? What was your great-grandfather up to?'

She studies the paintings she's seen before – the pleasant country scenes. It strikes her that none of these is of Wales, or at least, *this* part of Wales. They remind her of Constable copies but without the finesse. Rather basic, she thinks, wondering if she's being unkind. She moves the top layer to one side and finds more of the same. She digs deeper, Jamie squirming in her arms. She wraps her cardigan tighter around him, then pulls a canvas out from the back. This one is so unlike the others she almost drops it. She's glad Jamie's facing towards her, not looking at the painting, because it's, well … she can't quite work it out. She sets it down and steps away to view it properly.

What she sees is *violent*. Two bodies, entwined. Except 'entwined' is the wrong word for it. There's a sense of movement but it's hard to make out exactly what she's looking at because the painting is a close-up, like a blurry photograph. But she sees the face of the woman lying at the bottom of the canvas, lying beneath the man. Or rather, she sees the blood-speckled forehead, the hair fallen over her eyes.

The memory of her nightmare sweeps into the room, seeming to stir the dust motes and her hovering breath. She hushes Jamie against her chest although he isn't whimpering – he can't possibly realise what she's remembering: lying on her bed in the halls of residence, checking her alarm clock, hearing someone knock on the door.

She closes her eyes. For a moment, she's back there, in her room at university, pushing back the duvet, checking her make-up in the mirror, opening the door.

'Danny?'

But it isn't Danny who stares back.

Jamie makes sucking noises, pulling her back into the present, into the room in the tower. He's hungry, overdue a bottle. She opens her eyes and turns the painting around so no one can see it. No one can see that horrible writhing flesh. She catches her foot on the bucket as she leaves, sending it toppling. Rainwater seeps across the bare floorboards, towards Kyle's grandfather's paintings, threatening to ruin them.

She knows she should find something to mop it up. She should move the paintings out of the way. But she can't. She won't. As she runs down the stairs, shushing Jamie against her chest, she realises she doesn't care what happens to them.

13

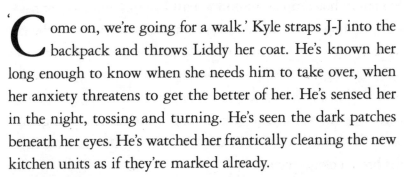

'Come on, we're going for a walk.' Kyle straps J-J into the backpack and throws Liddy her coat. He's known her long enough to know when she needs him to take over, when her anxiety threatens to get the better of her. He's sensed her in the night, tossing and turning. He's seen the dark patches beneath her eyes. He's watched her frantically cleaning the new kitchen units as if they're marked already.

'I don't know—'

'Look.' He gently levers her off the stool where she's been sat for an hour, bent over her sketches. 'We'll leave Martha here, if you like? Go for a proper hike. I can show you the stream, where I'm planning the forebay.'

'Aren't you meant to be working?'

'Internet's down again.' He runs his hands through his hair, masking his frustration. 'Anyway,' he sets his mouth into a deliberate grin, 'you're more important than work.'

He waits for her in the garden while she gets ready, telling J-J about his morning, and the walk they're about to do, and the view from the tower. The mist has lifted, and the view is astonishingly clear. It's like drinking the purest, freshest glass of water. Turning in the direction of the summit, he catches sight of the old choke lead, the one given them by Emlyn, glistening in the grass a few feet in front of him. For a moment, he thinks it's trying to tell him something: the way it's laid out in a straight line, pointing at the old farm building directly above the tower. But then, he realises that's stupid. He picks it up and tosses it in the dustbin, hearing it snake to the bottom, wondering why Liddy left it on the lawn. 'Silly Mummy,' he says to J-J.

As they stride along the track, Liddy beside him, he feels a hundred times better. It's not just Liddy who needs the exercise. He's been holed up all morning with a dodgy internet connection, wading through mounds of emails, apologising to clients for keeping them waiting. He's still a stack of things to do, not least getting his business launched in Wales, but it'll have to wait. He needs the headspace. They walk through the farm, then take the mountain path leading upwards. It's hard going with J-J on his back, but he doesn't say anything, just watches his breath cloud the air.

'This way,' he says, taking the path to the right.

Liddy runs a few paces to keep up with him. 'The cottage?'

He frowns. 'The stream. But yes, you're right. You need to pass those old buildings to get to it.' He knows she doesn't like it; the place she imagines she's seen the light. But he needs her to realise it's perfectly safe. 'They probably keep sheep there. It was a shepherd you saw before.'

'They don't keep sheep that far up. Emlyn Jones told me that.'

'And you believe that man? Probably said it to frighten you.'

He slows a little, taking care not to slip with J-J on his back, but he knows the route better now. He's been up here a few times when Liddy's been asleep, J-J snuggled beside her. He knows where to tread so his feet don't slide, where rocks lie hidden beneath the wiry tuff. This time, his feet find the places easily, naturally, like he's known this all his life.

Nearing the yard to the old farm buildings, the gate swings open. It's almost as though they're expected. As if someone's waiting for them there. Behind him, Liddy hesitates. She pulls off her jacket and ties it around her waist. 'Shouldn't we turn around?'

'I haven't shown you the stream yet. And let's have a nose around the old cottage.'

'Won't it be trespassing?'

'Hardly. This place doesn't belong to anyone. Or, if it does, it's long been abandoned. Look at the state of it.' He knows he's contradicting himself from earlier when he talked about the shepherd, but he *wants* to go in. He feels strangely drawn. It's like an itch on his back that he has to scratch.

The cottage is small, box-like, despite the fact the ceiling reaches to the rafters. He finds the torch on his phone and lights the way – the way he's been several times before – running his fingers over the seat of the spindle-back chair. To the left of it, the fireplace breathes into the sky and to the right, beneath a wooden ledge like a hayloft that conceals a third of the roof, is a line of shelves. He moves the torch up and down, finding a stone pot labelled 'Penglais marmalade', a green bottle embossed with some sort of sign, a heap of yellow candles swathed in cobwebs. Snug beside the shelves, reaching up to the ledge, is a huge wooden compartment. He looks through the wide gap in the panelling, as he's done before, shines the light into the corners. There's nothing there, just a platform swathed in cobwebs.

'What's that?'

He's almost forgotten Liddy's there too, leaning around him, pointing at something on the far wall of the compartment. He moves his torch until he sees it clearly: a carving of a skeleton with its arms raised high and its mouth spread into a wide grin. Next to it, forming a horizontal column, lines are scored deep in the woodwork. Something about the rhythm of the lines makes him uneasy. It's like something he knows but can't quite untangle. Like someone's been keeping a tally.

'It's a bed.' Lydia sounds relieved, as though she'd expected something else. 'This thing. This construction. It's a box-bed. To keep out the draught, I suppose. It's probably hundreds of years old.'

'It's too short to be a bed.' But now that Liddy's mentioned it, it sort of makes sense. The platform. The carved headboard. The hinges that suggest there was once a door. 'I guess people were shorter back then. But why the marks?'

'No idea. How anyone could sleep beneath a carving like that!'

He looks at the skeleton and then the lines, those rhythmic lines. 'You don't think,' he laughs, 'they're like notches on the bedpost?'

Liddy shivers in response. 'I don't like it here. There's something about this place that's not right. Can't you feel it?'

'It's just old, that's all. All old places feel weird.'

'No. It's more than that.'

He turns away from the bed, sits down in the chair, resting the weight of the backpack against the spindle back.

'No!' Liddy grabs hold of him, pulls him to his feet.

'What? I'm knackered.'

'You can't sit there.' Her face is serious and deathly pale.

'Why ever not?'

'I don't know, it's just . . . it doesn't belong to you.'

She drags him outside and he has the impression she wants to say more but won't. 'All right,' he says, holding his hands up in surrender. 'Let's explore out here instead.'

They nose around the back of the buildings, and the stream to the far right. He tries to explain his plans to Liddy, about the hydroelectric system, but he can tell she's not really listening. She's distracted, glancing nervously behind her at the cottage. For God's sake, he wants to shout out, there's nothing there!

Eventually, he relents, and they make their way back to the farm, then along the track to the tower. Lydia strides ahead, seemingly desperate to get back, but he follows more leisurely, hampered by Jamie, not sure whether he's fallen asleep or not, pointing out the other mountains he's memorised in the range. When the back door is opened, Martha darts between their legs, and he offers to follow her into the garden, keeping an eye as she squats on the lawn.

'Kyle!' Liddy calls from the kitchen. *Kyle!*

He runs inside. 'What is it?'

'This.' She points to the coving at the bottom of the kitchen island. The *new* kitchen island that cost them a bloody fortune. There are scratches in the wood, crossing over one another.

'Jesus Christ.'

'Martha must have done it. She must have got freaked out by something. When I came in, she was whining. I could see it in her eyes. She was terrified.'

'Perhaps she needed to pee?'

He gathers the splinters in his hand. The scratches are deep. Scored by a knife, he thinks, not by a puppy, but he can't say that to Liddy. He runs his fingers across his chin, over the patchy stubble, and looks around. No other disturbance. No sign of a break-in. It *must* have been Martha. And yet . . . he can't get the thought of those marks in the cottage from his mind. They're not the same. The marks in the kitchen seem completely haphazard. *Angry.* But when he turns his head and looks out the window, he can see the cottage. See it clearly, though usually it's just a blur, a mar on the landscape. Which makes no fucking sense.

'It doesn't matter,' he says, trying to keep his voice level. 'We'll just have to be more careful when we leave Martha alone. She must have got bored, that's all. We were too long. We shouldn't have stopped in that old cottage.'

14

L ydia spends the next afternoon in her studio. She's working with clay, sculpting a cat, trying to get the eyes right.
She likes clay, its versatility, the way it sinks and lifts and
smooths beneath her fingers, just as she'd once liked the rigid-
ity of stone, the magic of transforming something inflexible
into a thing of beauty. The eyes change with the movement of
her thumbs. She makes them soft, playful, then alert and dangerous. The cat is ready to pounce, head close to the ground,
tail mid-twitch. It's seen something in the long grass – its next
meal or plaything – and it's only a matter of seconds. She makes
the eyes wider using the ball stylus, shaping the lids so that the
cat looks up at its prey.

Straightening her back, she admires the finished product.
An hour has slid by and she hasn't noticed. Her mug of coffee,
sitting on her workbench, has long grown cold. She knows she

should have been working on the pieces for Stanley Harris, but she'd wanted to do this, something she loves doing, just for the sake of it.

She picks up the coffee and takes it into the house. Kyle is out shopping for the housewarming party, taking Jamie with him, and it's good to be on her own for a change. No responsibilities except for Martha curled up in her makeshift den. Still, she can't help her eyes straying to the bouncy chair, the pile of freshly laundered baby clothes on the worksurface, Jamie's favourite toy giraffe abandoned on the floor. Kyle's right when he says she never stops being a mother, even for a moment.

'Right,' she says, talking to the puppy, 'let's get this house in order.'

She attacks the lunch things first, then sorts the wine glasses and runs a tea towel over the plates. She sweeps up her sketches from the kitchen island and dumps them in the bin. They're still no good. Despite the initial euphoria, the commission work sits like a weight on her shoulders, something she doesn't want to do but knows she must. She'd thought she was done with sculpting humans, preferring cats and wild animals, and she'd thought she was done with stone, the way one slip can ruin an entire piece. But she has no choice, they need the money.

Where the sketches had sat on the kitchen island, there's a brown stain in the middle of the white marble. It's in the exact same spot where the old worksurface had been, where the old stain had been. As she stares, it seems to sprawl outwards, seeping beneath the surface of the marble rather than skimming on the top, until it's at least the width of her palm. Without taking her eyes from it, she grabs a dishcloth and goes over it once, twice, three times. But the stain remains stubbornly where it is, not wet like liquid, but like something ingrained. She covers it with a tea towel, not wanting to look – why would a stain appear in exactly the same place as before and how is it that it appears to be *inside* the marble? She drapes the dishcloth over the edge of the sink. It's one of the first times she's been on the mountain on her own, and everything seems magnified: the drip of the tap, the cold seeping through the kitchen window, the dramatic countryside rising just a few metres beyond the house.

She looks up, out of the window.

The light is out there – she *knew* it would be there – a glowing ember in the afternoon mist. It's almost as if it knows she's alone and is seeking her out as it moves across the landscape, left to right, right to left, pausing occasionally. She thinks of the open space on either side of her; the way the tower can't be seen from the village in the mist. A beacon and yet it can't be seen. Anything could happen to her up here and no one would know. Only the light. The one other sign of human activity, and yet it doesn't feel human, it feels – she swallows hard, the word hovering on her lips.

The light stops moving directly above the tower, shining steadily, focusing on something, finding something. She feels a deep dread whispering down her spine. A light should be warm and friendly, but this feels just the opposite.

It's found *her.*

She yanks down the blind and turns to Martha for reassurance. But Martha's ears are pricked, as if she's picked up something too. 'Good girl.' Her voice sounds hollow as she bends down and allows the puppy to bite her hand, little nips that don't hurt.

It's just someone on the mountain. It's just a stupid stain.

She powers up her laptop and checks the internet connection – stable, medium speed – then opens Google, fingers hovering above the keyboard, unsure what she's looking for. Information about the tower? The cottage? Stories about the local area? Something else?

She types 'Mynydd Gwyn' into the search engine and presses return. The first entry is a Wikipedia page she's read before:

> Gaer Fach is a picturesque village in South Snowdonia, traditionally a farming community, later serving the local slate quarry. The church with its Victorian weathercock is of historical interest with a number of medieval wall paintings. Overlooking the village, Mynydd Gwyn is an easy climb with good footpaths.

There's nothing about the cottage or the farm or the tower, only photographs of the trig point and the view towards the village. Photographs that don't do the area justice. She closes the page and scans the other results, all of which are related to the church or local walks or the Owain Glyn Dŵr pub, rated mostly one-star on Tripadvisor. The word she's been trying to ignore circles through her mind.

Hesitating, she types 'Mynydd Gwyn paranormal' into the search engine. Her eyes flash again to the window, the blind fully closed, not even a crack of afternoon sunlight. She presses return. The internet connection disappears, reconnects, disappears again, the results loading slowly, haltingly. She scans the page, but only one result refers specifically to Mynydd Gwyn, a walking blog, last updated three years ago:

Hello, I'm Outdoor Markey, fan of everything to do with the outdoors. Fields, hills, beaches, old railway tracks, mountains. You name it. I walk it.

Listed at the top of a menu of walks is 'Wet ramble over Mynydd Gwyn'. She clicks the link. Words appear first, followed by photographs. At the top is a view of the valley, the same view as from the lounge window. Markey must have been standing right outside the tower.

Outdoor Markey's verdict: 5 miles, pretty easy. At 500 ft, Mynydd Gwyn isn't strictly a mountain, more a large hill, but don't mention that to the locals! There's only one really steep climb from the metalled track to the OS marker. Worth it for the stunning views, even in the rain! Pint afterwards in the grubby Owain Glyn Dŵr (avoid).

There's a long description of the walk, accompanied by Markey's upbeat appraisal. The photographs that accompany it are views she recognises: the trig point, the steep descent and valley to the other side, the quarry, the farm and the track leading to Sunny Hill. At the bottom is a photograph of Markey and a girl huddled in waterproofs, sitting on the stone wall outside the cottage. The clarity of the photo makes her tense, the gate, the cobbles, the trough outside the shed.

The accompanying description reads: *Selfie taken between showers!!!*

She looks back at the window, wondering if the light is still out there beyond the blind. Just someone walking on the mountain, she tells herself. Someone with a head torch, prepared for the imminent darkness. She turns back to Markey's photograph, breathing consciously, the way she's learned. One deep in-breath, hold for the count of four, one long exhale. It's only a photograph. But Markey's blog has brought the cottage nearer. Into the house. Into the new kitchen.

Her throat feels dry. She fills a glass with water, downs it in one, turns back to the blog.

Markey's young, early twenties, blond hair and sparkling blue eyes, complementing the buoyant tone of his blog. The girl sitting next to him has pale skin, hair swept back in a ponytail, slight figure. Markey looks relaxed, whereas the girl looks slightly frayed.

She scrolls to the bottom of the page. There's a comment by someone called Dave: *Looks amazing. What's with the ghost in the doorway? Lol.*

She feels pinpricks on the back of her neck as she flicks back to the photograph. Markey and the girl obviously had a selfie stick or a stand because she can see the entire cottage behind them: the shed to the left, the thick stone walls, the open doorway. Is there something there? She zooms in, heart hammering. Dave's right. There's something there. *Someone* there. But unlike the digital clarity of the rest of the photograph, the colours are faded. It's like looking at an old print, degraded by the sunlight. She zooms in and out, trying to focus: a man with a long, serious face, slit colourless eyes, a white shirt open at the neck, dark trousers that disappear at the ends. No boots. Nothing supporting him. She has the incongruous impression he's hovering about a foot above the ground. He's holding a cigarette, and she can see the trail of smoke against the black of the doorway. If it wasn't for the cigarette, she could have told herself it was rain. Water on the lens. But the smoke is indisputable. Someone's there. Someone's watching Markey and the girl. Emlyn Jones? But no, the man is slighter, less angular. And his clothing, though indistinct, seems to come from a different time.

She scrolls back to the comments.

Outdoor Markey: *Lol. We didn't see that until we came back. Freaked Jenny out. Obvs just one of the locals, but still pretty scary. Always walk in pairs, guys. You don't know what psychos are out there.*

She flicks to the top of the page, passing quickly over the photograph, and clicks on Markey's email address. She writes hurriedly, without pausing, without allowing herself to question what she's doing.

> Hi Markey, I hope you don't mind me contacting you. I'm doing some research into the history of Mynydd Gwyn above Gaer Fach in Snowdonia, and stumbled across your blog. You may remember, you walked this way a few years back? I'm wondering if you could tell me more about your walk, specifically the photograph by the cottage? Any information would be helpful.
> Kind regards,
> Lydia Stein

She hits the send button and closes the laptop, then reaches for the old radio Kyle found in the cellar, turning the knob until she finds a channel – someone singing in Welsh. She feels slightly better, filling the room with the sound, but it's only four-forty; Kyle and Jamie might be gone for another hour yet. She leaves the radio playing and goes upstairs. Running the shower, she wraps herself in a towel, and roots through the bathroom cupboard for a razor. Her hands land on something else, something she swears she hadn't seen when she'd cleaned out the bathroom a few days ago, sweeping all Kyle's grandfather's things into the bin. But it *must* have been there. An old earthenware pot labelled 'Penglais marmalade'. Just like the pot in the cottage. Only, Kyle has filled it with their things. *Her* things. Hairbands, mascara, stubby tubes of lipgloss.

She takes the pot in her hands – it's cold to the touch, the letters faded – and, impulsively, tips the contents into the sink. Then she tosses the pot into the bin, hearing it land with a clunk.

Behind her, the shower runs hard, like rain on the roof, the steam filling the bathroom. She pulls the cord of the ineffective fan as the steam from the shower catches at the back of her throat. It smells bad. Not steam, but the pungent smell of a cigarette.

Her vision blurs, she reaches for the door handle, but can't quite grasp it. Her hands are slippery. Her heart pounds.

A panic attack. I'm having a panic attack. I need to stop it before it really starts.

She places a steadying hand upon her chest, takes deep deliberate breaths, but her thoughts race. She can still smell it: the distinct stench of a lighted cigarette, and it's moved, no longer behind her, but coming from the room next door. Coming from the bedroom she shares with Kyle and Jamie. Only Kyle doesn't smoke and it's impossible anyone else is in the house. The door leading to the outside is locked, the windows bolted. And yet she can smell it. Not deep in the walls, a memory as she'd thought before, but something real.

She tries again, this time managing to grab the door handle, pushing the door wide. But the bedroom is empty, just as she left it. Just the smell of fresh bed linen and cheap detergent. She takes a step forwards. Had she imagined it? Had she imagined that smell? A door slams downstairs. She tenses, listening hard; she swears she can hear something moving. Martha? The radio? She strains to hear above the sound of the shower still running next door, and the faint whir of the bathroom fan, and the thumping of her own heart.

And then she hears it clearly: the unmistakable sound of footsteps. Big heavy boots.

She grabs one of Kyle's long T-shirts and pulls it on, then picks up a book, the nearest thing to hand.

'Kyle?' She reaches the stairs, feeling in the dark for the banister, too terrified to reach for the light switch. She can't hear the radio, only the footsteps, someone crashing about. Not Martha, not a dog, but a person. She feels her way down the stairs, one step then the next, slowly, stealthily. Cracking open the door at the end of the lower corridor, her whole body shifts gear, ready to fight. She grips the book tightly and throws wide the door.

Everything changes. The lights are blazing in the lounge. The radio is still chattering. And through it, she hears the cheerful sing-song voice of Kyle talking to Jamie. She drops the book, runs through to the kitchen, pounds him gently with her fists.

'Hey!' Kyle pulls her back. 'What's up?'

She catches sight of Jamie on the playmat, happily reacquainted with his giraffe.

'You're early,' she says, remembering the shower still running upstairs.

Kyle grins and points at the crate of Prosecco and trays of canapés on the kitchen island. 'Fancy a drink?'

She crams her face against his shoulder. He smells of the town: traffic, people, bright October sunshine, the dust of crushed leaves. When she looks down, she sees he's already pulled off his shoes and is wearing slippers. No boots. She must have imagined that too.

'Yes,' she says. 'A large one.'

15

Kyle tops up their glasses, catching a drip of Prosecco as it slides down the side of the bottle with his finger. It's eight o'clock, half an hour into the housewarming party and no one's showed. The evening is rapidly descending into a disaster, all that wasted time and effort, not to mention the expense. He glances at the stack of unused plates and wine glasses – most of them retrieved from the boxes heaped with his grandfather's things – then turns his attention to Liddy. She's sitting with J-J on her lap, feeding him a bottle, absorbed in her own thoughts. She's hardly touched her wine, but he drinks deeply, wishing the alcohol would take effect.

'I suppose,' he says, eventually getting to his feet, 'we'd better start clearing this up . . . '

There's a gentle rap on the back door. He leaps to open it,

to find only the shop lady, Eleri, with a box of Thorntons and a bunch of flowers.

'Welcome,' he says grandly. 'Take a seat. There's plenty of space.'

Liddy winces, but he can't help it. He's fucking angry. He did all this for Liddy, for J-J, went to the trouble of buying bubbly and canapés, and only one person's bothered to show. He kicks a stool leg as he passes. Maybe he's drunker than he thought.

'Sorry, Jon couldn't make it. Had to put the kids to bed.'

'Of course,' Liddy says more generously. 'We should have thought. It seems inconvenient for a lot of people and it's so far up. I suppose people don't want to make the journey in the dark. Here, let me take your coat.'

Eleri unzips her puffer jacket. 'Brrrr, it's cold out there.' She hands Liddy the flowers. Wilted chrysanthemums in a cellophane wrap. 'These are from Mari.'

'Mari?'

'Silver hair. You bumped into her in the shop.'

'Of course,' Liddy says, and Kyle realises they are referring to something he's not involved in. 'That was kind of her.'

Liddy puts the flowers in the sink and offers Eleri a tray of canapés that suddenly seem far too fancy for the occasion.

'Thanks, I'm starving.'

'I'll show you what we've done to the house so far, if you like? Not that there's much, but I can talk you through our plans.'

Eleri hesitates, bites into a twist of pastry, catches a stray olive before it hits the floor. Kyle wonders what she's thinking, whether she'll rise to the challenge, because right now he gets the impression – or is he just imagining it? – she's only here out of politeness and would rather be anywhere but. She wipes her lips. 'Yes, sure. Why not?'

He hears them trudge around the house, up to the top room and down again, Liddy no doubt going through her elaborate plans – the colour scheme, the soft furnishings, the giraffe-themed nursery – then they go back to sitting at the kitchen island, drinking Prosecco. It's a quarter past eight. He averts his eyes from the canapés, the bowls of crisps, the paper napkins, all laid out on the worksurface and the kitchen island.

'Really, I shouldn't, I'm driving,' Eleri says as he leans over and tops up their drinks. 'But go on. Just a bit.'

There are a few false starts at conversation. He makes a bad joke, Eleri laughs, Liddy bounces J-J on her lap, Martha chases a toy. The kitchen clock hands edge towards eight-forty-five.

'Is it something we've done?' Liddy says, leaning over J-J, twirling the stem of her glass. He thinks she's going to cry. 'Or do they just not like strangers? The English? I posted an invite through every door in the village.'

'I'm sure it's nothing personal,' he hears himself saying. *Bullshit. Of course, it's personal.* 'The house is too far out. We've been unreasonable expecting people to drive all this way.'

Eleri pops a crisp in her mouth and crunches audibly. 'It's the mountain.'

He stares at the shop lady in surprise.

She wipes her fingers on her jeans. 'It's silly really, but the villagers are, well, how should I put it? Superstitious.' She turns to Liddy. 'You remember I told you the tale of the two dragons?'

Liddy nods, and he leans forwards, interested. 'Do tell me more.'

'An old Welsh myth about two dragons fighting. The red dragon of Wales, the white dragon of England. The mountain's all wrong, you see. This tower's all wrong. Built by an Englishman, dominating the landscape.'

He scoffs and, not for the first time, feels an ache for the man he hardly remembers, the man his mum barely talked about when she was alive. Did his grandfather have to put up with this bullshit too? He thinks back to his childhood, but his memory is pitted: a man who didn't look much like his mother, but who spoke the same, the same southern accent; a man leaning over him as he painted, showing him how to mix the colours, how to apply a wash before adding the detail; a tall man with fair hair. His grandfather would have stuck out like a sore thumb in Gaer Fach.

'Who carved the cross beneath the kitchen window?' Liddy says, clutching J-J. Kyle remembers her showing him the mark on the lintel outside and the dried-up rowan berries, convinced it was some sort of ritual.

Eleri shrugs. 'I don't know.' She looks genuinely clueless. 'Maybe it was Edward? He went a little bit crazy up here. He was a painter, as you know, and prone to fancy.' The implication sits between them: there's not much difference between a painter and a sculptor; between his grandfather and Liddy. 'But it could also have been one of the villagers. As I said, some of them – the older ones especially – are superstitious. Maybe someone was trying to ward off evil.'

Kyle laughs, but the word *evil* rings in his head. 'One minute the tower's English, the next it's evil.'

Eleri swallows the dregs of her Prosecco. 'Silly nonsense, of course.' She scrapes back her chair.

'You're not going?' Liddy sounds panicked.

'I'm sorry. Jon will need help tidying up.'

He knows it's a lie. The shop lady can't wait to get the hell out of here. He glances at the window as she pulls on her puffer jacket. The blind is open – had he done that or Liddy? – and it's dark outside, starless. He stands up to shut it all out again, knowing Liddy doesn't like it.

Eleri smiles her thanks as Liddy presses a bottle of Prosecco into her hand, insisting she take it with her. 'They'll come round. Please try not to worry. Jon will have a word with Griff, if you like? He's not as heartless as he'd like people to believe.'

They listen to Eleri's car grumbling into life and grinding down the track, the engine growing fainter and fainter. Eventually, there's nothing left but the sound of the wind and J-J murmuring softly in his sleep. He picks up his glass and knocks back the Prosecco in an attempt to lessen the band of tension around his head.

'I hate it here.' Liddy's eyes fill with tears. 'Let's go back to London. Let's just pack right now. We could be home in a few hours. Stay at my parents', go out for breakfast, put the house up for sale first thing on Monday morning, leave it in the hands of an estate agent. Never step inside the place again.'

'We can't,' he says simply. He's thinking of his plans, his scheme for the hydroelectric system, his vision of J-J growing up in the country. He thinks of his work, his efforts to pick up local contracts – the targeted online ads, the ad in the local paper. He *will* make his mark here, even if it kills him. 'We moved here for a reason, remember? For peace and quiet? Because you couldn't hack being in London, the panic attacks, the claustrophobia. Because you had a vision for this house, for what we could do with it. We moved for you.'

She wipes the tears from her face, and stares him straight in the eye like she can't believe he just said that. 'There's something wrong with this place,' she says. 'The house. The mountain. I thought I'd be better here, but I was kidding myself. I'm *worse*.'

The word somersaults through the air and lands like a slap. 'It's just the adjustment. It takes time—'

'Didn't you hear what Eleri said? The villagers hate the place. They hate *us*.'

'Now you're jumping to conclusions.' He feels a swell of irritation. 'They just need time, that's all. *We* need time. I'm not going to let the likes of Griff Fucking Davies throw us out of our dream home.'

Liddy breathes in through her teeth, and he knows she's counting in her head, counting up to four. It's like watching a balloon gradually filling with air. Sometimes he wants to stab at it. 'It's not just the locals,' she says, letting it all out with a loud sigh. 'I've been having those nightmares. I've been thinking about things that happened *ages* ago. That I haven't thought about in years. And then there's the cottage further up. I found something on the internet. A photograph, a ghost—'

'A ghost?' He grabs another bottle of Prosecco, pulls at the foil wrap, wishing it was something stronger. 'You shouldn't believe everything you read online.'

'You haven't seen it. A man in old-fashioned clothes. Let me show you.'

She reaches for her laptop, but he catches hold of her. 'Liddy. Listen to me! Don't do this to yourself. To us. There is no ghost. No dodgy vibe. It's just the mountain. Some freaky neighbours who don't like the idea of so-called foreigners moving in. Neighbours whose minds can be changed.' He lets go of her and slams back against the kitchen island.

'Why won't you listen to me?'

He pops the cork and watches the wine spill over the side of the bottle before filling his glass. 'Because it doesn't make any sense.' He rubs his temples, trying to get rid of the horrible squeezing sensation. 'All this has to stop. Can't you hear us? Can't you see what's happening? We're driving ourselves mad. We're become exactly what Griff Davies and his cronies want us to become. Two insane English people living on a Welsh mountain.'

16

Lydia stares at the ceiling above her head, wide awake, unable to sleep, the drink inside her making her heart race. Her mind spins back twelve years to 2004. This time, the memory is precise in its detail as if it's only just happened. She's back at university, lying on her bed, the taste of cheap lager on her lips, her head drumming, threatening a hangover. She turns on her side and sees her alarm clock. 2.30 a.m. Images of the evening crowd her mind: the DJ booth, the dance floor, the nausea-inducing rounds of tequila, the argument she had with Danny.

The argument. She groans at how stupid she's been. Danny had bumped into his ex at the bar, bought her a drink, chatted to her for a while. Lydia had accused him of flirting, a stupid accusation that had started as a joke and blown up into something bigger. She closes her eyes and tells herself it doesn't matter. Danny and she are sound. He'll know it was just the drink talking, that she overreacted. She'll apologise over breakfast, and everything will be okay again.

She drifts into sleep, her eyes unflinching as the clock flashes the hour. But then, there's a knock on the door. Groggily, she sits up, wondering if she imagined it, smoothing her hair. A quick check in the mirror to ensure her mascara hasn't slipped. Then she pulls back the covers and opens the door, expecting Danny.

'Oh.' Not Danny at all.

Matt Trevithick is standing in the corridor. *Matt Trevithick, her lecturer.* She's so surprised she doesn't say anything immediately. She's just conscious of her night T-shirt and her messy hair and her lager-tinged breath. 'I thought you were someone else.'

Matt holds something up, swings it in front of her eyes: her wallet. 'You dropped this in the club,' he says. 'I didn't want you worrying about it when you woke up and found it missing. And I don't have your phone number, so I thought I'd come and find you instead. I hope that's all right? I hope I'm not intruding?' He peers around her at the empty room, the duvet crumpled on her bed, the empty bottle of wine on her desk, crowning a stack of library books.

'Thanks.' She takes the wallet from him and smiles politely. How *did* he find her? She remembers seeing him in the club, briefly speaking, but she's sure she didn't mention her address.

'Can I come in?'

'Sure.' Though this doesn't feel right. Doesn't feel remotely appropriate. But what else can she say? She takes his class after all.

He sits down next to her on the bed, on the duvet cover Mum

bought her for university, a stylish duvet cover with big floral swirls. He pulls out two cans of Red Bull from his manbag and passes one over.

'I hope you don't mind me saying,' he looks uncharacteristically nervous, 'but I was worried about you earlier. In the club, you were drinking a lot.'

She shrugs. 'It's Saturday night.'

'I don't like the way he treats you.'

'Who?'

'Your boyfriend. Daniel Chapman. I've heard rumours about him. Not nice rumours, I'm afraid.'

She's taken aback. 'It was just a silly argument. My fault, actually.'

'I'm worried about you, especially with your exams coming up.' He cocks his head on one side and flicks his fringe.

He sounds drunk rather than worried, but he's young and good-looking, and despite herself, she wants to impress him. She listens to him talking about Danny and her exams, but she can't keep up. Her head feels muzzy and not quite right. She doesn't even shake off his hand when he lays it on her thigh.

'I'm sorry,' she says, feeling incredibly tired. 'Can you repeat all that?'

The memory disintegrates into colours and sounds. She turns on her pillow in Y Twr Gwyn, trying to get away from it, trying to get away from the feeling of Matt laying her back against the pillow, his hot white skin against hers, the blue of his jacket, the sound of the duvet beneath her, the yellow light overhead. But nothing feels right in the tower either. It's too dark in this house. It was never dark like this in London, always a streetlight gleaming through the curtains, or the headlights of a vehicle, even in the early hours. She'll buy a nightlight for her side of the bed; it will be easier that way when Jamie wakes and she needs to fetch him a bottle.

When she finally sleeps, it's not Matt she sees, but the cottage on the mountain, calling to her, drawing her back. She still has the sense of it hanging over her when she awakes at first light and creeps out of bed to find her running kit.

Outside, the air is damp and woody. The mountain is cloaked in golden light and the woodland beneath the farm is tinged a deep orangey red. From the track, the cottage is merely a mark beneath the rocks, something that has to be sought out rather than easily observed. She runs steadily, shaking off the dregs of sleep, crossing the farmyard, alert for the dogs. Relieved when none appears, she takes the steep path upwards until she finds the sheep track to the right. From here, above the low-lying mist, the view is endless. There are no tourists at this time of year. No families with picnics. No children piggybacked to the top. Now that the weather is changing, the mountain is theirs.

A few minutes later, she's standing in front of the ruined cottage, the space around her shimmering in the half-light, the cobbles like shells. But something's not right. She sees it immediately she lifts her head. Letters have been painted in bright red on the exterior wall of the cottage. English words, so that the message is clear.

KEEP OUT

A crow swoops overhead and the air changes, the cold suddenly more penetrating. Ignoring the painted message, she takes her mobile phone from her zip-up pocket and switches it to torch mode. She enters the cottage. It's empty as before, just the chair, the candles, the box-bed, the bottle and pot on the shelf. She takes the bottle outside and examines the embossed symbol. It's a skull and crossbones. She lays it on the stones and turns to the shed.

It's locked, fastened tight by a shiny new hasp and padlock. She twists the padlock one way then the other. The wood behind is rotten with age, and with effort she can probably rip the whole thing off. The lock digs into her fingers. She yanks harder, feeling the nails of the hasp pulling away, hearing the wood splinter. She falls backwards as it relents, crying out. The door swings open. A long low creak. She gets to her feet and looks for her phone, scanning the cobbles. It's dropped where she'd fallen, the screen a crisscross of broken glass. Cursing, she picks it up. Beneath the glass, the display is undamaged, though harder to read, and the torch still works.

She inches inside, examining first the floor — nothing but wisps of ancient hay — and then the walls. To her right is a line of farm implements: spades, forks, a pair of rusty shears, a hook on a long pole. She moves the torch to the opposite wall. There's a line of heavy objects suspended from chains. She takes a step forwards. The objects follow a similar pattern: a length of metal with a spring, a curved jaw and clamped iron teeth. *Animal traps*. She feels a wave of nausea as the torchlight falls on a trap at the end of the wall. Bigger than the others. Too large for an animal such as a rabbit or fox. Large enough for a human.

Martha.

Her heart thuds. She covers her ears with her hands. She didn't imagine it. That same voice. That same name. She *knows* she didn't imagine it. She should have stayed away from here. She shouldn't have paid attention to her dream.

Martha.

Behind her, there's the sound of footsteps on the cobbles. Heavy, deliberate feet, walking in boots. She freezes as the door widens behind her, as sunlight streams in, then she forces herself to turn, wrapped in horror, unable to breathe.

Martha, Martha, Martha.

A figure is blocking the doorway, silhouetted against the morning sun. She screams.

Emlyn Jones strides towards her, grabs her by the shoulders and pushes her into the yard.

'Get out!'

'I'm sorry, I was just—' She tries to think. Do the Joneses own the cottage? Is she trespassing? Did Emlyn watch her make her way up here from the farm? Follow her deliberately? Was it Emlyn calling that name, 'Martha'?

'Go on,' he shouts. 'Get out of here! Can't you read the sign? Get the fuck out of here! Cer o'ma! Sais busneslyd!'

Her heart races but she holds her ground, just for a moment. 'Why?' Her voice trembles. 'Does it belong to you? If so, I'm sorry. I didn't mean to trespass.'

'No one owns this cottage. Not any more. Not for a long time. That's all you need to know. Now, scram!'

She runs across the yard, hearing the door of the shed slam behind her. Reaching the gate, she glances back at Emlyn fiddling with the broken hasp.

She runs all the way back to Sunny Hill. Kyle and Jamie are still in bed, but Jamie opens his eyes when he sees her, and stretches his arms. She takes him downstairs to the kitchen and makes an effort to be cheerful, singing as she makes him his baby porridge. As she spoons it into his mouth, she tries to shake off what just happened, but she can't: the strength of

Emlyn against her shoulders, the sound of the hasp wrenching from the door, the sight of the traps. Those monstrous traps. Emlyn's traps? She's dizzy-sick tired, aching from the downhill run, but she wishes she could pack all their things right now and drive back to London.

Instead, while Jamie smashes his spoon up and down on the table of his highchair, she powers up her laptop. Immediately, her inbox pings into life with an email from Outdoor Markey:

Hi Lydia, thanks for your message. What exactly did you want to know about the mountain?
Cheers, Markey

She emails back:

Hi Markey, thanks for replying. Did you find out anything about the man in the photograph? The one standing in the doorway of the cottage on Mynydd Gwyn?
Kind regards, Lydia

By the time she's cleared up the splatters of baby porridge, there's another email waiting in her inbox:

Hi Lydia, no not really. My girlfriend, Jenny, was freaked out about the whole incident. She thought it was a ghost. I edited the photo, using different filters etc., and there was *definitely* something there, but I wasn't sure what. I asked at the village if there were any local ghost stories, just to placate Jenny, but the villagers didn't want to talk about it.
Cheers, Markey

Lydia:

Thanks Markey. I don't suppose I could talk to Jenny?

Markey:

Sorry. Jenny and I aren't together any more. We split up soon after this holiday. I doubt she'd want to talk about it anyway. As I said, she was freaked out. It got to her a bit. She started having nightmares. It seemed a bit irrational at the time.
Cheers, Markey

A dead end. And yet, it's more than that, it's confirmation. It's what she's been feeling herself: freaked out, disturbed by nightmares. She stands and stretches, realising how tense she's become, leaning over her laptop. The kitchen is only half-tidied from the night before, and the scratches on the woodwork at the bottom of the kitchen island look longer, deeper. She runs her fingers along them. Deliberate marks, not the frantic pawing of a puppy. Is someone – Emlyn Jones or one of the villagers – trying to scare them away? Perhaps Emlyn has a key to the house from the time of Kyle's grandfather? They ought to change the lock, bolt the door at night, check the window catches, just in case.

'You shouldn't go there,' Kyle says later when she tells him about Emlyn. 'Promise me you won't go there again? It's not safe. I shouldn't have encouraged you when we went for that walk. The roof is falling in for a start.'

'You didn't encourage me.'

He gives her a hug and writes 'new lock' on his shopping list. But he's cheerful today, the exasperation of the night before dissolved in a decent night's sleep. It's as if last night didn't happen; as if Eleri didn't say all those things about the mountain. He butters his toast and changes the subject, telling her about an email he's just received, a party they've been invited to in London: Charlie is celebrating his thirtieth birthday. The thought of London is like a warm drink. She holds on to it, imagining what it will be like being back, being among people they know, walking through crowds, pressing into coffee shops, strolling through manicured parks.

'Of course, I said we wouldn't go.'

She stops flicking through Jamie's first-words book. 'What? Why?'

'Well, we're here for a start. We moved to escape all that.'

She puts the book down. 'But, just because we're here, doesn't mean we're invisible, doesn't mean we don't exist!'

Kyle holds up his hands. 'Whoa! I didn't mean to upset you. I didn't think you liked Charlie?'

She runs her hands through her hair, wondering if she really is being irrational. 'I *do* like Charlie, sometimes at least.' She bites back the thought that Charlie's a bad influence – all the partying, all the drinking and God knows what else. But she needs this. Incongruously, she realises, she needs London. 'I'd like to go. It would be nice, being seen, talking to people. And Mum could babysit Jamie. She'd love that.'

He steps towards her and massages her shoulders, easing her jumper from her neck. She feels the warmth of his fingers, the wetness of his lips as he kisses her shoulder blade. 'Shouldn't we get used to being here first before running back to London?'

'We're not running back. Please, Kyle. I need this.'

She lays her head on his chest, hears his heart beating through his jumper. Kyle's dream of moving to the country includes being part of a close-knit community, a different kind of company to the one he'd kept in London: calmer, soberer, more grown-up. She'd been impartial on the matter – she wasn't the social one, after all – but now that the village seems positively hostile, she finds herself craving London.

He strokes her hair, inexplicably making her want to cry. 'All right. I'll tell Charlie we've changed our minds, that we are going after all. Okay?'

She reaches up and kisses him. 'Thank you.'

He takes his coffee to his study, and she tries to work, sifting through her sketches. But she's too tired, too preoccupied. Admitting defeat, she takes Jamie into the lounge and sits with him on the sofa. She feels herself drifting as she flips through his first-words book, knowing it's dangerous – the one thing that was drilled into them at parent and baby class: whatever you do, don't fall asleep with your baby on the sofa – but she can't help it. She's exhausted from the stress of moving and everything that has happened since. She lifts her legs onto the sofa, Jamie nestled in her arms.

Suddenly, she jerks wide awake. A sense of time having moved on, the sunlight brighter through the bay window, the room marginally warmer. Did something wake her? A movement? A fleeting smell? A cover has been pulled over her shoulders and a cushion placed beneath her head. Jamie's gone. She throws off the cover and runs into the kitchen, panic ringing in her ears. There's a note on the kitchen island in Kyle's hand.

Taken J-J and Martha for a walk. Didn't want to wake you x

Beneath the note is the stain. She reaches out, fingers hovering above it but not quite touching. She can smell the cigarette again and the racket in her ears is worse. With it, the stain seems to shift, inexplicably creeping through the marble. It's as if the tiny particles of stone are moving and darkening before her eyes. Impossible yet mesmerising. For a split second she's somewhere else: standing in the doorway of the shed beside the cottage, seeing the traps, animals caught in the iron teeth, bloodstained fur, shocked lifeless eyes. There's someone standing over them. A figure holding what looks like a metal chain. Not Emlyn Jones but someone else: the man in Markey's photograph.

She staggers backwards, knocking the mug from the kitchen island. Splashes of cold tea and broken china on the flagstones. She gathers up the pieces, feeling sick, cutting her hand. A welt of blood rises on her palm. She takes the first-aid box from the cupboard, dumps it on the workstation next to the telephone, her eyes falling on the handset left behind by Edward Jeffreys, with names and numbers scrawled on a cardboard slip: the vicarage, the GP, the dentist.

Blood still dripping from her palm, she lifts the receiver and dials the first number.

17

I hear him calling to me in the dark, the light of his lamp drip-ping orange-yellow down the stone, illuminating the white of the cottage walls.

'Martha?' he calls, the desperation in his voice palpable. 'Is that you?'

I remain stiff against the side of the animal shed, not wanting to give myself away. He stumbles across the cobbles, catching his boots on the legs of the mangle, clumsy with drink. I should go to him; I know I should go to him. It is not safe on the mountain and he is worried about me. He's imagining me tumbling over some unseen boulder, falling into the stream, my body carried away, ripped to pieces on the rocks. I know he is thinking these things for he has told me many times before.

But I like it out here. I like to breathe with the mountain. He will never understand that I need this space away from our little cottage, away from our lives. Out here, I can imagine another world.

A *world full of cities and castles and people in fine clothes. A life without hardship.*

'Please!' I hear the drink in his voice and feel ashamed of my childish fantasies. 'Please, Martha, you know it is not safe.'

Not safe. It is what our parents always told us. Not safe on the mountain. Not safe in the village. Not safe anywhere but here in the cottage.

He turns back inside, taking the light with him, and I let out a long even breath, the mountain breathing with me. For a moment, the darkness is complete, an impenetrable depth. But then, I look upwards and trace the star-studded sky, a sky I have known almost all my life, since we made the journey here from the smog-cloaked city in the north of England. I see it as if for the first time. A night sky full of possibility.

A gust of wind cuts through the valley, stinging my cheeks. I press myself harder against the shed. Beyond the stone, I imagine the pig snuffling in her sleep, the chickens lifting and settling their feathers. From this altered viewpoint, the darkness is not so complete as I had thought. My eyes are drawn to the lights of the village. I imagine Morgan Lloyd's house, the warmth from his fire, his mam frying Welsh cakes, his siblings squabbling over well-loved toys. Morgan, now the man of the house, sits by the hearth, reclining his head. Clean clothes, so welcome after the dust of the quarry. He closes his eyes as the day unwinds, his dreams punctuated by laughter and his mam's gentle fussing.

But no. No! I knock my head against the side of the animal shed, punishing my folly. How can I think of Morgan after what he and his kind have done to my brother? I look back at the sky and realise I have ruined it all. Ruined it with my wicked thoughts.

I cannot stay out here. The wind is bone-chilling. I pull my boots from the bog, making a squelching sound. The door of the cottage flies open and the light is thrown outwards. I wait for William's desperate calls, but instead all I hear is the gentle padding of the bull terrier.

'Here, boy.' I hold out a handful of dry toast from my pocket.

Bracing myself for the scolding I deserve, I turn back inside. The lantern burns steadily on the table but the fire is almost out, just a smouldering heap. I need not have worried: my brother is fast asleep in his chair, one hand cradling a pitcher of beer, the other trailing towards the floor. His presence seems to take up every inch of our tiny cottage: the white walls, the fireplace with its cooking pots, the table Ma brought with us from England upturned on a cart. I trace his features with my eyes, his square jaw flecked with stubble, his deep-set eyes, green beneath the lids recalling our father, the early grey in his hair. I feel a jolt of pity: what I see is hardened by work and poor living.

He snorts in his sleep, causing the pitcher to tremble.

'Brother?' I whisper, but he does not flinch. 'William?'

I take the pitcher from his hand and tuck a blanket over his knees. Then, trying to make as little noise as possible, I climb the ladder to the crog loft, listening to the rasp of my brother's snoring and the wind howling a storm across the mountain.

18

'Hello?' A tall woman with neat bobbed hair stands in the open doorway of the vicarage.

Lydia tries to shrug off the uncertainty that has plagued her from the moment she woke up, that has gradually got worse during the course of the car journey. 'I telephoned yesterday,' she says. 'I made an appointment with the vicar.'

The woman beams. 'You're in luck. You found her.'

'Oh, I'm sorry, I thought . . .'

'Alison Seymour.' The woman offers a hand. She has a distinct English accent. 'The Reverend Alison Seymour. It was my husband you spoke to, *Mr* Seymour; he's an electrician.'

'Of course. How stupid of me!'

'Happens all the time. You must be Lydia? And this is Jamie? And Kyle . . . ?' Alison peers behind her at the car on the driveway as if Kyle might be lingering somewhere behind.

'Couldn't make it in the end.' She thinks of Kyle outside the tower, building his shed. Earlier he'd busted his thumb with the hammer, but he'd carried on regardless.

'No worries. Come on through.'

The vicarage sits behind the church in the town, a 1970s building with a large sweep of lawn and a driveway built to accommodate several cars. But today, apart from hers, there's only one: a yellow Ford Ka matching the primrose colour scheme inside. Lydia follows the vicar to a large functional lounge filled with bookcases and mismatched armchairs. She takes the seat by the window, settling Jamie on her lap.

'So,' the vicar takes the chair opposite. 'Tell me what brought you to the vicarage today. Baptism? Wedding? No, wait,' her eyes flash observantly to Lydia's ring finger, 'you and Kyle are married, right?'

'Right.' Lydia fishes Jamie's giraffe from her bag and bounces it along her knee. 'It's to do with the house we've just bought.'

'Okay.' Alison smiles encouragingly.

She lands the giraffe on Jamie's stomach, making him giggle. 'There's something wrong with it.'

'Wrong?'

She sighs, wondering where to begin. 'I've been hearing voices.'

'Go on.'

'Just one voice actually, calling a name. Martha.' She looks up, expecting some sort of surprised reaction, but Alison's eyes are steady and encouraging.

'And is it only you who hears this voice, or does your husband—?'

'He thinks it's in my head.'

'I see.' Alison flexes her fingers and Lydia hopes she won't dismiss her, insist she sees a doctor instead. 'Anything else?'

Lydia bounces the giraffe again. 'Just little things. Scratches on our new kitchen units. A stain that won't go away. The house is old, 1930s, and halfway up a mountain. The villagers are superstitious about it, a lot of them won't come near the place. There's a cottage higher up. A ruined cottage. I found animal traps in the shed.' She trails off, unsure how the two things are connected, *whether* they're connected. 'I suppose it's not much. At least, it doesn't sound much now I'm saying it out loud. But living there, it's,' she hunts for the word, 'different.'

Alison fishes a mince pie from a box on the table, offers one to Lydia but she shakes her head. She doesn't have much of an appetite.

'It all sounds very mysterious,' Alison says lightly. 'How do you think I might help?'

'I don't know.' Earlier, Kyle had told her he's going away for a few days to meet a client, and the thought of being on the mountain without him makes her stomach clench with anxiety. 'Maybe you could come to the house? Say some prayers?'

Alison catches crumbs with her hand. 'A blessing?'

Lydia nods. 'Do you think it would help?'

'It might make you feel more comfortable. Lots of people ask for it, especially in an old place. How about I come over this afternoon?'

She waits for Alison in the studio, wanting to be out of Kyle's way. Over lunch, he'd laughed off her trip to the vicarage. The last time either of them had stepped in a church was for Jamie's christening and, even then, Lydia had had a hard time persuading Kyle it was the right thing to do. Today, he'd made her feel stupid, like she was wasting Alison's time. But there was something beyond the humour, a look in his eye, a shadow of unease. Was he starting to believe there was something wrong here too? They'd moved around each other awkwardly after that, making polite enquiries about each other's work, taking turns to spoon pureed food into Jamie's mouth. After they'd eaten, she'd dived into her studio with Jamie, but now that she's here, she can't settle at her work. Jamie's fallen asleep and, despite the storage heaters, the air is brisk with cold. She's wrapped him in a blanket, but she keeps glancing over, checking he's okay.

Standing in the middle of the studio are the granite blocks for the commission. She runs her fingers over the mottled grey and white. She hasn't worked with stone for a long time, deterred by the brutal physical effort it involves and the possibility of error. But Stanley Harris has been unmoving on the matter. She's decided to create three figures: three women with postpartum figures, linked by their experience of childbirth. Strong, triumphant, carrying on. Her fingers linger over the stone, trying to feel its energy, it's willingness to be moulded. She tells herself, the beauty's there, waiting to be chipped away, she just needs to find the strength, the self-belief.

A car pulls up outside, a welcome interruption. Gently, she lifts Jamie into her arms and goes out.

Alison Seymour is standing at the end of the track, inspecting the exhaust pipe of her Ford Ka. She straightens up. 'Sorry for the delay. I didn't realise it was this far out. Gaer Fach's my furthest parish, I've six in total, and I've never been up the mountain. I think my car just about survived.'

'I should have warned you. Sorry.'

Alison smiles and collects a bag from the passenger seat. 'So this is Sunny Hill?'

'We were optimistic when we named it.' She looks apologetically at the tower. It seems more desolate than ever, the pebbledash grey rather than white, the planks of pine in the garden making the place look messy and abandoned. How had she ever thought she could transform this place into a dream home? It's an ugly scar, a blip on the landscape. No wonder the villagers are hostile towards its inhabitants.

Alison pulls her coat tight. 'You didn't tell me you lived in a tower. It's lovely.'

'It's remote.'

'That's one way of putting it.'

They linger in the kitchen while Lydia makes coffee, and Kyle stands with his back towards them, fidgeting with a set of spanners.

'How long have you lived in the area?' Lydia asks for something to say.

Alison takes a clear glass bottle from her bag along with a Bible and prayerbook – what they're about to do will happen regardless of small talk. She shakes her head. 'A year. I was a curate in Portsmouth, then I was five years in Birmingham. This is a whole different challenge. Give me inner-city kids any day. I've tried learning Welsh but failed miserably.' She snaps her bag closed and waves the bottle in the air, the liquid inside it catching the light from the window. 'Holy water. Blessed in the church. So, are we ready?'

Kyle grunts from the other side of the kitchen but follows anyway, leaving Jamie asleep in his bouncy chair. They start in the lounge, Alison opening the prayerbook and reading aloud.

'Lord God, you sent your Son to live among us and you have

filled us with the Spirit who dwells with us. Help us to be attentive to your word . . .'

She opens the bottle, takes a little brush from her pocket, flicks water around the room.

Lydia feels herself tense. Apart from the christening, it's a long time since she last went to church, and this feels so alien, so old-fashioned. What if it's dangerous? What if it does the reverse and awakens something it shouldn't?

They walk into the hall, down into the cellar, up to the rooms on the first and second and third floors. But nothing happens. Nothing at all. She relaxes, imagining the words from the prayerbook brushing the walls, wriggling into the spaces between the furniture, doing good. She feels Kyle stiffen as they enter the study, sees the horror in his eyes as holy water splashes on his monitor, his keyboard, his iPad. But there's a serenity about Alison that's reassuring, that convinces her the prayers and the holy water are necessary.

'For thus says the Lord the God of Israel, the jar of meal will not be emptied and the jug of oil will not fail until the day that the Lord sends rain on the earth.'

They're back in the kitchen, and Lydia sees Kyle grin as rain patters lightly against the window as if in response. He squeezes her hand and she squeezes back, feeling the connection. Things will be okay from now on, she thinks.

'Prepare us for the banquet of heaven and seat us at the table of the saints. Through Jesus Christ our Lord. Amen.'

Lydia echoes the Amen and nudges Kyle to do the same. Then they sit around the kitchen island, drinking the coffee that's been brewing.

'Thank you,' Lydia says, smiling at Alison. 'It felt like the right thing to do. It felt important.'

'You're welcome.' Alison leans down and plays with Martha, letting the little puppy chase her fingers. 'The house feels all right. When I was blessing the rooms, I didn't feel any resistance. I think you'll be happy here eventually. It might take some getting used to, that's all. I'm not an expert, but I didn't feel there was anything wrong.'

'I told you, didn't I?' Kyle cups his coffee and turns to Lydia. 'I told you there was nothing the matter. It's just the locals. They haven't been exactly friendly. It's going to take some settling in.'

Lydia sighs. 'As you can see, we don't quite agree on the house.'

'No. Well,' Alison tickles the puppy's tummy, 'in my experience, men and women don't agree on many things.'

They talk for a little longer, about unconnected things – moving to Wales, the Welsh weather, trying to pronounce the Welsh place names – then Alison makes her excuses to leave. When she's gone, the yellow car jolting down the potholed track, Kyle clears away the coffee mugs and Lydia lays her head on the cool marble of the kitchen island. Is this it? Is it all over? She looks across at her sleeping child and tells herself she has to believe that it is.

Water splashes into the sink as Kyle pours away the coffee grains. He's not spoken since Alison left, but she can sense he's relieved the vicar's gone; he doesn't like people he doesn't know meddling in their affairs. He screws the tap off and comes towards her.

Suddenly, he's kissing her hair, brushing his hand against the nape of her neck. She giggles at the touch of him, 'Stop, you're tickling me.'

The light changes as a cloud passes over the summit and the

rain dashes the window pane. Kyle looks up briefly, then kisses her again, this time firmly, insistently, his fingers finding her skin beneath her jumper, pushing beneath her bra.

She leans away from him. 'Shouldn't we do this later? Jamie might wake.'

But he pulls her from the stool and drags her to the floor. The cold flagstones shock her as he wriggles down her jeans.

'It's all over now,' he says, tugging at her knickers. 'You heard the vicar. All this nonsense with the house. It's over.'

The flagstones beneath her are as hard and uncompromising as the granite. She closes her eyes, trying to breathe with Kyle, trying to move in sync with him, trying to want him as much as he obviously wants her. She hears Martha growling. The floor is too hard, Kyle's hands are too rough, her body won't yield. She tries to satisfy him quickly, glad that he's impatient, not bothering with her. She arches her back, giving him what he wants, anchoring her mind on her studio, the work she should be doing, her tools and gloves lying in wait on the bench.

When she opens her eyes again, Kyle's breathing heavily on her chest, eyes fixed on the flagstones, Martha's tugging at the sleeve of his jumper, and she can see the mountain through the kitchen window, silently watching them.

19

An hour later, Kyle spreads his latest drawings on the makeshift desk in the cellar. He's felt uneasy since the vicar left and Liddy took J-J back to the studio. He doesn't buy into all that crap about there being something evil here. It's just the villagers making up stories, the likes of Griff Davies trying to get rid of them. And yet, he can't shake the niggling thought – a thought he wouldn't dare breathe to Liddy: they've just made things a whole lot worse.

He remembers the feeling when they'd walked upstairs, following the vicar into his grandfather's painting studio, then down again into the kitchen. A feeling that someone was standing right next to him, marking his footfall. A shadow that disappeared as soon as he turned his head. A shadow mocking their efforts to rid the tower of this thing. Except he doesn't believe in all that nonsense, does he?

He takes a Biro from his pocket and starts embellishing his sketches, connecting pipes from the stream to the generator, the generator to the central heating system. As he works, he remembers the feel of Liddy on the floor beneath him, his head pressed against her chest, Martha growling and biting his jumper. The memory doesn't sit right in his belly. It's like he's done something wrong.

Looking down, he realises he's pressed the Biro right through the page, into the old crate beneath. He runs his fingers through his beard, then takes up a fresh sheet of paper and starts again. He needs to get this right. He needs to take control of the tower, control of their lives.

He uses his ruler to draw it all out, the exact proportions of the entire hydroelectric system, ignoring the bruised feeling in his thumb where he hit it with the hammer. He feels better mastering the situation. Funny, down here is the only place he feels remotely himself. This mouldy old cellar, deep in the ground, where he can't look out of the window. Where he can't see the mountain. The only place where he didn't sense that shadow.

Suddenly he freezes, pen in his mouth.

That noise again! That noise in the kitchen. The same noise he heard when he was painting the house, before Liddy and J-J arrived. He stands up slowly, making as little sound as possible, not wanting to upset whatever it is, whatever is making that noise like a metal chain being dragged over the stone. He creeps up the cellar stairs, pulling himself up by the banister, his legs stiff from sitting so long in the cold.

He holds his breath as he pushes wide the cellar door into the corridor. This time he'll catch it, whatever or *who*ever it is, he'll catch it and throttle the hell out of it.

The hallway is silent. The front room is silent. Then, there's a split second of sound like splintering glass, cut so short he's not sure if it's real or imagined.

He tiptoes to the archway and peers into the kitchen. Everything is as he left it: the plates stacked high on the draining rack, the cafetière resting upside down in the sink, the little table that clips on to J-J's highchair waiting its turn to be washed with their lunch things. Nothing broken. Then he moves his attention to the kitchen island and notices shards of glass on the marble. It takes him a moment to realise what's happened: the vicar must have left her bottle of holy water behind, and, although it doesn't explain the sound of metal, it explains that other noise. The bottle has been smashed on the marble top, the water spilling into a glassy film, almost, but not quite, reaching the stain. The stain they can't get rid of. The stain as large as his outstretched hand.

He walks towards it and picks up the largest, most lethal pieces of glass, piling them one on top of the other, trying to get his head around how a bottle could have smashed on its own like that. He shudders involuntarily as he thinks what damage the glass shards could cause in the wrong hands. How they could hurt Liddy. How they could hurt little J-J. It's unimaginable. Horrible. And yet, he's thinking it anyway.

20

⚬⚬⚬

*I*t is early summer, a warm leisurely day. The heat shines my cheeks as I walk towards the church, swinging my empty basket. I have sold all my eggs and I have just this one thing left – to lay flowers on our parents' grave. I stop beside the hedgerow and pick the brightest of the foxgloves – whites and purples – careful not to let the sap seep on my fingers, ruining the only pair of gloves I own.

I stoop to clear the old flowers. William has only been here twice, for the funerals, but I visit every week. The grave is at the back of the churchyard, hugging the fence, Ma's name sharp and angular in the stone beneath our father's. I feel a beat of sorrow for the man I hardly remember, who would raise us on his shoulders and show us the world. He was killed shortly after we arrived here. An accident in the quarry, killing five others, but of course they blamed him, blamed the Englishman. He should have seen the stones falling. He should have raised the alarm.

The memory sours the fragrant air. I think of the men who car-ried his body back to the cottage, to the yard where I was playing, my short stumpy legs not big enough yet to climb to the summit. He got what he deserved, the men muttered to themselves as they turned their backs on the cottage and walked away as fast as they could, as if it might curse them. I think of William working in that same cruel quarry, toiling alongside the same men who were glad that our father was dead.

'You are together now,' I say to our parents, laying the foxgloves on the earth, before picking up the vase for filling at the river.

Running behind the churchyard, the river is a bright swirl of silver where the mountain stream collects. Ma used to let me paddle there. I remember the water rippling between my toes, clear as glass, weeds and sticks drifting around my ankles. I would hitch my skirt and petticoat above my knees, but they would still get wet.

There's a rock protruding above the rushing water. I lay the vase on the bank and step onto it, knowing how William would scold me if he saw me now, taking such a risk. It is dizzying looking down, the water faster and deeper than I remember. I stretch my arms to steady myself and feel the cool spray against my face. Then I close my eyes.

Someone grabs me from behind.

My eyes flash open, sure it is my brother come down from the moun-tain to find me. I turn around, taking care not to slip from the rock. I am dazed by the glare of the sun, the way it shimmers off the water.

But it is not William at all. Morgan Lloyd pulls me onto the bank. 'Forgive me,' he says, releasing his grip. 'You almost fell.'

I raise my chin defensively, feeling the sun burn my cheeks, the rim of my bonnet too shallow to offer much shade. 'I was perfectly safe.'

He stoops to retrieve the vase, dips it in the river and fills it with water.

'I saw you in the churchyard,' he says.

I want to know if he followed me here deliberately, but I cannot ask. Instead, I lower my chin. 'It is the anniversary of Ma's death.'

He lays a hand on the rough sleeve of my dress. 'I am sorry.'

The tears well before I can control them. I fling his hand from mine and wipe my face, sullying my gloves. What does Morgan care for me? Is this a tale for him to laugh about with his friends?

'Please,' I say, thinking of William alone in the cottage, 'you must let me pass. My brother will be expecting me home.'

'You should stay. Sit down. I will keep you company. You seem unwell.'

'I am not unwell.' I am indignant. 'I am in perfect health. But I have a long way to walk.' My eyes flash to the mountain, to the cottage that from here is just a blemish on the landscape, unnoticeable to most who would look that way.

He follows my gaze. 'You should not live up there.'

'It is my home.'

'But a young girl! A young woman!'

'And what would you have? That I live here among men who accused my father of causing the death of others? Who beat my brother?'

I snatch the vase and push past him, our bodies brushing against each other.

'Martha!' he calls after me, but I will not go to him. I cannot go to him.

Then something happens. Morgan runs after me, pushes me against the hedgerow. I feel his hands on my waist, the heat of his breath in my face. The vase drops silently to the grass below. Water splashes down my skirt.

'Forgive me,' he says again, his cheeks burning with shame. He steps back so that my path is free, but still I do not move. 'It is just . . . you must believe . . . not everyone wishes you ill.'

He retrieves the fallen vase from the grass and pushes it into my hand, his fingers touching mine through the gloves, just for a second, while I try desperately not to think about what William would say if he saw us together like this. Then he turns and walks away from me, the flapping of his coat as rapid as my heartbeat.

21

Lydia wakes the next morning knowing something's wrong. Last night they'd ploughed their way through the leftover Prosecco, needing something to numb their minds after Alison's visit. But although the drink stirs inside her, threatening to resurface, it's not that which had awoken her but the light outside, flickering, strobe-like. They'd been too drunk to draw the curtains, but there's never a light on this side of the house, only natural sunlight pouring over the valley. She glances at her phone. It's only quarter to six. Quarter to six in mid-October. It should be pitch black.

She shakes Kyle. 'Wake up.'

'What?' He sounds decidedly groggy.

'Something's not right.'

But the light disappears. She stretches her arms but can't see them, can't see Kyle either; she still needs to buy that night-light. She switches on the bedside lamp instead.

Kyle groans. 'What the fuck?' He glances at the cot at the foot of their bed, at Jamie fast asleep. 'My head hurts.'

'There's something up. I saw a light.'

She rummages among her clothes from the night before, dropped on the floor where she'd left them. Memories float through the fog: showing Kyle the photograph on the walking blog; Kyle analysing it, dismissing it; the two of them arguing drunkenly, something about Griff Davies and the vicar; Kyle pouring more Prosecco, storming into the kitchen with a glass in his hand, pulling up the blind, letting the darkness stream in like water from a tap, drowning them both.

There's a foul, acidic taste in her mouth. She runs to the bathroom, clutching her stomach, and throws up in the toilet bowl. A noise startles her from behind. She swings around and the whole room spins.

'Hey, have a tissue.' Kyle leans over and pulls off a ream of toilet paper. 'I think we rather overdid it last night.'

She wipes her mouth as the bile rises again.

'Come back to bed,' he says.

'No. I think I need fresh air.' She stands up, unsteadily. 'I'll take Martha out.'

'But it's the middle of the night.'

'It's early morning. I'll be okay once I'm outside. Honestly. Go back to bed.'

He shrugs and leaves her to it. She cleans her teeth and examines her face in the mirror. Red hung-over eyes, tangled hair, anaemic skin.

Ugly. Fat. Unlovable.

The words come from nowhere. Words inside her head.

Words she has to chase to recall where they came from: her first university; just after she and Danny split up. She turns away and brushes her hair, determined not to think about any of that.

Downstairs, she puts Martha on the lead, then walks along the track. The sun is rising, tinging the sky red, and, at the far end, the farmhouse is lit up, lights in every window, lights glowing from the barns. The feeling that something isn't right intensifies. The Joneses are always up early, but she's never seen all the lights on like this. She glances back at the tower, seeking its reassurance, but it's just a dark shadow against the barely lit landscape. She runs towards the farm, Martha pulling in front, nose to the ground. Turning the corner into the yard, she sees an ambulance. She breaks into a sprint, not even thinking of the dogs as she enters the yard. There's a stretcher and a couple of paramedics in front of the farmhouse. Emlyn is standing in the middle of it all.

'What is it? What's happened?'

He turns, stoney-faced, hands pushed deep into the pockets of his boiler suit. 'Dad collapsed.' He eyes the stretcher, the pale slight figure beneath the blanket. 'Pig-headed bugger,' he mutters. 'I told him not to go there. I told him.' He strikes out with his foot, sending a metal bucket clattering across the yard.

'Collapsed? Where? How?'

'They say it's his heart.' He laughs, a cold hollow sound.

'I'm so sorry. That's awful. Such a shock.' She thinks of Kyle's grandfather, Eleri finding him on the doorstep. 'I wonder—'

He waves a hand to silence her, 'Dwi ddim angen dy cydymdeimlad,' then walks towards the barns, away from the ambulance, away from his dad.

She calls after him. 'Shouldn't you go with him? Go with the ambulance. Shouldn't you—'

'No!' The vehemence in his voice shocks her across the yard.
'But he'll want you. He *needs* you.'

'There's too much to do here.'

She looks around desperately, catching sight of the henhouse.
'I could help. I could feed the chickens?'

He opens the barn door and disappears inside.

She waits with the ambulance until it leaves, then stands
alone, wondering what to do. Stay? Go home? Eventually,
with no sign of the other dogs, she coaxes Martha into the
farmhouse before returning to the yard and inspecting the
henhouse. The chickens cluck impatiently. She follows her
instinct, finding a metal scoop and filling the feeders from
the sack by the door, changing the water, letting herself into
the shed at the back. The nesting boxes are stacked against
the far wall. She digs inside, feeling the smooth warmth of
fresh eggs, then looks for something to carry them in. There's
nothing she can make out that will do, so she lays the eggs in
a well at the bottom of her jumper. Something shifts above
the nesting boxes. A mouse? A rat? Unnerved, she withdraws
to the farmhouse.

The kitchen is a mess. There are plates piled high in the sink
and packets of food crammed on the table. She gets to work,
battling the dishes, scrubbing the blackened frying pan, scour-
ing the cutlery. Another flush of nausea sends her in search of
the bathroom. She finds it at the head of the stairs: a bathroom
suite in avocado green daubed with a greasy film of dirt. She's
sick again, hitting the toilet bowl just in time, feeling weak
and dizzy and better all at once.

Downstairs, she attacks the dishes with renewed vigour,
heaping half-eaten bowls of breakfast into the bin, pouring cold
tea down the drain, tackling the worksurfaces with a crusted

bottle of cream cleaner. The whole place reeks of neglect but, by the time she's finished, the kitchen is gleaming.

Emlyn walks in, trampling something foul-smelling across the floor. He finds his cigarettes and narrows his eyes. 'What the fuck's gone on here?'

She shrugs. 'I tidied up.'

He throws himself into the armchair beside the fire. She wants to tell him she's fed the chickens too, and changed their water, and collected their eggs, but she can't. The compulsion to get away from him is too great. She calls to Martha and lifts the latch of the door as silently, as unobtrusively, as she can.

'Where are you going?'

Her heart hammers. 'Home. Unless there's anything else?'

He lights up and inhales deeply. 'No,' he growls between his teeth as the smoke escapes. 'There's nothing for you here. Isn't that obvious?'

22

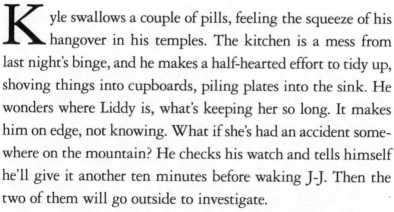

Kyle swallows a couple of pills, feeling the squeeze of his hangover in his temples. The kitchen is a mess from last night's binge, and he makes a half-hearted effort to tidy up, shoving things into cupboards, piling plates into the sink. He wonders where Liddy is, what's keeping her so long. It makes him on edge, not knowing. What if she's had an accident somewhere on the mountain? He checks his watch and tells himself he'll give it another ten minutes before waking J-J. Then the two of them will go outside to investigate.

He jams the Prosecco bottles into the overflowing bin, pushes the whole lot down to make them fit, then grabs the two sides of the bin bag in an attempt to make a knot. The bag splits. A bottle of Prosecco clatters onto the floor and rolls towards the kitchen island. He watches it rotate to a standstill, the green of the glass catching in the overhead light. There's a renewed quiet, the depth of which is almost palpable, like someone holding their breath.

He pauses where he is, hands resting on the rubbish, his chest tightening. The hairs stand up on his arms beneath his shirt. There's someone here. Someone standing silently behind him in the room. Someone he can't see, can't hear, but he knows they're there all the same. He thinks of all the things Liddy's been saying about the tower, all the nonsense she spilled to the vicar. He's not believed it before, not really; he's pushed it to the back of his mind because it doesn't fit with his plan of making a life for themselves here. But what if she's right? He thinks of the noise of the metal chain, the smashed bottle of holy water. The things he's made a conscious effort to rationalise. What if? What if?

He swings around, confronting his own stupidity.

A shadow moves across the floor. He can see it clearly: the shadow of a man. It's exactly like the shadow he saw when the vicar blessed the house, only this time it's slower, pausing on the paving so that he can make out the arms, the legs, the chest. He steps away from it, knocking the bin behind. A cascade of empty cartons hits the floor. The shadow disappears.

He bends down and shoves the cartons back in the bin, telling himself over and over to stop imagining things. To stop being so bloody stupid.

23

A week later, Lydia stands in the shop, breathing in the smell of coffee and cleaning fluid. She fingers sleep from her eyes and tries to look cheerful, but she's been awake since Kyle left at five-thirty and is starting to flag. It had come as a surprise when he'd announced he was going away: three days in London to meet a potential new client.

'*Only* three days,' he'd said that morning in bed, holding her tight, squeezing out the remnants of their latest argument. She knows how frustrated he feels by the lack of work he's picked up in Wales. He needs this client. 'And then I'll be back. I promise.' Promise. As if he'd considered *not* coming back.

Half an hour later, she'd watched the car he'd hired for the trip disappear along the track, the mist wrapping around her like a cloak.

'I wonder how Emlyn will cope,' she says to Eleri. They're

talking about the farm: the day after he'd collapsed, Mr Jones had died in hospital.

Eleri lugs a pile of Halloween decorations onto the counter. 'He'll be fine. Emlyn's strong.'

'He scares me.'

'Emlyn?' Eleri untangles a heap of cardboard skeletons. 'To be honest, you're not alone. A lot of the villagers keep a wide berth. His mum died of cancer when he was a kid and it messed him up. I remember him at school getting into trouble. He was always really angry.'

'He's *still* really angry.'

Eleri smiles, leans over and strokes Jamie's cheek. 'Thanks for the other night by the way. Jon was thrilled with the bottle. It's not often we drink Prosecco. And about what I said, I've been thinking.' A pause while she smooths Jamie's hair. 'I feel bad about what I told you about the tower. About the villagers keeping away. I probably made it sound worse than it is.'

'It's fine. Don't worry. It explained a lot. Helped us make sense of the situation.'

The situation. It sounds so ordinary put like that. So clinical. A situation that can be worked upon. That can be resolved. She thinks about Alison and the blessing, the way things have been strained between her and Kyle since Alison's visit. They've been polite with each other, *too* polite, like strangers at times. And, although nothing's happened at the tower since, it feels . . . she searches for the right word . . . it feels as if the house is *waiting*.

'I didn't want to scare you, that's all,' Eleri says.

'You didn't scare us.' But she's lying. She *is* scared. 'But there's one thing that's been bothering me.'

'Oh yes?' Eleri sounds cautious.

'You said Edward Jeffreys went crazy on the mountain. I

wanted to ask more at the time, only I didn't want Kyle to get upset. Things have been a bit difficult lately.' She chews her lower lip.

Eleri picks up one of the skeletons, folds and unfolds the limbs. 'Well,' she shrugs, 'I suppose you'll find out eventually, if not from me then from someone else. Before the heart attack, Edward Jeffreys went mad.'

'*Mad?*'

'Angry. Violent. Upsetting the villagers. He came into the pub one night and swiped drinks off the table, shouted abuse, accused people of spying on him, which was nonsense, of course.'

'Why was it nonsense? Maybe he was telling the truth.' She thinks of the light that shines through the kitchen window. 'Maybe someone *was* watching him.'

Eleri shakes her head. 'No one goes that far up. Only hill walkers and tourists. One day Edward came here to the shop. I was alone. Jon was out with the kids, thank God. Edward started swearing, calling me names. Bitch. Whore. Worse than that. There was a hardness to his eyes I'd never seen before. He started yanking things from the shelves. A whole unit crashed to the floor. Luckily Griff Davies was outside, on his way to the pub. He came in and manhandled him out of the shop.'

'Did you call the police?'

'I was going to report the incident. Jon wanted me to anyway. But there wasn't any real damage, just superficial stuff. I'd made up my mind to talk to his doctor instead. The next day, unbeknown to Jon, I went to see him, to ask his permission to speak to his GP. And that's when I found him on the doorstep.'

'You visited him in the hospital,' Lydia remembers. 'After

what he'd done to you, I'd have thought you were the last person who wanted to see him.'

'I felt sorry for him. He had no friends to speak of, only me. No one to look after him. What happened here was completely out of character.'

'Perhaps he had a breakdown? Perhaps he was a schizo-phrenic and forgot to take his medication? Perhaps he had a medical condition that made him confused?'

'I suppose.' Eleri smiles sadly. 'But he was also a recluse. He spent all his time up in the tower painting. Who knows what was really going on?' She slides a bag of toffees towards her across the newspapers, signalling the end of the conversation. 'These are on the house.'

'No, really I couldn't.'

'Yes, you could. It's a thank you for the other night. And with Kyle being away, you know you're welcome here, don't you? I mean it. Anytime.'

The story of Edward Jeffreys plays on her mind, but the days without Kyle pass without incident. She's careful to close the kitchen blind, and she scrubs away at the stain on the marble worktop whenever she passes. She even tries sanding the bottom of the kitchen island, but the scratches are deeper than she'd imagined. The whole plinth needs replacing. She takes a pen and marks the ends of the furthermost scratches, just in case.

On the second day, she makes a promise to herself: no more procrastination, no more excuses; other than attending the memorial service for Mr Jones and looking after Jamie, she'll work steadily on the pieces for the commission until Kyle comes home. She sets herself up in the studio, placing the storage heaters next to Jamie's playpen, making up flasks of hot tea and carrying them over. The remoteness of the tower seems even more pronounced within the thin walls and she can't help thinking of Edward Jeffreys, all alone painting in the tower, slowly descending into madness. The wind rattles the loose windows and whispers through the gap at the bottom of the door. As Jamie bats his baby mirror and Martha chases a ball into the dusty corners, it occurs to her that Alison didn't bother with the barn or the garage. This part of the property isn't blessed.

That night, too tired to shower, with clay in her fingernails from making maquettes for the commission work, she falls asleep immediately. It's a night full of dreams, nightmares, waking her sporadically, spiralling her into a state of semi-conscious panic. Dreams about Matt pushing her onto the bed. Dreams where she's looking up, seeing the madness in his eyes. Dreams where Danny's confronting her, demanding to know why she broke up with him. She wakes up, heart pounding, breathing rapidly into the bedclothes. Her hair is damp with sweat though the room is freezing, and the memories cascade through the darkness: Danny pestering her, pleading with her behind the closed door. 'I'm sorry, Lydia. Whatever I've done, I'm sorry. I love you! You love me too.'

In her mind, she's back in the university halls, back in 2004, turning up the stereo, blocking Danny out. Louder and louder until the desk drums beneath the speakers and someone thumps on the ceiling below.

But she can't get away from him. Danny's everywhere she goes: in the supermarket when she's buying bread; outside the lecture theatre when she hangs back to tie her shoelace; on her way to the gym. Then there are the letters, written on Basildon

Bond with a fountain pen, making her ache with regret, with guilt. Eventually, her friends grow tired of asking what's wrong with her and why she doesn't go out any more. Tired of the same reply, 'I'm fine. I'm just bored of the same bars and clubs. I want to concentrate on my work.'

She avoids Matt like the plague and changes her class. She cuts her hair short, buys new clothes, stops wearing make-up. In the end, she transfers to another university, on the other side of the country. It seems so much easier than facing the daily possibility of bumping into Matt Trevithick. She picks a different subject, something she's always been interested in, but never had the temerity to pursue until now, because now feels like she's already standing on the edge of a precipice anyway: Bachelor of Fine Arts. She thinks it will all end there – she can release herself in her passion – but it doesn't. She starts getting panic attacks and seeks help from her GP, who refers her to a therapist. But she doesn't tell the therapist the truth. Rather, she sorts things in her own way, focusing on her work, getting her name known for the right reasons.

Now she tries blocking the memories from her mind, tries forcing herself to sleep, but nothing works. The harder she tries, the louder the memories become.

In the morning, she drags herself out of bed to make Jamie his breakfast, then somehow battles through the other chores before driving to the village again for the memorial service. Dropping Jamie with Eleri, she walks to St Teilo's Church. There's a handful of villagers she recognises, but the rest are friends or relatives she doesn't know, only Emlyn, alone on the front pew, wearing a shabby black jacket.

She leaves the church first, intending to slip away before anyone sees her, but the relatives follow quickly, linking arms, smoking and sharing muted jokes. She escapes around the back, into the churchyard. No one will come this way, not with the sky threatening yet more rain. She watches from a distance, as they filter one by one into the Owain Glyn Dŵr. She thinks about joining them, imagining the freshly scrubbed tables, the pint glasses stacked in waiting on the bar, the plates of crisps and sandwiches. But she knows she'd feel alone. She'd feel the outsider.

Instead, she lingers in the churchyard, surveying her surroundings through the light drifts of rain. The graves are old, sinking into the ground. She wonders how long before they disappear completely, before the lives of all these people vanish as if they'd never been. The dates on the stones are mainly nineteenth century, a few older ones, but nothing from recent years. All the new graves lie in the town next to the crematorium.

She wanders to the far edge of the churchyard, to a grave on its own, leaning against the fence. It draws her attention because it looks so different to the others, plainer and of a lighter stone. The inscription is covered with moss, but, with persistence, she can read it:

GEORGE HELFORD,
DIED 1894, AGED 30

MARY HELFORD,
DIED 1908, AGED 42

MARTHA ELIZABETH HELFORD,
DIED 1910, AGED 20

Martha. Her eyes rest on the name. She thinks about the other graves in the churchyard, the elaborate inscriptions. Here, there are no comforting words about angels and heaven.

Nothing that suggests Martha Helford was missed by anyone, or loved by anyone. An English name, she realises with terrifying clarity. A single family of Helfords among the Joneses and Davieses and Williams.

'It's an illusion.'

She spins on the spot, dropping her handbag. Behind her is the vicar, sheltering in the arc of a huge black umbrella. Not Alison, but the older clergyman who'd taken the service. He extends an arm. 'I'm sorry, I didn't mean to startle you.'

She forces a laugh and picks up her bag from the sodden grass. It's only now she sees the line of berries on top of the headstone, small dried berries like the ones at the kitchen window.

'You're soaked. Here, come and join me under the umbrella.'

She hadn't noticed until now how heavy the rain had become. The vicar turns in the direction of the path and she follows.

'You're not from around here?' he says.

'No. We've just moved in. Sunny Hill. Up on the mountain.'

'Ah. Yes. I've heard about you from Alison. The Steins?'

'That's right.' What else has Alison told him?

'It's Y Twr Gwyn really,' he says. 'Twr, as you can probably guess, means tower, and Gwyn means white. Though why anyone would want to build a tower up there, at the mercy of the elements, is beyond me.'

'We wanted to change the name.'

'Wise.'

'Why do you say that?'

The vicar stops walking, the rain drumming on the umbrella, splashing her uncovered shoulder. 'It's always good to make a fresh start, don't you think?'

She remembers the cross carved into the lintel like a protective symbol.

'Superstition,' he says as if following her train of thought. 'Why do you think I'm here today? I'm seventy-five years old, but the villagers would rather me take the service than a woman half my age.' He leans closer, and reduces his voice to a whisper. 'Just wait until they ordain women bishops.' He chuckles.

'Tell me about the grave. Why did you say it was an illusion?'

'Martha Helford? She committed suicide, or so they say. There was a lot of talk at the time. Her body was found drowned in the river, but they also found poison where she lived, in the cottage on the mountain. Y Bwthyn Gwyn it was called back then. The White Cottage. But now it's just a ruin. I suspect the post-mortem examination was rather half-hearted. Even if someone had decided to do away with her, no one would have cared.'

'Why not?'

'They say she was a witch.'

She laughs. It sounds so medieval.

'The Helfords moved into the cottage on the mountain. They were English, came here to seek a better life, to find work in the quarry. But the parents died and it was just the two of them left, Martha and her brother.'

'Why did people think she was a witch?'

'Even as a child, she was arrestingly beautiful. Bewitching, some would say. I guess the local girls were jealous. Soon after the Helfords moved into the area, accidents started to happen. There was a crush at the quarry killing the father and several other men. A bad winter when there wasn't enough food. A couple of babies died. Then the Helford mother succumbed to a fever.'

'But what did any of it have to do with Martha?'

'A stranger in the village. A bewitchingly beautiful one at that, one who seemed to threaten the natural order of things. As I said, the villagers are superstitious. Always have been. Always will be. By 1910, suicides were allowed in consecrated land, but that didn't stop the locals. Rumour has it, they drove a stake through her heart, to stop her spirit from wandering.'

She shudders, glancing back at the grave, at those lonely names.

'They say her spirit wanders anyway. On the mountain where she lived with her brother.'

'Her brother?'

'William. Five years her senior. He was mortally wounded in Belgium in 1915, fighting for his country. He was one of the first recruits, a volunteer. Signed up as soon as the First World War was declared. I suppose he was lonely without his sister. Or maybe he'd had enough of the villagers. Enough of their tales. He'd moved from the area by then, but mud sticks.'

'And what do you believe about the tales?'

'Coincidences. That's all. People die all the time but we make it into something unusual. We look for answers where there aren't any.' The vicar smiles, his dog collar flashing beneath his thick woollen trench coat. 'As for the stake through the heart, I know there's no truth in that either.'

'How do you know?'

They reach the lych-gate and he pushes it open, allowing her to step through. 'My grandfather was sexton here until 1930. He told me what happened. He'd got everything prepared. The coffin was waiting in the church, the grave dug. But William insisted he take the body away, said Martha belonged to the mountain. They waited until dark, and then my grandfather helped him carry it there, with only a lantern to lead the way.

The cart would only go so far up the mountain road before they had to walk, carrying the coffin between them. Then, William dug the grave himself and paid my grandfather, and presumably the vicar, good money to keep it all quiet. He didn't want anyone to know. He thought people might try to dig her up, mistreat her in death as they had in life. That's why the grave is an illusion.'

'But where is the real grave?'

The vicar looks upwards, tilting his umbrella. 'Somewhere up there. Up on the mountain. It was marked with a stone, my grandfather said. A white stone. But there are hundreds of white stones on Mynydd Gwyn. She could be anywhere!'

Back at the house, she keeps herself busy, walking Martha, playing with Jamie, trying not to think about the grave on the mountain. Jamie falls asleep and she takes him upstairs, laying him gently in his cot, arranging a blanket over his little body, tucking in his toy giraffe. Then she checks the baby monitor is turned to full volume and busies herself in the kitchen, purposely clattering pans, talking to the puppy as she works.

'I'm baking a cake for Kyle. Marmalade cake. Do you like cake, Martha?' She bends down and scratches the puppy's head, more unsure than ever about her name. Is it too late to change it? But Martha responds as usual to being called, wagging her tail and playfully nipping her fingers. Lydia takes a bag of raisins from the cupboard and glances upwards at the blind, reassuring herself it's closed. A solid wall of muted green. 'Maybe Emlyn fed you cake in the farmhouse,' she says.

The baby monitor crackles on the other side of the archway. She pauses with the raisins in her hand, hearing a faint whir through the speakers. She stiffens, alert to every sound, the wind down the chimneys, the birds crying outside. She puts the raisins down, wipes her hands, then walks purposefully through the lounge, down the corridor and into the stairwell. The noise is suddenly louder and she knows what it is: the mechanical whir of the bathroom fan. She runs up the stairs, thinking she must have forgotten to turn it off when she showered, and somehow she didn't notice it when she put Jamie to bed. She tiptoes past his cot, reaches for the cord around the bathroom door, gives it a tug. The fan clatters to a standstill.

'Sleep tight, Jamie,' she whispers as she tiptoes out again.

She opens the door to the stairwell and freezes. The noise is still there. The smooth whir-whir of a fan, only dimmer, this time emanating from the washroom on the second floor. She can't explain it. She *knows* she hasn't been higher than the first floor since Kyle left for London. It's impossible the fan has been left on all this time. Even if Kyle *had* left it on for a reason she can't fathom, she would have heard it.

Her stomach tightens as she grips the banister and forces herself to climb the second flight of stairs. She reaches the door to Kyle's study and takes a deep breath before pushing it open. She walks quickly, past his PC, past the empty beer bottles lining his desk, to the washroom door. She hesitates, hearing the moan of the fan from within, then turns the door handle. The room is freezing cold. Icy tiles meet her fingertips as she steps forwards, grabbing the end of the fan cord, pulling it hard. The fan whines to a stop, but the noise is still there, still whirring above her head. She looks upwards to the ceiling, dotted with mould spores: the washroom on the third floor.

It's just another fan. It means nothing. Kyle must have left them on before he went.

She retraces her steps through the study, then tiptoes up the next flight of stairs. In the room at the top, the room with Edward Jeffreys' paintings, dust motes hover in the dying afternoon sunlight. The door to the washroom stands ajar and she can hear the vague clanking of the fan within. She runs the final few paces, unable to bear any more.

She can't locate the fan to begin with. She casts her eyes across the cream tiles, the old-fashioned lavatory, the empty shelves. The room is even colder than the one on the second floor and reeks of damp. Eventually she sees it, high above the mirror. An old-fashioned wall fan, older than the ones on the first and second floors, with a Bakelite surround, probably original to the house. The mirror too is old, not one of their own. The glass is mottled with age, so that what she's looking at is part her own reflection and part black spots. She reaches upwards, pulls the frayed fan cord, listens to the gradual cessation of sound.

Even as a child, she was arrestingly beautiful.

Suddenly, she's too afraid to look in the mirror. What if it's not her reflection staring back? What if it's someone else's? She shields her eyes with her hands, seeing in her mind that face again, the face from her dream: the long black hair, the forehead splashed with blood. Her heart races. She can smell it again, the bitter stench of a cigarette.

She tries to breathe through the fear, the smell, the overwhelming horror. Someone's in the room. Someone's behind her. Then, something pricks her arm. A searing red-hot pain.

She gasps and pulls her hands from her face, but there's nothing to see, only her own reflection, distorted in the antique glass.

She runs, taking the stairs two at a time, grabbing Jamie from his cot on the first floor. He cries into her shoulder, baffled by the sudden awakening, as she takes him outdoors, into the barn, calling Martha to follow.

'We're waiting in here for Daddy. He won't be long. Then everything will be okay. Everything will make sense again.'

24

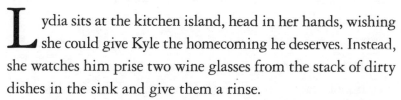

Lydia sits at the kitchen island, head in her hands, wishing she could give Kyle the homecoming he deserves. Instead, she watches him prise two wine glasses from the stack of dirty dishes in the sink and give them a rinse.

'The fans,' she says. 'The extractor fans. Not just in *our* bathroom, but in the washrooms on the second and third floors too. They were all turned on. And then, I felt something, a presence in the room, an image in my mind. Someone I've seen before in a dream.'

Kyle flicks a tea towel over the glasses. 'It was me,' he says simply. 'I just remembered.'

'What?'

He sets the glasses on the kitchen island. 'It was me who turned the fans on before I left. I'm sorry, I should have told you. There's so much damp up there. I thought it would help.'

'Oh.'

He laughs. 'You sound disappointed. Almost as if you wanted a haunted extractor fan?'

She smiles, but she's not convinced. Is he lying to make her feel better? She watches him pull up his sleeves and uncork the bottle he picked up in a service station.

'Hey, what did you do to your arm?' he says, reaching out.

She frowns and looks down. Above her wrist, just showing beneath the sleeve of her jumper, there's an ugly red mark. 'I don't know. I thought I felt something earlier . . . '

'You must have burned yourself cooking.'

She shakes her head. She's sure that's not true. It's something to do with the house, the washroom. She's about to say more, but she stops herself. After a long drive, she's being unfair, she ought to be asking Kyle about his time away rather than talking about the tower. 'So, how was London?' she asks half-heartedly.

'Oh, you know. The same old.' He sits down next to her, his suit sleeve brushing against her jumper. In front of them is her sketchbook. Her eyes fall on the lines of pen covering the open pages. Just scribbles on paper. She's spent hours working on these, but looking at them now, they aren't what she envisaged. It's like she's got a mental block.

'Look,' Kyle says, following her gaze. 'You've had a hard day, a memorial service, not exactly a barrel of laughs. And you've been stressed with the move. I'm sorry I left you alone. I was worried about you. It's a big thing, all this. Moving house. Moving to Wales. You said yourself you were having night-mares. Memories you've long ago buried. The move is bound to bring stuff back. It's bound to make you imagine things.'

'What about the scratches?'

'The scratches?'

'Here,' she bends down and points at the plinth at the bottom of the kitchen island. She's doing it anyway, talking about the house. 'We haven't discussed those properly. We've just put them down to Martha.' She flinches at the name. All afternoon, shivering with Jamie in the barn, she'd been thinking of alternatives – Jess, Poppy, Flax – but none of them had seemed quite right, and, although she hadn't known why, she'd felt guilty even thinking about it. 'But she's only a puppy and I've been looking at them. I don't think it's possible.'

He rubs his arm through his sleeve. 'Martha probably saw a mouse and went crazy. I found droppings beneath the sink. We'll set a trap. There's a few old traps in the cellar.'

He pours the wine, the comforting glug-glug-glug that these days seems to be his answer to just about everything. Then he changes the subject, telling her the story of his week: his morning pancakes, his evening stroll along the Thames, drinks with Charlie and Benedita, the new contract. She feels herself withdrawing and puts it down to tiredness; looking after Jamie on her own has sapped her energy. Eventually, when they've finished the bottle, he leads her to bed.

'I've missed you,' he says.

She changes into her pyjamas with her naked body facing the wall, but she can feel him watching her, watching and wanting in the nightlight she's bought. She lies down and stares at the shadowy ceiling, feeling his hand move up her thigh. Not in the mood, she rolls away from him, pulling the duvet with her.

'What?' he says. 'Is it the time of the month?'

She shakes her head. It hasn't been the time of the month for a long while, not since before she fell pregnant with Jamie. He leans over her and kisses her eyebrows, her eyelids, the tip of her nose, the stain of red wine around her mouth. But she doesn't want it, though she can't explain why. Maybe she's jealous of his time away in London? Maybe it's the way he lied about the fans?

'I'm tired,' she says. 'Sorry, not tonight.'

But he doesn't give in. 'You'd tell me, wouldn't you, if something was wrong? I don't mean the house. I mean wrong between us?'

She nods silently, and creeps a little further to the edge of the bed.

The next day, she drives the eight miles to the town. Something Kyle said last night is bothering her: *you'd tell me, wouldn't you, if something was wrong?* Something *is* niggling her, not just the house; something on her mind that she wants to put to rest. She parks the car, then walks to the pharmacy, pretending to look at make-up until the place is deserted. Then she heads to the family planning section and picks up a pregnancy test.

Back at Sunny Hill, she hides herself in the bathroom and opens the foil wrapper. It doesn't seem long ago since she found out she was pregnant with Jamie. She'd been a bundle of nervous excitement, back then. Kyle had waited for her in the living room in the flat, and she'd run from the bathroom and held the test out to him, beaming. Now, she does this alone: Kyle and Jamie are downstairs with no idea what she's doing. She pees on the stick and watches the digital egg timer flash on the screen. She tries telling herself it's ridiculous. Jamie's not even seven months old. She's only just stopped breastfeeding. Her hormones are out of whack, that's all.

Flash, flash, flash.

She glances up at the bathroom fan, down at the baby-blue

bathmat. She thinks of the washrooms, the layout of the house, the way the rowan trees shade the barn.

The flashing stops. She holds her breath, feeling her whole body tense as she stares at the screen. Her stomach flips. There's no denying the word in black digital letters:

Pregnant

She opens the bathroom door in a daze. Now it all makes sense. The reason she's imagined all this stuff in the tower, the reason she's been having nightmares, the mood swings and sickness. She remembers when she'd been pregnant with Jamie, how difficult it had been to concentrate on anything but the pregnancy; she'd forgotten things, made silly mistakes. She sits down on the bed, her mind racing, wondering how on earth she's going to tell Kyle. Present him with the pee stick? Wrap it in tissue paper? Tell him over a bottle of wine? And then the guilt: God, she's been drinking a lot recently, too much, still has a vague headache from last night. It's the reason she thought she'd been sick. She prays she hasn't done it any harm. It. *It?* A baby. A human being. A brother or sister for Jamie.

She holds her head in her hands. How will Jamie cope? Will he feel pushed out? How will they afford the extra expense? Is she even strong enough to carry a baby so soon after Jamie? They'd been drinking so much with the move, they'd had sex without thinking, presuming they were safe because her periods hadn't resumed after the birth. They'd tried for months to conceive Jamie; it had become compulsive, tracking her cycle, doing her utmost to look after her body. She knows it had driven Kyle to distraction, the way she'd obsessed over it. And now this has happened, just like that.

She hears Jamie crying for her downstairs. He's hungry. She can tell that just by the sound of his cry, and for some reason,

Kyle isn't listening to him. She goes downstairs and finds Kyle scrubbing the stain on the kitchen island, rusty red again – the stain that remains no matter how many times they spray it with bleach – his forehead creased in a deep frown. She grabs Jamie from his bouncy chair and presses him against her chest. 'I'm pregnant,' she says.

Kyle looks up as Jamie bawls.

'What?'

'I'm pregnant.' She flings the test on the kitchen island, watching it skid to a halt on the stain. The frustration on Kyle's face distorts into shock. He picks the test up slowly, as though it might hurt him. 'I don't understand.'

'We haven't been exactly careful.' She turns to find the tin of powdered milk on the workstation and opens it with one hand. 'It's okay, little fellow. Mummy's here now.' She counts scoops of powder into a bottle.

'Jesus Christ.' Kyle stares at the test. 'This is totally crazy.'

Jamie stops crying and tries out his latest sound against her shoulder, *Ma, Ma, Ma.* Her heart melts. She leaves the bottle and leans into Kyle. 'We'll be all right won't we?'

For a moment, Kyle doesn't do anything, just stands rigid, arms at his side. She even wonders if he's going to push her away. She feels the prickle of his beard against her scalp.

'It doesn't seem real,' he says, his voice faltering. 'It isn't possible. I thought we were safe.'

She begs him. 'Please, Kyle, tell me we'll be all right.'

He wraps his arms around her, kisses her cheek and tentatively touches her stomach. 'Of course we will. It's just a bit of a surprise, that's all.'

*

The week continues in a strange dream-like state. She registers with the GP surgery and makes an appointment with the midwife. She swallows her folic acid and multivitamins, forgoes wine and morning coffee, alleviates the now almost constant sickness with ginger tea. She thinks about confiding in her parents, or Eleri, or one of their London friends, but tells herself it makes more sense to wait until after the scan. She doesn't need to tell anyone yet, only the GP. If she doesn't tell anyone, then it's not really true.

Sometimes, she wakes in the middle of the night, clutching her belly, eyes seeking out Jamie by the soft glow of the nightlight. She calculates in her head for the thousandth time: by the time the baby's born, Jamie will be sixteen months old, taking his first steps, exploring on his own. He'll need her undivided attention. She won't be able to take her eyes off him for a moment. Sometimes, she even tiptoes to his cot, strokes the fine wisps of hair from his forehead, checks the zip of his baby sleeping bag, re-tucks his blanket. If he awakes wanting milk, she cherishes the time with him, the need he has for her. She doesn't even mind, creeping downstairs, trying not to wake Martha in her crate, heating the milk, tiptoeing back again. Only the smell, the smell of the lighted cigarette, that seeps through the darkness, finding her when she's alone in the kitchen, or in the stairwell, or leaning over Jamie's cot, then just as suddenly disappearing, reminds her that things in the tower aren't right.

Some days, the better days, she feels determined to make a life for themselves at Sunny Hill. She accepts an offer of a drink in the pub with Eleri, and sits as far as possible from the bar and the eyes of Griff Davies. Sipping Diet Coke, she talks about things unconnected to the house: her commission, their old

London flat, her attempt to learn Welsh, this time via an app. She drives home with a sense of accomplishment. She *can* do it, even without a real drink. She can learn to live here, learn to belong here. Time, that's all, like Kyle insists. She only wishes she could talk to him more, let him know what it feels like to be carrying another baby, but he moves around her like a fragile object, skirting the subject, as if this time it's him and not her who's afraid of what might go wrong.

25

⟨⟨⟩⟩

*T*he days are becoming shorter, the nights rolling in too fast. Hurrying home from the village one day, eager to beat the dark, I hear footsteps behind me. I turn on the mountain path, clouding the sharp air with my breath, and see that it is Gwenllian, Morgan's sister.

'You frightened me,' I say, setting my basket on the path.

Gwenllian giggles. She is not more than a child, but her waist has been laced tightly into a shapely silhouette and her chest is noticeably curved beneath her jacket. 'I came to give you this,' she says.

It's a crumpled piece of paper. My heart flutters as I unfold it, as if it knows already what it will find: black ink, multiple crossings out, spots where the nib of a pen has rested. I cannot understand what it says, for I have never learned to read well, only to trace and copy the alphabet. Not wanting to admit my ignorance, I will the words to make sense, but the most I can make out is my name: Martha.

'Morgan wrote this?' I settle on the only possibility that springs to mind, praying Gwenllian will not notice the tremor in my voice. Recently, Morgan and I have been meeting in secret, walking in the fields, or alongside the river, though William does not approve. He thinks I am a fool, that Morgan is bad news. 'He'd sooner feed you to the lions than marry you,' William had said when I'd shared the hope of becoming Morgan's wife.

Gwenllian nods. 'Yes, the letter is from my brother. Only, he did not finish it. Morgan is so silly! He threw it away.'

I thrust the paper back at her. 'Then you should place it back where you found it.'

'It was on the fire. He must have placed it there, intending to burn it, yet it fell from the grate. Do you not think that it is strange? It is as though the letter wanted to find you.'

I fold the page, pick up my basket and tuck it beneath the tangles of evergreen. 'It is cold out here. We should not stand about talking. I have to get back. It will soon be dark.'

Gwenllian smiles, her cheeks blushed from the uphill climb. She opens her mouth, as if to say more, then shakes her head and buries her chin in her scarf.

'Good day,' I say, turning.

'Is there no message for him?'

My heart jolts. I think of Ma in the last years of her life, how silent she had become, how guarded. Would she have argued with William for me if she were still here? Would she have told me to follow my heart? 'You may give your brother my regards. I will see you all at the Christmas services.'

'But—'

'Please, Gwenllian! I have a long way to walk. You should go home now. You look frozen to the bone!'

In the cottage, I lay the fire, heaping sticks in the hearth, the smallest ones first followed by logs, crisscrossing them in a pile. I take a match from the ledge, bend down and strike it, then watch the flames lick the wood, little darts of light. Rubbing my hands together, I turn into the room and admire my handiwork, imagining what William will say when he sees it. Earlier, I studded oranges with cloves, and now with the evergreen, the air is rich with leaves and spice. This will be a merry Christmas, I am determined to make it so. There has been enough sorrow.

With the fire warming my back, and the light dancing along the holly at the window, I take the letter from my basket and smooth it on my lap, I struggle with the words, sounding them out.

My dear Martha,
Forgive me for writing, I had hoped to talk
I think about you all the time. Is it possible that two people, so different, could be one unite? You asked me once why I was so kind, why I do not shun you like the others do in the village. But the others are stupid and I care not that you are different. You are beautiful.
If only

There's nothing more, just ink marks. I clutch the note to my heart, not fully understanding the words, just enough to guess the sentiment. I know that it was never intended to be read. But how can this be wrong, this feeling that swells inside me? How can it be sinful? Whatever wrongs Morgan has committed in his past — my mind wanders to the scars that mark my brother's arm — were they not the misdemeanours of youth? Surely a man who writes so ardently, cannot be a tyrant?

I am still crouched beside the hearth when the door swings open, and William returns red-faced from the cold. His lantern casts shadows around the cottage, warming the wood of his chair, warming the *panels of the box-bed. He knocks his boots against the door, spraying mud across the freshly swept floor.*

'I saw Gwenllian on the path,' he says. 'I told the silly girl to go home.'

'You did right.' I heap coal onto the dying embers. 'It is dark out there, dangerous.' The words repeated to me so many times. 'She could have tripped, fallen.'

William sniffs the fragrant air and surveys my efforts at making merry. 'A young girl like her should be at home.'

'Indeed.' I usher him to his chair, help him pull off his boots and socks. The lie comes easily: 'I wonder what she was doing this way.'

He smiles, bends forwards and runs a hand gently against my cheek. 'You are so innocent, Martha.'

The gesture startles me, the feel of my brother's rough skin, the calluses upon his fingers. Heat flashes through my body. What is he talking of? Surely he does not mean . . . ? My mind reels. I have seen Gwenllian before on the path. I have seen her watching the men return from the quarry, her eyes trained on the tail end of the column, seeking out one man in particular. William. I had thought I had been mistaken, but is it possible?

I rise to my feet, the realisation making me careless. The letter falls from my pocket and lands at my brother's feet. He picks it up and frowns at the untidy words, his ability to read no better than mine. 'What is this?'

'Nothing.' I make to snatch it from his fingers, but he moves it from my reach. 'Just a note from the coal merchant. But I have already paid him what we owe.'

He grunts, satisfied, then crumples the letter in his hand and tosses it into the hungry flames. I watch it unfurl into a burst of yellow, the fire burning a little fiercer as William throws his weight into his chair, and stretches his legs, and warms himself by its glow.

26

⸻ ∞∞∞ ⸻

I t's like someone's flicked a switch. Lydia starts sleeping well, no more nightmares, no more feeling sick. Pregnancy seems to suit her for a change. She was never this well with Jamie; with Jamie the sickness never left her for the entire nine months. She spends quality time with Kyle: lunch out in town, choosing tiles for the bathroom on the first floor, shopping for matching waterproofs, a size bigger for Lydia to accommodate the inevitable bump. She and Kyle laugh together like in the old days, showing a genuine interest in each other's work, watching films late into the night, taking it in turns to rock Jamie to sleep. In the mornings, she gets up early and spends the hours before breakfast in her studio, ramming the ineffective heaters up to maximum. She finishes outlining the figures in pencil, then takes to the stone with an angle grinder. Steady, steady cutting of the stone, warning herself not to rush, not to make a fatal error. Dust in her hair, mist beyond her goggles. Nothing else in the world but herself and the stone.

'Should you be doing that?' Kyle appears one morning without Jamie, bed-hair up on end. She switches off the machine and the grinder whirs to a halt.

She pulls off her ear protectors. 'What?'

'That.' He points to the stone, the rough carving of a woman: arms, breasts, neck, hair. 'I said, should you be doing it?'

'It's my job!'

'I know, but isn't it dangerous?' He nods at her stomach.

She laughs, 'I'm not eating it!' She hasn't told him, but it's so much easier this time; she doesn't worry about every single twinge or sensation. 'And we need the money, remember? I have no choice.'

He wraps his arms around her and fondles the imaginary bump, making her promise to take more care.

Later, to placate him, she emails Stanley Harris and hints that the work will take longer to complete than she'd thought. She asks for more information about where the sculptures will be exhibited, the advance he promised but which still hasn't materialised. He replies immediately. The plans she's sent aren't detailed enough. He wants exact dimensions. He wants context. He wants to *understand* her. The advance will arrive only when he's satisfied.

The email plays over and over in her mind as she sifts through the rest of her mail, all her old insecurities spiralling inside her. Maybe she's not up to this? Maybe she can't deliver what Stanley Harris wants? She considers mentioning it to Kyle, but he's stressed enough with his own work and she doesn't want to worry him.

A notification flashes on the screen: a new email from Outdoor Markey.

Thought you might like these. Lol.

Beneath the script is a series of photographs. Or rather the same photograph, copied over and over, filtered through different lenses. The same photograph she'd seen on Markey's walking blog, the man standing in the cottage doorway, watching the two hikers on the yard wall. Except the photograph has been cropped, so that the man's face, his open shirt, his hand reaching upwards with the cigarette, and his disappearing trouser legs, are magnified. Green eyes leap out at her through various filters. Monochrome, contrast, nostalgia, pencil, illusion.

She snaps the laptop shut. Why the hell has Markey sent her such a thing? Is he trying to freak her out? Instinctively, she glances out the window, seeking the light through the mist, but there's only a flicker, like sunlight on glass, and the cottage is just a smudge amidst the green. But it seems to feed into the house. The more she thinks about it, the more it seems real. If she had a ruler long enough, she'd be able to draw a straight line: the cottage to the tower, the kitchen, the archway, the fireplace in the lounge.

Something catches her eye on the edge of the lawn.

She goes outside, not bothering with a coat, shivering against the cold. It's early November, and the ground is crisp with frost. She wonders at what point the snow will fall, reminding herself of all the things they need to do before it does: stock up on food and logs, buy that four by four Kyle has promised. At least when the new baby arrives, it will be summer and an easy run to the hospital. The thing on the lawn is a cardboard package sodden with ice, addressed to Lydia Stein. She wonders why the postman left it there, why he hadn't bothered to knock or leave it on the doorstep. It's almost as if he panicked and made a hasty retreat. She's only met him once in the whole time they've been here, a bald-headed Welshman who'd given her the impression he didn't want to hang around, who'd seemed only too pleased to hand over his bundle of envelopes and get back inside his van.

She takes it inside, slits open the box, pulls at the bubble wrap. Something falls out, sliding from the bubble wrap onto the stone floor. It's a slate sign, like the broken house sign out-side, engraved with a single word: *Welcome.* Only the 'Welcome' is split in two – 'Wel' 'come' – severed by the landing. At the bottom of the box is a note in her mum's hand:

Thought you might like this for the new house. Can't wait to visit!
See you soon.
Mum and Dad xxx

Holding the note in her hand, staring at the broken slate, the two halves like jagged blades, she feels her eyes well with tears.

Later, she heads to the shop with the excuse of needing more milk. The shop is busy for a change, and there's no time to chat to Eleri, but she's not ready to go home yet. Every time her mind drifts, she sees the broken sign in her mind, or worse still, the man in the photograph, his eyes seeking her out. She wanders instead, taking the footpath through the churchyard to the river. The ground is patchy with ice and she uses the hedge to steady herself, feeling the prickles of frosted holly through her gloves. She's almost at the river when she loses her grip, landing heavily, the milk carton splitting on the solid ground.

'Ti'n iawn?' Footsteps behind her, then someone bends down and lifts her up. She looks over her shoulder. It's Griff Davies.

He nods – in acknowledgement or embarrassment, she's not sure which – then turns away from her and walks up the path.

'Thank you,' she calls after him, then remembering the Welsh she's learned from the app: 'Diolch yn fawr.'

'That was a nasty fall.'

She swivels in the opposite direction. Mari, the old lady she'd met in the shop, who'd sent her flowers on the evening of the housewarming party, stands up from a grave and admires her handiwork. 'My husband,' she says, gathering a pile of stems. 'I leave him flowers every week. They don't last long in the bad weather, but I like him to know I'm thinking of him.'

Lydia smiles sympathetically.

'Why don't you come for tea?' Mari says. 'My house is just across the way, and it's cold.'

'That's very kind, but I wouldn't want to intrude.'

'You wouldn't be intruding. I'll make us a pot.'

Mari picks up her flower basket and beckons Lydia to follow. She doesn't really want to – she's not in the mood for small talk – but she reminds herself, it doesn't hurt to make friends with the neighbours. She shoves the milk carton into the churchyard bin, then follows Mari across the road.

'Don't mind the dogs,' the old lady says as she opens the door of a small terraced cottage. Immediately, two terriers rush at them, pawing Lydia's jeans and sniffing her trainers. 'Come through to the living room. Make yourself at home. Take a seat while I make the tea. I've been wanting to talk to you for a while.'

The living room is a tiny, cluttered space. Squeezed between mismatched armchairs are a couple of glass-fronted cabinets housing an array of holiday souvenirs. Photographs are displayed on the mantelpiece and the big-box television. As the terriers settle in their basket in front of the fire, Lydia studies the largest photograph: two children, a boy and a girl, clasp ice-creams under a cloudless sky. She knows the boy instantly, something about the shape of his forehead, the rosy cheeks, the wry smile.

'You know my son, I'm sure?' Mari startles her from behind, setting the tea tray on the table. 'He helped you in the church-yard just now. Everyone knows Griff.' The pride in her voice is unmistakable. A mother's pride, unable to see her son for what he really is.

'Griff Davies is your son?'

'That's right. That's his sister next to him. She died not long after the photograph was taken. She was only six. It's just me and Griff living here now.'

'I'm so sorry.' Despite the stifling heat, she feels a shiver of cold.

Mari indicates for her to sit down. 'He's a good boy, my Griff. He takes care of his old mam. Moved in to look after me.'

'He drinks too much.' She bites her lip, hoping Mari won't mind.

But the old lady laughs. 'It's the rugby. All the rugby boys like a drink. There's no harm in it, it's just their way.' She pours the tea and hands Lydia a cup. 'That's his father there. Also a rugby boy in his time. Been dead ten years. And that's his grandfather, my father, who fought in the war.'

'You've quite a family history.'

'That one, over there, is my grandfather, Griff's great-grandfather. He fought in the First World War.'

Lydia makes out the distinctive uniform, the puttees, the cap, the tunic, reminding her of the soldier-doll. Only this soldier's face is long and grave, and the white of a scar runs from his eye to his chin. Someone has written in pen, at the bottom of the photograph. She leans forward to read it:

Pte. Morgan Lloyd 1917.

'The wars were terrible, but my family were lucky. We didn't lose anyone.'

'You remember it?'

'I was a child in the second one. I remember my grandfather's face when my father announced he was joining the army. Here's a photo of the two of them much later.' She reaches behind her, takes another framed photo from the shelf: two men with the same long faces, both smoking cigarettes. 'After what my grandfather had been through in the trenches, he thought my father was stupid. But then, as I said, we were lucky.'

Lydia nods, only half-following. Through the window, she can see the pub. It dawns on her: she's in Griff Davies's house, taking tea with his mother, delving into his family's history. What if he comes back?

'So, you're from England?'

'That's right. London.'

'We don't get many English around here, apart from tourists.'

'I know—'

'I never learned English myself, not to write, I mean, only to speak. A lot of the old folk are like that, but we don't mind the English in our family.'

Lydia smiles politely, thinking about Griff – does Mari not know what a bully he is? She sets her cup down. 'You said before, it was a shame we'd moved to the house on the mountain.'

'I was thinking about the cottage.'

'You know about the cottage?'

Mari looks at the tea tray. 'I'm sorry. I should have brought biscuits. You should have said. How silly of me!'

Lydia protests, she's not long had lunch, but Mari potters to the kitchen anyway and returns with a packet of Bourbons. 'You were talking about the cottage. The cottage on the mountain, above Y Twr Gwyn?'

Mari tumbles a pile of biscuits on the tray. 'I shouldn't be talking about it.'

'Why not?'

'Griff. He doesn't like me to, he thinks it's bad luck.' They both glance at the pub, but the street is silent. 'You go to church?' Mari says.

'Sometimes.'

Mari nods, as if that's good enough. 'Well, I guess it's only talk. What harm can talk do?' She brushes imaginary crumbs from her trousers. 'A long time ago, a very beautiful girl lived in the cottage. My grandfather's first love. Her name was Martha and she had deep brown eyes. She was an Englishwoman like you. The family moved here to find work. The quarry was hard, backbreaking work, but at least it offered steady employment and the people who worked there considered themselves lucky.'

Lydia feels dread in the pit of her stomach. That name again. 'What happened,' she swallows hard, 'what happened to Martha?'

'She died. Drowned herself. They found her body in the river, washed down the stream, battered from the rocks.'

'I've seen her grave in the churchyard. Martha Helford.' She thinks of the puppy, the way 'Martha' seems to suit her regardless of her attempts to change the name.

'That's right. The family grave, all by itself. No one wanted anything to do with it. It was left to the weeds and the moss, and no grave was placed near it.'

'Do you know anything about the cottage? Is there a reason I shouldn't go there?'

The terriers shuffle in their basket, whining in their sleep. Mari pulls a thread from her trousers and twists it around her finger. 'Griff will be home soon. He was only popping to the pub for one. This was a bad idea. Griff's a good boy, but he has a temper on him sometimes. And you'll be wanting to get back to that baby of yours.'

'My husband's looking after him. It's fine.'

'No, it's not fine.' The force in Mari's voice is unsettling. 'You need to get home.' She stands and hands Lydia her coat, then walks into the passageway.

Lydia has no choice but to follow. Part of her can't wait to get out of the cottage, away from the muggy heat and the threat of Griff, but the other part of her wants, *needs*, to know. 'Please,' she says as she steps down into the street, into the biting cold. 'Can you just tell me one more thing? Why did Martha kill herself?'

Mari stares at her hands, twists them together. 'All I know is what my grandfather told me,' she says softly. 'I was nineteen and in love, contemplating my own marriage. My grandfather told me to follow my heart, that if I didn't, I might regret it. We all lived together, here in this house – people did in those days. Mam and Dad and my grandparents and my two siblings. My grandfather used to have nightmares. I could hear him through the walls, calling for Martha in his sleep. It was years after it happened, years after he'd married my grandmother. But he never got over her. You might call him obsessed. He thought he should have saved Martha, stopped her from killing herself, but he didn't.'

27

She can't get the story of Martha from her mind as she wipes down their travel bags – dusty after only a few weeks – and packs for the party in London. Her clothes are damp-smelling from hanging in the wardrobe with Edward Jeffreys' old shirts, the ones Kyle won't part with, and she has to run the worst through the washing machine. As she zips up the case, she realises how much she's looking forward to the London trip, seeing friends, sleeping at her parents' house with its power shower and reliable wi-fi. She's looking forward to the noise and buzz of the city; all the things she'd thought she didn't want any more, but which she can't stop yearning for.

'I'm glad you're getting away,' Eleri says when she eventually drops Martha at the post office. To Lydia's relief, the puppy runs into the house without a second invitation and settles down in the lounge. 'It will do you two good,' Eleri says as they follow her. 'Get away from the house for a bit. It can't be easy when you're renovating.'

Renovating. God, if only they were. They haven't touched anything in the house since the new kitchen arrived, all their plans ground to a standstill. 'We're looking forward to it,' she says, trying to hide her desperation; she can't wait to get away.

Eleri feeds Martha and her own dog, Pwtsyn, a biscuit. 'Go catch a show, or whatever you do in London.'

'It's just a party. Meeting up with old friends. Kyle's friends really.'

'But it's good to get away, isn't it? Have a break from . . .' Eleri glances at the mountain through the window, 'all that.'

'*All that?*' She thinks about the stuff Eleri told her about Edward Jeffreys.

Eleri sighs and pulls her gaze away, turning to Martha and Pwtsyn playing a game of tug of war. 'It wasn't just Edward who went mad, you know. It had happened before.' There's a long pause while Lydia senses Eleri battling with the decision of whether or not to continue. 'The previous owner, a Scotsman, another arty type – this time a writer – also went mad. Killed one of the Joneses' dogs, shot a couple of sheep, came into the village and accused the women of selling themselves. I was only a child at the time, so I don't remember much. But it's the same pattern. A quiet, unassuming artist – a foreigner – moves into the tower and goes mad.'

'And you think the same will happen to us? Just because we've moved here from England? Because,' she swallows hard before verbalising the thing that's been worrying her for days, 'I'm a sculptor?'

'No, of course not. I'm sorry. It's not the house. It's just being alone up there, miles away from anything. It sends some people a bit crazy. I know it would me. Just enjoy yourselves in London, won't you? Make the most of the time away.'

Back at Sunny Hill, she trails Kyle around the house, double-checking everything: the windows are bolted, the kitchen blind down, the modem working, the bathroom fans turned off. Satisfied, they bundle their case into the car and strap Jamie in the baby seat. She can hardly believe it: they're going, really going. On their way to the station for a wonderful weekend in London. No more Sunny Hill. No more mountain cottage. No more silly stories.

Kyle insists on carrying Jamie in the baby backpack when the train arrives at Paddington, the scenery of November-grey replaced by a multicolour of commuters and fast-food places. 'You shouldn't be carrying anything heavy,' he says, taking hold of their case.

'It's fine. I feel fine.'

'Feeling fine and being fine are two different things.'

She tries to remember if he was like this when she was pregnant with Jamie, but that part of her life is a blur. All she can remember is being terrified of doing the wrong thing.

'What first?' she says. 'I mean after we've seen my parents.'

'Don't you want to rest?'

'I've been sat on a train for five hours!'

'Let's go out for dinner then, before going to Charlie's. It's going to be big, I'm afraid. He's booked a DJ and a massive sound system.'

'I know. I don't mind.'

'Just don't say I didn't warn you.'

They walk hand in hand, Kyle pulling the case behind them,

Jamie already asleep in the backpack. A pigeon swoops over-head, causing a commotion. She breathes in the complex tang of petrol fumes and fast-food places, and can't help thinking she's back where she belongs.

Three hours later, Charlie meets them at the door of his flat in Notting Hill, the place gifted to him by his parents at graduation, which he renovated with their money. Lydia's only been in the flat once or twice before and it's stylishly devoid of character: modern art prints framed in white against white walls, white sculptures of indeterminate objects, white book-cases housing immaculate copies of Dickens. Today, the hallway is crammed with people. Lydia feels all her good intentions slipping away – her determination to relax and enjoy herself – as she scans the wasted faces. It's immediately clear what sort of party this is.

'Good of you to come,' Charlie winks at Lydia, 'consider-ing . . .'

She turns to Kyle accusingly, wondering how Charlie knows. She doesn't know Charlie and his girlfriend well, though Charlie had been Kyle's best friend at university and later his best man. When they'd lived in London, she'd had her own group of friends, professional arty types; no one close, just friends to have drinks with. Her interactions with Charlie had consisted of waving goodbye as he'd swept Kyle out for yet another night out, and making him coffee whenever she found him sprawled on their sofa in the morning. Why would Kyle tell Charlie about the baby when they'd both agreed to wait until after the scan?

Charlie plants a glass of wine in her hand. She softens, real-ising her mistake. He doesn't mean the pregnancy. He just means, good of them to come all the way from Wales.

'Just the one won't do any harm, will it?' she whispers to Kyle, knowing she needs the drink to steady her nerves.

He shrugs. 'Probably not. You ready?' Already people are noticing them, raising hands, calling them over. She squeezes his hand.

In the lounge, the plush sofas have been moved aside to allow for a dancefloor and two enormous speakers. Lydia spots Benedita, Charlie's girlfriend, in the crowd, a stylish silhouette in black, rocking in time to the music. It's too loud to hold a proper conversation, but people are talking anyway, shouting at each other, goading each other to drink, joking with Kyle, asking Lydia questions about Wales. About the house. About the mountain.

'I need the toilet,' she mouths at Kyle.

She finds her way to the bathroom, pushes wide the door. Benedita is bent over the toilet lid, lining white powder on a mirror.

'Oh, sorry.' Lydia turns back again.

'It's okay. I wasn't about to pee or anything. Come in.' Benedita points at the mirror. 'Want some?'

Lydia shakes her head, watching as Benedita snorts a line of coke through a twenty-pound note. Benedita lets out a satisfied gasp, picks up the mirror and sets herself down on the toilet lid. 'So tell me,' she says. 'How's Wales?'

'Great.' She feigns a smile. 'Thanks for asking.'

Benedita tilts her head on one side as if she's not entirely convinced, then she stands up and checks her make-up in the mirror above the sink. 'Why don't you use the loo and I'll meet you in the kitchen? Let's get ourselves a drink.'

The kitchen is calmer, quieter. People come and go, helping themselves to the contents of the fridge.

'Wine?'

'No, actually, I'm still breastfeeding.'

'Oh, what a shame.' Benedita hands her a J20. 'Tell me about Wales. What's it really like?'

'Quiet.' She's only met Benedita a couple of times before, but she seems nice enough and, maybe it's the earlier glass of wine after two weeks of not drinking, but suddenly she wants to tell someone, to normalise what's happening. 'To be honest, it's a bit lonely. The locals are standoffish. It's hard to break through.'

'Have you thought about learning Welsh? There're apps you can get. Charlie learned Portuguese in three months.'

'I'm trying, but it's hard. Languages aren't really my thing.'

Benedita glugs wine into a pint glass. 'I was nineteen and terrified when I first moved to London. I'd just split up from my boyfriend, a right prick called Flavio. I got a job in a café flipping burgers. Three years later, just when my life was going nowhere, Charlie walked in, ordered a kebab, our eyes met. Bam. Life's never been the same again.' She sweeps back her hair, golden like the rest of her. 'Things work out, you see. They always do.' She pushes a pint glass towards Lydia. 'I think you should give the baby a bottle tonight and have a drink.'

'I can't.' Her eyes flash to her stomach.

'Oh shit. Wow. Congratulations. I would never have guessed.'

Immediately she regrets it, divulging their secret. She can almost hear the unspoken question on Benedita's lips: *isn't that a bit soon?* 'It's early days. We haven't told many people.'

'I won't say a word. You look positively skinny, not pregnant at all. How are you feeling?'

'Good. Really good. I was sick at first. Horribly sick. And there were a few weird things. But now I feel fine. Better than normal.'

'You look great.'

'Thanks.'

Benedita reaches for her cigarettes. 'We had a scare before Christmas. Turned out to be a false alarm. Thank God. Imagine having Charlie's child!'

Lydia giggles. 'I'm sure he'd make a great dad.'

'We both know that's a lie.' Benedita lights up, looks at Lydia, then stubs it straight out again. 'Hey, next time you're down we should hang out. Go shopping for baby stuff or something. I know you've got a little boy already, but what if it's a girl?'

'I guess—'

'It will be fun, I promise. And I promise I won't let Charlie get Kyle completely plastered either. Kyle needs to behave now he's a father of two.'

The evening wears on. Kyle is drunk, deep in conversation with Charlie, casting Lydia apologetic glances. She feels sick from the amount of J20 she's drunk, sick and tired. She switches to water and tries to pull Kyle away, but he wants to dance, wants to drink more, wants to talk. He hasn't spoken to his friends for ages. The DJ turns up the speakers and the music makes her brain hurt. She sees Charlie pass Kyle a little white pill and her heart sinks. It's the side of Kyle she hasn't seen in a while, the side of him she doesn't really know, doesn't want to know. She tells him she's going back to her parents, back to their son, and rings for a taxi.

'Hi, love, good night? Jamie's been a darling.' Her mum's in slippers and dressing gown at the door, smothering a yawn.

'Great. Thanks.'

'Kyle not with you?'

'Still catching up with friends.'

Her mum turns and pads towards the kitchen, the dressing gown flapping, revealing a pair of snowflake pyjamas. 'Well, let me make you a cup of tea.'

'No, Mum, really, you go to bed. It's late.'

'It's the least I can do. You've got to let me look after you sometimes, you know.' Irritation flecks her voice, but when she turns back again, she looks concerned rather than angry. 'It's my prerogative as a mother.'

They sit across the kitchen table, the chequered wipe-clean table cloth that Lydia remembers from her teenage years when they lived in the house in Norwich. Her mother hugs her cup of tea, and she imagines all the questions she wants to ask about her and Kyle, about why Kyle's still at the party when she isn't. Wants to ask but won't. Just like all those other times in the past, the time when Lydia changed university and when she was seeing the therapist.

'So how are you getting on with the renovations?'

The question jolts her into another space. In a heartbeat, she's back in the kitchen on the mountain, looking out the window, the hard top of the kitchen island beneath her fingertips, the wind rattling the window latch and the outside door, the incongruous feeling, despite Kyle and Jamie, she's alone.

'Slowly,' she says, forcing a smile, knowing her mother meant it as a safe topic. She stands and picks up her cup of tea. 'Sorry, Mum, but I think I'll go to bed now, if you don't mind. I'm exhausted.'

'Of course, love.' Her mother's eyes crease with concern. 'Maybe we can have a proper chat tomorrow?'

'Sure.' She leans down, hugs her mother goodnight. She thinks about saying something else, blurting it all out about the pregnancy and the sense something isn't right in the tower. But she can't. She never does. She hasn't allowed herself to open up in years. She's afraid that if she does, she might unravel completely.

28

'Sorry about last night.' It's Sunday lunchtime. Kyle feels decidedly like shit as he picks at a steak burger. It was Liddy's mum's idea for them to go out before the journey home, treat themselves to lunch while she babysits J-J. 'I should have left the party when you did,' he says, not meeting Liddy's eye.

It was four o'clock in the morning when he finally made his way back to the spare room at her parents' house. He doesn't remember how he got there or who let him in; he doesn't remember falling into bed still with his clothes on.

'Maybe I'll give up alcohol too, until the baby's born.' He smiles guiltily at his beer, his hair-of-the-dog, and deliberately changes the subject. 'Do you miss London?'

Liddy looks out the window and shrugs. There's a couple on the other side of the street, drinking wine outside the bar opposite, and sharing a cigarette.

He selects a sachet of vinegar from the condiments tray and tears at it with his teeth. 'What's wrong, Liddy? You haven't been yourself for a while. I do notice some things, you know. I'm not a complete bastard.'

She smiles and looks down at her food, barely touched. Then she picks up her fork and prods her lasagne. 'Since moving to Wales, something's changed. The thought of going back to your grandfather's house, me doing my work there, sculpting in the barn . . . well . . . it makes me uneasy.'

He reaches over their plates and massages her fingers. 'It's not his house any more, not his barn, remember. It's ours.' He looks down, over the table, thinking of the bump that isn't a bump yet by any stretch of the imagination. Another baby. It hardly seems possible, but a sibling is exactly what J-J needs, someone he can play with, whom he can protect and vice versa. As an only child, moved from place to place, from school to school, he knows only too well what it's like to be lonely. Lonely and bullied.

Liddy draws her hand away and he wonders if she's still pissed off about last night. 'Tell me again about your grandfather. About why he was so distant.'

He sips his beer. The memories have been coming back to him recently. Memories of his childhood. 'All I know is the bits and pieces I picked up before Mum died. He was born in 1935. His father fought in the Second World War and he lost an uncle and two older cousins. His grandmother was killed in the Blitz. And then his daughter, my mum, went and did the worst thing imaginable in his eyes: married a German. They'd had a difficult relationship before that by the sound of things, and that was the final straw. They stumbled on for a few more years, the occasional family get-together. I remember visiting my grandfather's house in Suffolk. I remember playing with the toy soldiers. He had this set left over from the war. Did I tell you, he looked after me for a while when I was born? Dad was ill by then, though he didn't yet know it was cancer, and Mum had post-natal depression. I can't remember it, of course, but I get the impression my grandfather was protective of me. Had ideas about my upbringing that Mum didn't agree with. After a while, the rift got too much, and they didn't talk to each other at all.'

'But your grandfather left you the tower?'

He shrugs. 'Maybe he felt guilty after all those years of silence? Maybe it was his way of making amends?' He thinks of the shadow that's been following him around the tower. He's seen it a few times now, but he hasn't mentioned it to Liddy because he knows she'll freak. Sometimes he wonders if it's his grandfather, keeping watch. He supposes it's kind of comforting, a guardian angel. Or rather, it *would* be comforting. But there's something about the shadow that doesn't feel right. His grandfather, from what he can remember, was tall but skinny, whereas the shadow is wider, looser.

'It's the same thing, isn't it?' Liddy says. 'Your dad and your grandfather? Us and Wales?'

He picks at his skin through the elbow of his jumper. 'What do you mean?'

'In Wales, we're outsiders, tolerated at best. Sometimes it's worse than that. Sometimes it feels,' she scrapes at the cheese sauce on the top of her pasta, 'it feels like I'm on my own. Like you're in the house but not really there. Like I can't trust myself to look after Jamie. Everything feels so *unsafe.*'

He reaches for her hand. 'It's just the winter. We weren't prepared for how cold it is, how bleak. Next year it'll be better.

We'll know what to expect. We'll plan it all out. We'll have the house up and running just the way we want it.' He thinks of his shed in the garden, taking shape. It's the first time he's attempted anything like that, and, even if it's decidedly amateur in places, it gives him a sense of satisfaction, feeling the sturdiness of the frame, seeing how his painstaking calculations are paying off. He likes working out there. He likes looking up at the cottage. He doesn't want anyone to take it away from him.

'We'll make this work,' he says, his voice softening. 'I really am sorry about last night. I didn't mean to get drunk at all, though I suppose it was inevitable. You know what it's like with Charlie. He's my best friend. He's always been kind to me. Always accepted me. But, at least, when I'm in Wales, we're away from all that. We can concentrate on each other. On being a family. Let's give it a few more months and if it's still not working out after that, we'll think of a Plan B.'

29

Eleri answers the door in her pyjamas, book in one hand, hot water bottle in the other. 'Come in,' she says, stifling a yawn.

'Sorry we're so late,' Lydia says. 'The trains were delayed.' She's grateful for the muggy warmth of the Calor gas heaters in the lounge. Compared to London, it's freezing in Gaer Fach.

Eleri smiles sleepily. 'It's fine. I'm always the last to bed, and I'm a light sleeper. You can call me anytime, you know that, don't you?'

Martha jumps from the sofa, paws Lydia's clothes and licks her hands, while Kyle stands stiffly behind. Lydia bends down, setting Jamie's car seat gently on the rug, letting the puppy nip her fingers. 'Good girl. That's right. Fuss me, not the baby.'

'Stay over,' Eleri glances at Jamie fast asleep. 'We've a spare room and that road will be treacherous. It's past midnight.'

'We can't, I'm sorry.' Kyle sounds determined as he lays a hand on Lydia's shoulder. In the train, after she'd worked her way through a lesson on her Welsh app, she'd told him the story of Martha and William, how it was rumoured the villagers had driven a stake through Martha's heart. She'd shown him the photo of the cottage on Markey's blog once more, this time when they weren't both drunk, but Kyle had laughed it off again – just another silly tale and a badly taken photo. His verdict: 'Someone's trying to mess with your mind.' He'd made her promise not to contact Markey again, but he'd been on edge ever since, snapping at her for no reason, refusing to take turns with Jamie.

'It's very kind of you,' Lydia says. Suddenly, the room feels stifling. Is Eleri thinking about Edward Jeffreys and the previous owners again?

'But we should be going,' Kyle finishes the sentence for her, and retrieves Martha's lead from the sofa. 'Thanks very much for looking after the pup, but it's way past J-J's bedtime, and we've still that drive up the mountain. You ladies can catch up another time.'

Eleri shrugs and wraps her arms around her pyjama top. 'It's really no inconvenience. But if you must go, I want you to know, you're always welcome here, whatever happens, whatever the time.'

Kyle's silent as they drive up the mountain road. Martha circles the footwell of the passenger seat, unable to settle. Lydia wants to comfort her, but she's too tense herself, unable to shake away the sense of foreboding that has followed her ever since she stepped off the train. She reaches out, squeezes Kyle's hand as it rests on the gear stick, but he jumps at the touch of her.

The tyres slip on ice as he swerves around the bends. She wants to tell him to slow down, to take more care. Instead, she grits her teeth. They pass through the farm: no lights, no dogs, only a stray chicken trying to get into the henhouse. She yells at Kyle to stop, gets out and runs across the frozen yard. As she lifts the latch, the smell of the henhouse hits her. Hay and shit and the woody smell of pellets. The smell of the country.

She gets back in the car.

'What did you do that for?'

'It would have died. It's so bloody cold out there!' She's shivering though she's only been outside for a minute. This place is so exposed.

Kyle shifts the car into second gear and they crawl up the track to the tower. She can sense Sunny Hill in the distance: the tower and the barn and the garage shrouded in darkness. It's almost worse, knowing it's there, but not being able to see it. Martha scrambles onto her lap and paws at the glove compartment.

'We're here.' Kyle touches the brake pedal and the house lights up in the pale moon of the headlights.

She steps out and unbuckles Jamie from his seat, shushing him to sleep again over her shoulder. She wants to get inside. There's something deeply unnerving about being on the mountain at this time of night, the summit crouching unseen in the blackness, the deceptive silence, the space. Kyle takes an age unlocking the door, whistling as he does it, acting casual, but she can sense the fear behind it; he's just as nervous as she is.

The smell of damp hits her as soon as she walks into the kitchen. The cold seeps through her coat and jumper. Taking Jamie with her, she goes into every room, switching on the lights. It's just as they'd left it apart from the kitchen blind, which has sprung open a crack, leaking darkness.

Kyle heats up a bottle of milk and offers to take Jamie to bed. He's still groggy from the night before and the beer he had at lunchtime. 'Good night,' he says, pecking her on the cheek, pressing Jamie into her for a cuddle.

After he's gone, Lydia stares at the crack beneath the blind. Suddenly, she can't bear it any more, she can't bear the way this house seems determined to get the better of her. She won't become like Kyle's grandfather and the others before him. She buttons up her jacket and braves the outdoors again. Beyond the glare of her torch, she can't see a thing, and yet she knows it's up there: the cottage, the spindle-back chair, the open fireplace, the memory or ghost or imprint or whatever it is of the man in the photograph. Whatever Kyle thinks, right now, she believes it's real. She believes there's something here on the mountain. Something unnatural. Something that changes the people who attempt to live here. She can *feel* it in the air. A heaviness. A sense of oppression. But she won't be beaten by it. She won't let this thing inside the tower, not even by a crack.

The garage door judders as she pulls it back, squealing overhead, slamming into position. She blinks in the glare of the electric strip light, and walks through the empty space to the shelves at the back. Pulling down the old toolbox belonging to Edward Jeffreys, something clatters to the floor. She jumps backwards. It's the dog chain from Emlyn, the one she thought she'd thrown out with the rubbish. Kyle must have found it, resurrected it from the bin. But why?

Back in the kitchen, she positions a nail beneath the blind. The plaster splinters as she hammers it in. She hits harder, pounding out her frustrations. Then she ties the cord of the blind around the nail.

That night, she barely sleeps. When she does, it's fitful and unsatisfying. She wakes up crying, grabbing on to Kyle, but Kyle doesn't stir. When she sleeps again, Matt Trevithick's in her dreams, leaning over her, pinning her to the duvet. Her dream-self pushes him away. She runs from her room, down the corridor, out through the revolving doors of the halls of residence, into the night. Not the university, not London, but Myndd Gwyn, the mountain in Wales. She realises she's on the sheep track, running away from the cottage, not daring to slow, because the man's behind her. The *other* man, the man in the photograph. She can hear his footsteps. She can smell his cigarette.

She screams herself awake again, and this time Kyle throws an arm across her body and shushes her back to sleep.

By the time she struggles out of bed in the morning, it's late and Kyle's already up. She lifts Jamie from his cot and takes him downstairs, still wrapped in his blanket. Goosebumps prickle her arms, and she can see her breath in the air. She calls for Kyle but there's no answer and his coat's gone from the hook on the door. Sunlight spills through the kitchen window though the space inside is still cold, and she notices the nail has wrenched itself from the wall, leaving an ugly gash in the plaster. She curses inwardly – she should have done the job properly with an electric drill – and places a row of spent wine bottles in front of it, behind the sink, to cover up the mess.

Back upstairs, she lays Jamie on the mat in the bathroom with his giraffe, and runs the shower. The water is ice-cold, tingling against her skin, numbing her scalp. She runs it faster, harder, turning the dial as far as it will go, but still no warmth. She gets out, shivering, and wraps herself in a towel.

'No bath for you today, little man,' she says, bending down, tickling Jamie's tummy. He giggles. 'It's far too cold.'

Leaving the door open, she goes into their bedroom and surveys her chest of drawers. It's a mess: clothes, underwear, running kit muddled together. Clothes she's never worn in Gaer Fach, picked up in quirky London boutiques. Clothes she might never wear again. Unexpectedly, she feels herself welling up. It's like they've never been away. Like they'll never go away again. She swipes at her face and the towel slides to the floor. The freezing bedroom air jabs against her skin as she looks down: a spot of blood, no bigger than a five-pence piece, sits magnified against the white of the towel. Frantically, she checks herself. No sign of injury, no blood, thank God, between her legs. She bunches the towel in her hands, not looking again at the spot of blood, and buries it deep in the wash pile. Then she glances at Jamie, still chewing his giraffe on the bathmat.

But no, it's not his giraffe. He's found something else.

It's a soldier-doll made from wood, wrapped in swathes of moth-eaten khaki. The same uniform as the soldier on Mari's television. Only this is a horrible ugly thing, its face faded with age, its tiny pinprick eyes staring right at her. It must have belonged to Edward Jeffreys, one of the set Kyle used to play with. He must have found it and dropped it on the floor. She runs towards him and prises the thing from Jamie's fingers.

He wails, reaching his hands out to grab it.

'No!' she says, more firmly than she intended. 'It's a horrible, horrible thing.' But he won't stop crying, desperate, frustrated tears. She buries the doll beneath a heap of tissues in the bathroom bin, picks him up and rocks him gently against her shoulder. 'It's just a mangy old toy. Nothing to get worked up about. Shush, shush, shush.'

But she still has the image of those pinprick eyes in her mind.

30

'*My* sister,' Morgan *looks over his shoulder at the group of women gossiping at our back, 'my silly sister, Gwenllian. She showed you a letter. It was never intended—*' He coughs apologetically into his gloved hand.

We are standing in the churchyard after the morning service, on the edge of the milling parishioners. A robin hops on a nearby grave and I imagine my face flushed the same colour as the bird's chest.

'I do not know of any letter,' I say, deliberately keeping my voice level.

Morgan lifts his eyes to mine and sighs; he knows I am lying to save him. 'She only told me this morning. I thought I had destroyed it, but it seems she snatched it from the flames.'

My cheeks burn despite the chilling wind.

'Can I ever hope,' Morgan wrestles with his hands, 'that you will one day return my feelings? The feelings I expressed so badly in the letter? Can I ever hope that one day we will be joined as man and

wife in this very church?' His eyes dart to the villagers, perhaps sensing my disquiet. 'Or if not here, somewhere else? Somewhere far from this village and these people? Is that too much for me to dream, Martha?'

My corset seems suddenly far too tight. I turn my gaze from his, seeking the robin, now hopping on the frost-laden grass. The memory stings worse than the cold: another winter morning when I was just a child, sitting on a rock on the mountain, wrapped in my coat and muffler, playing with my rag doll.

I heard the men before I saw them, struggling along the path, cursing their burden. I remember feeling annoyed – these men were disturbing my game – but as they neared the cottage, I saw that the thing they were carrying was not, as I had imagined, a sack of coal, but my brother.

Ma came out to meet them and I could hear the worry in her voice even from a distance, recalling, no doubt, the time they brought our father home. By the time I had scrambled down from the rock, the men were gone.

'What is the matter?' I said, bursting into the cottage. 'Who were those men?'

William was sitting in my father's chair, the chair that had not been occupied since his death the year before, the seat and the spindles still polished as if he might march in any minute with his big boots and big smile.

'Men from the quarry.' Ma bustled about, filling a basin with water, tearing a cloth into strips. 'Look what those boys have done to your brother!' She pulled up the left sleeve of Willam's shirt, and I saw that his arm was striped with blood.

My young eyes widened. 'Those men did that?'

'No. Those men found him. Some young lads from the village did this to your brother. They beat him and tied him up in a chain. That's how the men found him, barely conscious. Bound in a dog chain.'

'*But why?*'

'*Because boys can be wicked. And we are not the same as them. We are outsiders, always remember that.*'

I watched as she gently dabbed my brother's wounds and mopped his forehead as he held the pain valiantly between his teeth. In the months and years that followed, he told me the truth about those boys, whispering their names as we lay together on the crog loft. Geraint, John, Morgan . . .

'*Martha?* Martha?' I hear Morgan calling my name, drawing me back to the frozen churchyard. The breeze tugs the little wisps of hair around my face and startles the robin, who flies to a nearby tree. '*I have asked too much. Hoped too much.*'

'No!' I reach out a hand, not quite touching him, only too aware of the parishioners nearby. All those years ago, Morgan was but a bystander, that's what William told me. And does not the Bible teach us to forgive?

'You may hope,' I say, lowering my voice.

Then I turn away and push through the crowd, afraid of what the villagers might think, of what they are already whispering behind our backs.

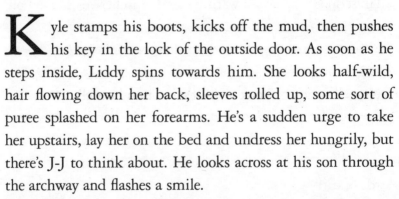

31

K yle stamps his boots, kicks off the mud, then pushes his key in the lock of the outside door. As soon as he steps inside, Liddy spins towards him. She looks half-wild, hair flowing down her back, sleeves rolled up, some sort of puree splashed on her forearms. He's a sudden urge to take her upstairs, lay her on the bed and undress her hungrily, but there's J-J to think about. He looks across at his son through the archway and flashes a smile.

'Thank God you're all right,' Liddy says. 'I was starting to worry about you. Normally you leave a note.'

He pulls off his gloves, walks to the fridge, lifts out the milk and gulps straight from the carton.

'Where did you go?'

'The mountain.'

'The summit?'

He doesn't answer – it's like he doesn't hear her though he catches the words clearly, notes of accusation in his head – instead, he dives into the pocket of his waterproof and battles with the flap, pulling out the old green bottle embossed with the skull and crossbones.

'Look what I found,' he says, searching for somewhere to put it. 'I thought it would look nice . . . ' he catches sight of the empty wine bottles behind the sink, 'there!'

'What? No!' She snatches it from him, smearing puree on his hands. He flinches at the gooey mess. 'Where did you get it?'

He flings himself on a stool at the kitchen island. 'That old cottage.' He gulps more milk. His head is hurting, a blinding, stabbing pain, and his chest is tightening. He needs an asthma inhaler but he doesn't have one. He hasn't really had asthma since he was a kid.

'I'm serious,' she says, a warning tremor in her voice. 'I'm not having this thing in the house.'

'Why not? It's just a stupid bottle. I thought you'd like it. You like antiques.'

'Not *all* antiques. Look at it. It's a poison bottle!'

She marches towards the door, bottle in hand, and before he questions what he's doing, he's grabbing her, yanking her towards him. The bottle slips and shatters on the floor, big shards of dirty green.

The pain in his head feels a hundred times worse. Beyond the kitchen window, he can see the cottage clearly. He can see the door wide open, the beaten earth floor.

'Now look what you've done.' He shoves her backwards and bends to the floor, picking up the pieces, hair tumbling across his brow. He tries to salvage the larger pieces first, thinking he could glue it back together. It's only when he looks up with a pile of broken glass in his hand that he realises Liddy's on the floor. He must have pushed her harder than he thought.

He feels bad for the rest of the day, sitting in the cellar, pretending to work on his plans for the house – isn't that why he went up to the cottage in the first place, to ascertain the exact dimensions of the forebay and where he'll lay the pipe? – listening to the sounds above him: Liddy's feet on the stairs, the closing of doors, J-J crying for his bottle, the scuttle of Martha's paws as she chases a ball. He's never done anything like that before, never touched Liddy in that way, and he hates himself for it, hates the fact J-J was in the next room, sitting in his bouncy chair, watching his bully of a dad through the archway. Absentmindedly, he flicks through one of his grandfather's notebooks, landing on a page with just a couple of written lines.

The doctor gave me pills and says he'll run some tests. But I know it won't stop the voices. I phoned the vicar.

He runs his fingers over the words. Running some tests sounds consistent with his grandfather's dicky ticker, but the voices bit is confusing. A schizophrenic? He racks his memory for clues, but draws a blank. The last time he saw his grandfather, he was five years old.

He shuts the notebook and goes upstairs, habitually checking his phone. No emails, no eager new clients enquiring about his custom-made websites. It pisses him off, all that effort of placing ads and paying for a decent Welsh translation, and he's not gained a single local customer. He stows his phone back in his pocket. The house is silent, but he can see the lights in the barn. He doesn't want to think about his grandfather's notebook, he doesn't want to think about Eleri's words, so he gets to work, clearing the kitchen, chopping onions, defrosting mince, trying and failing to shake the saturating chill of the cellar from his bones. An hour later, he pokes his head through the barn door. Liddy's studying some papers. J-J's on his playmat, fast asleep.

'Hope you're hungry,' he grins, still feeling like a complete and utter bastard. Frowning, she lifts her eyes to his, and he realises how mad she still is, how it's not going to be that easy. 'I've made spaghetti bolognaise. And I'm sorry about earlier. I overreacted.'

32

⸺⊶⊷⊶⸺

The next afternoon, after working in her studio, Lydia finds a note from Kyle:

Taken Martha and J-J for a walk.
Back soon.

She makes herself tea and sits at the kitchen island, scrolling back through the emails from Markey on her laptop. This time, the images he sent download instantly: the man in the doorway leaping into the room through various filters. In each image, she's drawn to the eyes, narrow green slits.

I could hear him through the walls, calling for Martha . . .

She tries to remember the face of the First World War soldier on top of Mari's television, the scar running across the soldier's left cheek. She zooms in. Is it the same man? But the picture's too blurry and there's no visible scar – perhaps the injury had occurred after the photograph was taken?

She shakes her head. She's being silly. This *isn't* an old photograph. This was taken recently, a hundred years after the First World War. This has been taken on a modern-day camera, with a modern-day selfie-stick, by modern-day people. So what is she seeing exactly? An imprint of something from a different time? A memory etched in the stone?

She emails back.

> Hi Markey, thanks for the photos. Sorry it's taken me a
> while to reply. Lots of things have been happening.

She paces around the kitchen, tugging up the blind, feeling an immediate shaft of cold air on her hands and face. Just a leaky window, she tells herself. They'll get new ones, replace every damn window in the house.

She returns to the email, accidentally knocking her tea cup, splashing lukewarm liquid over the keyboard. Quickly, she dabs up the spills with a tea towel, then sits down to write. She's an irrational desire to pour herself out to Markey, a man she's never met, and is unlikely ever to meet, in a way she can't right now with Kyle.

> We bought the house beneath the cottage. I don't know
> if you remember it? Sunny Hill, or Y Twr Gwyn. It's quite
> distinctive: a 1930s tower. But it seems it was a mistake.
> Strange things have been happening. There's a light
> that shines from the mountain, and a strange energy, a
> sort of bad energy, that emanates from the cottage. I'm
> afraid for us. Very afraid. We seem to be falling apart.

She hits send before she can question herself, then goes to the barn and picks up her chisels. She works hard, nervously chipping at the stone, scared of making a mistake as she shapes the eyes of the first woman for the new collection. Half an hour later, with no sign of Kyle and Jamie, she stands upright, aching. It's getting dark. Wherever they've gone, they'll struggle to see their way back. She can hardly see the track through the window, hardly see the tower apart from the light from the kitchen. And then she remembers: the blind. She needs to get in, pull the cord, tighten it around the screw that Kyle has fitted properly. She can't let the darkness into the house. She pulls off her goggles and runs from the barn, glancing up the track for Kyle and Jamie, but there's no one there.

When she unlocks the door, she sees her laptop still open on the kitchen island. But something about it is odd, the way it's half-positioned over the stain, the backlight lit up. Had she left it like that? She walks towards it and stares at the screen. There's a crack in the bottom right-hand corner that wasn't there before, a dark splodge reaching outwards. Cold creeps up her spine as she imagines someone else in the house, someone watching her, laughing at her seeing the laptop the way it is. Except it's not just her imagination. It's a feeling, a knowledge. *Someone's here.* She steps forwards, hardly daring to breathe. Her emails are still open and Markey has replied to her message:

Hi Lydia. Sorry to hear things aren't good. I think I told you I split up with Jenny. We haven't been in contact since, but I still have her email address. Might be worth getting in touch? She was really disturbed by the photo. It might be an old email address by now, but you could try.

As she stares at the screen, the crack at the bottom of it seems to spread, rippling beneath the glass, reaching to the opposite corner, running through Markey's message. The same shape, the same deep brown as the stain beneath it. She presses the escape button in case it's something internal rather than the screen. The cursor flickers. Around the stain, covering the emails, a single typed letter repeats itself over and over, as if someone is standing right next to her, pressing the key:

MMMMMM

She bashes the M-key, confused, thinking somehow it must be stuck. But it makes it worse. Far worse.

MMMMMMMMMMMMMMMMMMMMM

She stumbles backwards, breathing fast – *M for Martha* – then runs to the outside door and yanks it open. The darkness is complete in the short time she's been inside. She can barely see more than a metre in front of her. But she needs to get out. She needs the open space.

'Kyle?' she calls out, pinning her eyes on the weave of a light along the track. She thinks of that other light and looks up. It's there, as she knew it would be, higher up on the mountain, mimicking the one below. 'Kyle,' she calls again, desperate, panicked. 'Is that you?'

33

'Something happened,' Lydia says as soon as Kyle walks in. He bends down, lets Martha off her lead, then tugs off the baby-backpack. Jamie's fallen asleep, nose dripping but snug in his snowsuit. 'I came in from the studio and found my screen broken.' She points at the right-hand corner of her laptop, at the splodge that seems to have shrunk again, but then she remembers the email she sent to Markey, the one about her and Kyle. Quickly, before he has chance to read it, she flips down the lid.

Kyle frowns. 'You must have damaged it.'

'No,' she shakes her head. 'I didn't do anything. I didn't even touch it. What if . . . ' the thought makes her stomach turn. 'What if there's someone else in the house?'

'Did you hear anything?'

'No.'

'Did you see anything?'

'No. Just the screen.'

She thinks of the spilled tea. Maybe she damaged the screen when she knocked the tea cup? She opens her laptop again while Kyle's busy with Martha's lead. Her emails are still open, but the damage is different to how she remembered, a neat black splodge in the right-hand corner. The repeated letter M has completely disappeared. It's like she imagined it.

'Well?' Kyle interrupts her.

She closes down her emails. She can't risk him seeing her messages, knowing she emailed Markey after she promised she wouldn't. 'You're probably right. It probably was me. But do me a favour, just in case? Check the tower? For a moment, I thought I felt someone watching me.'

'Jesus.' Kyle pinches his forehead. 'We've been through all this before.'

'This was different—'

'It's almost as if you're trying to find fault with the place. Like you don't want us to be happy here.'

She stares at him in disbelief and wonders where he's been, where he's taken Jamie. 'Of course I want us to be happy here. But please, Kyle, check the house with me? Every room? Every door? Every window? Just to be sure.'

He hands over Jamie and plants his hands on her shoulders. 'You stay here. I'll check the house. No point you jumping at every shadow.'

She holds Jamie tight, whispering to him how much she loves him, how she'll do anything to keep him safe, as Kyle stomps around the tower. She hears him go into the cellar, through the corridor then up to the top room.

'There,' he says, reappearing in the kitchen. 'I've checked everywhere. There's no one here. Satisfied now?'

It's not until much later when Kyle and Jamie are asleep that she carefully crafts her message to Markey's ex-girlfriend. The thought that someone else might understand, that someone else had been as disturbed as her by the mountain, gives her courage.

Dear Jenny,

 I hope you don't mind me contacting you out of the blue. I was given your email address by an old friend of yours, Markey. I saw a photo of you and Markey online outside a ruined cottage on a mountain in Wales. Mynydd Gwyn, do you remember it? In the photograph there's someone else there, standing in the doorway of the old cottage. We've recently moved into a house on the same mountain (you might remember the tower house along the track from the farm?) and things are happening that I can't explain. Somehow it seems connected to the cottage and the photograph you took. I'm wondering . . .

She glances at the kitchen blind – closed – the cord tightly wrapped around the nail. But she has the impression the cord is straining, determined to spring loose.

. . . if you'd be able to talk to me about it? Anything you can remember about the mountain, anything at all, might be useful. Please respond. Please don't just delete this email. It's important. It's very important. We're a family with a little boy and another baby on the way, and I need to make sense of what's happening before it's too late.

She signs off and goes to bed, dozing and waking at intervals. At one point, she checks the time on her phone, through the cracked screen she hasn't got round to replacing, the cut glass rubbing against her thumb every time she swipes. It's not even midnight though it feels much later. She sleeps again, a short fitful sleep. She's trying to get rid of the baby, beating her fists into her stomach, battering it out. It seems logical, necessary. She *has* to get rid of it. It's the most necessary thing in the world. 'Devil's child,' she screams at it, over and over, as she beats her stomach.

She wakes up, rigid with terror, listening to her body. There was something else, wasn't there? Not just the nightmare, there was something real. She waits and waits until she feels it again: an ache, sharp, short-lived, like a period pain.

She throws back the duvet and stands up. The pain comes again, low down near her pubic bone. Lightheaded, she stumbles towards the bathroom, remembering the dream again. *Devil's child.*

She switches on the bathroom light, sits on the toilet and carefully touches her stomach. Is she just imagining it feels tender? As though she really was beating herself in her sleep? She pees and wipes herself, and the paper comes away covered in blood. *Oh God. God no!* She stands up again and the pain strikes a little stronger, the blood soaking her pyjama bottoms bright red.

'Kyle!'

The room blurs. She crumples to the floor. So much blood, it can only mean one thing. When she looks up, she sees Kyle's concerned and sleep-addled face hovering above her.

'I'm ringing nine-nine-nine,' he says.

She tries pushing herself up. The room swims. Kyle lays a steadying hand on her arm. 'I'm calling an ambulance now.'

'No!' She remembers Mr Jones on the stretcher, wrapped in a blanket, jolted about by the ambulance crew who didn't know the best way to skirt the potholes. 'No, not the ambulance. You can drive me to the hospital.'

'I can't. Look at you. Look at the blood!'

'I'm losing the baby.' Suddenly, she feels clear-headed, removed from the situation, as if someone else is speaking. 'It happens all the time. One in five pregnancies. I don't need an ambulance. I just need you to help me.'

'Right.' Kyle leans over her and she can tell he's desperately trying to master the situation. 'What do you want me to do?'

'I need a towel,' she says. 'Something small I can put between my legs. And a pair of loose trousers, and my coat. And we'll have to take Jamie with us. You'll have to wake him. Put him in his snowsuit. What's the time?'

'Ten to midnight.' There's panic in his voice. They need to get to the hospital for Kyle as much as for her. Whatever is happening will happen regardless, but Kyle needs the reassurance of machines and beds and uniformed professionals. He needs to be able to look back on this night and think they did everything they could to save the baby, even if, as she already knows, the situation is hopeless.

'Eleri might still be awake,' she says calmly. 'If we hurry, she might be able to look after Jamie.' Another gush of blood, but this time no pain. Life flowing out, as naturally and completely as it had flowed in. 'Please,' she says, feeling suddenly weak again. 'I feel weird ... dizzy ...'

34

I t's five o'clock in the morning and Kyle is still wide awake. He'd driven back from the hospital in a mild state of shock, his mind working overtime, trying to process everything that had happened. He'd pulled off the main road, taken the narrow country lanes through the valley to Gaer Fach, parked outside the shop and walked around the back. The back door had been left on the latch and he'd found Eleri in the lounge, nodding over his sleeping son. He'd felt a sudden anger. Why had she allowed herself to nod off like that when she was meant to be babysitting?

He'd scrawled a thank-you note and lifted J-J into his arms before tiptoeing out again. Then, somewhere between the village and the tower, J-J had woken up and started screaming. He'd tried everything to shut him up, turning up the stereo, blasting the car with hot air. But it had only made him worse. Back at Sunny Hill, it had taken him a full hour to get J-J off to sleep again – he'd not been able to find that damn giraffe anywhere – pacing back and forth across the bedroom, singing lullabies. Eventually, he'd laid him in his cot as gently as he could, whispering to him not to wake up again because Daddy needs his headspace.

An hour later, he's like a live wire, twitching, unable to even contemplate sleep. He sits at the kitchen island, absent-mindedly stretching his hand over the stain, a perfect fit, as he replays the evening over in his head.

'It's nothing you did,' the nurse had said to Liddy, wearing a professional sympathy-smile. 'It's just one of those things. Lots of women presume it's something they've done, or something they didn't do, when in fact it's just nature doing what nature does. Next time you'll be luckier.'

Kyle had squeezed Liddy's hand, trying to keep his eyes from the cannula in her arm, the cannula they'd used to give her a blood transfusion. The thought of someone else's blood inside her made him feel sick.

'The consultant will want to speak to you in a minute,' the nurse had said, gathering her notes, squaring them up against her palm. 'I'll leave you two together for a while. I'll just be outside if you need me. You can ring the buzzer.'

Liddy had nodded. 'I'm sorry,' she'd said when they were left alone.

He'd remembered the Prosecco, the wine at Charlie's party, the sneaky cups of coffee. *It's nothing Liddy did.* 'It's not your fault,' he'd said regardless.

'I had this dream. I beat myself. Beat my stomach.'

'Shh. Shh.' He'd stroked her forehead. 'Don't stress yourself out.'

'You don't understand.'

'There's nothing *to* understand. You heard the nurse, it's not your fault.'

She'd closed her eyes and seemed to withdraw, and he'd felt all alone in the room with its ultrasound machine and boxes of latex gloves. But after a few minutes, despite everything that had happened, he'd also felt himself nodding.

'So, this was your first pregnancy?' The consultant had startled him, hovering above them, flipping papers on her clipboard. To his surprise, Liddy was sitting upright, alert.

'No,' she'd said, and Kyle had squeezed her hand again at their shared knowledge of J-J. 'No. We have a little boy. He's almost eight months old.'

The consultant had arched her eyebrows and written something down, then Liddy had looked weird, almost sheepish. 'And I had an abortion when I was nineteen.'

He'd dropped her hand, stared at her in shock. In horror. What the fuck? She'd never mentioned anything about an abortion. They'd been married five years, known each other for six. He'd thought he knew everything about her.

The consultant had smiled encouragingly. 'So, this is your second planned pregnancy?'

'Not quite. It was an accident.'

'I see.' The consultant had tapped her clipboard with her pen, and he'd felt an irrational desire to punch that stupid smile off her face. 'Well, there's not much else we can do, I'm afraid. We'll keep you in overnight, keep an eye on your blood pressure. You've lost a lot of blood and we don't want you haemorrhaging again. It's lucky you came in rather than trying to manage it at home.' She'd glanced at Kyle, as if to say, well done for bringing her in, then turned back to Liddy. 'We also need to check we've got all of it out.'

It. It? It wasn't an it. It was a baby.

Kyle had stood up, accidentally sweeping a box of tissues to the floor. 'Is there a place I can get coffee?'

'There's a machine in the foyer.'

'Right,' he'd said, looking Liddy straight in the eye. Is there anything else he doesn't know? Anything else she's neglected to tell him? 'And then I'll need to get home for our baby.'

In the tower, he opens the cupboard where they keep the wine and stares at the near-empty shelf. There's only one bottle left. He makes a mental note to get supplies in, finds a pint glass and fills it to the rim.

The kitchen blind is open, the way he likes it, and the night spills into the dimly lit space. It's colder with the blind up like that, but he doesn't mind. Recently the cold has ceased to bother him. It's like he's acclimatised to the conditions on the mountain, whereas Liddy's forever laying fires and fiddling with the thermostat.

He takes his wine to the kitchen island, then goes back to just sitting there, scratching the skin above his left elbow. Half a pint of wine later, his head feels better, calmer; his muscles have quit their involuntary twitching. Just over his shoulder, he can sense the shadow, a dart of movement every time he twists his head. *I know you're there, I know you're watching me.*

He pulls open the drawer he's sitting against, and fumbles for a knife. Just a short blade, but it's deadly, one of the professional chef knives he bought Liddy before J-J was born. He tests it against his thumb until he feels a sharp prick, sees a small welt of blood. Then he leans over and makes a mark in the panel of the kitchen island beside his right leg. A long, deep notch in the wood.

35

Spring time. My favourite time of the year. Everything feels fresh and new. There are light green shoots on the trees and lambs dancing in the fields. The colours are dazzling after the grey of winter. Hard to believe we have just been through a hard frost, followed by snow. I shudder at the memory of waking early, taking an axe to the water trough, feeling my way with my fingers. The hollow smash of ice. Splinters in my face.

But not now.

Now, I am striding up the hill with my egg basket, enjoying the heat creeping down my back, and the stretch in my legs, feeling alive, thinking about the sunshine, thinking about Morgan. I cannot stop grinning when I think about him. His smile. His laugh. The way his eyes shine when he looks at me.

We are careful how we meet — I do not tell William — usually at his mam's house for tea, or the path near the river, or the graveyard after church. Places where William does not go, where he would not think to find me. I will make him see in the end that Morgan has repented his boyhood wrongs. He is a good man, and we are right for each other. When we marry, things will be well again. But I am biding my time, waiting for the right moment, when William is sleepy with beer.

Marry Morgan! The thought sings in my head. I forget I am almost at the cottage, that I will soon be making dinner, and scrubbing pans and feeding animals. I do not care about any of those things. In my thoughts, I am as free as the birds sweeping low over the hillside.

In the yard, there are signs of life: a bucket of slops, an abandoned tin mug catching the sun. I look for William, thinking he must be home, but cannot see him anywhere. I pick up the mug and throw dregs of beer across the stones, then I push open the cottage door and step within.

Something smashes into me from the side. A bolt of pain pierces my head, striking through my eye. I stagger, fall. I cannot think. Only the crushing, debilitating pain and the knowledge that something is very wrong.

I come around slowly, realising I am lying on the earth beaten floor. The pain is still there, in the side of my head. A searing, dizzying pain. I try to focus. The fireplace. The chairs. A pair of big heavy boots, once worn by my father, and now, his son.

William.

The pain shifts as I move, regathering behind my eyes. He is sitting in his chair, watching me, with his gun in his lap. Through a cloud of blood, my gaze focuses on the barrel first, then travels slowly down to the stock. Instinctively, I know that's what jammed into my head. He must have watched me climb the hill. He must have hidden himself behind the door, waiting. I know what this is about too.

Morgan and I had met by chance on his way home from the quarry and wandered arm in arm to the river. But I'd had a sense we were being watched, something about the shadows and the rustle of the hedgerow, though when I'd looked over my shoulder there had been no one there.

Pulling myself upright, I put a hand to my head. My eye is sticky, and when I draw back my fingers they are bright red. I take a few faltering steps, dragging myself into the yard, stumbling towards the wash bucket. I have to clean myself up. William will be wanting his dinner. He will not want blood all over his food. I lean over and splash water on my face. The nausea rises, flushing through me, forcing itself out. Over and over. When I am finished, my hands are shaking, but at least the pain is not so bad.

Somehow I make it back to the cottage. The light hurts my eyes but the kitchen is dark and I know my way around. William is still sitting in his chair, watching as I stagger to the table, trying to make sense of the various utensils.

I take big rasping breaths. I have to make food. That is what I have to do. Sweet Jesus, help me! He watches me all the while, scratching his skin, the place where scars twist up his arm, courtesy of Morgan's friends. He does not say anything, he does not need to say anything. The message is clear. I pick up a knife, still shaking. Despite washing my face, blood drips from my eye, onto the table, staining into the wood. A neat red stain that grows larger and larger. I look at the knife and think about all the things I could do with this weapon in my hand. All the things I could do but will not.

'I lost my job,' he says eventually. 'Some bastard had it in for me, and he,' he spits the word 'he' and I know it can only mean one person: his supervisor, Morgan, 'was only too happy to oblige with the formalities.'

I clutch the knife tightly, trying not to look at the blood on my hands, the blood on the table, trying to follow what William is saying, but no longer able to think above the strangled hissing sound in my head.

36

When Lydia gets back to Sunny Hill, everything feels different. The house is in disarray, and nothing's been cleaned. There's blood on the bathroom tiles. Her pyjama bottoms are still dumped in a heap. A sodden nappy lies discarded on the mat next to a pile of dirty wet wipes. She goes through it all with a bottle of bleach, wrapping the pyjamas in a plastic bag, carrying them out to the dustbin.

'You shouldn't be doing that,' Kyle says from the sofa, then punches something into his phone.

She takes pasta from the cupboard and boils it on the hob. She's thinking about the baby. A girl. She's sure it was a girl, although the nurse had said it was too early to tell, only ten weeks or so. She decides she'll give her a name, an English name. She'll bury her on the mountain beneath the purple moor grass. Then in the summer, when everything's green and the fields are bathed in sunlight, she'll be close to her. Mynydd Gwyn. *Her* mountain. Tears roll down her cheeks, into her mouth. She's part of it now, regardless of wherever they go, whatever they do. She'll never be able to shake the mountain off. She doesn't even want to.

Kyle startles her from behind, drawing her into a hug. It's the first time they've hugged since it happened and it feels awkward like they don't quite know what to do with their bodies.

'What about we take a holiday?' he says, reaching up, wiping a tear from her cheek. 'Go see your parents? Or friends?'

She shakes her head. The last thing she needs is company right now, her parents fussing and piling on sympathy. 'Sorry,' she says, 'I couldn't face it.'

'Just a day out, then? Go somewhere nice. Go out for lunch.'

'I couldn't. Not now. I feel wiped out. I feel as though I could sleep for a week. I'm better off staying here. Besides, I'm behind with my work. I've had another email, a rather demanding one. You and Jamie go out if you want to.'

He brushes her cheek with his lips, his beard irritating her skin, as the pasta bubbles furiously. 'Why didn't you tell me about the abortion?'

'Because it doesn't mean anything, not any more. It was a long time ago. I was a different person back then.'

'And the boyfriend?'

She turns down the hob, clatters pan lids and spoons. 'Just an ex. We weren't going anywhere. It wasn't meant to be.'

'I see. I'm sorry. Can't have been easy, having to go through all that, then having to relive it again yesterday.'

'It felt like the right thing to do. The only thing to do. It wasn't the right time.'

He picks up a spoon, stirs the pasta slowly. 'But what I

still don't understand . . . ' He reaches over her, grabs the salt, grinds a couple of flakes into the pan, picks up the spoon again. 'What I still don't understand is why you didn't tell me. When we were trying for J-J you were obsessed with doing everything right. You even talked about seeing a specialist at one point. And all that time, when you read the rule book at me, when you were tracking your cycle, and creating the perfect conditions like,' he clatters the spoon down, draws his hands down his face, 'like a fucking laboratory, you *knew* you could get pregnant naturally anyway. That it wasn't an if, but a when.'

'I would have told you at some point. I guess I was worried you'd judge me.'

He looks at her quizzically. 'I hope the boyfriend, whoever he was, was supportive.'

She takes two plates from the drying rack, wipes them with a tea towel, trying to ignore the note of jealousy in Kyle's voice. 'By the time I found out, we weren't together any more.'

'Oh—'

'Please, let's not talk about it now. I'm tired. I need food, sleep, an early night.'

She spills twirls of pasta onto plates, then takes a bowl of apple puree from the fridge for Jamie. They sit at the kitchen island, picking at their food. Lydia spoons puree into Jamie's mouth, catching it with a cloth when it dribbles down his chin.

'But you *did* discuss it with the boyfriend, didn't you?' Kyle says, not letting it drop. 'It was a joint decision?'

She scoops a dollop of fallen puree from the floor. 'Why does it matter?'

'Just because . . . ' He plays with his pasta. 'Because it does.' He rests his fork on the side of his plate, reaches out a hand, runs his fingers over hers, but it feels too late and not quite enough. 'I thought we told each other everything,' he says with a note of bitterness.

'We did. We *do*. Only this was different.'

'How?'

She sighs. 'It was before us. It wasn't about you. And perhaps, I felt guilty.'

'Guilty? Why? You said it wasn't meant to be. That it wasn't the right time.' He scratches the skin above his elbow. He's wearing a T-shirt though it's cold in the kitchen. It's cold everywhere in the house regardless of what they do.

She closes her eyes, not wanting to think about it. At that point, she'd known it was just a bundle of cells, not really a baby, but she'd still been confused. She'd had no one to talk to. No one to help her process her feelings. The guilt was all part of the patchwork of emotions.

They tidy away the plates, the mood between them sullen and unpredictable. Kyle offers to take Jamie to bed while she sits at the kitchen island, hugging a mug of hot chocolate. She doesn't want to sleep because she doesn't trust her dreams. She wants to sit here, knowing the light is outside, because it's strangely comforting: Morgan's light searching for his lover, calling her name in the darkness – *Martha, Martha, Martha* – never letting up; knowing that things go on and on regardless of whatever happens. But she hears nothing beyond the vague hum of electricity.

She runs her mug under the tap, leaving it to soak, too tired to clean it properly. Too tired, she hopes, to dream, to lie awake thinking about the baby or what might have been. She fishes the bottle of wine from the fridge, the one Kyle must have opened last night, and pours herself the remaining half-glass, hoping to numb the areas of her brain that are still searching, still questioning.

The next morning when she awakes, Kyle and Jamie are gone. She darts upright. Had she heard Jamie crying for her in her dreams? Heard him crying, but not done anything about it? *Devil's child.* The words sound in her head. She presses her hands to her ears and scans the room: the clothes on the floor, Jamie's sleeping bag slung over the side of the cot. Kyle has evidently got him up and dressed without her hearing a thing. She pulls on a jumper, shivering in the ice-cold room, and runs downstairs. There's no one there either, just a note on the kitchen island.

Couldn't sleep. We've gone walking. Don't worry about us. K x

She feels hollow inside as she makes herself coffee. There's an emptiness to everything: the ritual of selecting a mug, the steam escaping from the cafetière, the complex smell of ground beans. She places her hands on her hips, working her way to the dip of her stomach. She's still bleeding, but already it's less, a memory of the last forty-eight hours rather than the process itself. A stain like the stain on the kitchen island.

She takes her coffee with her as she goes through the house. The emptiness is everywhere. In the bathroom, changing her sanitary towel. In the bedroom, among the heap of clothes, none of which seems right when she tries them on, settling for an old baggy jumper. In Kyle's study, where she flings the information from the hospital, not wanting to look at it again.

In her studio, staring at the vast stone blocks she's worked on so carefully, that are taking shape, becoming human rather than granite. But, today, the arms look misshapen, the heads bulging, the stomachs hideous, the breasts too large. They're ugly, she thinks, swirling the remaining coffee around in her mug, just like this house is ugly. She'd wanted to portray confidence, acceptance of the post-partum figure, self-love, but instead she's created monsters.

She finally lets go, sinking to her knees, splashing coffee on the concrete floor. Tears run down her face as she hugs herself tight, shuddering under the weight of what's happened.

She goes back to bed and sleeps, only vaguely aware of things happening around her: a hand pressed against her forehead, Kyle asking if she's okay, Jamie crying. She's aware of curtains being pulled on their runner, a sense of the day becoming night. Dreams of the man in the cottage doorway, holding the lantern high, looking for her. Dreams of drowning, swallowed into a mist of freezing water, weeds trapping her feet. Dreams of running across the mountain, hearing footsteps behind her on the rocks, turning around and seeing the woman, the woman with hair all over her face.

On the third day, she gets up to please Kyle, who insists she'll feel better for it, shuffling into the lounge. She looks at Jamie in his bouncy chair, playing with his mirror, and flushes with guilt.

'Hello, little one. I've been a bit of an absent mummy, haven't I?'

A moment later, she hears Kyle's voice from the kitchen. 'She's in the lounge. Come on through.'

It's late morning and bright sunlight pours through the window, making her head hurt. Kyle appears in the archway with splodges of baby food all over his T-shirt. Behind him is Eleri, dressed for the cold. Lydia struggles to her feet but something's not right. Her head feels like it's swimming. The room sways.

She hits the carpet, knees first, knocking her head against the side of the sofa. It's a moment before she comes to, fighting the urge to be sick. Someone's next to her, pushing a cushion beneath her head, stroking her brow.

'It's all right. You fainted,' Eleri says.

Kyle kneels beside them. 'I'm not surprised. She hasn't eaten for days. Maybe you could persuade her?'

Eleri nods and Kyle heads to the kitchen. She hears him boil the kettle as Eleri helps her onto the sofa and pulls a blanket over her knees. Kyle returns a few minutes later with sandwiches and cups of tea, then he takes Jamie upstairs. As soon as he's left, Eleri unzips her coat and loosens her scarf.

'Kyle asked me to look in on you,' she says, her voice full of concern. She seems on edge, playing with the zip.

Lydia takes a bite of the peanut butter sandwich but it lodges in her throat. She feels self-conscious. Her hair is stuck to her cheeks where she must have dribbled in her sleep, and she can't remember the last time she brushed her teeth.

'He said you weren't eating, that you wouldn't get out of bed.'

She forces herself to swallow. 'Kyle went to see you?'

'He was really worried. He was ... ' Eleri zooms the zip up and down, 'not quite himself.' She shivers. 'It's freezing in here. Shall I light a fire?' Without waiting for an answer, she kneels down and screws newspaper into cones. Then she lays them in the grate with bits of kindling and breaks up pieces of fire starter.

They sit in silence, drinking tea, eating sandwiches. Eleri

fusses over Martha and throws more sticks on the fire, but it all feels awkward, like Eleri's only here out of politeness. Lydia wishes she could tell her everything, about how it feels, this sudden inexplicable emptiness when she didn't even know she wanted another baby, at least not so soon. And the guilt she feels about Jamie. How she knows she's not a good mum right now. How she's not well enough to look after him. But it's all so terrible, she can't bring herself to say any of it. Instead, she listens to Eleri, talking about the shop and the village.

'Thanks for checking in on me,' she says when Eleri gets up to leave.

'You're welcome. It's the least I could do. Promise me you'll pop down to the shop for a coffee soon?'

'I promise.'

After Eleri's gone, she goes in search of Kyle and Jamie. They're in the study, Jamie sitting upright in the comfy chair, chewing fistfuls of paper. She settles him onto her lap, pulling soggy paper from his mouth, then watches Kyle work. She doesn't understand what he's doing, but it's comforting just sitting there, being close to him, watching the movement of his hands across the keyboard.

After half an hour, he switches off the desk lamp and swivels the computer chair towards her. She notices how unkempt he is, not just the daily mess of looking after Jamie. His beard is untrimmed and his eyes are ringed red as though he's been awake for days. Next to the monitor, there's a stack of dirty pint glasses. She wonders what he's been doing since she's been ill. Now that she thinks about it, she can't remember him lying next to her in the bed, even in the middle of the night. She can't remember turning over in her sleep and sensing him there.

His voice breaks the silence. 'Feeling better?'

She nods. 'I just needed to eat something. Sorry if I gave you a fright.' More silence while Jamie chews her finger. 'What did you do while I was ill?'

'Oh, you know.' He picks flecks of food from his T-shirt. 'Changed nappies. Washed clothes.'

'You didn't come to bed.'

'Course I did. Just you were sleeping.'

His pupils are wide, shining; the skin of his face loose around his jaw. He's put on weight, she thinks, as he swivels back again, crushes an empty can of lager into the wastepaper bin. It's as if he's thriving here whereas she's curling up on the inside.

'Oh, and I played with Jamie,' he says, turning back again, reaching for Jamie's hand, shaking it up and down. 'Didn't I, J-J?'

She watches the two of them, Jamie giggling as Kyle pulls funny faces. It should be a beautiful picture, one she cherishes: a dad bonding with his son. But something about it makes her blood run cold.

37

⸻ ⚬⚬⚬ ⸻

T wo days later, as promised, Lydia takes Jamie to the shop. It's afternoon, already dark, and the rows of terraced cottages sparkle with festive lights. Christmas is four weeks away, but she hasn't talked about it to Kyle, where they'll be or what they'll do or what presents they'll buy each other. Jamie's first Christmas and they haven't prepared a thing.

'Come through to the back.' Eleri throws her an encouraging smile and turns to her husband. 'Jon, you're in charge for half an hour, okay?'

They sit in the kitchen, drinking mugs of instant coffee. The table in front of them is heaped with projects: maths homework, half-finished drawings, a cereal box that's being turned into a spaceship. Lydia surveys it all with an ache in her heart. A proper family. A unit of four. She looks away. 'Have you ever felt you were being punished?'

'Punished?'

'For things that happened in the past?'

Eleri dunks a chocolate digestive into her coffee. 'What do you mean?'

Lydia looks down at Jamie chewing her finger. She can't find his giraffe anywhere and her finger seems to be the next best thing. 'I had an abortion when I was nineteen. I didn't handle it well. I bottled it all up, didn't talk to anyone at all, started having panic attacks. I didn't even tell Kyle until recently.'

'Oh, I'm sorry.' Eleri lays a hand on her arm.

Lydia blinks back tears and shakes her head. 'Don't you see? I don't deserve it. I don't deserve sympathy. The miscarriage is a punishment.'

'It's not punishment. It's guilt. Don't get me wrong, you haven't anything to feel guilty about. But if you feel that way, then that's what matters, what needs to change. I'm sure you had your reasons, it's not a decision anyone takes lightly. I had an abortion too, when I was sixteen.'

Lydia moves her arm away and fusses with Jamie's collar, trying to hide her surprise. For some reason, this terrible, weighty secret, had seemed just hers.

'We were far too young. We discussed it with our families, and they agreed. Jon's mam came with me on the day because Mam was working and couldn't get the time off.'

'It was Jon's?'

Eleri blushes. 'He's the only boyfriend I've ever had.'

'Gosh.'

'What about you?'

'An ex.' Lydia closes down. She doesn't want to talk about what happened. She doesn't want to remember the knock in the middle of the night, the denim jacket flapping in her face, the banging of the door behind him as he'd left. She's spent so many years purposely blocking it out. The doctor hadn't asked either, hadn't wanted to know. Or perhaps he'd been pushed for time, fed up with students getting knocked up and wanting a quick way out. He'd avoided eye contact, studied her medical notes and asked in a monotone whether or not she wanted to keep it.

'Did you ever feel bad about it?' she says. 'Did you ever imagine the person it could have been?'

Eleri shrugs. 'I must have done, once or twice. But to be honest, I haven't thought about it in years. When I got pregnant again, I was twenty-five and married. I knew I wanted to be with Jon for the rest of my life, and this time I felt old enough, responsible enough, to be a mother. Things were completely different.'

'I'm sorry. I shouldn't have brought it up.'

Eleri pushes the packet of biscuits towards her, urging her to take one. 'Of course you should have. But you've got to start believing that whatever you did when you were nineteen has absolutely nothing to do with what's happening right now.'

She nods, swallowing back her tears. 'There's something else.' Her voice is a whisper. Somehow this is even harder. 'Something that's been bothering me. Something that seems more important since the miscarriage. I can't get it off my mind.'

'Go on.'

She hesitates, looking down at Jamie, thinking about what Eleri told her about Kyle's grandfather, and the others before him, the ones who went mad; and the way the tower is overshadowed by the ruins, how the two things feel connected. 'That cottage on the mountain, the one above Sunny Hill. Do you know anything about it?'

Eleri snaps a digestive in two and plunges one half into her coffee before sucking off the melted chocolate. 'I suppose you mean what happened in the sixties?'

Lydia frowns 'The sixties? I'm not sure . . . ' She shakes her head. This thing, whatever it is, feels much older than that.

'The little girl? Griff's sister?'

She shrugs, but it rings a bell: the sister who died.

'There was an accident up in the cottage and the little girl, Cerys, was killed. I'm afraid I don't know the details. No one really talks about it, not openly, not with Griff thinking he rules the roost. No one goes there either. It's a bad place.'

'Why?'

'It's structurally unsound. Rotten through and through. Please don't go there. I'll only worry about you if you do.'

Back in the tower, she finds Kyle sitting at the kitchen island, flicking the ring pull of a can of lager. She lays Jamie fast asleep in his car seat on the floor, then steps towards him. 'What are you doing? You don't like lager. It's not even twelve. I thought after London you were going to take it easy on the drinking?'

Foam spills from the top of the can as Kyle cracks it open. 'There's no rule I can't have a drink before lunchtime, is there?'

He pushes back his chair and comes towards her, breathing beer on her neck.

'Oh God. How much have you had?'

'Why? Is there a problem?' His voice is slurred.

She glances at the mountain. The blind is half-open and she can just about see the cottage, sunlight pooling on the broken roof. She attempts a laugh. 'It's just that it's Friday morning – you're usually working.'

'Fuck work.' He spins the blind up as far as it will go. 'Isn't this the whole point? Moving to the country. Doing what the hell we like!'

He nuzzles into her, breathing her skin. 'No,' she shakes him off. 'I've got work to do even if you haven't.'

He looks crestfallen, just for a moment, then his eyes harden. 'Had I known it was going to be like this.'

'Like what?'

'You always working, me just wanting a bit of fun. Fun. That's all I'm asking, not the earth.'

She stiffens. 'I'm still recovering from ... from what happened.'

He puts down his can and opens the back door. Fresh air breezes into the room, rattling the empty wine bottles, clinking them together.

'Perhaps you're right,' he says, looking out at the frost-laden garden. 'Perhaps this is just the way it is. Different people needing different things.'

He steps outside, not bothering with a coat, closing the door behind him. She watches him in the garden, seemingly oblivious to the cold, ducking into his partially made hut, staring up at the cottage through the planks, scratching his skin. It takes her a moment to recognise the shirt he's wearing. It's one of his grandfather's – stained off-yellow cotton, rolled to the elbows – and it unnerves her, seeing him dressed that way when he has plenty of his own clothes hanging in the wardrobe. It reminds her of the man she doesn't know; the man whose house they inhabit. He steps out again, crosses the garden onto the track. She knows he'll be gone for a while, he'll go walking on the mountain, wild and windswept and drunk. She hates it. Hates the sound of the beer can still fizzing in her head, that look in his eyes.

She sits at the kitchen island, smoothing a piece of paper over the stain. Martha settles beside the baby seat, looking up at her, tail wagging, probably desperate for a walk.

'As soon as Jamie wakes up, we'll go out, okay?'

It feels right to handwrite the letter rather than type it. It feels more personal. Still, she doesn't really know what to say, whether any of the staff at St Dyfrig's Care Home will even remember Edward Jeffreys. He hadn't stayed there long. His illness had been short-lived. But it's been on her mind to write for a while, ever since Eleri mentioned where he died, and the address had been easy enough to Google. She sucks the end of her pen and looks down at the paper. She can see the stain beneath it, seeming to grow darker, spreading outwards to the corners of the page.

Suddenly, she knows exactly what to say. The pen flows easily as if it has a mind of its own. By the time she's finished, she feels strangely content. What she's written feels right. *She* feels right. She signs her name and folds the page into its envelope, noticing the stain has marked the opposite side. A dirty splodge of faded red.

38

I am healing, from the outside, at least. No pain any more and the dizzy spells are fewer. I have not been to the village. There is still a bruise around my eye, a watercolour of purple, yellow and green. I could not go down to the village even if I wanted to. William has made sure of that. Though he barely speaks to me other than to grunt orders, he follows me everywhere. Into the shed to feed the animals, onto the mountain to scavenge the last few berries before the frost. Always hanging a few yards back, waiting for me to make a run for it. Daring me to make a mistake. I know the mountain better than he does, and he knows that, the little paths that lead down to the valley on the other side, the shortcuts through the fields.

I think of Ma, slaving in front of this same hearth, sweeping the same earth beaten floor, dusting the same shelves, the same furniture, the same few ornaments. I remember the terror in her eyes, the silent

obedience. Scared of her own son. How had I not realised it before?
How had I not seen what William had become?

I try not to think about Morgan, but he is with me anyway as I
scrub the pots and sweep the ashes and concoct meals from our scant
supply. But there is no hope now. No hope of ever marrying. Of ever
getting away from the cottage or the mountain. I see it clearly: William
will never allow it. I have been a fool to let myself dream.

I think of breaking free, slipping away, not taking the obvious route
through the farm where William will find me, but one of the lesser
paths, meeting the wood and the quarry and eventually the town. I
could take a train to the south, to Cardiff or even London, find work
in a laundry or a shop. Anywhere where I could be someone else. A
nameless face. A nobody.

I am thinking it right now, as I scrub the boots, hands black with
muck and polish. It is a rare moment of freedom – William trudged
out this morning and has not returned.

Run for it, Martha, *I tell myself.* It could be your only chance.

I glance around the room. It would only take a minute or two
to throw everything together. I haven't many things. I could use the
egg basket to carry essentials: money from the stone pot in the eaves,
a shawl and clean undergarments, rags for my monthly event, a
loaf of bread. I am almost decided on the matter, when the door
is pushed wide. William clatters in and throws something on the
table. An iron contraption with teeth like a rabbit trap, only much,
much bigger.

Pain flashes through the side of my head. 'Dear God, what is that?'

'A mantrap. I have four of them strapped to the horse.'

'The horse?'

'Hired it from the farmer.' William nods backwards at the yard.

I stare at the vicious, devil-like contraption, my heart full of fear,
wondering where he managed to purchase such a thing. I remember

Ma telling me a story from our old town in England: a child got his leg caught in a trap and lost his foot. Mantraps are banned, but this was a forgotten one deep in the woodland, left over from a bygone era.

'We cannot trust people,' my brother says, throwing himself into his chair.

I wonder how he found the money. Devilish though these things are, they must have cost a penny or two. We haven't much left, and our supplies are dwindling. William has not worked for over a month. I still do not know what happened at the quarry and I do not like to ask. All I know is that a fight broke out and he lost his job.

'I sold the pig,' he says, as if he hears my silent question.

The pig! I hand him a bottle of beer, thinking how I have not checked on the pig since first light.

'We do not want people snooping around. Trespassers. Thieves. Murderers.'

The last word lingers in the air. I turn back to the boots and continue my polishing, but my hands shake and I cannot rest with that thing in the room. I think of running away again, running to the workhouse, begging for mercy. But what is the point in that? Better to rot on the mountain than there. William would find me anyway, however far I ran, however hard I tried to hide. Even if I changed my name and cut my hair, he would find me and bring me back.

He tosses the beer bottle onto the floor and grabs the ghastly trap with both arms, shedding rust onto the table.

'I am going to lay them now,' he says. 'Before it is too late. You must keep to the cottage, Martha. You must not look from the window. If I see you peeping . . .' He draws a hand across his throat, then stands up and draws the shutters, leaving me in darkness.

I feel limp, helpless, the breath squeezed out of me. It is too late to escape. Too late to hide. The force of what my brother is doing hits me harder than the stock of his gun. No one can get in. I could die up here and no one would ever know. I could waste away, shrivel to nothing, sorrow and fear eating me up from the inside.

No one can get in. And no one, only William, can get out.

39

⸺⸘⸙⸺

The café is in a narrow side street in Aberystwyth.
Lydia sits at the window, beneath sagging wreaths
of tinsel, watching the pedestrians through the rain. She's
dressed in jeans, a black jacket and a red scarf. The scarf
is deliberate, the way she'd told Jenny to identify her. Not
that there's anyone else in the café she could be mistaken for,
just an older lady reading a book and a group of teenagers
ordering all-day breakfasts. Halfway through her second
cappuccino, she starts to wonder whether she's wasted her
journey. Jenny's half an hour late. Outside, the rain is mer-
ciless, giant grey sheets that slash against the kerb, not the
sort of weather that invites you out unless you really have
to be somewhere. She packs away her wallet and phone, and
stands up to leave.

The café door swings open and the girl from Markey's

holiday snap walks in. She recognises her instantly. Taller than she'd seemed in the photograph and not quite so slender, but Jenny nonetheless.

'Lydia?' Jenny shivers in a cheap-looking raincoat.

'That's right. Jenny?'

The girl pulls off the sodden coat and pushes a satchel under the table. 'I thought you'd be different,' she says, looking pointedly at Lydia's stomach. Lydia blushes, remembering she'd told Jenny she was pregnant. 'Sorry about the delay. My seminar overran.'

'No problem. Thanks for agreeing to meet up. Can I get you coffee?'

'Black. Two sugars.' The girl peels hair from her cheeks, sits down and drums her fingers on the tabletop while Lydia buys another drink. In her email, she'd told Lydia she was a student at the university, studying drama. She didn't mention anything about the cottage or Mynydd Gwyn, only that she was happy to meet.

'I won't keep you long,' Lydia says, returning with the coffee.

The finger-drumming continues. 'So, this is to do with the photograph, right?'

'That's right. The cottage on Mynydd Gwyn. In the background, there's a man standing in a doorway. A man smoking a cigarette, with trousers that disappear at the ends. You must have used a selfie stick or something. You can see the mountain and the courtyard and the shed.' She wishes she'd brought the photograph to the café, but maybe she can find it on her phone? She reaches for her bag.

'It's impossible,' Jenny says, stopping her.

'Sorry?'

'The photograph. It's impossible. That's what really freaked me out. Not the man in the doorway, although that was spooky enough. But the photograph itself. We didn't have a stand or a selfie stick or anything to mount the camera on, and we couldn't have held it out that far with our arms. I remember taking photographs, but we didn't take that one. It's like it appeared by itself. I remember, afterwards, lying on the bed in the youth hostel, flicking through the camera. It was raining that day. We'd made our way down from the summit to the cottage, but we didn't stop for long. We *might* have sat on that wall, we *might* have briefly admired the view, but we didn't stop to take photos. I'm sure of it. Markey suggested sheltering inside the cottage until the weather cleared, but I didn't fancy it. The place was really creepy.'

'Are you sure about the photograph?'

'Dead sure. I pointed it out to Markey and he just laughed, said we must have taken it. Men are so bloody logical, aren't they? It wasn't until later, when Markey was uploading it onto his blog, that I saw the man.'

'So, you don't remember seeing a man in the cottage?'

Jenny sets her jaw. 'There wasn't a man.'

'How do you know?'

'We had a good look inside. The place was tiny. If there was anyone there, they'd have had nowhere to hide. I remember Markey shining his torch into the old bed, waving it up at the rafters. There was this loft thing, like a platform, but no way to get to it. We checked the barn next to it too. The whole place was desolate, it hadn't been lived in for years, decades. There was no one there, no one at all. I swear on my life.'

'So how do you explain the photograph?'

Jenny shrugs. 'Something weird. Something . . . supernatural. A spirit, a ghost, a phantom. Whatever you want to call it.

Someone who had lived there a long time ago. Someone who remains there, trapped. Someone evil.'

Lydia tenses. 'Why evil?'

Jenny plays with her empty sugar sachet. 'I don't know. I'm not sure. Just a feeling.'

'Markey said you had nightmares after the holiday?'

'Oh yes?' Her eyes dart upwards. 'And what else did Markey tell you about me?'

'Nothing. Just that the two of you split up.'

'That's right. To be honest, I was surprised when I got your email. I haven't been in contact with him since we split. I've moved on. Markey wasn't ... how should I put it?' She twirls the sugar sachet. 'Let's just say, he wasn't the nicest boyfriend I've ever had.'

'Oh, I see, I'm sorry—'

'Took advantage, that sort of thing.'

Lydia thinks of Matt Trevithick and immediately pushes him away again. 'Do you mind telling me about the nightmares?'

Jenny sighs. 'They began the same night. We were staying in a youth hostel. I can't remember exactly. It was more a feeling than anything else. Shapes, shadows, a sense of being followed. And always, somewhere in the dream, the man in the photo, looking out of a window or a doorway. Always looking, searching for something. There was some sort of metal contraption. Chains and metal teeth. I can't describe it properly, but I think there was something similar hanging in the shed. It doesn't sound that bad, does it? There's nothing specific, just the man and the metal thing. But I'd always wake up screaming, with this horrible sense I was drowning. Markey couldn't take it after a while. It was happening every night. It's partly the reason why we split.'

'Did you ever get a sense of a girl? A young woman? Martha?'

'No.'

'You never heard someone calling the name? Martha, Martha, Martha. Like that?'

Jenny slurps the top of her coffee. 'No.'

'Only the man?'

'Always the man. He was the only person there except for me and Markey. There was no girl.'

'And this man, did he have a name? Morgan Lloyd? Something like that?'

Jenny shakes her head. 'I don't know about any name. Why do you want to know all this anyway? You said you'd bought that old tower. That things were happening?'

Lydia nods. 'Not happening exactly. Just a sense, like you felt.'

'What about your husband?'

'He doesn't really believe it.' She thinks of their latest argument that morning, a stupid thing about the washing-up. 'He thinks I've gone Christmas shopping.' She pictures Kyle with Jamie on his knee as he tries to work. 'Actually, things aren't so good right now. We don't agree on the house. Kyle thinks it's all in my head. He's changed . . .'

Jenny pushes her coffee aside, slopping it onto the saucer. 'I'm sorry.' She stands up abruptly and fishes for her satchel. 'I've just remembered, I've got a lecture.'

'But it's lunchtime. And it's still pouring with rain. Can't you stay a little longer?'

A hiss of steam escapes from the coffee machines behind them, plates rattle as they're stacked. An old man walks in, tutting at the weather, shaking a newspaper from the folds of his coat. Lydia anticipates the lunchtime rush, students and office workers and Christmas shoppers running in out of the rain.

Jenny pulls on her raincoat, still dripping with water. 'To be perfectly honest, I don't want to talk about it any more. It was only three years ago, but it feels like a lifetime. I was a different person back then. A very different person. I've moved on, changed.'

Lydia nods, something resonating. 'Well, thanks for speaking to me anyway. I'm sorry for taking up your time.'

Jenny zips her raincoat. 'Thanks for the coffee.' She bends to retrieve her satchel, tangled wet hair sliding across her back. When she rights herself, she flashes a smile. 'It was nice to meet you.'

She watches through the window as Jenny disappears in the direction of the promenade. The girl's coffee is still steaming, barely touched. She'd seemed desperate to get away from the café, to get away from her questions. She sits there for a moment, doing nothing, then impulsively fishes for a pen from her bag and looks for something to write on.

Outside, the street is almost empty, just a few lone shoppers hugging their umbrellas. It's easy to spot Jenny among them, waiting at the traffic lights.

'Jenny!'

The girl turns. Impossible to be certain with all the rain, but Lydia wonders if she's been crying. She presses a paper serviette into her hand.

'My number. Just in case you remember anything else. Or in case you ever need to talk. And if you think of anything to do with the cottage or to do with Mynydd Gwyn, then please, please, let me know.'

The lights change. Jenny sprints across the road, swallowed

into the mist along the seafront. Lydia imagines the serviette clutched between her fingers, the edges wet, the numbers blurring, eventually dropped in a gutter, sailing like a boat into the rubbish and leaves.

40

⌒⌒⌒

*I*t is the dead of night. I am lying in my bed on the crog loft, trying to focus, trying to shift the sleep from my eyes, trying to understand what awoke me. I lie still and wait. A sound. A tinkling sound. Bottles clinking together. And then I hear William moving about below me. I wonder what the time is and what he is up to. It is winter and dark, even when we rise, but I have a feeling it is not time to get up yet, not for hours. He is drunk, that is for sure. The bottles clink again. I can hear them rolling about on the floor between the sound of his footsteps. Clumsy feet, still in their boots. He groans and swears. He will lie down in a minute, I am sure of it. I will hear him open and close the door of the box-bed and soon he will be sleeping deeply beneath the skeleton carved so many years ago by the bedmaker as a reminder of our mortality.

'Martha, are you there?'

I freeze. I can feel the wood beneath me through the mattress. There is a tonne of blankets on top, making up for the lack of padding, and a bed warmer at my feet. The blankets smell of hay, making me feel safe and cocooned. The loft is a place where William never goes, not any more. A place where I can still dream, still imagine a life beyond here. A life with Morgan.

'Martha, you little bitch. Where are you?'

I breathe deeply into the old wool and tell myself to let him wear out his anger. He will soon go to bed and let me sleep again. I will soon hear him snoring. Rasping, beer-fuelled snores.

When I hear the twitch of the ladder, my heart stutters. William would not come up here, surely? He has not been up here for a long time. Not since he cast Ma out and took the bed. He wouldn't, would he? Would he?

The ladder sighs and creaks, sighs and creaks, not used to his weight.

'Martha!'

His voice cuts through the brittle air. He reaches the top rung and throws his stomach and arms onto the ledge, panting heavily before drawing up his legs. Do not move, I tell myself, whatever you do, do not make a sound. He will think I am asleep, he will soon creep down again.

Do not move! Do not move!

I feel his hands on the blankets, pulling at them, tossing them aside. I wonder what he is doing. What can he possibly be doing? The chill night air kisses my neck, my hands, my ankles. There's just my nightgown to protect me. I scream, despite myself, letting him know that I am awake and at his mercy.

'William, what are you doing? Are you ill? Go away! Please!'

It is so dark, I cannot see a thing, but I sense him leaning over me and feel flecks of spittle on my cheek. I taste his breath, warm and acidic. He fumbles with my nightgown, pulling it above my knees, striding over me.

'*What are you doing? Please, William, go away!*'

'*You are just like her,*' he says, breath sharp in my face. '*Just like Gwenllian. Begging me to take her.*'

'*Gwenllian?*' I do not understand, but my voice tremors. '*What do you mean?* What do you mean?!*'

He smacks my face, sending my nightcap flying. I gasp, tasting blood, catapulted into silence. Into pure terror. I cannot see anything. I cannot guess what he will do next. I wish Ma was here. I wish. I wish. I wish. I try to think logically, but my brain burns with a million terrifying thoughts.

He pushes my legs wide and forces his way between them, fiddling with his clothes. I hear the buttons pop on his trousers, material being wriggled down. Then, there is a sensation I have never felt before, something thrust between my thighs, a cold sharp pain, so brutal it could be a knife. But the humiliation is even worse. A deep burning shame though I still cannot grasp quite what he is doing. Deeper and deeper he goes. Pounding. Grunting. Not caring that I have found my voice again. Not caring that I am screaming.

At last, he lies back, breathing heavily. I stare into the blackness, more confused than ever. Only one thing is certain: whatever has just happened is horribly, horribly wrong. I wonder whether he has fallen asleep, but then he mutters beneath his breath, as if justifying everything, '*Little bitch.*'

I curl into a ball, nursing the soft swollen place between my legs. No longer screaming, but silent, numb. This is what it must feel like to be dead, to be nothing, to be nobody. When he rises again, I prepare for the worst, telling myself that nothing else can hurt me. I am beyond pain. I am beaten, broken. But he does not come. I hear the sigh-creak, sigh-creak of the ladder, then the door of the bed being opened below me.

I wait, still curled in my ball. There is a noise that I cannot quite *fathom. I lie as silently as I can, trying to work it out, trying to anticipate if this means more danger. Eventually, half-asleep with exhaustion and fear, I work it out.*

It is a knife making deep scores in the box-bed.

41

L ydia awakes to the sound of tapping. She sits upright, feeling an immediate shaft of cold air on her shoulders. She
reaches for Kyle, but he isn't there. Instead, she rubs the chill
from her arms and listens. A faint tap-tap-tapping comes from
somewhere below her. She throws back the duvet and stands
up. It's the depth of night and the glow from the nightlight
illuminates the way to the stairs. She hesitates as she passes
Jamie's cot, bends down, listens again. Just the unnerving stillness of a baby deep in sleep. Impulsively, she reaches down and
touches him, feeling the warmth of his forehead and the rise
and fall of his chest beneath his sleeping bag. Reassured, she
tiptoes out onto the stairwell, alert to everything: her breath,
the creak of the floorboards, the cool wood of the banister, the
tapping sound getting louder and louder. And the smell. The
smell of a cigarette.

She finds Kyle sitting at the kitchen island, the cigarette-smell replaced by the slightly off-smell of the downstairs rooms. But something's not right. He looks dishevelled, his hair over his eyes, his beard untrimmed. The dog chain – the one she was sure she'd thrown out – is wrapped around his wrist and he's flexing it up and down on the marble.

'Kyle,' her voice is little more than a whisper. 'What are you doing?'

He looks up, but doesn't seem to register she's standing there, just keeps flexing his wrist, causing the chain to tap against the marble. It's almost as if he's looking through her, seeing someone else.

She screams, 'Kyle! Please! What the fuck are you doing?'

He stops, confusion clouding his face. He shakes the chain free, and it falls to the floor, a snaking clatter as it hits the stone paving.

'I couldn't sleep,' he says, rubbing his forehead. 'And I've got to go to London.'

'What?' She notices his text messages open on his phone.

'Charlie's got more work for me. Website of a friend of his. Wants me to start on the project as soon as possible. I won't be long, a few days at most.'

Goosebumps rise on her arms. 'When?'

'Tomorrow.' He looks at his watch and laughs. 'It's tomorrow already, isn't it? What I mean is, today.'

She sinks onto the stool next to him and holds her head in her hands, wanting to feel his warmth, his arms around her, but she doesn't know how to ask. 'What about Jamie? What about Christmas? We haven't planned a thing. And I can't just up and leave now, however much I'd like to. I've got work to do. Stanley Harris has asked for yet another report before he pays the advance.' She swallows hard. The last email she'd received about the commission had been abrupt: her plans still weren't up to scratch. She'd felt sick as she'd read and re-read Stanley Harris's words, wanting to walk away from the whole thing, but knowing she couldn't, not with their finances the way they were. And she'd not told Kyle because she was ashamed. Ashamed to admit she might not be good enough. 'After what happened with the baby, I'm behind,' she says now.

'Stay here then.' His tone hurts more than his words. 'I'll be back well before Christmas anyway.'

'Can't you just say no?'

'No!' He bangs his fist on the kitchen island, catching the edge of his phone, causing it to jump. 'I have to go. I can't stay here. Don't you understand?' He tucks his phone into his pocket, then offers a sheepish smile. 'Hey, sorry. I didn't mean to snap. Just, I've got a lot on.' He places a hand on her knee. 'Turns out the last contract was a cock-up. My fault, should have read the small print. Anyway, this one promises to be substantial. The guy's offered money upfront. But he wants to meet me first.'

'What about Stanley Harris? I could ask him for more money?' Although he still hasn't approved her plans and the thought of asking him for anything turns her stomach. 'I could tell him the materials were expensive or I had to buy new tools or . . .'

He moves his hand up and down her thigh, up to her crotch, and for a moment she thinks – but surely not, not so soon after the miscarriage? 'I can't just turn work down because I feel like it. Besides, it might do us good, having some time apart. We haven't got on so well recently.' He looks around the kitchen, the cramped space that feels no better with the new units. 'No wonder, just the three of us, and no one else for miles. We need time to breathe, to be ourselves.'

She nods, on the brink of tears, wondering if he's right.

Five hours later, she drives Kyle to the car rental in town. Their farewells feel hurried and superficial. Kyle spends most of the time throwing Jamie in the air, catching him and making him giggle. Three days, he reckons it will take him to sort the contract; he'll be back in time to help her decorate the house for Christmas, buy a tree, find something special for Jamie. She plays along with it, trying to sound upbeat: she'll order a turkey, go shopping for tinsel. At the last minute, she almost jumps in the hire car with him – she can stay at her parents', go shopping in London – but then she remembers how far behind she is with her work. Three days is perfectly manageable.

The rain turns to hail as she drives back home and turns up the mountain road. A hollow, tinny sound drumming on the car roof. Halfway along the track, she's forced to stop. Emlyn Jones is standing in the middle of the road, facing away from her. She beeps the horn, hoping he'll move. But it's like she's not there. Or he doesn't care. Or he's blocking her way deliberately.

She buzzes down the window, shouts through the rain. 'Excuse me.'

Emlyn turns. Balanced on his forearms is a fragment of paving slab. Fear snakes down her spine as she imagines it meeting the window, shattering the glass. She glances in the rear-view mirror at Jamie in his car seat, then fumbles for the wiper switch and turns it to maximum speed. *Slash, slash, slash.* Emlyn takes a step forwards, raises the paving slab.

Please God, no. No!

She tries and fails to throw the car into reverse, her hands clumsy on the gear stick, grating the gears. Then Emlyn laughs. Laughs into the rain, a sound she can't hear, only guess by the glee in his eyes and the tremor of his jaw. He drops the paving slab into a pothole and walks casually to the side of the track.

She feels his eyes on the car as they bump the rest of the way home, her heart in her mouth. He could have done it. He could have killed them both. She keeps her eyes from the rear-view mirror. Ahead, at the far end of the track, Sunny Hill is ugly and menacing, its walls more grey than white, nothing like its name. She pulls up the hood of her waterproof as she bolts to the door, clutching Jamie who shrieks as a gust of hail smacks around the side of the building. As soon as they enter the kitchen, Martha jumps up, proudly bearing a chunk of wool from the sheepskin rug. She looks around, close to tears: wisps of white dot the flagstones and the lounge floor. She just wants it all to end. She wants to blink, open her eyes and find herself back in London. When Eleri phones, inviting her out for a drink, suggesting that Jon could babysit Jamie and Martha, she jumps at the chance.

'Perhaps he didn't hear you?' Eleri suggests when she recounts the incident later. The pub is practically deserted, just Lydia and Eleri and a couple of locals whom she recognises from the memorial service.

Lydia shakes her head. 'He knew I was there all right. When he turned around, he wasn't surprised. I thought he was never going to move. I felt,' she picks at the beer mat, ripping it to shreds, 'I felt threatened.' She thinks about the painted red letters on the cottage walls, so careful, so deliberate. The message perfectly clear: *Keep Out.* She sighs. 'Sometimes, I think we'll never fit in. It's a constant battle. We get through one thing, and then there's another just around the corner.'

The door of the lounge opens. Griff Davies walks in, plants himself at the bar and jokes with the landlady. Eleri throws Lydia a sympathetic smile. 'Talking of which, I think we need another drink. Another glass of red? You need to relax.'

But she can't relax, she can't ignore Griff. She wants the evening to end, even as the alcohol wraps around her, even as she tries to lose herself in conversation with Eleri. Griff Davies is always there, in the corner of her eye, blowing froth from his pint, causing ripples that run down the side of his glass onto the beer mat.

'I think I'd better call it a night,' she says after the fourth glass. 'I feel a bit sick.'

'Me too.' Eleri downs her pint and giggles.

They bump into each other as they search for their bags.

'Eleri Thomas,' Griff Davies catches Eleri's arm as they pass. 'I'd have thought better of you. Hanging out with the English family.'

Eleri shakes herself free. 'Leave it, Griff.'

'I'm just looking out for you.'

The landlady mops the counter, head down, intent on her work, but there's a smirk on her face that's barely concealed.

'After what happened last time, I'm surprised, that's all.' Griff reaches for his beer. 'I'd have thought you'd have learned your lesson by now. Jeffreys was a nasty piece of work. Would have had his wicked way with you if I'd not stopped him.'

Eleri adjusts the strap of her handbag and says something in Welsh. She pulls Lydia towards the door. 'Come on, let's go.'

'I'm only trying to protect you,' Griff calls after her. 'I've seen the way he looks at you.'

Eleri frowns. 'Be ti'n siarad am dan?'

Griff drinks deeply, then wipes his mouth with his sleeve. 'Kyle Stein. That's who I'm talking about.'

'*Beth?*'

'You heard what I said.' He looks gravely at his pint, and Lydia realises he's speaking in English for her benefit: he wants her to understand every word he's saying. 'I've seen him hanging around the shop, the way he talks to you, Eleri bach, the way he invites himself into the back. I saw—'

'What do you mean?' It's Lydia who speaks, shocked at the sound of her own voice. Images flash through her mind, making her head hurt. Images she doesn't want to see: alone in the bedroom at Sunny Hill, turning over in the dead of night, feeling the sheet beside her still cold; Kyle last night when she'd found him in the kitchen, unable to sleep, making an excuse to run away from her. The change in him. The drink. The lies.

Griff shakes his head. In disgust? In amusement? 'I mean, little Sais girl, you ought to keep better track of your husband. Where's he tonight, for instance?'

'He's in London.'

'Doing what?'

She hesitates. Truth is, she doesn't know, she's only had a text from him earlier saying he'd arrived. 'He's working.'

Griff smiles at his pint. 'You don't know, do you? You don't even know where he is right now!'

'Stop it!' She presses her hands to her ears, feeling like a child. She's giving the wrong impression, that she's out of control, but she doesn't care. She wants it all to stop. The house. The mountain. Griff. *Stop it. Stop it. Stop it.*

She feels Eleri behind her, dragging her backwards, forcing her into the street. 'Are you okay?'

'What did he mean?' she gasps. Her skin tingles with cold. 'What did he mean about Kyle? He was speaking in English. He wanted me to understand.'

'Nothing. He's drunk. Don't listen to anything he says.'

'He said that Kyle had been snooping around the shop, looking at you.'

Eleri hesitates. 'Kyle was concerned about you, that's all. Griff must have seen him come round after the miscarriage. I thought Kyle had told you?'

'He mentioned something.' But she can't let go of it. In her mind she sees a key, a door inched open, the pair of them, Kyle and Eleri, whispering in a corridor, Kyle leaning across, drawing Eleri close. Her stomach lurches, the foul taste of alcohol resurfacing in her mouth.

'Griff will do anything to make a scene. He thrives on the attention,' Eleri says. 'Please don't worry about it.'

They walk in silence to the shop while she tries desperately not to throw up. Eleri digs in her handbag for her keys, drops them onto the pavement, reaches down. 'Oh shit.'

Lydia stares at the back of her, at her hips, at the gap between her trousers and top, at the pasty roll of flesh.

The door swings open. Swathes of tinsel drift into the night.

'Lost your keys?' Jon grins. He turns to Lydia. 'Stay the night if you like. Pwtsyn and Martha are getting on just fine. Jamie's settled in Iwan's old crib. And by the look of things, you might need me to make you coffee in the morning.'

But Lydia shakes her head, thinking about Griff and his accusations. 'We'll be fine. If you don't mind driving us back?'

Jon hesitates. 'Are you sure?'

'I'm sure.'

She says as little as possible in the car on the way home. Jon talks about the kids, the nightmare of Christmas shopping, the school nativity play. As they reach the track, he rams the car into first gear. 'Jesus, this road. We used to play up here as kids, though we weren't supposed to. The road was just as bad back then. That's why I didn't like it when Eleri took the job with Mr Jeffreys, though the money was useful. Shall I see you in?'

'Thanks, but we'll be fine. And thanks for looking after Jamie and Martha.'

He pulls up outside the tower and she takes Jamie's car seat from the back and calls Martha to follow. Then she turns and waves goodbye. But Jon's already manoeuvring the car, brushing the hedge with his three-point turn. Lights drift away from her down the track, replaced by the ever-present sense of isolation. Opening the back door, she switches on the kitchen light and sets the car seat on the floor. Then she draws down the blind, shutting out that other light, shining from the mountain. This time, it feels a little brighter, a little closer. She shudders, picks up the telephone and dials Kyle's mobile.

42

K yle doesn't notice his phone vibrating in his pocket, not at first. He's had a skinful and he's deep in conversation with Benedita. They're sitting in Charlie and Benedita's flat, and, in front of them, on the coffee table – a circle of glass supported by a hunk of wood that's shaped to resemble tree roots – are numerous empty bottles. Not just wine but whisky, vodka, gin. Charlie is passed out on the leather beanbag and it's just the two of them left talking. He hasn't spoken much to Benedita in the past, but she's intelligent and engaging and, although she's not personally his type of woman – too lithe, too made-up, too *young* – he can see why Charlie is attracted.

'Maybe you should move back to London?' Benedita says.

He struggles to chase the last ten minutes or so of their conversation. What were they talking about? The mountain? Liddy? He remembers saying he's scared, that time away from the place has made him see things more clearly. But what those things are, he can't quite remember. Just tendrils in the mist.

'Actually, I'm going to suggest it after Christmas.'

Benedita leans forwards, picks up a bottle, shakes it. 'Shit. We drank it all. Wait here, I'll bring another.'

It's then that he feels his phone vibrate. He takes it from his pocket: three missed calls from the house. He telephones back, desperate to hear Liddy's voice, to know she's okay. 'Liddy?'

'Hello?' The line crackles. He pictures Liddy in the kitchen, cradling a mug of tea, J-J on her lap. His Mini-Me. God, he misses that kid. 'You okay?'

'No. Not really.' She sounds like she's been crying and he feels such a dick, being miles away in London, unable to sort whatever needs sorting.

'I'm missing you, I'm missing you so bad,' he says, knowing he sounds drunk, but he doesn't care. She has to know. She has to know how much he loves her. 'I've been an arse recently, haven't I? I haven't looked after you properly. After the miscarriage, I withdrew. I was confused. I'm sorry. I'm sorry.' The alcohol is making his head spin. He leans against the back of the sofa.

'You went to the shop the other day.' Her voice cuts through the spinning.

'What?'

'You went round the back. You went to see Eleri.'

The line fizzes then clears. He can't think straight. Can't even begin to formulate a response.

'You went to Eleri's house. You invited yourself in.'

Something twists inside him: the old self, the old him. 'Are you all right?' he says, managing to sound a whole lot more sober than he is. 'You sound tired.'

'I'm not bloody tired.' Is she crying for real now?

'All right, all right, calm down. You're not tired.' He stands up, wills his vision to remain steady, then paces across the room, back and forth over the polished floorboards. Everything's so stylish, so coordinated, so bloody expensive. 'Yes, I went to see Eleri. I was concerned about you, I didn't know how to help you. You wouldn't get out of bed.'

'You could have just asked?'

Kyle groans, his concern replaced with an anger he can't control. 'You weren't exactly easy to talk to. Besides, you were asleep most of the time.'

'I'd just lost a baby. I'd had a miscarriage.'

'I know.' He stares out the window at the wide London street. There's no one there, but he's a sense of people crammed in around them, in the flats and the houses and the traffic nearby. 'It was my baby too.'

Silence.

He hears Benedita in the kitchen, the pop of a cork, drawers being opened, glasses taken from the dishwasher. His head spins. Suddenly, he feels sick, swallowing hard, fighting the urge to actually throw up. Something that's been niggling at the back of his mind, that he's suppressed until now, lurches forward before he can stop it. 'You knew it wouldn't last, didn't you?' he says, frowning at the realisation. 'One in five pregnancies, you said.'

'What?'

'One in five pregnancies ends in miscarriage.'

'I read that on a website. I—'

'Read about it? Why? Why were you reading about miscarriage? You should have been reading about how to keep the baby healthy after getting pregnant again so fast, how to have the best birth possible.'

'Kyle—'

He remembers the blood transfusion, the cannula in Liddy's arm. 'You wanted it to happen, didn't you?' He feels fucking clever working it out. 'It was too soon for you after J-J. You drank wine at the party, you even asked my permission to make yourself feel better. Oh God, Liddy, what have you done?'

The line goes dead. He lets the phone slip from his hand, hears it slide and knock against the leg of the sofa. He staggers backwards, head spinning, seeing the bottles on the table, Charlie half-buried in the beanbag. God, how much had they drunk? And what the fuck has he just said? It's like he's not in control of his own mind. It's like . . .

'Hey babe,' Benedita pushes a glass into his hand. He looks down. It's a glass of water. 'I thought you might want a different kind of drink. Everything all right?'

He shakes his head, and the movement makes everything so much worse. Bile floods his mouth. He swallows it down, but it leaves a sharp tang at the back of his throat, telling him tomorrow's going to be rough. 'I have to go back,' he says, pulling the keys of the hire car from his pocket. 'I've done something terrible.' He holds his head in his hand, stabs the car keys into his temple. 'I need to go home.'

43

Lydia's asleep on the mountain, half-dreaming, half-remembering. It's twelve years ago and she's standing in a car park in front of a tall building. Everything's white: the walls behind her, the pavement, the skin on her arms and hands. Even the things with colour – the cars, the ambulances, the staff in their blues and greens – have a sheen of whiteness. Everything's sterile, including herself: wiped clean, tidied up, the nasty business of the baby sucked out of her, carted away to a lab or an incinerator. She didn't ask what would happen to it, but she has an image of the child suffocating in a glass bottle like the old-fashioned ones used for milk, face and hands pressed outwards, squashed into a pulp of pinkness. She knows it isn't really like that. The thing would have been tiny, negligible, but she can't get the image out of her mind.

'Where you going, love?'

The taxi driver seems to sense her misfortune, opening the door for her, packing her in, playing surrogate-dad. She's grateful for his kindness, for the way he chats aimlessly about politicians and some celebrity's new hairdo. It doesn't matter after all that she lied to the nurses, told them that a family member with a fear of hospitals is waiting for her outside, that someone will be staying with her overnight, that there will be people around to look after her and call if there are any problems.

'You'll be all right?' says the taxi driver, pulling up at the university halls. It's the summer holidays, almost three months after the night in her room, and the place is practically deserted, only a few conference guests and one or two students who, for convenience or, in her case, necessity have chosen to stay on and pay the additional rent.

She smiles and thanks him and hands over a ten-pound note, refusing to take the change. 'I'll be fine.'

Three hours later, there's a knock on her door. She doesn't want to answer it, but the person won't give up. 'I'm coming,' she says, crawling out of bed, thinking to get rid of them as quickly as possible. Probably the cleaner or one of the summer conference guests who's lost their way.

Instead, she finds Danny.

'Hey,' he says, awkwardly holding out a bunch of white roses. 'I heard you'd been ill.'

She sighs. He must have driven all this way from home. Someone, probably Kess, must have told him she was here, must have said she was ill although she hadn't disclosed the details. She rubs her forehead. She can't deal with this right now. 'I'm sorry, Danny, it's not a good time. And I'm not ill, I'm fine.'

'Please? Can I just come in? I just want to talk to you.'

'No. It's over. I told you. There isn't anything left to say.'

She closes the door and leans against it, breathing heavily, feeling like the worst person in the world. She'd meant to tell him the truth, but she can't. She can't bear to say the words. *I got pregnant by someone else. I can't really remember what happened. Maybe it was my fault. Maybe it was his. I got rid of the baby. I don't deserve you.* It's then that she thinks about moving on, transferring to another university, running away from herself.

She turns to the sink, splashes water on her face, looks up into the mirror. The words jump out at her: *Ugly. Fat. Unlovable.*

A moment later, she's wide awake in Y Twr Gwyn, groping in the dark for her phone, reaching down to switch on the nightlight she'd forgotten to turn on earlier. What time is it? Is Jamie okay? Why hasn't he called for her in the night for milk? Or maybe he did. Maybe he woke up and screamed and she slept right through it. She finds her phone shoved beneath her pillow. It's 7.00 a.m. She sprints across the room and finds Jamie's fast asleep, hands balled into fists. She puts a hand to his chest, feels the reassuring rise and fall. He looks so content, he must have slept right through: a first. She should be celebrating, marking all these little milestones.

She reaches for her phone again. There's a text from Kyle, sent three hours ago, a muddle of misspelled words and predictive text asking if she's okay. Her head pounds as it all comes back to her: the tears, the angry words, Griff Davies in the pub. Reaching for the blister pack of paracetamol by the bed, she realises it's empty. She grabs a jumper and runs downstairs, landing in a puddle, then switches on the light. Puddles everywhere, dotting the corridor. Martha! She'd been too drunk to let her out last night. She steps between them, trying not to mind when Martha jumps up at her pyjamas, paws wet with her own urine.

She heads to the kitchen for something to wipe the floor. The blind has sprung loose though she's sure she knotted it around the nail. It's the last thing she remembers doing before stumbling to bed. Then again, she'd been drunk. She must be mistaken.

You wanted it to happen, didn't you? The words come back to her, stab right at her core. Kyle's words, slurring down the phone.

Her head pounds. Martha circles her feet looking for somewhere to squat. She grabs her trainers, attaches Martha's lead to her collar and drags her outside. The wind stings her eyes, and it's still inky black, only just enough light from the kitchen window to show her the garden. Shivering, she stares at the space in front of the garage where the car should be, and remembers it's still in the village, still nestled between the shop and the pub. They're totally alone, cut off from the outside world. Just the mountain and the endless darkness and whatever's lurking nearby, the things she can't see, only sense.

'Hurry up, Martha. Please, hurry up!' The puppy shuffles in the long grass near the barn. She jumps up and down for warmth. 'Hurry up. Please!'

She glances at the kitchen window. She can't see the cross on the sill in this light, but she knows it's there, protecting the house, protecting Jamie inside. But is it? *Is it?* She thinks of the vicar, the blessing, the holy water. They're meant to be protected but, last night, she'd seen it again, hadn't she? That light on the mountain, shining through the window, entering their space. Martha pulls on the end of the lead, pulls towards the barn. She's only just realised the door's wide open, a shadow in the dark.

She hesitates. She wants to go back inside the house, check on Jamie. But she can't leave the barn door like that, not with her work and equipment inside. She must have forgotten to lock it and somehow, incomprehensibly given the stiffness of the hasp and the way you have to ram it to fasten it, the wind has fingered it open.

'What is it, Martha?' The puppy disappears behind the open door, the lead unravelling like a kite string. She steps inside, momentarily grateful for the shelter. Martha's wagging her tail as she switches on the lights, a beat against her pyjama bottoms as though she's seen something or someone she recognises. Except there's no one there, only splinters where the door's been forced, and daubs of red paint on the floor, forming a trail to her workbench, her chair, her sculptures. Not just the ones she's been working on, but her collection, favourites that remind her of her past. And the pieces for the commission, the three postpartum women, barely taking shape, their rounded stomachs, their swollen breasts. Her eyes flash to her workbench. Hundreds of pounds' worth of equipment: her tools and aprons and goggles. Her notes, her sketches. Everything slashed with bright red paint. And above it all, on the far wall, in unapologetic letters that drip like blood:

Saesneg. English.

Tears stream down her face as she makes connections. Griff Davies in the pub. The laughter following her into the street as they'd left. She drags Martha back to the house. She has to take photographs, telephone the police, tell them to take fingerprints, tell them where to find Griff. She runs to the telephone and finds the handset off the hook, buzzing gently, another reminder of her conversation with Kyle. She lifts it to her ear and presses the receiver button to clear the line.

At the same time, she's distracted by something on the kitchen island. She lowers the handset. It's the green bottle standing in the middle of the stain, the green bottle with the skull and crossbones. The bottle Kyle smashed, which he said he'd glue together. Only he hadn't, as far as she knows, and the bottle is unbroken. There's no trace of any cracks, any dents. Was it there earlier? Was it there when she came in last night?

Kyle's words come back to her: *someone's trying to mess with your mind*. For a moment, she wants to believe it. Wants to believe this has some rational explanation, that someone's been in the house playing tricks, because the other possibility is too twisted, too disturbing to contemplate. Yet her fingers are trembling as she picks up the handset again, and the number she calls isn't the police, but the vicarage.

'You were lucky to catch me.' Alison Seymour is dressed in her coat. 'I was just going out. Last minute Christmas shopping.'

Lydia smiles her appreciation. After she'd found the bottle, she'd hurried Jamie through his breakfast, then bundled him in the backpack and started the long walk to the village to collect her car. As they'd turned off the track onto the mountain road, Emlyn had driven past and almost run them over. Brakes had squealed, muck had sprayed from the wheels of the old Land Rover.

Emlyn had rolled down the window. 'Get the fuck out of the road.'

'I'm sorry.'

'Fucking twpsyn!' He'd spun away without offering them a

lift and it had made her wonder: what if it had been Emlyn in the barn and not Griff?

'So tell me,' Alison says when they're sitting once again in the vicarage lounge, 'why did you come back?'

Lydia drags her fingers through her hair, wishing she'd brushed her teeth and washed her face. Jamie's on the floor, trying to push himself up, and the thought flickers through her mind, through all the other crap, that he'll soon be crawling. She hangs her head. 'I'm not really sure. It's all such a mess. I can't seem to think straight.'

'Start at the beginning. That's sometimes easiest.'

'You're not busy?'

Alison sits back. 'Actually, today's my day off. Last day of freedom before the Christmas rush.'

'Oh, I'm sorry . . .' Lydia stands up to leave, and looks for a place to plant her tea mug. 'I didn't mean to take up your time.'

But Alison waves her down again. 'What I mean is, I've got plenty of time. Tell me your story. This time, *all* of it.'

Lydia glances at Jamie, batting a plastic ship Alison's dug out from the parishioners' playbox, and babbling happily. She takes a deep breath and begins, telling Alison how Kyle inherited the property, how it had always been their dream to live in the country, the little things that have happened since they've moved, the stain on the worksurface, the scratches, the blind, the light that shines through the window, the cracked laptop screen, the feeling of being watched, the voice in her head. 'It's as if someone's looking for me, as if he won't leave me alone.'

'And this someone, this "he" as you call him, is he real?'

Lydia shakes her head, certain of one thing. 'Not in the sense of flesh and blood. More a spirit. A wandering spirit.'

'A lost spirit?'

'Not lost. He wants something. He wants revenge.'

'Why?'

She shakes her head. 'I don't know. I don't even know why I said that.'

'You've never seen him?'

'Only in a photograph, but that could have been someone else.'

'I see.' Alison pushes her glasses up her nose. 'Usually in these cases it's something to do with the person experiencing the disturbance. In this case, you. There's something about you that this spirit, for want of a better word, has latched on to. A reason why you're vulnerable. Have you any idea what that reason might be?'

She thinks of the dreams she's been having about Matt Trevithick. Sometimes she manages to escape from him, but other times he catches her, holds her down, rapes her again. Sometimes he rams his jacket in her mouth and puts his hands around her throat and hurts her so bad the pain's still there when she wakes. But that's her past, or a distortion of her past, it's nothing to do with the mountain. 'The only thing I know is that it doesn't feel right. *He* doesn't feel right,' she says. 'He feels evil.'

'And what does Kyle think?'

'He won't talk about it any more. He's gone off to London again. Another contract. He's ... ' she searches for the word, 'changed. I can't describe it. It's just, he doesn't seem like Kyle at all.'

Jamie starts to cry, frustrated on his tummy. Alison bends down, lifts him into her arms and rocks him back and forth. To Lydia's surprise, he doesn't seem to mind, like he senses he's safe there. 'Do you want me to go back? Say more prayers? I'm free this afternoon.'

'But it's your day off—'

Alison beams at Jamie. 'There's no such thing as a real day off for a parish priest, especially at Christmas. And honestly, I want to help.' She hands Jamie over.

Lydia makes ready to leave, zipping Jamie's coat, following Alison through the corridor of primrose yellow. 'The vicar who took the memorial service for Dai Jones was a man. I was surprised. I'd presumed it would be you.'

'That would be the Reverend Cadoc Hughes. He's retired.' Alison opens the front door to a clear winter's day, the sky a wash of white. 'Lots of the older folk request him. I'm from Portsmouth originally, I can't get my Welsh consonants to sound authentic, and I've got boobs. Two damning attributes.'

Lydia laughs.

'Two o'clock then?'

'Perfect.'

44

I carry on doing all the things I used to do, washing, cleaning, cooking, taking care of the animals. But it is different now. No more singing, no more dreaming. I do not go to church. I only walk to the village to buy our food, keeping to the main road, not daring to take the paths where William has laid his traps.

In the space of a few weeks, I hardly recognise myself. My brother calls me to serve him day and night, to nurse his cuts and bruises when he falls down drunk, to lie with him. At first I resisted. Dear God! If I am ever brought to trial, they must believe that! I dug my nails into his back, tore his flesh, kicked out with my feet. But it only made him worse. Brutal. Livid.

'Do I have to restrain you, Martha? Do I have to use my belt?'

Better to lie still, better to let him get on with it, turn my face to the wall, or bury my head in the pillow, depending on whichever way he takes me. I did not know how many ways there were before this. I did not know men could be so cruel, so carnal. Afterwards, lying on the crog loft, crying until there are no tears left, I hear him running his knife along the wood, scoring our sins.

The seasons come and go. It is spring again. He tells me to take my basket of eggs to the village, we have the rent to pay, and bills to settle. He will not be far behind, he says, landing his belt on the table with a slap. He will be watching every step.

'Do you hear me?'

He scratches that place on his arm as a warning. I nod. I have learned not to speak, not to answer him back. Silent and obedient like our mother became.

'What did you say?'

I manage a whisper, 'Yes.' Then I pull on my shawl and head out. It is warm, but like an old woman I feel the cold, every breeze, every cloud across the sun. I will not last long in the mountain cottage. One day it will be winter again and the frost will take me with it. I am too weak to survive and I have no willpower left. At least that is something. How gloomy to look forward to death!

At Morgan Lloyd's house, his mam looks at me kindly. 'We heard you had been ill,' she says.

She beckons me inside, but I shake my head. I have only come to sell eggs, nothing else. William is watching from the public house, and I dare not stay long. She buys half a dozen and starts to close the door, but there is movement within.

Morgan bursts forth, pushing his mam aside. 'Martha!'

My heart gladdens and then sinks, remembering all the things I have done. Remembering what I have become.

His face drops. 'You poor thing.' He reaches out and places a hand against my cheek. I pull away, but his touch lingers, and I wish I could move my cheek back against his fingers, stay there for ever.

'Come inside,' he says. 'Come and rest.'

I must look ghastly, that is why he is asking. I haven't looked in a mirror for weeks and the walk to the village has taken it out of me. I shake my head.

'I am busy. I have eggs to sell.' My voice comes out as a croak, a thing unused. I turn away, huddled in my shawl.

His voice follows me into the street, oblivious that people are watching and whispering, pointing their fingers.

'Martha, come back!'

And I want to. Every fibre of me wants to turn and run. To belong with Morgan and his mam and his rowdy siblings, even Gwenllian and her silly ways. To allow them to take me in, to nurse me back to health, to bathe me in their love. But how can I, after everything I have done?

I keep on walking, dragging my feet from house to house, selling my eggs, praying that William did not witness what happened. I will not go back, I tell myself, I will not go back to Morgan. He is an angel by comparison. I would only sully him, destroy him. I cannot go back. William has taken everything from me, and I will not let him destroy Morgan as well.

45

Lydia drives back to Sunny Hill feeling lighter, no longer afraid. She can manage whatever it is, the ghost, the evil spirit, the real human being trying to scare her, until Alison arrives. She tidies a little, then sorts through the post – mostly junk mail, still no response to the letter she sent to Edward Jeffreys' care home – before counting down the hours, keeping to the lounge as much as possible, keeping the television tuned to CBeebies. At one point, her phone buzzes. It's a text from Eleri not mentioning the night before, just saying she's found Jamie's giraffe shoved beneath the sofa; he must have dropped it the time she babysat. Lydia texts back, promising to drop by next time she's passing.

She puts the phone down, and surveys the lounge with a sense of dismay. The space she'd intended to cultivate as her own, to transform into a dream family home, is just as damp and decrepit as when they first arrived. The cobwebs have regathered in corners, Kyle's paintwork is streaked with damp, the bay window rattles with every gust. On top of the bookcase is the plastic tub from the hospital, fixed with a thick white sticker. She takes it down and reads the typed note: just her name and hospital number.

Now is as good a time as any, she thinks.

Leaving Jamie fixated on the TV, she goes outside and takes a spade from the garage. Then she scans the garden, catching sight of something swinging from the half-erected generator shed. Confused, she shields her eyes from the winter sunlight. It's a large metal trap with rusted teeth arranged in a circle, like the one in the cottage-shed further up. *A mantrap.* Her stomach churns at the sight of it. How on earth did it get there?

Using the handle of the spade, she tries levering it off, but it's wedged high up, looped over one of the upright stakes, and she has images of it suddenly flinging free and falling on top of her.

She turns away, struggling to think straight, conscious of that awful thing at her back. Her eyes land on the rowan trees behind the barn, like the rowan trees at the farm. Apart from the graffiti, the barn has always felt a safe place, and though she's never thought it before, maybe it's something to do with the trees? She walks across the lawn, keeping her back to the shed. The air is bristling with cold, and her fingers are already numb around the spade. She looks down at the pot in her hand, at the white label, the printed letters: her name because there'd been no other. *Devil's child.*

She hates the words in her head. Hates the way they repeat over and over as she pushes the spade into the frozen earth beneath the rowan trees.

Devil's child. Devil's child. Devil's child.

'No!' she screams at the mountain, screams up at the trig point, at the buzzard circling overhead. She lays the earth back over the pot, hoping for some sort of solace, a sense of completion at having buried her child. But – maybe it's the knowledge of that trap behind her, skewing her judgement – all she feels is an immeasurable guilt.

Two hours later, Alison takes a bottle of holy water from her bag. 'Round two. This time double strength. From Walsingham.' She waves the bottle and picks up her Bible. 'Ready?'

Lydia looks down at her son, seated on her lap at the kitchen island. He's wide awake, grasping her chin with his two fat fists. 'Will it be okay, you know, with Jamie?' She doesn't want to risk anything that might hurt him.

'It's perfectly safe. These things – ghosts, spirits, whatever you want to call them – affect the whole family. So it's entirely appropriate for the whole family to join in. But if you'd rather stay here?'

'No, we'll come with you.'

They follow Alison around the house, the same prayers as before, blessing every room, this time the barn and garage too, sprinkling holy water. Twenty minutes later, they're back in the kitchen, drinking coffee. Alison reaches in her bag and pulls out a cake wrapped in clingfilm.

'I was baking today,' she says. 'I thought you could do with something to cheer you up. Hope you like almonds!'

'Thank you. That's really kind.' Lydia finds plates and carves a couple of slices while Martha plays at their feet, chasing her tail.

'I just don't feel there's anything wrong with the house,' Alison says, when they've finished eating. She licks her fingers. 'I'm sorry, I feel as though I'm failing you, as though I *should* be finding something.'

'Not at all.' Lydia looks out the window, at the rowan trees, just in sight around the corner of the barn. The blind is up again. She can't remember opening it, but then she can't remember *not* opening it either. 'Perhaps you're right. Sometimes, I think it's all in my head. Sometimes, I think I'm going crazy.'

'You're very isolated. Apart from the farm, there's no one for miles. Do you go out at all?'

'Not much.' She runs a hand over the side of the cafetière, feeling the burn against her skin. 'Actually, things got a bit messed up. I found out I was pregnant, and then I miscarried, and everything came to a standstill.'

'I see, I'm sorry.'

'Which explains a lot, don't you think? I've been imagining all this?'

'Maybe.' Alison follows her gaze to the mountain and shivers. It's still cold in the house though Lydia's cranked the central heating up to maximum. Alison picks up the milk carton and moves it to one side, revealing the stain on the kitchen island. She traces it with her fingers, then stands up and walks to the window. 'Rowan trees. The berries are symbolic of the blood of Christ.' She leans further over the sink. 'But what's that further up? There's something out there.'

Lydia's suddenly conscious of the row of empty wine bottles standing behind the sink. 'There's a cottage if you look carefully, the one I told you about, but it's derelict. Hasn't been lived in for years.'

'It's up there, isn't it?'

'What do you mean?' Her voice comes out as a whisper and Alison doesn't seem to hear. Darkness is creeping down the mountain, inch by inch. Soon it will reach the cottage. Soon, Lydia knows, she'll see the light again, searching through the fields.

'It reminds me of something,' Alison says. 'A feeling I've had before.'

'What sort of feeling?'

'My last parish in Birmingham. A modern church. Twentieth century. The old church had burned down in the sixties. There was one place in the church where I never felt comfortable. An area in the south transept. It felt sad. Tragically sad, if you know what I mean? If I ever had to go there, I'd do it quickly. I mentioned it to a member of the congregation, and he told me that it lay on the site of a mass burial pit from the time of the Black Death.'

'What happened?'

'I blessed the transept and the feeling disappeared.'

'Just like that?'

Alison nods. 'I've never experienced anything like it since, at least not until today. I thought it was a one-off. I don't want to be one of those people who senses things. But here, I feel it. It's in this part of the tower. A sort of negative energy.'

Lydia thinks of the light through the window, the line of energy that seems to run from the cottage to the window to the kitchen island. She thinks of the bathroom fans on the first, second and third floors. *This part of the tower. The most vulnerable part.*

Alison turns back into the room and gathers her things,

suddenly practical. 'I'm sorry, I don't think I can help you any more.'

Lydia feels a rush of panic. 'Please. You are helping, just by being here. Please stay.'

'I'm sorry, I can't. It's getting dark. I won't be able to see the road. My husband was expecting me home half an hour ago.'

'Then, at least, tell me what I should do?'

Alison sweeps her Bible to her chest. 'As I said, it's out there on the mountain. Stay away from it. Don't go out unless you have to. You think the house is dangerous, but it's not. Sunny Hill is your friend. Lock the door. Lock the windows. Don't let anyone in. As soon as you can, get away from here altogether. Is there anywhere you can go?'

'London. I can go back to London. To my parents. I can drive tonight.'

'Good.'

'But can't you stay? Just for a bit longer? I know it sounds crazy, but can't you bless the entire mountain?'

Alison reaches for the latch on the outside door. 'I'm sorry. I've got a carol service. I'm already pushing it as it is.' She blushes and Lydia guesses it's a lie. She's scared, she thinks. This thing – whatever she just sensed – on the mountain terrifies her. A shaft of icy air bites into the room as Alison lifts the latch. 'Feels like the weather's taking a turn for the worse. Take care when you leave, won't you? They don't grit the roads as much as they should.'

The Ford Ka spins away from the tower. Lydia clutches Jamie and calls Martha to her heels. She pulls the kitchen blind lower than before, anchoring it with a row of books, hefty volumes of artwork from her student days, then she switches on the television in the lounge, finding a comedy show, turning the volume up so that laughter obliterates the sound of the wind. Then she takes Jamie upstairs, talking to him as she drags a suitcase from beneath the bed, throwing in clothes and toiletries for the two of them.

'Right,' she says, zipping the case. 'We're leaving.' She lifts Jamie from the bed, cradles him in one arm, pulls the suitcase with the other, bouncing it down the stairs. It's stupid, dangerous. She knows she's being reckless, she could easily trip, but she needs to leave as fast as she can. In the kitchen, she grabs a few essentials, then puts Martha on the lead and unbolts the outside door. The sharp air makes her gasp. Jamie screams.

'It's okay, it's okay. We're going to London.'

She fastens Jamie in the car, then rams the suitcase into the boot and settles Martha on the passenger seat. She turns the ignition key once, twice. Nothing. *What the fuck?* She groans, a tight pain stretching across her forehead, then tries again. This time, a slow whir-whir then nothing. She counts to three, willing her breath in and out, willing the engine. She flicks the key. The car starts immediately, reversing with a jolt, causing the suitcase to slide across the boot. Martha digs in her claws. She laughs wildly. 'It was cold. It was just cold.'

Through the windscreen, she sees the light in the kitchen, a steady beam thrust outwards at the garden. But she's not going back. It will have to remain that way until they return – *if* they return – just like the TV she hasn't switched off. And then the realisation: there should be no light, because she's closed the blind, secured it with books. Fear and confusion spiral through her as she reverses the car onto the track, then bumps forward, setting off towards the farm, driving too fast for the road, more than once riding up against the bank at the side. She *has* to reach the farm. As long as she reaches the farm, she'll be okay, civilisation of sorts. She revs the engine. There's a bang followed by a fast hiss of air. The car lurches to one side, rolls unsteadily and comes to a standstill.

46

---

*T*wo *days later there is a knock on the door. Immediately William jumps for his gun and the bull terrier starts barking. It is only the farmer's wife, I think, come for the rent. We still haven't the money, but she has always been kind. I will beg for a few more weeks.*

I lift the latch.

Morgan is standing in the yard, red-faced from the climb. 'Martha!'

My pulse quickens but there is no time to act, no time to think. William steps in front of me and shoves me backwards, closing the door so that he is outside with Morgan and I am within. I run to the narrow window, open the shutters, press my head against the central bar.

I hear him laughing bitterly. 'Why have you come here, Morgan? Do not tell me you are here to offer me my job back!' I wince – Morgan was William's superior at the quarry – and, not for the first time, doubt gnaws my bones. Morgan must have known what it would mean to me, reporting the fight my brother was involved in, causing him to lose his job. On the very day we had walked together hand in hand!

'I am here to see Martha.'

'She is ill. You are not to bother her.'

'Liar!' The force of Morgan's voice carries into the cottage.

Feet scuff the cobbles. A bucket rolls over. I see William raise his fists. I see the flash of a chain. I lean through the window, straining to see. It is the chain he uses to tether the dog, except now he is throwing it into the sky, and it whooshes down like a streak of lightning. There is a sharp cry that is immediately cut short. I cannot bear to watch any longer. I cannot bear to remain silent. I fly from the cottage, hands clasped to my mouth.

'There,' William points at me, his breath clouding the air. 'Ask her yourself.'

Morgan is on the ground, blood running from his face. There is a deep cut that slashes his cheek in half. I glance at William, the end of the dog chain wrapped around his wrist. Small mercy it missed Morgan's eye!

'Well, Martha?' Morgan says, his voice etched in pain.

I try to speak but my throat is dry. I want to scream and run and tend to Morgan all at once.

My brother laughs. 'See? It is as I told you, she does not want you.'

'Is it true?' Morgan pleads with his eyes, and I can tell by the pain in them he is fighting the darkness.

William laughs again. He will kill him, I think. He will kick him in the head. He will wield the dog chain again.

'It is true,' I say, staring down at Morgan, at the blood pooling on the cobbles. 'Please go away and do not come back.'

'Say you do not want me. Say it!'

'I do not want you.' The words are like stones in my mouth. 'I have

no need of you. I have my brother. He looks after me. Protects me. I have no need of any other.'

Bewilderment clouds Morgan's eyes and, for a horrible sickening moment, I think he is going to challenge me. But then he pulls himself to his feet and sways towards the path.

'So be it,' he says, wiping blood across his face. He stumbles to the gate and pulls it wide. 'I would have given up everything for you. My reputation. My life here. But no, you will not have it.'

I watch as he staggers along the ridge, his figure depleting with every step. Soon, he is just a speck, an illusion of what might have been, and it takes every ounce of my being not to run after him and tell him the truth.

47

Lydia jumps out of the car and stares at the flattened tyre and the line of deep potholes behind her. Darkness is falling steadily, the sky beneath it pinky-red. She needs to act fast, think fast, except she can't bloody think. Her brain seems frozen along with the rest of her. All she knows is that Sunny Hill is nearer than she thought, eighty metres or so, the farm another few hundred. But perhaps she can make it if she drives slowly?

She gets back inside the car and starts the engine, inching forwards, hearing the wheel grind on the road and a slow slapping from the blown tyre. The car dips on the uneven track, scraping its undercarriage. She grips the steering wheel tighter, manoeuvring between the potholes. There's a tricky bit where she knows there's a row of them, scattered unevenly. But the car feels heavy and slow to respond. She turns the wheel to the right, avoiding a pothole on the left, then immediately the other way. The car dips before crunching to a standstill. She revs the engine but, this time, the car refuses to move.

'Please, please, please!'

She checks her phone. No signal, no internet connection. The farm buildings are shadows in the dying light. She needs to change the tyre, except she's never done it before. She gets out of the car again; she needs to locate the spare tyre and the tools to jack it up.

God, it's freezing. Alison Seymour was right, the weather's turned.

She looks beneath the car and then into the boot, lifting the carpet, finding the spare tyre and some sort of pulley. She grabs both, heaving the tyre over the carpet. It lands on the ground with a thud. She wipes her forehead with her sleeve. What next? What next? The jack! She searches various compartments until she finds what she's looking for.

It's dark now. Evening dark. Taking the wrench in her hand, she walks to the front of the car, crouches down, positions it around one of the nuts on the driver's side wheel. Already, her hands are raw with cold, her cheeks numb as the wind whips her hair. She presses down on the wrench but it refuses to budge. She presses harder, the muscles in her forearms straining. The darkness crowds in; she can barely see a thing. Perhaps the nuts are clogged with dirt? She uses her mobile phone as a torch, angling it so that it shines upwards at the wheel, then she tries another nut, using her foot this time to move the wrench. Some small give. She tries again. Nothing. *Fuck.* She digs her fingernails into her forehead, knowing she's defeated, for tonight at least. It's too dark to attempt a job she's never done before and Jamie's crying. She's shaking with cold, more vulnerable in the open, doing exactly what Alison Seymour told her not to do: *it's out there on the mountain. Stay away from it.*

'Come on, Jamie. Come on, Martha. We're going back. We'll have to walk.'

The puppy trots to her side. It's too awkward to put her on the lead as well as carrying Jamie, so she risks it, lifting the suitcase from the boot, taking Jamie in her arms. One trip's better than two, she thinks, gripping the handle of the case with one hand, Jamie with the other. Then she starts along the track, dragging the case back to the house, Jamie wailing, too cold without his snowsuit.

The wheels of the case catch in the potholes. She considers turning around, walking in the opposite direction, walking to the farm, but she'd feel even less safe there, alone with Emlyn. So she stumbles onwards to the tower, Jamie still howling, face pressed against her coat. She thinks about dumping the suitcase, but it contains their essentials: Jamie's milk powder, the steriliser, the dwindling supply of nappies. She pushes on, focusing on the track, one step at a time, seeing her way with the light of her phone, held awkwardly in the same hand she's holding Jamie.

Ahead, Sunny Hill is shrouded in darkness. She remembers the light shining from the kitchen window, illuminating the garden; the blind she anchored with books so that light can't get in or out. It doesn't make sense. It *should* be dark because the blind is down, but how does that explain the earlier light? She almost turns around there and then, but she's nowhere to go except the car, and she remembers what Alison Seymour said: *You think the house is dangerous, but it's not. Sunny Hill is your friend.*

She picks up the pace, yanking the suitcase. Tears course

down her cheeks, chilling her all the more. Jamie buries himself deeper into her chest. *Get inside the house, bolt the door, don't let anyone or anything in.* She'll cope for one more night. She'll sort the car in the morning. By lunchtime tomorrow they'll be in London. Not long now. Not long.

She fumbles for her house keys and opens the door.

48

When Kyle wakes up, it's dark outside, almost evening, and someone's knocking on the bedroom door. He can't remember the last time he felt so rough. He's only surfaced a couple of times in the last fourteen or so hours to throw up in Charlie's designer bathroom. Snatches of the night before come back to him: Charlie on the beanbag; Benedita filling his glass; talking about the tower, Lydia, the miscarriage. He remembers Benedita prizing the car keys from his hand. 'You're not in a fit state to drive anywhere, babe.' Where the hell had he thought to go at that time anyway?

The knocking comes again, doubling the incessant pounding of his brains.

'Come in,' he groans.

Benedita enters, looking immaculate, fluffy slippers slapping the polished floor. She sits on the edge of the bed, balancing a tray on her lap, and the smell of fatty food drifts towards him. His stomach turns, and he's conscious that, apart from the duvet, the only thing between him and Benedita is his boxer shorts.

'Hey, babe,' she smiles. 'Thought you might like a sandwich.' She points at the gooey mess of bread, fried egg and melted cheese. 'My speciality.'

'I don't think I could.'

'Go on, just try it. Charlie's had one.'

He forces himself upright, grabs a couple of pillows and wedges them behind his back. The light hurts his eyes but at least he feels slightly more human. He takes the sandwich in his hands, the grease slipping down his fingers.

'What did I say last night?'

'What do you mean?'

'What was I talking about? And where was I trying to get to when you grabbed my keys?'

Benedita frowns. 'I can't remember much, to be honest. You were talking about your grandfather. About your family. How your grandfather treated your mum. Actually, on that account, I've done some research.'

'Oh?'

She stands and he catches the complex scent of her perfume. 'Have your sandwich, then get up. I'll be in the kitchen. I'll show you.'

He forces down the food, telling himself it's doing him good, then pulls on his crumpled jeans and T-shirt. Charlie's in the kitchen, sitting at the breakfast bar, drinking beer. 'All right, mate? Help yourself.' He waves the bottle.

Kyle shakes his head. He'd rather a cup of tea or a glass of water. He'd rather he'd spent the whole of yesterday evening sober. He hates all this, the endless cycle of drinking, the person he becomes after one too many. But it draws him back every single time. Is this what it's like to be an addict? Knowing it's wrong but doing it anyway? Even moving away from his friends hasn't helped. If anything, he's been worse in Wales, drinking in secret as well as all the other times.

He sits next to Benedita and helps himself to the fruit bowl, attempting to feel clean in some way. Benedita flips the cover of her iPad, scrolls through a few pages until she lands on what she's looking for.

'Here it is,' she says, handing the screen to Kyle. 'What you were talking about last night, about your grandfather and the tower. Seems like you were on to something.'

49

⸻ ⬗⬗⬗ ⸻

Lydia flicks the light switch. The kitchen is in a state of disarray: the books she'd used to anchor the blind are strewn across the floor; the wine bottles she'd placed to the side of the sink are smashed in lethal shards; Martha's water bowl has been knocked over; olives from a jar she'd left on the workstation stare up at her from the flagstones like black eyes. In the background, the television blares as if nothing's happened.

She staggers backwards against the door, clutching Jamie. Something's been in the house, turned the light off, created chaos. A whirlwind. A rage. A monster. She lets the suitcase fall, slapping against the stone. The sound startles Jamie who immediately cries out, and looks up at her with his big blue eyes.

'It's okay, little one.' But she can't get the thought out of her mind: someone or something has been in the tower.

She thinks of the mantrap hanging outside on the generator shed, and yanks down the blind, knotting the cord tightly around the nail. Then she breathes in and counts to three. Her whole body trembles from cold or fear or both. She breathes out again as slowly as she can. There's a leak somewhere, a place where the wind gets in and creates havoc. It's the only possible explanation. Her eyes dart to the outside door. She thinks of the car stranded on the track. She doesn't have a choice. She has to stay the night. Somehow, she has to make this bearable.

She shoos Martha into the lounge, afraid the glass will get caught in her paws, sits Jamie in his bouncy chair, then gets to work, taking a dustpan and brush from the cupboard, sweeping up the mess, her hands shaking and clumsy. *It's the wind. Just the wind.*

Martha whines over the TV.

She dashes into the lounge. 'What is it, Martha?' She finds the puppy's collar and persuades her to follow. 'Come on, we're going to check this place out.'

They go into every room, peering into every cupboard, beneath every table, beneath every chair.

'Just the wind,' she tells herself as she inspects the dark space beneath the bed, crammed with old suitcases and boxes, as she climbs the stairs to the second and third floors, as she flicks the light switches in the washrooms.

There's a bang from somewhere below her. Her heart thumps, thinking of Jamie alone in the lounge. She stumbles downstairs, but Jamie's fine, kicking his legs up and down, giggling at the TV. A second later, a blast of cold air slams through the archway, rustling the papers on the coffee table. She runs to the kitchen: the outside door is wide open, buffeting back and forth. She closes it firmly and slides the bolts. Sinking against it, she laughs, close to hysteria. She must have left the door on the latch. 'See, Martha,' she says, looking down at the puppy. 'Didn't I tell you, it's just the wind?'

But she's shaking, unable to dislodge the fear from her mind. She opens Google on her laptop to search for local taxis. A message flashes up: You're not connected, check your network cables. She groans, then remembers, when they first moved in, spying a damp copy of the *Yellow Pages* in the study. It seems a lifetime ago now, though it's only been weeks: all their hopes and dreams of creating a perfect life for themselves vanished into thin air. Upstairs again, she rummages through Kyle's papers, heaps and heaps of notes to do with his work. She finds a scrap of paper with a telephone number scribbled in an unfamiliar hand and recognises it instantly – she's recently typed it into her phone herself: Eleri's number. She crumples it into the bin, trying not to think why it might be there, before spying the *Yellow Pages* stuffed in the bin with a pile of old papers.

'Hello, Dai's taxis.' The voice on the end of the phone floods her with relief. She's an overwhelming desire to pull the woman down the line and hug her.

'Hello, I need a taxi. Y Twr Gwyn in Gaer Fach. Halfway up the mountain.'

'Dai's busy at the moment. He'll be about an hour.'

She nods. An hour doesn't seem so bad, not compared to spending another night in the tower. 'Tell him to be as quick as he can. It's urgent.'

She sits in the lounge, cradling Jamie, trying to focus on the TV. An hour turns to an hour and a half. Jamie dozes and she feels her own body dipping into sleep, weighed down by pure exhaustion. She changes the channel in an effort to stay awake, and it's then that she remembers: her car is blocking the track. What if the taxi driver turned back when he saw it? Didn't bother walking the final stretch to the house? She runs outside, flashing the torch on her phone. The desolation strikes her. No cars, no lights except the vague glow of houses in the village, not even starlight. With the car on the track, she's more cut off than ever before. She turns back indoors, calls the taxi firm again.

'Sorry, Dai's been held up. Problem with the motor. He won't make it tonight.'

She claws her fingers through her hair. 'Are there any other taxi firms in the area?'

The woman laughs. 'This isn't bloody London.'

She replaces the handset, snatches it up again, dials Kyle's number and speaks to his answerphone. 'Phone me back. Please. I need to talk to you. It's important.'

Then, impulsively, she calls the vicarage. A teenager answers. 'You want Mum? Just a sec, she's in her study.'

Footsteps, voices, something falling. The teenager comes back on the line. 'Sorry. My mistake. Mum's out at the moment. Carol service. Can I take a message?'

'No, thank you. Just say that I called. You got the name?'

'Lydia Stein?'

'That's right. Thank you. Goodnight.' The line goes dead.

She sits in front of the TV, trying to watch a romantic comedy, but she can't keep her eyes open. She forces herself up, piles the art books back against the kitchen window, this time using only the heaviest books, ones that can't be moved by a freak draught. Piling them higher than before, reaching halfway up the window. She catches sight of the stain on the kitchen island and slams a book on top of that too. There. Nothing can get through the window and the stain isn't visible.

She lifts Jamie from his bouncy chair and hesitates. Usually, Martha sleeps downstairs in her crate, but tonight she wants to keep her close. She needs all the protection she can get. She calls her upstairs and goes to bed. The taxi isn't going to come. Kyle isn't going to phone. No one is going to rescue them.

So tired and yet she can't sleep. Tossing and turning beneath the duvet, Martha too hot against her legs, her mind flooding with memories. It's her second year at the new university. She's doing well, no more therapy, the abortion is behind her, Matt Trevithick is behind her. She's made new friends. Not close friends, but friends she can at least go out with, get dressed up with before hitting the bars. She's careful, always careful, never leaving her drink in places where it could get spiked, carrying a rape alarm, avoiding the men who try to chat her up, using the same get-out line, 'Sorry, I've got a boyfriend.' Her friends think she's being picky or she's a lesbian or both. She laughs it off, they can think what they like. Eventually, she starts seeing a boy called Dean. She's intrigued how he will make her feel, how she will react if he tries to kiss her, touch her, have sex with her. In the end, she doesn't go much beyond kissing him before making her excuses.

'You really must be gay,' concludes Cara, a girl on her course. 'Dean is *so* fit.'

'Maybe I am.' Though she knows she isn't. Or rather, she's not attracted to anyone any more. The thought of getting close to someone again, allowing them to share her bed, to run their fingers all over her body, to whisper in her ear, makes her feel sick. Then, one day, in the computer room, she's distracted. Outside it's snowing, fluky April snow, startlingly bright.

Students are throwing snowballs and building snowmen in the quad: a snowman with a penis, a snowwoman with breasts. Someone has blown up a condom for the snowman and shrieks of laughter carry through the breeze-block wall.

'He's hot.'

'What?'

Cara points at her screen. It's open on her Facebook page and in the notification bar is a friend request from Matt Trevithick. The room spins. She tastes her lunch. Cara leans over and clicks on his profile picture. Matt with a pint of beer in his hand, surrounded by nameless students. She recognises the Sports Bar at her old university, she recognises the jacket he's wearing, she recognises his thumb ring. It's all horribly familiar. She thinks she'll have to run to the toilet, but somehow remains seated, staring at the screen. Cara clicks the confirm friends button.

'Cara, no!'

'Why not? He's gorgeous.'

'You don't know him.'

'Who is he?'

'A lecturer from my old uni, that's all.'

'A lecturer?' Cara giggles and raises her eyebrows.

She closes down her Facebook account after that, refusing to have anything to do with social media, not until years later, not until she needs to promote her work. And even then she's reluctant.

She lies awake in Sunny Hill, thinking about it all. Thinking about Cara and the time in the snow, remembering all the friends she hasn't kept in touch with since marrying Kyle. The nightlight glows steadily against the wall. She can make out the pattern on the wallpaper, indistinct swirls like ribbons of pasta, muted green against green. She can feel the cold in the room, even beneath the duvet. She thinks about Cara. She thinks about the Facebook request. She remembers Matt Trevithick in the Sports Bar, beaming into her world. She turns over, and screws her eyes shut, and tries not to think about any of it.

Outside, the wind howls around the tower, the crows shelter in the rafters of the old cottage, and the sky beneath the darkness washes whiter and whiter.

50

Spring turns to summer, summer turns to autumn. Leaves fall from the trees creating a rich patchwork of red and orange and brown upon the path. One day, as I look from the cottage doorway and see the cobbles on the yard glistening with frost, I know at last that it is here: winter. The winter that will take me with it, that must take me with it because I cannot last much longer. Another year, another spring, another summer seems impossible. I want to go. I have to go. This is my time.

It is a Sunday. I have not been to church for months. I think of the women in their bonnets, the quarry workers with their faces scrubbed clean, the children shuffling in their blackened boots, the scent of hymn-books and medieval stone. But it is no longer mine. I do not belong there. I have never belonged there. Have they not always stared, whispered, judged? I was a fool to believe I could ever be one of them.

I belong only to William, now. To the mountain. To our cottage.

On this holy day, I go about my chores as if it is any other, feeding the animals, carrying my bucket of slops across the yard. Halfway across, my boot laces send me flying. I land face down, knocking my chin, tasting blood in my mouth, reminding me cruelly that I am still alive, still breathing, still pumping fresh blood. The bucket clatters and rolls to a standstill as I lie there with my hand to my mouth. Despite everything, I seem to be growing stronger, more resilient, physically at least. I cannot just will myself to succumb to the elements; it does not work like that.

It is then that I know, with my face against the icy cobbles, and blood bubbling between my teeth, and my gloves staining red. I know I will not die this winter. Far from it, in fact.

The realisation makes my head spin: I am carrying my brother's child.

I stand up, wipe down my skirt, and gingerly touch my stomach.

Ma told me what it was like. I remember her stories about sickness and the missed monthly event. Horrifyingly it all adds up: the constant fatigue, the dizzy spells, the random pains, the way my breasts hurt when I roll over in the night. I had put it down to the fact I am ill. How can I have been so blind?

I rescue the bucket from where it landed when I fell, then go indoors to find a rag to press against my mouth. William is sleeping beside the range, though it is midday and there is plenty of work to be done. I stare at him with disgust. My brother! The one person in the world who should protect me! Between us, what have we created? A demon? A monster? No natural thing, that is for sure. I remember the story of Lot's daughters in the Bible, the preacher slamming his fist as he delivered his message, a warning to us all. At the time, I did not understand. But now . . .

Impulsively, I grab a knife from the table, the one I use to chop the vegetables and scrape meat off the bones. Then, I stand over my brother, the handle raised, the blade pointing downwards.

I could kill him.

I could plunge the knife deep into his heart.

My brain thrums, my ears pulse. I grip the blade tightly. How easy it would be. How easy I can imagine it: his blood splattering upwards, spraying across my face, dribbling down my blouse. But, what then? What would I do with his body? I would have to dig a hole, conceal it on the mountain. It would be too heavy for me to drag more than a few yards. What if someone saw me, a hill walker or the farmer's wife or Morgan come to see that I am still alive? What if his body resurfaced in the rain, a macabre relic?

I drop the knife, stumbling backwards, reaching for my neck. How can I have imagined such a thing? How could I even have contemplated it! I think of the gallows. No one would believe me, would they? No one would believe that this was the lesser sin. I catch sight of the vague swell of my belly, and think of this other thing, this devil's child. I heard something once, about a servant girl who got into trouble and managed to get rid of it. How did she do it? I cannot remember. I feel dizzy as I glance around the cottage, my eyes returning to the knife on the floor. I imagine lying on my back, reaching inside, skewering the thing and flinging it out. But I am not sure that is possible. I would not know how far I'd have to go. I realise, after everything that has happened, I do not even know the basic anatomy! Something else then, not a knife, but a crochet hook or a knitting needle?

That night, I lie awake on the crog loft, heart thumping beneath the blankets. I run my fingers along the thin metal of the knitting needle, then part my legs, finding the place where he invades me. The needle feels cold and alien, and only goes so far before it meets resistance. At the first twinge, I draw it out in alarm. I cannot do it. I am too terrified of the blood, of the pain, of doing it wrong. No, this monster has to die, but not by me.

I start to cry, afraid William will hear me, burying my tears in our mother's pillow. In my mind, I see the doors of the workhouse in town and, next to it, the iron gates of the foundling hospital. But I will not let it come to either of those things. They would throw me in prison first anyway for the evil that I have become.

I shake myself to my sensibilities. No good crying. There is only one thing to do. I need to find someone to help me.

51

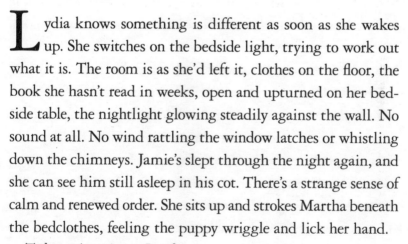

Lydia knows something is different as soon as she wakes up. She switches on the bedside light, trying to work out what it is. The room is as she'd left it, clothes on the floor, the book she hasn't read in weeks, open and upturned on her bedside table, the nightlight glowing steadily against the wall. No sound at all. No wind rattling the window latches or whistling down the chimneys. Jamie's slept through the night again, and she can see him still asleep in his cot. There's a strange sense of calm and renewed order. She sits up and strokes Martha beneath the bedclothes, feeling the puppy wriggle and lick her hand.

Today we're going to London.

She plans it all out: they'll have breakfast, then swap the tyre for the spare. It will be easier in broad daylight, following instructions she'll memorise from YouTube. Then they'll drive all the way, surprise Kyle and, later, her parents. They'll be all right, her and Kyle. They'll forget about their argument, or rather, he'll apologise and she'll put it down to too much drink. She'll explain about the house and he'll reassure her about Eleri. She'll make Kyle understand she can't go back to Mynydd Gwyn; neither of them can go back. They'll arrange for someone else to collect their things. After that, they'll put Sunny Hill on the market, look for somewhere in London. A ground-floor flat, preferably modern.

She pulls back the duvet and shivers. The floorboards are icy beneath her feet and the radiator is stone cold. She fiddles with the valve at the bottom, waiting expectantly for the tick-tick of pipes, but still there's nothing. She pulls on a jumper and tells herself it doesn't matter; they won't be here much longer anyway.

Downstairs, everything is as it was last night: the kitchen floor still sticky with brine, the blind secured around the nail and half-obscured by art books, the outside door bolted. Martha scurries towards it, tail wagging. She draws back the bolts to let her out, pulls wide the door and gasps.

The world is wintry white: snow is stacked a foot deep against the tower, concealing the roof of the garage, weighing down the boughs of the tree, banked up against the drystone wall. Beyond the wall, the mountain is hazy. It's as though someone's taken a paintbrush and scrubbed everything out. She can't see the trig point. She can't see the rocks. She finds her trainers, grabs her thickest winter coat, and goes out.

Martha follows her into the garden, squats down, then runs back to the door. Lydia lets her in before continuing alone, printing footsteps until she reaches the car. Cold sears her hands as she clears a half-moon on the windscreen. But already she knows the task is pointless. Snow has drifted against the tyres and it's impossible to make out the line of the track – only the farm buildings ahead of her, blobs of white against white. She gazes down at the village, shading her eyes from the dazzling snow. Only the church spire is distinct against the haze. Turning back to Sunny Hill, a gust of wind sweeps over the mountain. She feels a steady feathering of snow on her hands, nose and lips. Amidst the startling beauty, the tower is an ugly off-white scar. A stain against the purer white.

To her relief, Jamie's still asleep when she gets back inside. She throws on an extra jumper and sits on the floor beside the cot, watching the rise and fall of his chest. She takes stock of the situation. They're trapped – until the snow melts, there's no chance of getting away. They're low on fresh food, low on nappies and baby wipes, and the house is freezing. She reaches out, touches the radiator. It's stone cold. Perhaps she turned the valve the wrong way? She screws it in the opposite direction, the numbers too faded with age to read, but nothing happens. Downstairs, it's the same – the radiators freeze against her fingers. The ancient boiler sits in a cupboard in the corridor, the door sagging on its hinges as she opens it, threatening to pull away. But the dial indicates the heating is turned to maximum. Next to it, there's a large red button. She presses it once, twice, three times, hearing the empty click of something inside. Is the tank out of oil? Has the pump failed? She remembers Kyle checking the sight gauge in the garden. Enough oil to last the winter, he'd said, so it must be the pump.

Trying not to panic, she assesses the log pile in the lounge. There's enough kindling and logs for a couple of burns, more in the garage. She heaps kindling in the fireplace and flicks the lighter. The wood won't catch. She tries again, lighting a coil of paper first, using it to torch the smaller pieces. She makes a small blaze, then reaches for her laptop – no internet signal. She tries ringing Kyle on the landline instead – silence, not even the hum of connection – so she rings him from her mobile and leaves yet another message.

'When are you coming home? Please, we're snowed in and freezing. Everything's down. The internet. The phone line. We need wood and supplies. We love you.' Her voice dies on the last words.

She puts her phone in her pocket and crouches as near to the fire as she dares, listening to the wood crack and hiss. She throws on another log and prays it will take, thinking she should pin something – a sheet or a cover – over the archway to trap the heat. Soon, she'll have to go to the garage, dig the snow from the door, fetch more wood. How much is in there? She hasn't paid the log pile as much attention as she should – it's always been Kyle's thing, not hers. How long can they last? She reassures herself: snow never stays for long. By tomorrow the roads will be clear. By tomorrow, she'll be able to make it to the village, walking if necessary with Jamie in the backpack.

52

<hr>

*M*rs Lloyd opens the door, glances over my patched-up clothes and red-ringed eyes, and ushers me inside. I am relieved to discover there is no one else about, only a cat licking its paws on the windowsill, oblivious to my presence. All of the children are old enough to work now, the youngest being twelve, and they will not be back for hours. It is washing day, and there are shirts hanging on a rack near the hearth. One of the shirts, Morgan's by the size of it, flaps at me as we enter. The cotton is threadbare, patched at the elbows, but still more serviceable than the rags on my back.

'He is working,' Mrs Lloyd explains, following my gaze.

I know that. In the early days, when things were different, I would deliberately visit in the evenings or Sundays. But it is just after midday and Mrs Lloyd's lunch — a slice of bread and a sliver of cheese — is perched on a sideboard.

'Sit down,' she says, picking up a pile of sheets and making space *for me on Morgan's chair. She looks pointedly at my empty hands. 'I see you have no eggs to sell today. Let me get you some cake. You look tired.'*

She moves around me, hanging my bonnet and shawl on the coat stand, planting tea-loaf in my lap. Her kindness makes everything so much worse, so much harder.

'How have you been?' Her face is a picture of concern.

I look down at the tea-loaf and start to cry. I cannot help myself.

'Now, now,' she says firmly. 'None of that.' She hands me a hand-kerchief from the wash pile, a large one – one of Morgan's – and it is then that I tell her, sobbing my eyes out with my nostrils full of starch and cleanliness and tears.

'I am in trouble,' I say. 'Big trouble.'

She stands up and lays a hand on my shoulder. 'Whatever it is, it cannot be that bad.' I shake my head, grateful for the touch of her, but knowing I do not deserve her mercy. She has not understood me. I will have to spell it out. 'I am with child.'

The kindness in Mrs Lloyd's eyes dissolves into disbelief. She lifts the tea-loaf from my lap and delivers it back into its tin. God knows they cannot afford to waste food. 'Who is he?'

I look into her eyes and, for a moment, think I can tell her. I think I can tell her everything about William. But of course, I cannot. Better for her to believe anything than the truth.

'Is it Morgan?' she whispers hotly.

I shake my head. Morgan has not even tried to speak to me since the time at the cottage, since the time William struck him. He thinks I never loved him and I have been glad on his behalf. It is better this way. 'I am not at liberty—'

'I know he got into a fight,' she raises a hand to her own cheek, indicating the scar that is writ on her son for ever, 'but he will not say how or with whom.'

'It was not Morgan,' I say, wishing with every fibre of my being that it was.

Her shoulders dip with relief. 'So, why are you telling me?'

It seems so futile, but what else can I do? 'Because I need your help.'

'My help?' Her eyes widen with incredulity. The cat stops licking her paws and jumps from the windowsill, stretching and arching her back. 'What exactly do you expect me to do?'

'I thought you might know someone? Someone who could help me?'

'Why on earth would I know anyone like that?' Her tone is sharp, defensive. In the background, in the shadow of the door that leads to the pantry, I see someone else. Gwenllian. Only, not as I know her. Not the gay child with her silly ways and pretty smile. But a child grown into a woman, clutching her stomach in the way I have started cradling my own.

The tears fall again, running into my mouth. 'Since Ma died, I have had no one else to turn to. No other woman from whom to seek counsel.'

Mrs Lloyd attends to the washing as if I am not even there, pulling it down from the rack, folding it into squares. She pulls Morgan's shirt down last of all, flaps it out, puts it onto a pile for ironing. I stand up to leave, fetch my hat and shawl, knowing I have no business here. How foolish to think that I did!

'Thank you,' I say, wiping the tears from my cheeks. 'Thank you for listening.'

Mrs Lloyd opens the door and the cold howls in. I wonder where William is, whether he followed me, whether I am in for a beating. But he has grown slack of late, drinking more and watching less. In his lucid moments, he tells me there is work for him again in the quarry. But I do not believe him, and the rent is months behind. He will have us starve before the winter is out.

The wind catches my breath and I know it is going to be a long trek to the cottage. I feel the older woman sigh beside me. For a moment, *it is just the two of us in the world looking out into the bleak street, feeling the rain and the first dash of hail against our faces.*

Mrs Lloyd speaks softly. 'Come back in a week. I cannot promise anything. But I will see what I can do. You are not the only one with troubles.'

I think of Gwenllian in the shadows and wonder if it is possible. Has William done this too? Are we sisters together in our misery?

Outside bracing myself for the storm and for the long walk home, I realise that I am still clutching Morgan's handkerchief.

53

Lydia sits with Jamie in the lounge, the only warm room, spooning him puree on her knee. At one point he stops and reaches for something on the mantelpiece, screaming at her until she hands it over. It's the soldier-doll with the pinprick eyes; it makes her think of the photo on top of Mari's television, the lover-cum-soldier, Morgan Lloyd, who used to call for Martha in his sleep. She swears the doll wasn't there before. She swears she'd dropped it in the bathroom bin. As soon as it's clasped in Jamie's little fingers, he stops crying. She looks down at him, hating the doll, hating the way he finds comfort in the thing. But it's only a toy. No hazardous smaller parts. What harm can it do?

She waits until he's asleep before assessing the log pile in the garage, shovelling snow from the door, levering it open, ducking inside. It's late afternoon, still just enough light to assess the situation: enough wood to last several days. She carries a bucket-full back to the house, then takes stock of the fridge. There isn't much: a carton of milk that's two days past its sell-by date, a wrap of cheddar, a bottle of rosé, a punnet of grapes mouldy at the bottom. In the bread tin, there's half a loaf of sliced white and the remains of Alison's cake. She opens Jamie's tub of powdered milk – three-quarters full, at least that's something – and then she remembers: the cellar is crammed with tins. It's the one thing Kyle *has* done, stocked up on tins in case there's ever an emergency.

A blast of cold air rushes to meet her as she opens the cellar door. She's only been down here a handful of times, and she doesn't like it: the cold, the exposed pipework, the bare bricks that leave a fine coating of dust on her fingertips. She moves quickly to the stack of tins against the back wall, grouped into categories: baked beans, spaghetti hoops, tomato soup. She lets out a sigh of relief; Kyle hasn't been very imaginative, but at least they won't starve. She looks around for something to carry the tins and catches sight of a pile of upturned crates. There's a chair beside them and a stack of paper on top. Evidently, Kyle's been using the crates as a makeshift table. She takes a quick look at the papers: Kyle's notes for the generator – careful drawings of the turbine, the pipes, the weir, the stream, the cottage. *The cottage.* He's drawn it over and over, sometimes connected to his hydroelectric system, other times alone. She feels goosebumps on her arms as she recognises the caving roof, the doorway, the window, the cobbles outside, all in meticulous detail. The pencil is dark, pressed hard against the paper, and next to the cottage, formed over and over, in various sizes – sometimes small and precise, other times large and comic – are question marks.

She flips the drawings upside down, then grabs another crate, empty apart from a notepad, piling it high with tins before retreating upstairs. She lines the tins next to the cooker, then goes back down into the cellar. Three more trips, until the tins are three rows high, then she settles in front of the fire, and wipes the dust from the notepad. It's the type she's seen in the shop, lined, wide-margined, still with its price sticker of 75p. Inside, in Edward Jeffreys' hand, are lists.

Jobs: clear gutters, unblock sink, remove dead bird from path

Appointments: GP Monday, dentist Thursday, library Friday

Items to buy: bread, milk, rodenticide

She feels a disquieting sadness. The loneliness of Kyle's grandfather's life seeps from the pages, the vacant company of doctors and dentists and shop assistants. She's yet to receive a response to the letter she wrote to the care home, and she has a feeling she'll never know more about him than this. This loneliness.

She flicks to the back of the book. Here, the writing's different, scrawled, spotted with dots as if Edward Jeffreys has been sitting with the notepad on his lap, tapping the book with his pencil. It's a list of names, occupants of Y Twr Gwyn since 1933, the year the tower was built. By the look of things, no one's stayed at Y Twr Gwyn for more than a few years and there are lengthy periods when the house has stood empty. Beneath is a list of occupants of 'The White Cottage – Y Bwthyn Gwyn'. The list contains just four names:

(Pre circa 1895 occupants unknown)
Circa 1895 onwards:

George Helford
Born England circa 1864
Died Mynydd Gwyn 1894

Mary Helford
Born England circa 1866
Died Mynydd Gwyn 1908

William Helford
Born England 1884
Wounded in Ypres 1915, gas gangrene leading to amputation
    of both feet
Died war hospital, London, March 1915

Martha Helford
Born England 1890.
Died Gaer Fach 1910 (suicide)

A log falls in the grate, causing her to jump. She looks up, her eyes landing on the toy soldier clasped in Jamie's hands. Suddenly, she knows she got it wrong. It's not Morgan standing in the cottage doorway, searching for his lover. It's not Morgan calling for Martha on the mountain. It's not his light she sees, searching for Martha in the dark. It's William's. William Helford, the brother. The man in the photograph who's not standing but hovering. *Hovering because he has no feet.*

She leans over and tries to prise the soldier from Jamie's hand, but he cries out in his sleep and scratches her arm. At the same time, Martha starts growling.

'What is it, Martha?'

She's drawn to the archway, to the change in the light. The bedsheet she'd secured over the gap earlier has pulled away from its pins and is lying in a heap on the floor.

'Oh God,' she laughs, hand to her chest, wondering how she hadn't heard it fall. 'It's okay, it's okay. It's just Mummy's silly DIY.' But Jamie's crying as she picks him up, clinging on to her jumper, his fists digging into her skin beneath. And Martha's on all fours, ears pricked. 'It's okay. Just a sheet. Silly Mummy!'

Her gaze is drawn to the space beyond the archway, the kitchen window, the books piled high, the blind closed behind them. There's something wrong. Something that sets her heart racing all over again: a glow of orange shining through the green blind, moving softly through the fabric. She feels a wave of lightheadedness as she stands and places Jamie in his bouncy chair, though he protests, though he screams at her to take him again. 'It's okay,' her voice trembles, knowing it's not okay at all. 'I have to check this out. I can't take you with me.'

The feeling is back again, the feeling of vulnerability, of being watched, of someone seeing exactly what they're doing. *I have to be strong.*

'Come on, Martha.' She fondles the puppy's ears, then gently pulls her with her.

She creeps into the kitchen as the light shines wider and fiercer through the blind. Trembling, she pulls the books away, tossing them on the floor, hearing them thump and skid across the stone paving, splitting at the spine. But she doesn't care. She won't let the light get away, not this time. She'll discover what it is, *who* it is. She flings the last of the books on the floor, finds the pull cord and releases the blind, sending it spinning upwards.

Martha, Martha, Martha.

She presses her hands to her ears as the word calls through the walls and echoes around the kitchen. She feels sick and giddy as she catches the scent of a cigarette. The smell envelops her so that she can barely think, barely breathe. She staggers backwards as Martha whines and paws at the outside door. But she won't open it. She doesn't dare open it. Instead, she gapes at the window.

There's a lantern on the other side of the pane, so close she can make out the wire cage around the glass, the flame burning steadily on the wick, the handle held upright, the lid glinting beneath. A Tilley lamp, the type she's seen before in museums. But there's no hand. No figure. Only the lantern. A terrifying ghostly glow.

For a fraction of a second, she stares unmoving, then she spurts into action, running to the front of the house, wrenching the boiler door from its hinges. She staggers beneath its weight, dragging the door through to the kitchen, Jamie still screaming.

Through the archway, she stops dead in her tracks, the weight of the door cutting into her hands. The kitchen is in darkness; the lantern gone, just a rectangle of evening-dark at the window. Resting the door on the paving, she flicks the light switch one way and then the other. The bulb fizzes orange then burns out. Everything is uncannily still, like waking from a dream, the cigarette smell vanished. Even Jamie has stopped crying.

Seeing her way by the light from the lounge, she lifts the boiler door and balances it on top of the sink so that it leans against the window, blocking it completely.

54

A week later, Mrs Lloyd ushers me indoors without speaking. This time things are different. She does not take my shawl or bonnet, or ask me to sit, or offer me tea-loaf. The cat is occupying Morgan's chair and makes no effort to move, rather studies me disapprovingly and flicks its tail. I seek Gwenllian in the shadows, but see nothing beyond the grandfather clock, marking out time, the time that is working against both of us. Mrs Lloyd goes straight to the side drawer and pulls out a wrap of paper.

'You are to take all the pills at once,' she says.

I hesitate before accepting, wanting to stall the moment, wanting to ask Mrs Lloyd for forgiveness, tell her that the child within me is a devil's child and can have no life, that it is not my fault, that I wish things were different. But there is nothing I can say that will change her heart. She has set herself against me and I can hardly blame her. Would it be better or worse if she thought it was Morgan's? I take the *packet and tuck it in my pocket, then draw out my purse: the few coins left from the egg sales. I have already prepared the speech – rehearsed it over and over – where I will tell Mrs Lloyd I will pay her back, penny by penny.*

Mrs Lloyd takes the purse, considers for a moment, then hands it back.

'There is no need,' she says, stooping to lift the cat. It regards me from the vantage point of her shoulder. Slit green eyes, as clear as water. Black cats are not well regarded around here, but Mrs Lloyd is not the sort to abide by superstition.

'Thank you,' I say, averting my eyes from the cat. And every ounce of me means it; we need those coins to survive.

She nods, a business agreement. I accept the packet and never bother her again. Never speak of her own troubled child, hidden within this very house. 'You are to use towels,' she says. 'Or a blanket. To catch the blood.' She hesitates, then turns to the pantry. A moment later, she is back with a small green bottle embossed with a skull and crossbones. She hands it over, averting her eyes from mine, then wipes her hands on her skirt as if she is glad to be rid of it. 'In the event it does not work,' she says.

The sky is angry black as I walk away from the village. One or two women pass, keeping their heads low as if they know, as if the devil inside is etched on my face. The clouds spit rain and there is a hole in the side of my shoe where the stitching has come loose. I need to get back before I am well and truly drenched. William will be wanting me; he will be calling for me by now. He thinks I have gone to the farm to beg for work and he will be watching the track, waiting for my return, wondering what has taken me all this time.

But, as I reach the mountain road, I turn back. There is something else I need to do, need to see: a grave behind the church sitting all alone, the grass around it left to grow tall, moss already blighting the lettering. A grave I have not visited for many months now. I take the little footpath around the side of the church, thinking of happier times, of Morgan, of our love.

I rub the grave with my sleeve as rain trickles across my cheeks, clearing away the worst of the moss. I think of Ma silent and pale as the years went by and wonder what he did to her. Only Ma would understand, I think, tracing her name with my finger. Only she would know I had no choice.

55

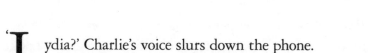

'Lydia?' Charlie's voice slurs down the phone.

She feels herself well with relief. 'Charlie? I've been trying to get hold of you for ages. Or rather, I've been trying to get hold of Kyle. The signal keeps dipping. Is he there?'

'Hang on a sec. We're in the pub. I'll pass you over.'

Lydia leans against the wall of the top-floor room – the room with Edward Jeffreys' paintings. 'Kyle?'

'Hello?'

The line crackles. She runs to the other side of the room, chasing the reception, knocking a pile of canvases with her foot. She can't lose him. She can't lose Kyle this time. Paintings cascade like dominoes across the floor. There's one she's never seen before. A glow of orange against a black background. Immediately, she knows what it is. He'd seen it too: Edward Jeffreys had seen the lantern light.

'Liddy? Are you all right? I'm sorry, I lost my phone. I wanted to ring, but I couldn't. I was hoping you'd eventually ring Charlie.'

More crackling. 'Someone came to the house. There was a light shining into the kitchen. Only, there was no one there.'

'What?'

'A lantern. It was hovering.'

'Hovering?'

'I know it sounds stupid. I know, I know. Logically, there *must* have been someone there. But I couldn't see anyone. It was dark. Almost nighttime.'

'It must have been Emlyn.'

'But why didn't he knock on the door? And why so late at night?'

'I don't know.' Kyle sounds distracted. 'But you know what he's like. Probably some sort of game.' She can hear noises around him, people talking, laughing, clinking glasses. 'Look, Liddy. I can't get back. The roads are closed. I wanted to come back. After our phone call the other night,' his voice falters, someone shouts in the background, she hears Charlie announcing another round, 'I desperately wanted to see you, to apologise. But then I lost my phone and the snow fell. There's something I need to tell you. Something important . . . '

His voice is swallowed in the hiss of the lost reception. She tries phoning him back, but the line is dead. Instead, she stares at the painting of the light, thinking of Edward Jeffreys, thinking of all the other people who've ever lived here, who didn't stay long. How many lives has this place destroyed? Awkwardly, holding Jamie in one hand, she pulls the first painting from the toppled stack. The painting beneath is of a woman. A woman with her head bent, her dark hair, streaked with gold, obscuring her face, her forehead pricked with blood. The woman from her dreams. Has she seen this painting before, buried it deep in her subconscious? Or had Edward Jeffreys dreamed the same thing she had? She turns it over, sending it clattering face down on the floorboards.

Later in bed, she hardly sleeps. Jamie's lying next to her rather than in his cot, and Martha's buried deep beneath the duvet. At one point she gets up, rummages through an old crafting box she's stored in the wardrobe, finds a stainless-steel carving tool with a pointed end. Good enough for a weapon if she needs one. She puts it on the bedside table and gets back into bed. But she doesn't feel any safer and she can't get warm; she's too scared to dream, too scared to stay awake. Instead, she tosses between the two. Fragments of dreams that mean nothing: the staircase, the fan in the upstairs washroom, the woman in the painting. Just as she feels herself drifting deeper, a sound drills through her thoughts.

She awakes fully, pulse racing, alert to the rustle of the duvet and the wind whistling down the bedroom chimney and the soft sound of Jamie breathing next to her. Had she imagined that other noise? She stills her own breath as she listens again. This time she hears it clearly: the sound of the landline ringing from the kitchen. She flings back the duvet and runs downstairs, through the lounge, into the kitchen, flicking the light switch on as she goes, only then remembering that the bulb has blown. She fumbles for the landline in the dark and lifts the handset.

'Kyle?'

'Hello, is that Lydia?' It's a girl's voice, not Kyle's. She almost cries with disappointment, and then with relief. Another person. In all this loneliness, another person!

'Yes. Who's calling?'

'Jenny.'

'Jenny?' A second to remember: Jenny, the café, the number scribbled on the serviette. The time glows above the dial pad: 3.00 a.m.

'You told me to phone, right?'

'Yes. It's just, I wasn't expecting—' She has an image of the girl in the coffee shop, her wet hair, her fingers drumming the table.

'I've been thinking,' Jenny says, as if they're continuing a conversation they've just been having. As though this isn't the middle of the night. There's a pause, the line crackles. Please God, don't let the line go again. 'There's something I didn't tell you about the mountain. About Markey.'

'Yes?' Another pause. She hears something else, but this time coming from nearby, just outside the kitchen window. A slow solid tapping sound. Her grip tightens on the receiver. 'Jenny . . . Jenny . . . are you still there?'

'Yes, I'm still here.' Another pause. 'He changed, that's all. After the holiday, something changed in him. And I don't know why, but I knew it was something to do with the cottage.' Jenny audibly blows her nose. 'Markey was always nice. A regular bloke. Used to take me out to the cinema, buy me flowers on my birthday, that sort of thing. But, after the holiday, when I started getting the nightmares, he changed.'

'Changed? How?'

'He was more demanding. He had this look in his eye like he wouldn't stop until he got what he wanted. We started having arguments, terrible arguments, said all sorts of things. Then he started getting violent. There were one or two times . . . ' Jenny blows her nose again.

'He hit you?'

'Let's just say, he got more demanding than he should have done. That's when we broke up.'

'I see.'

'No, you don't.' Jenny sounds determined. 'You don't see at all. It wasn't the violence, though that was bad enough. It was the nightmares. They were getting worse. It was like *he* was making them worse. I couldn't cope. One day he'd be nice, saying I needed help and should go see a doctor. The next day he'd be making a big joke about it all, calling me names, making me feel stupid. It was like there were two sides of him. Like someone was inside his head, flicking a switch.'

'But why did you think it was something to do with the cottage?'

'In my dreams, there was this other man. The man in the photograph. Sometimes it was Markey. Sometimes it was the man. Sometimes it was both. Like the two men were becoming the same person. And although nothing actually happened in the dreams, there was always this terrifying sense of evil.'

Kyle holding the skeleton of the crow. Kyle on the floor picking up the glass. Kyle accusing her of wanting to lose the baby. 'Go on.'

'That's it, really. I just thought you should know. You said you have a husband.'

'He's not here. He's gone to London. It's just me and the baby and the dog. There's no one else.' The wind batters the window, the sound muffled and distorted through the cupboard door. She's aware of how cold she is, her feet numb on the stone paving.

'You should get away,' says Jenny. 'That's why I phoned. I've been thinking about it all night. I couldn't sleep. You brought it back. I thought I'd got over it, but I haven't. You have to get away before it's too late. Before he makes things worse.'

'He? *He?*' The sound outside seems louder, more a thud than a tapping. 'Jenny, please, what do you mean by worse?'

But the line's already gone dead.

56

I swallow the pills with a glass of water, tiny spherical balls like the ones in the chemist shop in town. I wonder where they came from, what shame Mrs Jones endured on my behalf to procure them. Placing the glass on the table, I knock over one of William's beer bottles and quickly upright it before the contents spill. My brother is sleeping, passed out in his chair, beer bottles at his feet, too drunk to bother with me. A small mercy in the light of things. One of these days, he will drink himself to death, and then I will live here alone, growing as wild as the mountain, living off the animals I can trap and the berries I can scavenge. I will become a myth like the black cat, a creature rather than a human being. They will talk about me in the village. They will warn their children not to come here. Morgan will count his blessings that he escaped. I press his handkerchief to my lips, breathing deeply. There is no trace of his scent, just a faint smell of starch.

I leave my brother where he is and climb up the ladder, waiting for *things to happen. I have everything prepared, a blanket beneath me, and a jug of water by my pillow. I wait, wondering how long it will take and what it will feel like. Will the thing slide from me easily or will I need to push it out? Should I be doing something to help it? I press down on my stomach, on the swell between my hips. For the first time in months, I find myself praying. Praying that the devil child will slip out of me quickly, painlessly.*

I am woken in the middle of the night. There is an ache in the pit of my stomach. I do not remember falling asleep, but I must have done: it is completely dark and there is a sense of the early hours.

I hold my breath until the pain comes again. A short sharp stab. It is happening, thank the Lord! I pray that it will not take long. That it will be over by the time William wakes up and demands his breakfast. Another pain, greater than before. I grit my teeth, preparing for the worst. The pain rises, rises, then subsides. Three more, then nothing. I check the blanket between my legs. Bone dry. I panic it is not working, but then the pain comes again, sharper than ever. I catch my breath in my teeth.

By the time my brother stirs, I am up, boiling water on the range. He regards me from his chair, stiff from having slept there all night, angry because he is stiff, throwing a tin mug in my direction. It falls harmlessly against the folds of my skirt. He tells me to get a move on; he wants his breakfast. The bull terrier darts between my feet, knowing his master is in one of his moods.

Breakfast on the table, I make my excuses: I have to empty his chamber pot.

'Hurry up,' he barks as if the job is a liberty.

Outside, the view is beautifully clear: the village, the river, the mountains. I drink in the chill air and it rattles in my lungs, setting me into a fit of coughing. Doubling over, I lay the chamber pot on the ground just in time. A thick phlegm rises in my throat and I grip my stomach. Am I imagining it? A small popping sensation, deep within? But no. Everything is still. Stubborn. No pains. No gush of blood. Complete calm, like a storm that has raged itself quiet. Tears prick the corners of my eyes as I stare down at the village, at the church, imagining the moss-covered gravestone behind, and wondering how things have come to this.

And then it comes again. A butterfly brushing its wings against my skin. I think of William inside, devouring his breakfast. I think of the unsoiled rags between my legs, the unused blanket, the pains that started but then vanished.

The butterfly beats its wings again.

And then I know. I know with the certainty of a mother.

The child inside me is moving.

57

Lydia's teeth won't stop chattering as she boils the kettle. She can't warm up. She can't think clearly. After Jenny's early morning phone call, she'd spent most of the night awake, listening to Jamie breathing and Martha chasing rabbits in her sleep. As she'd wrapped herself tighter in the duvet, the cold had crept inside her, a saturating cold that she couldn't shake off, that she *still* can't shake off, that seems nothing to do with the temperature, however chill, in the house.

She's already used the last of the teabags, so she pours plain boiling water into a mug and holds it steaming between her hands. Beneath the kitchen sink, there's an old plastic tub of medicine. Clutching the mug for warmth, she rummages through it, pulling out various creams and cough syrups and ancient-looking Ventolin inhalers until she finds what she's looking for: an out-of-date blister pack of paracetamol. She swallows a couple of pills, hoping to alleviate her pounding head, then sets about her chores: bringing Jamie downstairs, making a fire, heating his breakfast.

At one point, working in the semi-darkness, she accidentally knocks the tub of Jamie's powdered milk from the workstation onto the flagstones. She panics, dropping to the floor, rescuing what she can. It's then that she catches sight of the plinth at the bottom of the kitchen island. Is it her imagination or have the scratches edged beyond the marks she made? She sets the powdered milk tub upright, then runs her fingers along the grooves, following the lines several inches beyond her pen marks. Further up, there are more marks. Marks she's sure weren't there before, cut into the panel beneath the marble top. But it's difficult to see. With the kitchen window still blacked out by the boiler door, she's only the sunlight filtering through from the lounge. She remembers Kyle in the cottage, the torchlight shining into the box-bed, illuminating the marks in the old wood. Someone keeping score, that's what he'd joked. She'd not liked the look of those marks though she'd not understood why. Just like Jenny had said, she'd felt the evil.

But this isn't the time to start imagining things. She takes another mug of hot water into the lounge and throws more logs on the fire. Then she wraps herself around Martha. Jamie's watching TV, kicking his legs up and down in his bouncy chair, seeming completely unfazed by their situation.

Her headache settles to a dull throb. Her eyes ache from lack of sleep. She tries to get comfortable, tries to feel truly warm, but she can't. It's like the cold has settled inside her bones. Like she'll never feel warm again in her life.

The hours drag by. She takes Martha into the garden,

brings her back in again, nestles down once more on the sofa. She heats another can of soup for lunch, drinks more hot water, throws the last of the nappies in the bin and uses a towel instead. At one point, she dozes and awakes with a start. The television is buzzing white noise into the room, the picture transformed into a fuzzy image of black and white. She switches it off. All around her: deadening silence, broken only by Jamie sucking loudly on the soldier-doll, and Martha running from the lounge to the outside door, whining, pawing at the wood.

'No, Martha, no. Not yet. Not again!'

She switches on the radio in the kitchen, once or twice almost picking something up, a stray voice, the tinny sound of a vintage recording, *Silent night, holy night*, but mostly the vacant crackle of white noise.

She switches it off. The white noise is worse than the silence, the possibility of music and voices that might materialise but don't. She sips her boiled water, trying to think, trying to keep calm, talking to Jamie, singing nursery rhymes. When she can't hold on any longer, she goes upstairs to the bathroom to pee, hurriedly unbuttoning and buttoning her jeans, not wanting to leave Jamie alone for longer than she has to. She flushes, listening to the rumble of water through the pipes, eventually settling to a hush. Another sound cuts through the stillness. She screws off the bathroom tap and listens, heart in her mouth, wondering if she imagined it. It comes again: a regular thumping sound.

Someone's knocking on the outside door.

'I'm coming,' she shouts as she runs. The banging becomes louder, more distinct. Tears slide down her cheeks. Someone has come to find them, rescue them, take them away. Someone has taken the trouble to traipse through the snow, someone better equipped for the weather than herself. They aren't alone any more. She's never going to be alone ever again in her life. All these years, she's pretended she's okay, pretended all she needs is Kyle, but she's been kidding herself.

The knocking is insistent. Or rather, not knocking as she'd first imagined, but thudding. Not the door, but somewhere else.

'Don't go away,' she shouts, confused. 'I'm almost there.'

She runs to the outside door, past Jamie who's fallen asleep in his bouncy chair, past Martha growling. She slides back the bolts and turns the key in the lock.

Wind slices into the house. She sees snowflakes, white swirling against white, the garden shrubs, the overgrown lawn, the oil tank, the wall. Everything bedecked in a perfect equal crust of white. Gaspingly beautiful.

There's no one there. No footprints. No sign of another human being. And yet she knows she didn't imagine it. She steps outside, wraps her arms around herself for warmth, a gesture that immediately feels foolish and futile. And then it comes again. The same rhythmic thudding she heard when she spoke to Jenny last night on the phone. Only last night, it had seemed otherworldly, whereas now it's something real. Something solid.

It takes her a moment to locate the noise as she turns to the right, into the garden: the mantrap has slipped down the stake, and is gusting back and forth in the wind. Thud, thud, thud against the planks beneath.

Martha!

She gasps as something pushes between her legs: Martha hearing her name on the wind, wriggling to get through, darting into the snow.

'No, Martha!' she shouts as the house door slams behind her, locking her out, locking Jamie in. The mantrap thuds violently against the frame, straining to get free. 'Come back!'

58

*I*t is a bitter cold day and there are flakes of snow on the cobbles. William is in bed with a bad cold, hacking his guts out. I make him broth, fetch him cigarettes, empty his chamber pot. Eventually he sleeps. I walk into the yard, shaking off the foul air inside the cottage. The child inside me rolls over. I think William knows. He keeps away from me now, does not lay a finger on me except to beat me, as if I disgust him as much as he disgusts me. A soiled thing, like the rag he uses to wipe his nose.

From here the village is a blur, but if I stare hard enough, I can make out Morgan Lloyd's house in the middle of the row of cottages, the thin line of smoke from his chimney, his mam outside working the mangle, his siblings jumping rope in the street. In reality, the house is too far away to see any of these things, and it is too cold for anyone to be outside unless they have to be. But I like to imagine that I can really see them: Morgan in his Sunday best with a girl wearing a *wide-brimmed bonnet. A clean girl in clean clothes. Pretty blue eyes, long combed hair, a pink ribbon on the bonnet to match the sash at her waist. I see Morgan on one knee, asking her to marry him, and when she says yes, the pink ribbon flutters its assent.*

I find myself wanting it. Wanting and yet hating. A strange feeling, tugged back and forth. I want Morgan to be happy, but the old self is still there. The self that believed we were meant to be together.

I lift my gaze to the river. From here, it is just a grey snake winding behind the church, but I imagine the white crests breaking over the stones, and the way it gets deep in places. I remember paddling there as a child, the water reaching my knees, the mud squelching between my toes. I did not feel the cold back then. Sometimes, in the summer, I would watch the village boys swimming, their skinny bodies flashing like eels, their shrieks carried all the way to the cottages. Ma would pull me away when she caught me. Not proper to watch, she would say, scolding. But I used to love it. The boys were like fish, so free, so buoyant.

Looking at the river, I suddenly know what I need to do. The answer to my troubles is so clear, it amazes me.

I take a deep breath and return to the cottage. William is snoring as I take down the sewing kit and a pair of scissors. Heavy, rattling snores. I could run away, taking the main road if I wanted to, but in my condition, there is only one place I could go — the workhouse — and that is unthinkable. I unfold my best blanket from the ledge and smooth the rough wool over my knees. Ma's blanket. I dream I can still smell her: warm milk, soap, sweat. Somehow, it seems appropriate, using this.

I hold the blanket tight and start to cut.

59

Lydia runs to the front of the house, checking the windows, knowing already they're locked, there's no possible way through. She peers into the lounge, seeing Jamie still asleep in his bouncy chair, then runs to the door again and throws her weight at it, but it won't budge. The wind whips her cheeks and sends gusts of snow across the garden. A proper blizzard. Through it, she sees Martha, a black smudge, making her way over the drystone wall towards the summit. She screams, calling her back again, but the puppy doesn't turn. What the hell is driving her up there?

Martha, Martha, Martha.

She loses sight of her, her eyes pulled to the rocks above the tower. To the cottage. The landscape is brilliant white. Lethal. She has no choice. If she doesn't follow Martha, the puppy will be lost, sink into a snowdrift, die of exposure. She'll bring her down again, then find a way of breaking into the tower, breaking a window if necessary.

Jamie's asleep. He'll be okay. She'll only be a few minutes.

She runs through the garden, kicking snow with her trainers, feeling it seep into her socks. Near the wall is the old dog chain. She grabs it, knowing she'll need something to pull Martha down with, trying not to think how it could have got there. How it came to be lying so perfectly on the snow.

She climbs over the wall and lands in the snow on the other side, the fourth side of the rectangle. Her trainers sink into the thick drift, meeting the ice beneath and the thick twists of heather. Ice rather than bog – it won't be easy, but finally the fourth side is passable. She makes out Martha's pawprints, heading upwards, treading the surface, as she calls into the wind, 'Martha!' Her voice jumps back at her, an echo: *Martha, Martha, Martha.*

She calls again, 'Martha!' and starts to laugh, a spontaneous physical reaction, her stomach in spasm, her lungs spluttering. *Martha, Martha, Martha* in rhythm with the thudding mantrap behind her. But it's not her voice that echoes this time, it's someone else's. That man again.

'Martha!'

Martha, Martha, Martha.

'Martha!'

Martha, Martha, Martha.

They could go on like this for eternity, her and the man, as tears spill down her cheeks.

So numb. So cold. Head freeze like diving into a river.

Her mind begins to drift until she's in some other place, some other time.

*

After the Facebook friend request, she didn't hear from Matt Trevithick ever again. Days went by when she didn't think about him. She didn't dream about him, for a long time. That was the last of him, she thought. She finished university and graduated with a first. Life opened up for her, a book with unwritten pages. The day after graduation, she walked down the high street, through waves of shoppers and businesspeople, considering her future. Strong sunlight. Summer. Three summers since the abortion. She didn't think about that either. She'd found ways of not thinking, focusing on her future, compartmentalising her youth. That was before, this is now.

'Lydia?'

She turned. A stranger in dark glasses. Long black hair. A girl, the same age as herself, freckles, T-shirt emblazoned with Calvin Klein: Kess from her first university, from the life before.

'Kess? What are you doing here?'

'My parents moved down this way. Wow, you haven't changed at all.'

'Neither have you.' Except it wasn't quite true, Kess looked older, more self-assured. Every time she moved, a snake of bracelets jangled up her arm.

They sat in the garden of a café, making small talk. Five minutes in, the conversation dried up like the coffee rings on the table. Lydia realised she didn't know Kess any more, perhaps she'd never really known her; they'd been two people thrown together by circumstance.

'I love this weather,' she said for something to say.

'S'pose you heard about Matt?'

'Matt?' Everything changed: the sheen of the metal tables, the green of the grass, the red of Kess's lips. Brighter, starker.

'Shit. I presumed you'd know. Matt Trevithick, the lecturer?

You remember him? I think you took his art class. You fancied him for a bit. *Everyone* fancied him.'

'I didn't. I just—'

'He was killed in an accident.'

'*What?*'

'Ben Nevis, a year ago. In the snow. He lost his footing.'

The bracelets jangled up and down as Kess sipped her coffee. Lydia saw it all, saw it clearly: Matt showing off – the same arrogance that had led him to sending that Facebook request – taking a step nearer the edge than he should have done. The open-mouthed onlookers. The rocks beneath. The deadly snow.

'Shit, sorry.' Kess's cheeks coloured. 'I shouldn't have blurted it out like that.'

'Thank you for telling me. I had no idea.' She felt numb.

'I went to the funeral. It was horrible. The place was jammed with students. Everyone was crying. You should have seen his mum.'

'It sounds awful.'

'It was. God.' Kess shook her head as if trying to dislodge the memory. 'Anyway, tell me about your plans. What are you up to?'

They talked about the future, vague plans for their careers, then they said goodbye and hugged, muttering vacant promises to keep in touch. Lydia knew they wouldn't; after the revelation about Matt the conversation had been dragged out for the sake of it.

'He never got over you, by the way,' Kess said, hitching her bag over her shoulder.

'Who?' Her heart beat hard like the beat of the sun.

'Danny Chapman. I still see him sometimes. He looks kind of sad.'

'We don't keep in touch.'

'Well, maybe you should give him a call?' Kess laughed. 'Though what do I know? My love life's a disaster.'

Lydia watched Kess walk away then sat back down at the table, feeling as though her whole life had been uprooted and set on a different course. She googled the accident on her phone. A hiking expedition that had gone horribly wrong. Matt had plunged several hundred metres into ice and rock. A tragic end for a lecturer with a glistening future, who, last year, had run the London Marathon, who had raised thousands of pounds for Cancer Research, who, two years ago, at the age of thirty-two, had been promoted to reader, just short of professor. His parents were devastated, couldn't believe it, still expected him to walk in the room. His photograph, a Christmas Day shot with tinsel and a manufactured smile, somehow looked like a man who was going to die. She switched her phone to silent, put it in her pocket, and deliberately didn't think about Matt Trevithick again for years.

But she thinks about him now as she trudges through the snow, as she searches for Martha on the slopes, as the voice calls around her, encasing her: *Martha, Martha, Martha.* She thinks about Danny, how she never called him. She couldn't have called him, not after the way she'd treated him. But Kess didn't realise that. Kess didn't know anything about Matt or the baby. And she'd been too ashamed, too guilty to admit the truth. A guilt that had weighed on her for years, eaten into her, destroyed the confident, happy person she'd been. Turned her into a shadow, hiding behind her husband.

She tries to dispel the thoughts from her mind, tries to

bring herself back to where she is right now, on the mountain in Wales. She just needs to find the pawprints, find the puppy, rescue Jamie, bring them both back home to London. Not here. Home was never here.

She looks up, taking her eyes off the prints. Beyond the next field is the cottage, and in front of it, shining steadily, the light glowing warm and orange against the snow. A light that draws her and yet chills her at the same time.

Someone is waiting for her.

60

⬗

A week later, William is much worse. He has not been out of bed
for days, only to use the chamber pot, and he has barely eaten
a thing, though I have been tempting him with broth. It has gone to
his lungs, he tells me, pounding his chest.

'Then I will fetch the doctor.' I move away from the box-bed, knowing
we cannot afford it, but he grabs me by the arm and draws me back.
For a moment, we stare at each other in the bare candlelight, his green
eyes steady on mine. He will pull through, I think, feeling the strength
of his grip. He will be back to his old ways before the week is out.

'I do not want that little ferret around here. Go buy me beer.' His
breath is rancid on my face, and the beard he has grown in these last
few weeks is matted with the medicine I have tried to spoon him.

'Beer will not cure you.'

He spits into the sheets, too tired to argue, and scratches the scars on
his arm. 'Hurry up. I will not wait for ever.'

I make a point of changing my clothes – I must look respectable if I am to go to the village, I say – wearing the skirt I have carefully altered for the occasion. His child turns inside me as I pull on my shawl, pull on my bonnet, tie my scarf. My fingers stumble. I am nervous, excited, scared all at the same time. I look at the fireplace, the fire almost out for we have not the logs to stoke it up, his chair with the spindle back, the table still stained from the time with the gun. A bloodstain that will not fade, regardless of how many times I scrub it. Like a stain on my heart.

Could this really be it?

William hacks into the bedsheet and I stare at him through the doorway of the box-bed, the ragged up-down of his chest, his hair sticky and unwashed, his shirt damp with sweat, the familiar arch of his shoulders shuddering with each cough. Fleetingly, I feel pity. Despite everything that has happened, he is still my brother. But then I see the marks on the boards, scoring our sin, and I look down and see the burn marks on my hands where, in his rages, William has pressed his cigarette.

'Goodbye, brother.' Swiftly, I push the bottle of medicine into my pocket and replace it with the one Mrs Lloyd gave to me. The green bottle with the skull and crossbones. In the event it does not work, she'd said. Had she known? Had she known what I might need to do?

'Do not forget to take your medicine,' I say, tying my shawl. 'It is here on the table.'

I bend to fondle the dog, then close the door softly before crossing the yard. I have done it a million times, maybe more. But this time, the simple act of walking is entrenched with meaning. The things that have marked my life: the cobbles, the cottage, the view. I wait to hear the muted squawk of the chickens, the whisper of the trees behind the shed, the cry of a bird. Everything sharp, punctuated.

I think of the happy, sunny times with Ma. I think of helping her on washing day, flapping the clean sheets into the breeze, pretending they are clouds. I think of walking with her side by side to the church, daffodils in our bonnets at Easter, holly at Christmas, reminding us of where the story ends, with the crown of thorns.

Then, as swiftly, as lightly, as if I am doing nothing at all, I close the gate behind me and whisper to my brother, 'Goodbye.'

61

Lydia's cheeks sting. Her ears ache. Her head throbs with the cold.

Her mind wanders to Christmas Eve five years ago, her first Christmas with Kyle. He'd found her antidepressants, fallen from her washbag, dropped on the bathroom floor.

'These yours?' he'd said, waving them in front of her.

She'd been peeling potatoes in the kitchen for Christmas Day lunch, and she'd looked up with the knife in her hand. 'Yes.'

He'd smiled and chucked them in the bin, down with the potato scraps. Then he'd brought her into a hug, moved his mouth to hers, and she'd tasted the wine on his lips. 'You don't need them. You've got me now. You don't need pills.'

After that, she'd stopped listening to her relaxation CDs, dropped her yoga sessions. She'd tried to believe she just needed Kyle, just like he told her. She was happy with her new life.

She didn't need anything else. Didn't need her parents. Didn't need the new friends she was making at the studio, who invited her for drinks after work. Kyle always picked her up anyway, escorted her from A to B. He made it clear all she needed was him. Until she decided she wanted a baby, and then he'd told her she was obsessed by the idea. Looking back, he was right. She'd tracked her cycle, kept a log, fixated on doing everything right, scared she'd had her one chance and blown it.

Martha, Martha, Martha.

She brings herself back to the mountain, knowing she needs to concentrate despite the pain in her head. She's almost at the cottage. The snow is much thicker here than at the tower, up to her shins, up to her knees when she takes a wrong step. The pawprints weave in front of her, lighter than her own, not always clear. She sees the broken cottage roof, caved at one end; the shed with the traps; the red paint on the walls; the gate yawning open, and through it fresh pawprints. She stands just inside the gate, staring at the snow-covered cobbles, then she looks down at the tower, at the light shining through the kitchen window.

The light. Her heart races. The cupboard door must have fallen, and now the light can get through, and the mountain can get in. And Jamie's in there on his own.

'Martha!' Her voice cracks with desperation. The wind stings her eyes, her hair lashes against her cheeks. She's trembling with cold, her jeans and jumper soaked through, her fingers painfully numb. She fumbles in her pocket for her phone, presses the power button, hoping, praying. A miracle of light. She scans the screen – battery low but working – and flicks to torch mode.

The pawprints lead both to the cottage and the shed, back

and forth as if Martha has been called in different directions. She checks the cottage first. Snow has inched inside where the wind has blown it. The chair has been knocked to the floor and there's a palpable air of oppression. She reaches for the box-bed, shines the light into the corners, revealing the skeleton on the headboard. A feeling of dread creeps up her spine, filling every inch of her. Just as Jenny said: this place is evil. She turns around and, for a split second, she sees a wooden table, a crock of vegetables, a bloodstain marring the surface exactly like the one on the kitchen island, filling the cottage with a deep metallic tang. But it's just an illusion. A moment later, there's nothing there beyond the chair and the bed and the cupboard, and the dark, earthy smell of decay.

She runs out again, out into the snow, into the clouded sunlight foretelling more bad weather, towards the shed with its shiny new padlock. Except the padlock is gleaming on the ground and the chain is hanging loose. She raises her phone, pushes the door wide, heart thumping, spasms of pain across her chest, the dog chain wrapped tightly around her arm.

The door creaks, but there's another, louder noise on the other side. A high-pitched moaning. She flashes the torch.

Martha, Martha, Martha.

The voice encases her. She breathes audibly, gulping the air, telling herself it's all in her imagination, that there's nothing there. The torchlight lands on the puppy, oddly outstretched, eyes reflecting back at her. Eyes full of fear.

'Oh my God, Martha.' She runs forwards, sweeping the torch along the puppy's body. Her back leg, the right one, is caught in a trap and her whole body is shaking. She drops the dog chain, and pulls at the metal with her hands. Martha snarls, snapping back, puppy-teeth biting into her arm.

'I'm trying to help you,' she cries, tasting tears in her mouth, wiping the hair from her forehead with her arm. She tries again, feeling the warmth of blood on her fingers. She flashes the torch into the corners of the room, looking for something that might help. There's a ping from her phone, a warning that her battery is about to expire.

Darkness.

She turns to the doorway, to the one source of natural light.

A man is silhouetted against the snow. A man she's never seen before except in a photograph. Except this time, he's real. Not a faded image. Not just a blurred possibility. Real legs; real feet that stand firmly on the ground; eyes lit up, iridescent. Fear shivers up and down her body. She catches the taste of his cigarette in the back of her throat as he walks towards her, swinging his lantern, the warm glow of orange light illuminating the walls and the traps hanging above her. So confident of his catch. So certain.

'Martha.' His voice is deep, resonant, and there's something about him that's eerily familiar. And then she remembers, she *has* seen him before. The man waving at her the first time they'd seen the tower. Although she hadn't seen him clearly then, she knows, *knows*.

She screams, somehow finding her feet. A moment of hesitation. She can't leave the puppy, but she can't stay here either. If she stays here, they'll both die. She gropes for the chain and hurls it at the man. It falls on the floor, a clatter of metal links, enough to distract him. She runs, darting beneath his shadow, hearing the lantern fall and roll on the floor behind her, casting a light that flickers and then dies.

Out into the blizzard. Stumbling. Gasping. More snow in her eyes. She can barely see. Snow up to her knees when she steps to the left. Where is it? The wall? The gate? The cottage? She turns, disorientated, ploughing forwards, onto the footpath towards the farm. Safer here than through the fields. But she feels the presence of the man behind her, his stride lengthening, his lantern relit. The strange ghostly glow of it over the snow. Something glistens ahead of her: water bubbling between rocks. The stream. The place where Kyle is building his weir. This isn't the footpath at all. She's going the wrong way.

She thinks of Jamie in the house alone. The puppy bleeding to death in the trap. *I'm going to look after you*, Kyle had said that first Christmas together, *you can't do this on your own. You need me.* And then closer, quieter, in the dead of night, *You're mine now, aren't you?*

She falls, tumbling down a hidden dip, dropping her phone. Images flash through her mind: Matt plummeting off the mountain, backpack flying through the air, unable to see clearly because of the snow. Kyle at the hospital when Jamie was born, so proud of her, so proud of the two of them. *His clan.* Her mum on the phone, asking what's wrong, gently persuading her to visit. The falling seems to go on for ever. The last few years replayed over and over.

She lands, sore, bruised, but alive. Whatever happens now, there's only one thing that matters: Jamie. She has to get back for him. She pushes herself up, stumbling against the stone that broke her descent, brushing the snow from the side of it. It's different from the rest on the mountain, somehow more upright, and there's a name chiselled roughly at the top. A name she knew she would find one day on Mynydd Gwyn.

MARTHA

She takes another few steps forwards, around the stone, heading downwards. There's a grating sound, metal against metal as an ancient mechanism, deep in the undergrowth, catapults into action. Pain grasps her foot, screeches up her right leg. She looks down through debilitating waves of agony: a spring, a semicircle of iron, fat metal teeth she can't shake off. Unable to move. Unable to pull away. Flashes of the kitchen at Sunny Hill, the rose-pink walls of their old flat in London, the painted breeze blocks of her university room. Bile floods her mouth, then darkness.

62

Kyle grips the edge of the polystyrene cup between his teeth. The coffee is scalding, but apart from water it's the only thing he's consumed since yesterday evening. His head throbs with another bad hangover, his eyes sting at the corners. But he needs to get home. He needs to get to Mynydd Gwyn. He hands over more money, buys a bacon sandwich. 'Do you know if the roads are blocked further up?'

The woman leans over the counter of her trailer, wipes her greasy hands down her apron. 'Where are you heading?' The Welsh lilt stirs something deep inside. Not just his memories but those of his grandfather.

'Gaer Fach.'

The woman laughs. 'You'll be lucky. The roads have been blocked that way since Wednesday.'

He turns to go, hugging his coffee, the taste of salty bacon on his lips.

'You take care now,' the woman calls after him. 'These roads can be death traps. Better to sit it out and wait until the snow thaws.'

'I can't,' he says simply, slopping coffee on his fingers. He thinks of J-J. His Mini-Me. The person he aches for.

Everything changed with J-J, didn't it? He'd thought he'd be jealous of his wife's distracted attention, but instead, right from the time J-J slid into the world, onto the white hospital towel, he'd felt something he'd never felt before: a love that was so intense it took his breath away. For a while, he'd been like any other new dad, so proud, so in love, unable to take his gaze away from the tiny bundle of pink flesh with the same shaped eyes as his own, that would one day be the same colour too. But it grew inside him, this *thing* that he couldn't explain, this overwhelming need to own his son, to own his wife. To control them both. Whereas other young dads showed their kids off to the world, he wanted just the opposite. He wanted to retreat, to take J-J and Liddy with him. *Us against them.* It unsettled him, this feeling, it kept him awake at night, twisting in his gut. He knew it was wrong and he tried his best to hide it from Liddy. He even tried to distance himself from J-J, knowing it couldn't lead to any good. It was the reason he started drinking heavily, agreeing to every night out Charlie suggested. The drinking was a mask. With a drink inside him, he could pretend to be normal. A normal happy dad. And when he drank too much, he was just a normal bastard like everyone else.

'Not even the emergency services can get through those roads,' says the woman. 'You'd be crazy even to try.'

'Maybe I am crazy.'

He feels her eyes on his back as he climbs into the hire car. *Mad English bugger.*

'Nadolig Llawen,' she calls after him.

But he merely raises his hand. He has an irrational desire to prove her wrong about the roads. He needs to get back to the tower, to be that other person. The person who drives him. The person he's strived to deny all his life. The person he knows he can't escape any more.

63

S he's floating away from the mountain, floating downwards, down a street towards the river. The winter sun is full in her face, snowflakes fleck her arms and stick to her hair. She shades her eyes and sees a newspaper headline: *Violent Scenes at Westminster; Suffragettes Arrested.* She sees an advertisement for Dunlop tyres; women with long skirts and baskets; a boy on a bicycle with wobbly handlebars.

The river is silent. It's a calm day despite the snow, nothing much stirs. She hovers, her attention shifting to the far bank where she sees a girl in a brown dress, a dress with pockets cut from an old blanket, standing at the water's edge. She recognises the river now, the one that runs behind the church, the River Teilo, and watches as the girl bends and fills the pockets with stones. The weight of them pulls at the waist of her skirt and she sees a flash of white blouse beneath the girl's patched-up jacket. The pockets sag but don't break. She's done a good job, good with her fingers. When she's finished filling them, the girl pulls something from her sleeve. A white handkerchief that flutters in the breeze.

This is the way it is, the girl says to her, without moving her lips. *This is my choice. They'll think I'm weak when in fact I'm strong. I left him the bottle. I hope he drinks. Or else. Or else . . .* She lifts the handkerchief to her face and holds it there as she wades into the water, unflinching despite the cold. The hem of the skirt swirls but only slightly, too weighed down by the stones to offer resistance. *Or else, it might never end.*

Deeper, deeper into the water. Lydia isn't sure, but she thinks the girl might be pregnant. Or is it just the shape of her clothes? Old-fashioned clothes from a century ago. She knows, more certainly, that this girl is Martha Helford, the name on the grave in the churchyard. Martha Helford who lived in the mountain cottage. Martha Helford who was loved by Morgan. Martha Helford whose grave she'd found on the mountain.

The water's up to Martha's waist but she still doesn't flinch, though it must be freezing. One last look towards the opposite bank, registering Lydia. Their eyes lock. *It wasn't meant to turn out like this, but I made my decision, I chose the better path.* Then she throws herself under like a giant fish, her body twisting in the icy water, her hands reaching upwards, her arms flailing. A moment of helpless defiance, then the water stills and closes over her, taking her secrets with it.

A white handkerchief drifts towards the place where Lydia is no longer hovering but standing firm-footed. When it lands on the bank, she picks it up and wrings it dry.

*

Something shifts. Her body feels heavy. She's aware of some-one leaning over her, pulling her upper half out of the snow. Something is thrown over her and she realises she must have been dreaming. She tastes the collar of a wax jacket against her lips and a nose nuzzles against her own. A moment later, she feels the wet warm lick of a dog. She turns expecting to see Martha, but instead sees a collie with a vacant eye.

'Dos i lawr, Blodwen!' Emlyn Jones stands over her, shotgun tucked beneath his arm. Despite the situation, despite the excruciating pain travelling upwards from her foot, she tenses, remembering the time with the paving slab. She knows she's trapped. There's no way out. Even if she could move, she doesn't have the strength to escape.

64

K yle stares at the road, or rather, the place where the road
should be. A mantle of unbroken whiteness. There's no
earthly way he can plough the car through that. He opens the
driver's side door and steps into the layby. Ahead of him, the
signpost to Gaer Fach is half-obscured by windswept snow,
but he knows it's there. Knows Gaer Fach lies just a little way
ahead. Knows the mountain road is only a couple of miles
from here at most. He imagines wading through the drifts,
crunching his way towards the farm, eventually taking the
track from the farm to the tower. He imagines the surprise on
Liddy's face when she opens the door. *See*, he laughs at her, *I'm
not as incompetent as you think.*

He takes a couple of steps forward, then stumbles down
some unseen dip beneath the snow, crunching his ankle. Pain
twists up his leg. Snowflakes flutter into his eyes, momentarily

blinding him. He groans and picks himself up, dusts the snow from his sodden jeans, then he takes a few steps forward. His ankle screams. He tries again, managing a metre or so before falling down another dip, his knees slamming into something hard beneath.

Enraged, he picks himself up again and turns back to the car. He knows it's impossible to drag himself to the tower like this. He can take the pain, but not the inability to fully weight-bear. He yanks open the door and thumps down into the driver's seat, then he glances up through the windscreen. There's that thing again, that shadow. Only, it's miles away, high up on the mountain, moving fast along the ridge. He laughs, knowing deep down it's impossible to see so clearly so far away, but believing it all the same.

He's not left Liddy and J-J alone after all.

65

Lydia clears her throat and tries to talk. Once, twice. Eventually, the words bubble out, a strange sort of whisper. 'My baby . . . the cottage . . . you. *You?* Why did you ruin my sculptures?'

Emlyn lays the gun in the snow, crouches beside her and moves her hair from her mouth. She knows he could end it all now if he chose, shoot her, or strangle her to death like he'd threatened to kill the puppy. Or perhaps he'll bide his time, leave her guessing, let her think she can escape before going in for the kill. She wonders whether he heard her and tries to speak again.

'Quiet,' he commands, and then softer, in a voice she's never heard him use before. 'You need to save your strength. If you're quiet and lie still, I'll tell you everything.'

She's confused and disorientated as he settles beneath her in the snow. She's half lying on his lap, on his sodden waterproofs. He strokes her forehead with his rough hands. 'I was trying to warn you off the mountain, but you wouldn't listen. You're too stubborn. Dad tried to warn you too. He carved the cross into the tower window and painted the words on the cottage. He planted the rowan trees, just like he planted rowan trees around the farm, and he made us say our prayers every night to ward off the evil. After Mum died, he became obsessed with the cottage, just like she did after the girl was killed.'

'The girl?' The pain makes it difficult to talk.

'Cerys. Griff's sister. The two of them were playing in the cottage but something went wrong. Griff ran away. He's never forgiven himself. Mum tried to find out the truth, but it changed her. They said it was cancer, but Dad knew different. This thing, this *evil*, was eating away inside her. After she died, Dad tried to make the place safe, finding the traps, locking them in the shed. But William was too strong for him despite the prayers, despite all the little rituals. Killed him too in the end. Dad was only trying to help. Dad was always only trying to help. The villagers keep away, but it's different for us. We have to live here.'

She struggles to follow him. 'The villagers know?'

'Enough not to come here.'

'But the traps. I thought they were yours.'

He shakes his head. 'They're his. William's. The man with the lantern.'

'But he's dead, isn't he?'

Emlyn says nothing, but the knowledge sits between them. She has so many questions. About the cottage, about Martha, about William, about what Emlyn's going to do to her now. But she's slipping again. She sees Emlyn talking into a mobile phone, talking in Welsh. The pain is too great even to attempt to follow it, even the odd English phrase makes no sense.

The snow glistens crimson. The sunlight dulls. She falls asleep, wakes up again. Someone shouts – a voice she recognises.

'Over here, boys!' It's Griff Davies wearing the same clothes he wears to the pub: a Welsh rugby shirt over dirty jeans. A hat is pulled low over his ears and a coat flaps as he raises his arms. 'Over here,' he shouts again, waving his arms.

Boots break through the snow. Radios crackle. A different man leans over her, a man she's never seen before in a fluorescent jacket. A paramedic. 'Lydia? Can you hear me?'

She tries to talk, but this time she can only whimper.

'All right, Lydia, we've got you. We'll have you warm again soon. We're just going to do some checks.'

Blankets. Movement. Griff Davis gasping, 'Bleeding fuck.'

Someone else, 'We've got to move her. Hand me the radio.'

'Jamie . . .' she struggles with her words.

'Quick, she's passing out again.'

She's muddled. Time is working in strange leaps. More people are bending over her. She sees Emlyn, Griff, Eleri; she sees the shock in their eyes. She hears Eleri trying to phone Kyle but unable to get through, and she wants to tell her he's lost his phone, only the words still won't come out. Everyone's panicking but trying to act calm. Is she dying? Is this the last look all people see? She tries to find the girl among the crowd, but then she remembers the girl's dead. Martha Helford's dead. She's seen her grave. She tries to talk to them again, to make them realise they're all in danger, that they need to get off the mountain before the man with the lantern finds them.

Darkness crowds the edges of her vision. 'Jamie,' she mutters, finding her voice. She's lightheaded and nauseous, but she needs them to know. She reaches up and tugs the paramedic's arm. 'He's in the house. I left him. My baby.' The tears chill her face.

'Don't worry, we'll get him.'

There's a jab in her arm momentarily distracting her from the other terrifying pain. She feels herself being lifted. She sees the man in the fluorescent jacket. She hears the crunch of boots on snow.

66

When she opens her eyes again, it's a different type of whiteness: a wall with cracked plaster, a line zigzagging through the white. It takes her a moment to realise where she is. She recognises the curtains, recognises the bed, the type with buttons that lift you up and down. *Hospital.* She tries to say the word out loud, but it won't form and there's a bitter taste at the back of her mouth. Instead, she tries to communicate with her eyes, locking them on to Kyle.

Kyle.

He leans across from the chair and squeezes her hand. She wants to get out of the bed, she wants to tell Kyle to take her out of here. But she's too weak to move and there's something else. Something about her husband that makes her uneasy. Wasn't there something she remembered on the mountain, something that started that first Christmas together? She stares at his familiar face, his beard trimmed for a change, but all she can recall is a vague sense of unease.

'I'll leave you two to it.' A woman's voice followed by the sound of a door clicking behind her. Kyle beams down at her like a kid with a bag of sweets.

'How long have I been here?' Her throat feels woollen and dry.

'A week.'

'A *week?*'

'You really scared me. I thought I'd lost you. You kept drifting in and out of consciousness.'

'Where's Jamie?' Her eyes dart around the room, expecting to find him.

'It's fine. *He's fine.* He's at your parents'.'

'My parents'?' She closes her eyes briefly, swallows hard – *Jamie's safe, he's in London, she needn't worry.* 'What happened?'

'You don't remember?'

'Not really. I remember the cottage and the snow. I remember Emlyn and Griff. I remember Eleri trying to phone you.'

'You fell in some sort of horrid mantrap. You almost lost your foot.'

Her eyes travel the length of the bed, relieved to see both feet planted firmly above the covers, the right one bulging in a brace. She notices other things too: the drip attached to the crook of her elbow, the blood pressure monitor on the other side of the bed, the bowl heaped with fruit.

'Will I be all right?'

'You'll be fine. You just need to be patient. You worried everyone for a time.' He ticks off on his fingers. 'Fractured fibula, osteomyelitis, hypothermia, dislocated shoulder, some weird fever the doctors are still arguing about. The thing you fell into, the mantrap,' he shifts his gaze to her foot in the brace, 'it was a hideous thing from the eighteenth century. Should have been in a museum, not lying about on the mountain. It was deep in the undergrowth where you slipped.'

A cold sweat prickles her forehead. She remembers that other mantrap in the garden. A warning. 'It was a memory.'

'What?'

'A memory of what happened there. A memory from a hundred years ago. The man who lived in the cottage, and his sister, Martha.' She swallows, her throat scratchy dry. 'I saw him, you know. I saw the man. And I've seen the girl, Martha, in my dreams. I think she's trapped there. I think she's trapped on the mountain for ever.'

'Shh.' He strokes her forehead. 'Don't stress yourself out. You need to keep calm. Get better. What happened was just an accident. I tried to get to you, you know? I was on my way back to the tower, but I couldn't get through because of the snow.'

He helps her to water from a straw, then waits until she closes her eyes, her mind already drifting, pulled by the drugs.

She's floating in a white cocoon, hemmed in by blankets and nurses in blue uniforms and drips that hurt her arm. But there's something else, something leaning over her, a pressure, oppressive, bearing down. She awakes in a sweat. Kyle's still there, picking at the ham in his sandwich.

'Hey, how you feeling?' he says when he realises she's awake.

'Better, I think.' She's remembering more now: being wheeled between wards, being dressed by people she doesn't know. She looks at her arm, at the tube leading into it, at the heaped bowl of apples and grapes on the table. 'Thanks for the fruit, but I don't think I could face it.'

'It's not from me. It's from that old lady in the village. Mari, I think her name is. Here, there's a card.' He hands her a cream envelope with her name on the front in spidery Biro. Inside, beneath the get-well wishes, there's a note.

There's something I should have told you. Fifty years ago, my daughter, Cerys, lost her life on Mynydd Gwyn. She fell into a trap, just like you did, but she wasn't as lucky, they didn't find her until it was too late. Griff doesn't like me to talk about it. He feels guilty because he was there. Because he didn't save her like he saved you. But now that he has, maybe things will be different.

She's still processing what this means when Kyle lowers his sandwich and takes her hand. 'I'm sorry,' he says. 'I haven't looked after you as well as I should have done, have I? I tried to get back to you, you've got to believe that, only things didn't work out. I twisted my ankle.' He glances down at his own leg. 'But things are going to be better from now on. When we go back to Gaer Fach—'

'The tower?' Alarm surges through her body. She tucks the note beneath the sheet. 'We can't go back there!'

'Not right away, no. Not until you're sufficiently recovered.'

'Not ever.'

Kyle strokes her fingers, looks at her with what seems like pity. 'You've had a shock. You're not thinking straight.'

'No!' She shakes her head. 'I'm not going back. I'm never stepping inside the house ever again. The tower, the mountain, the cottage – don't you see? – they're all connected. They're all haunted.' For a moment, she's there again, in the shed with the lantern light and the man blocking the way behind her. She swallows hard. Kyle told her, didn't he, when they first got together, that she needed him, that she was his to keep. Surely he's got to listen to her now? 'Ever since I stepped on the mountain, I knew it wasn't right. The locals know it too. Apart from the Joneses, they all keep away. That's why Griff acted the way he did, he was trying to scare us off the mountain. But we didn't listen. We didn't read the signals. I tried to believe it could be our home for your sake.'

Kyle rubs his cheeks, rubbing life into his pale skin. 'Not this again. I thought we'd been through all this already?' He picks up the sandwich, takes a bite. 'God, this is fucking awful.' He pulls back the thin white bread. 'No mayo.'

'Please,' she reaches out. 'Promise me we won't go back? I want to go home to London. I *need* to go home to London. I don't think I'll ever get better if you take me back to the mountain.'

He pushes the sandwich back into its plastic wrap. 'We'll talk about it later, okay? Right now, I need you to concentrate on resting and getting better.' He leans over and lifts the sleeve of her other arm, the arm not attached to the morphine drip. The skin is covered in small red marks, identical burns from her wrist to her elbow.

She gasps in horror. 'What's this? How—?'

'Don't you remember?' he says calmly.

'Remember what?'

'You did this to yourself. You found an old packet of cigarettes in the house. I found them on the kitchen island.' He lowers her sleeve. 'Don't you see? You're not well. You haven't been well for a long time. But don't worry. From now on, I'm taking control.'

She's moved from the private room to an orthopaedic ward, mostly older people with fractured femurs. The ward smells of overcooked food, talcum powder and shit, but she prefers it here, where she can see other people, hear other families chatting. The ache for Jamie is worse than the muted ache in her leg, but she knows it's impractical for Kyle to bring Jamie all the way from London. She just needs to be patient like he told her to be. The other occupants are nice to her, they seem to feel sorry for her, at least at first, but then the nightmares return. She tries to stay awake so they won't happen, counting spots on the curtains, listening to the nurses administering medication, and checking blood pressures, and helping patients on and off the commode. But inevitably exhaustion sweeps through her.

She dreams she's back on the mountain and the man with the lantern is searching for her. Sometimes he finds her cowering in the cottage. Other times, she finds herself falling down the slopes of Mynydd Gwyn. Other times still, she's back in Sunny Hill, crouched on the sofa with the duvet pulled over her head, Jamie cradled on her lap, listening to the wind creaking around the house, knowing that the danger is just outside, waiting to get them.

Every night, she wakes up screaming. The nurses take turns to calm her; they try to talk to her about it, try to get her to open up about the burns on her arm, but she just shakes her head. She hears one of the patients complaining, insisting Lydia be moved to another room. One night, she manages to stay awake until the morning. But the lack of sleep gives everything a surreal quality – the strip lights, the blue and white uniforms, the breakfast trolley – like lurching into a different sort of nightmare.

When Kyle arrives with his offering of sandwiches, she doesn't want to stop hugging him, but eventually she lets him sit down in the chair, and watches him talk, showing her pictures of Jamie on his phone, and telling her about the delayed Christmas he's going to give her.

'Please,' she says when he stands up to leave again. She holds on to his sleeve, looks him straight in the eye. 'I meant what I said about the tower. I'm not going back. I want to live in London. Or,' she laughs, 'anywhere. Anywhere but *there*.'

67

They rent a flat in Shoreditch. A friend of a friend of Charlie's needs lodgers while he backpacks around Thailand. Lydia likes the flat, it's modern and characterless: a stainless-steel kitchen, leather sofas, an enormous widescreen TV, art prints she doesn't care for. Not a flat to settle in, but a neutral space in which to recover, in which to wait while Sunny Hill sits on the market. 'No interest so far,' Kyle says when she asks a few weeks later, 'but it's early days. I guess it's more likely to sell in the summer.'

In Shoreditch, the New Year is in full swing. Between physiotherapy appointments and exercising the leg that refuses to heal, she sits at the window, watching the lights dazzling below her. She wants to go outside and lap up the optimism, drink champagne, get tipsy. But she isn't strong enough yet and they don't have the cash. Kyle is busy, desperately trying to make the money they need to pay the rent, taking on more contracts than he can handle. Most evenings, he sits in a corner of the lounge while she plays with Jamie, hunched over his keyboard, drinking tea rather than wine or beer. But at least he's there, a room away at most rather than two floors above. On his breaks, they sit on the leather sofas, taking turns with Jamie, or watching him on the sheepskin rug, grasping chunks of white wool as he crawls.

For the rest of the time, she has Martha. The little dog is making her own steady recovery, lolloping around the flat on her three good legs. Emlyn had found her just in time, saving her life if not her paw. Lydia's impressed by the puppy's resilience. She can run already, whereas Lydia's still limping. The flat seems taken up by her, her bowls and dog food, her toys and basket. A lasting link with the mountain, but one she doesn't mind: they'd been through this together and survived.

How are you doing?

Eleri's text arrives one day when she's scrolling through her phone. Jamie's fallen asleep on her chest and Kyle's busy working on his PC. For a moment, another world replaces the one outside. A world of snow and muck and waterproof clothing. She thinks of Emlyn and the farm, the Owain Glyn Dŵr, the smell of bleach and plastic in the shop. She knows Eleri feels guilty for leaving Lydia on the mountain in the snow. She's apologised to her several times already despite Lydia's insistence it was no one's fault.

Good thanks. On the mend. How's
things with you?

> Good. Kids were crazy over the holidays. Must
> come and see you sometime. The kids would
> love London.

For a second, she hesitates, glancing at Kyle, drinking his tea. Except for the time on the telephone, she's not confronted him about Eleri. But all that's over now.

She texts back: Yes do. We'd love to see you.

Eleri: Ok. May be in the spring?

The spring. Everything had been meant to happen in the spring, Kyle's generator system, the renovated studio, the decking in the garden. None of it will happen now. With the house on the market, it's an unspoken agreement: apart from to collect their things – she knows they'll have to eventually, they can't afford to pay someone else and she's fed up of wearing the same few clothes Kyle had grabbed while she was in hospital; besides, she needs her tools, her sculptures, her workbench – they'll never go back to the tower.

She switches her phone to silent, places Jamie quietly in his cot, and tries for the umpteenth time that day to sleep. But she knows she can't sleep without dreaming. Even in the daytime, the nightmares happen. The nights she spends tossing and turning, moving from one dream to another, scared she'll wake Kyle. Sometimes she moves herself into the lounge, spends the nights semi-conscious in front of the huge television, with the lights on.

Perhaps things would be better if she spoke to him again? All the things that happened between them at the house are still there, sloshing around her head. Kyle and Eleri. Kyle pushing her after she'd smashed the green bottle. Kyle accusing her of not wanting their child. In calmer moments, she knows it's nothing, just the house, the voice on the mountain speaking through Kyle. At other times, the panic sets in. A gnawing panic that sets her seeking his reassurance. *You do love me, don't you?* She knows one day she'll have to broach the subject. But not now. Not until she's strong enough.

'Shit, you look awful,' says Benedita one afternoon. It's early February, and everything's damp and grey outside. Kyle is out, doing their daily shop, and Lydia's spent the afternoon googling playgroups for Jamie. He's growing up so fast, becoming more aware of other people, and he needs to socialise.

'I bumped into Kyle,' Benedita frowns with concern. 'He told me to take you in hand.' Her eyes travel upwards from the ground: slippers, jogging bottoms, T-shirt, make-up-less face, messy hair. 'You need a hairdresser for a start. Highlights, I think. Come on.'

She wants to refuse but she doesn't. Stepping into the street, with Jamie in his buggy, she recalls something of her old self. A self that wouldn't have thought twice about going to get a haircut. She clutches her bag into her waist and tries to seem normal, even as pain twitches up her leg, even as she tries to bear weight equally on both feet. Benedita has already hailed a cab, and the pace of things makes her dizzy.

They visit a boutique studio off Oxford Circus, a place Lydia knows she can't really afford. But for once she's glad that someone else is making the decisions, that once again, like in the early days at the hospital, she doesn't have to think. As the hairdresser partitions her hair into foils, her thoughts dissolve. She no longer has to think about the house, about talking to Kyle, about setting things right. She simply has to sit.

'You look amazing,' Benedita says, returning three hours later with Jamie asleep in the buggy. Lydia stares in the mirror, turning her head one way then the other. She doesn't look like *her*. But perhaps that's good? Perhaps that's the whole point? She could be anyone with this new look. She could start afresh.

Benedita grins. 'Kyle will love it.'

The next day, despite a niggling headache from the bottle of wine she shared with Kyle the night before, she feels better. She sits in the sterile kitchen with Kyle, dissecting croissants and slurping coffee. Things feel good for a change. It's almost as if Wales never happened, like the arguments never happened, like everything that occurred had been a bad dream. She leaves Kyle to work and takes Jamie and Martha to the park, treating herself to a coffee from the kiosk. Martha lollops ahead, chasing something in the undergrowth, then changing direction, bounding towards a group of pigeons, dragging Lydia with her. The buggy jolts with the movement. Jamie laughs.

'Stop, Martha! You'll pull us both over.'

Coffee splashes on her hands. She laughs along with her son, spraying coffee on the path, allowing herself to be hauled into the chaos of flapping wings, forgetting about her leg. She feels like herself again. A moment of clarity, of contentment. She sits on a bench, clutching the paper cup, breathless from laughing, watching Jamie take it all in: the way the light moves between the trees, the toss of the leaves in the wind.

'It's beautiful, Jamie, isn't it?'

There are a couple of pings from her mobile phone: a line of kisses from Kyle followed by an email. She opens the email, suddenly deflated. It's Stanley Harris wanting an update. The money's there, waiting to be transferred into her account, she just needs to demonstrate real progress. Lydia swirls the dregs of her coffee. She's been thinking about work, meaning to get back to it, but making excuses: her sculptures and tools are still in Wales and she's still sick. But there's the matter of money. There's always the matter of money. Besides, today she feels different. Despite her leg and the headache from last night, she feels better. Today is the start of a new phase.

She responds:

Dear Mr Harris,

   I'm sorry about the delay. I had an accident but I'm better now. I can start working again, right away . . .

68

Kyle sits at the desk in the lounge in Shoreditch, staring at his PC and scratching his arm. He should be working, but he's not in the mood. Liddy's gone walking with J-J and Martha, and he's distracted, flicking through Google images of Mynydd Gwyn. He finds one of the cottage, a snapshot posted on a walking blog – the same one Liddy showed him before – and zooms in on the man in the doorway. *William Helford.*

He thinks how Liddy was obsessed with the cottage, obsessed with the man. He'd tried to tell her it was water on the lens, or the way the photograph had been developed, but he'd known all along he was kidding himself. Kidding her. There *is* something there. He's known it all this time. He'd *felt* it when he found that old trap, deep in the undergrowth near the stream – the one he carefully retrieved, and slung on the generator shed like a trophy. The same sort of trap that Liddy fell into.

He digs his fingernails into the skin above his elbow so hard it bleeds.

His grandfather had also suffered from eczema: he'd found the tubs of E45 in the medicine box, the inhalers too. It's like the tower had connected them in more ways than one. But it wasn't just the eczema. It was deeper than that. He remembers Benedita showing him the ancestry website. She'd been doing some research for Charlie's thirtieth birthday, signed up to the site and paid its premium fee. A few clicks and she had it: Kyle's great-great-grandmother was a lady called Gwenllian Morgan from the village of Gaer Fach in Snowdonia.

'Ring a bell?' Benedita had said, flicking through the database.

He'd frowned and bit into his apple. He'd never known he'd had a connection with Wales before, even less so Gaer Fach, other than his grandfather's house.

In 1914, Gwenllian married a man named William Helford in Cardiff, a man by whom she already had a four-year-old child. Then, when William was killed in the war, she married again.

'Any clearer?' Benedita had asked.

He'd sipped his coffee, his head fizzing, remembering the stuff Liddy had told him on the train, the photo she'd shown him. 'I'm not sure,' he'd said. 'But maybe, yes.'

Now, he stares at the man in the cottage doorway: his great-great-grandfather. The same bloodline, the same DNA. It's only the name that had changed. Helford had changed to Jeffreys when his great-grandfather – Gwenllion's son – had adopted his stepfather's name. And then *his* son, Kyle's grandfather, had researched his family history, discovered the connection to Wales, to Mynydd Gwyn, and moved there.

He zooms in further, adjusting the contrast. There's something in William's hand, not the one smoking the cigarette, but the other one, easily missed in the blur: a toy soldier.

He remembers playing with the soldiers in his grandfather's house, his grandfather sitting on the opposite side of the rug.

'You have to be prepared to kill,' his grandfather had told him as he'd knocked his soldiers down one by one. 'Protect what is yours whatever the cost.'

One soldier was different to the others, didn't fit with the set. It was larger and older, more like a doll, with tattered khaki clothing.

'My father gave me this,' his grandfather had said. 'It belonged to *his* father who was killed in the war. One day, when I'm dead, it will be yours.'

It hadn't meant much to Kyle at the time. Why would he want a mangy old toy? But now it makes sense, the way things are passed on and on and on . . .

He thinks of the people he knows, the ways in which they resemble their parents. How long does it take to imprint oneself on another? A lifetime? A few years? *A few months?* He remembers how his grandparents had looked after him when he was a baby, when his parents were sick. Long enough to make an impression. He'd always believed his grandfather had cut his mum off because she'd married a German, but what if it had been the other way round? What if it had been *she* who'd eventually broken the link, believing his grandfather – her father – had already had too much influence? That the men in her family were somehow bad?

But it had been too late by then anyway. The Jeffreys

trait – the *Helford* trait – had stuck: the belief he's somehow superior, the need to possess, to discipline his own. He's always felt it, but on the mountain, it was worse. Something about that place meant he couldn't hide any more. Hours would slip by when his other-self took over. Sometimes he remembered it. Sometimes he didn't. He wonders which is the real Kyle Stein. The one that wants a normal happy family, or the other one he doesn't completely understand?

The last night he'd spent in the tower, he'd woken to find he wasn't in bed but standing over it. Standing over it with the dog lead in his hand, the other man's shadow at his back, about to lash out. Lash out at Liddy to teach her a lesson. He'd almost done it. He'd been annoyed about her relationship with Eleri – *fraternising with the enemy* – and, for a moment, he'd been back on that rug, playing toy soldiers with his grandfather. His grandfather had looked him straight in the eye. Those bright green eyes he'd also inherited, but which seemed to have passed his mother by. *The dissenters need to be punished.*

Even now, he grimaces at the thought of Eleri standing in the hallway behind the shop, her husband and children sleeping soundly above them. He'd bumped into her in the pub in the days after the miscarriage when Liddy was sleeping, and bought her a few drinks. She'd scrawled down her number on a bit of paper, told him to phone if ever he was concerned about Liddy. Then, when she'd left to go home, he'd followed her, let himself in and put his hand down her jumper, just because he could, because it felt good seeing how far he could go, how easily he could destroy Eleri's perfect family.

He'd laughed when she'd slapped him, when she'd told him to keep the fuck away. Even then, he could have taken her if he'd really wanted to, he was stronger than Eleri after all. But he'd stepped away. Just like he could have struck Liddy with the chain, but he'd chosen not to. He remembers now what had stopped him: J-J in his cot, wriggling in his sleeping bag.

J-J. Oh God, he cradles his head in his hands, hating himself. *No, no, no.* He doesn't want all this for Jamie. This thing he carries. This burden. This trait. It's not a strength, it's a weakness. He remembers the notebooks in the cellar, his grandfather's lists, the name Jeffreys written repeatedly as if he'd been confused about who he really was. Who he really wanted to be. It's not too late to save J-J, is it? He won't go back to the tower. He won't step foot in Wales ever again. *Please God, don't let this happen to my son.*

And then, he hears that other voice, the stronger, more insistent one — the one he was only able to escape in the cellar, where he couldn't see the mountain, where he couldn't see the cottage, the cottage that had got so close it was like he could open the outside door and step right inside. *You know what you want, Kyle. What you've always wanted. It's within your reach. You can have it all. You can control them just like I did. You can control your family.* This *is strength.*

He pulls his hands away, sits up straight. He can't get distracted. He can't allow emotions to get in the way. He has to be the stronger version of himself. A Helford not a Stein. One day, J-J will understand. One day, J-J will be just like him. Even if he dies tomorrow in some freak accident, he's already made a lasting impression. *His Mini-Me.* He turns back to his computer, to the message just arrived in his inbox. Not his work emails, but the other account, the one he invented when they first moved to Wales, the name made up on the spur of the moment: Stanley Harris. Even now, he's not sure why he did it, except for the fact he'd liked the control, he'd liked watching

Liddy react to his every demand, even working with stone, which he knew she hated, covering his tracks by pretending he was worried. Had he sensed, even then, she was slipping away from him? Forging her own friendships, her own way of life?

He opens Liddy's message and begins his reply.

69

〜∞〜

Lydia sits in the passenger seat of the hire van, feeling
more and more unsettled as the countryside changes, the
mountains rising up on either side, the shadow of clouds drifting over. Sheep wander along the sides of the roads, occasionally
veering into their path, forcing Kyle to slam the brakes. Even in
the drizzle, the landscape is awe inspiring. At any other time, in
any other place, she'd be captivated. But not now, not here, so
close to Gaer Fach; as the roads become narrower and steeper,
she can't ignore the creeping sense of dread.

'Hey.' Kyle leans over from the driver's seat and pats her arm.
'What are you thinking about?'

'Oh,' she forces a smile and lies, 'just Jamie. I hope he's okay
with Mum. You know how clingy he is at the moment.'

Kyle grins. 'You're a typical mother. You never stop worrying.
It's only one night. We'll be back this time tomorrow. And you

know Stanley Harris wanted you to start on the work again straight away?'

She forces another smile, but really she feels sick at the thought of spending even a night in Y Twr Gwyn. *Y Twr Gwyn*, she always gives it its real name now; it was never really Sunny Hill. But it's not just the house. There's something else on her mind.

Yesterday, on her way out to Jamie's playgroup, she'd picked up the post from the mat: the usual bank statements and utility bills. Right at the back was a cream-coloured envelope. She'd been about to put it in the rack for reading later, when something had stopped her. Something about the envelope. More than that, the handwriting itself. *Her* handwriting spelling out the address: St Dyfrig's Care Home, Porth Colmen. Only the address had been slashed through with ink, and another hand, which she didn't recognise, had printed in capitals, RETURN TO SENDER.

She'd opened it – her own letter – afraid. The carefully folded page had slid neatly into her hands, and, on the back, she'd seen the grey-brown stain from the kitchen island. When she'd turned it over and opened it up, she'd seen her own neat handwriting. A single word repeated over and over:

Martha, Martha, Martha

She'd dropped the letter. How was it possible? How had a letter with no address, other than a care home in North Wales, found its way to the London flat? How was it that that word, *Martha*, appeared repeatedly? She'd remembered writing the letter, though it was something of a blur. She'd remembered sitting down at the kitchen island. She'd remembered the strange pull of the pen across the page. But she'd not remembered the words she'd written, only a dim recollection of folding the letter and putting it inside the envelope. As though someone else had taken possession of her hands. As though someone else had written it.

After that, she'd abandoned her plans to take Jamie to playgroup. She'd sat in the lounge, drinking coffee, her mind elsewhere: the kitchen at Y Twr Gwyn, the pen still in her hand, the letter written, ready to be stamped. The more she'd remembered, the more the space around her had seemed to shrink. Her breathing had become shallow, her vision had blurred. She'd thought of the burn marks still visible on her arm, the answerphone messages she'd been ignoring from the mental health nurse. She'd focused on Jamie, waving his rattle on his playmat, as she'd counted in her head, slowing her breath, using all the old tricks.

When Kyle had returned home, she'd begged him to return to Gaer Fach on his own – she was stressed and still unwell – but he'd flat-out refused. How was he to know what tools were important to her and what weren't? Besides, he wanted her company on the drive.

Now, she sits rigid in the hire van, unable to relax, unable to enjoy the scenery.

'Here we are,' says Kyle, pulling into the village, switching on the windscreen wipers. 'Bloody Welsh weather. Do you want to stop at the shop?'

The post office lights bloom into the empty street. She can see Eleri inside at the counter and part of her wants to go in, be welcomed, feel like she's been missed. It occurs to her that, in all these years since meeting Kyle, Eleri's the only real friend she's made. But already Kyle is unbuckling his seatbelt.

'You stay here. I'll pop in. Grab a couple of sandwiches and a bottle of wine.'

She nods, although she knows it should be her, she's Eleri's friend after all, but Kyle's already out of the van, and she's out of sorts. She watches through the windscreen instead: Eleri glancing up in surprise, somewhat nervous. She sees Kyle pointing at the van, Eleri frowning, and she wonders what they're saying, whether they're talking about her. *God*, when did she get so bloody paranoid? A moment later, Kyle's striding out of the shop and Eleri's running after him, shouting at the van, shouting at her, calling her name, 'Lydia!'

She's about to open the door, when Kyle jumps in and starts the engine. 'Ready for the tower?'

'But, Eleri. *What about Eleri?*'

'I said you'd catch up tomorrow.' Already, he's pulling away down the street, breaking the speed limit.

She doesn't know what to say, doesn't know what to think. She sits in silence, masking her confusion, masking the feeling she'll never be ready to return to the tower. Then she pulls herself together. She needs her equipment to work; she needs to be sensible. After all, she's got it all planned out. They'll pack this evening. Get going first thing tomorrow, pop into the post office to see Eleri. They'll breakfast on the way home, no need to stay in North Wales longer than they have to.

The mountain road is worse than she remembers. The potholes seem deeper, the road cracking in new places. She has a vision of the van getting stuck as Kyle swings it around the corners as if he can't wait to get there. The farm seems greyer and muckier: the tractor sports a flat tyre; the dogs who come barking are bedraggled and splattered with mud. The whole place shouts at them to turn around and get out.

'Nearly there,' says Kyle, ramming the van into first gear, turning onto the track.

Y Twr Gwyn looks unlived in even from a distance. More tiles have slipped from the roof. Patches of pebbledash have fallen away from the walls. A stray sheep bolts from the lawn as the van rattles to a halt outside. She looks up at the place she's been avoiding until now, knowing it's inevitable, that the more she avoids it, the bigger it will become in her mind. But the cottage is just a blur on the landscape. A dirty smudge.

'Got the keys?' says Kyle.

She fishes in the glove compartment, pulls out the bunch of keys she'd first seen Eleri use all those months ago, still with the faded leather tag, and hands them over. Kyle's house. Kyle can go first.

The door sticks for a moment before it opens. There's a smell of damp and disuse and unemptied bins. Kyle fishes for the light switch, but then she remembers the bulb in the kitchen's blown. She tells him to try the light in the lounge instead.

Still darkness, just the evening sunlight streaking through the rain.

'Shit,' Kyle knocks his forehead. 'They cut us off, didn't they?'

'What do you mean?'

'The bloody electricity company. We didn't pay the bill.'

The knowledge consumes her. The idea of a night in the tower in the dark, surrounded by the memories of what happened here. In the murky light, she sees a tin of soup open and unused on the worksurface. She sees a soiled nappy, the last one of Jamie's before she ran out and had to make do with an old towel, dumped beside the overfilled bin. Kyle had said he'd come in here to tidy up when she was in hospital, but there's no sign of any attempt to organise, to discard, to clean. Only the kitchen window has been cleared. No cupboard door. The blind removed. She wonders what happened, whether Kyle did all this. She turns to ask, but something else catches her eye. The marks on the kitchen island: they're everywhere, scoring the wooden panels, not an inch untouched.

'Oh my God.'

'What is it?'

He's by her side, his arm rubbing against hers. She points, unable to form the words, unable to express the horror.

'Rats,' he says, shrugging. 'The place is probably riddled.'

'I can't stay here.' She shakes her head. She's desperate. She *won't* stay here. She'd rather sleep in the van on the side of the road. 'Let's take a hotel room. Or drive back tonight. We could do that, couldn't we? We could pack all the stuff and be gone in a couple of hours.'

'You mean, *I* could pack all the stuff. *I* could drive back to London.' He looks pointedly at her foot, and she knows he's right. It's not fair to ask. 'Look,' he reaches for her hand, squeezes it hard. 'I don't know about you, but I'm knackered. That was a hell of a long drive. Let's eat and drink the wine and go to bed. We can get up early. We can do all this in daylight.'

'No!' She releases his hand. 'I can't. I can't stay here. You don't know what it was like when you were gone. It was,' she hunts for the word, fixes her gaze on the kitchen island, at the blood-red stain, '*horrible.*'

'But I'm here now, aren't I? I'm not going anywhere. Relax. You're not alone any more.'

They go to bed early. There isn't much more they can do in the dark, and they've burned the only candle they can find. She hopes she'll fall asleep straight away, but instead, she lies awake, staring into the darkness. The sheets smell of damp and cling to her body. She wants to throw them off, but even with Kyle lying next to her, she's unbearably cold. He's snoring loudly, obliterating the sound of the wind outside. She wants to wake him up again, she wants to talk, but she remembers the long drive he has to do in the morning. She closes her eyes and prays she'll eventually stop trembling, that the exhaustion she feels will soon sweep through her body. Next to her, on the bedside table, is the carving tool with the pointed end taken from her crafting box the last time she was here. The memory of it being there comforts her a little and finally allows her to sleep.

She awakes with a jolt.

It's dark, midnight dark. The wind is throwing a gale outside and somewhere in the house, a door buffets back and forth. There's a depth to the darkness, layer upon layer, as if she could peel it back, reveal the tower's secrets. Something else is here. Someone else is in the house with them. She can smell it. She can smell the cigarette. She slides out of bed, grabs her coat from the floor, grabs the carving tool, and creeps towards the door.

The feeling is even more intense in the stairwell. They're not alone. Someone's watching her. The vicar was wrong. It's not just the mountain that's unsafe. That thing, that malevolent presence, is here in the tower. Right here in the stairwell.

The feeling encases her. A feeling of oppression, of hatred, of pure evil. She hears the door banging downstairs, the fans whirring in every bathroom, the mantrap still hanging on the frame outside, thudding against the planks. She thinks of the cracks, the slipping tiles. The mountain getting in whatever way it can. She has a feeling she'll never escape this thing, whatever it is, wherever she goes, and then she sees the image in her mind again: the woman with the long hair and the blood-splattered forehead. Only this time, the woman raises her gaze, and her blonde-streaked hair slips back from her face, and she sees her fully, sees who it is, who Edward Jeffreys captured in his paintings.

Not Martha Helford, but her. He saw *her*.

She looks down into the dark depths of the stairwell and realises she's clutching something else in her other hand. She must have carried it here from the bed, she must have clutched it as she'd pulled on her coat, pushed it through the sleeves, and somehow not noticed until now: the toy soldier. She can feel its bulbous head, it's ragged clothing, the shape of its legs. It's *definitely* the soldier. Only this time – her fingers stumble in the dark trying to work it out – it has no feet.

Footsteps behind her. A door creaking open.

She drops the doll and turns, expecting the worst, expecting to see the man from the mountain, his green eyes seeking her out like lanterns. But then she realises by the tread of his feet and the sound he makes when he clears his throat, it's Kyle, *only* Kyle, come to see if she's okay.

She laughs with relief as she finds her husband, welcoming his arms around her waist, the feel of his beard prickling her neck, but there's something wrong, like the pieces of a jigsaw puzzle flying into place, the complete picture cracked and distorted. The wind howls. The mantrap thuds louder and louder in the garden.

'It's you,' she says, turning in Kyle's arms, her voice just a whisper. She thinks of Jamie miles away in London as she grips the pointed tool in her hand, feeling it's smooth length. The only thing that matters is to keep Jamie safe, to protect him in whatever way she can. It's not too late. She raises the tool so that it's almost touching Kyle's neck. It won't take much. A short sharp jab.

'What's wrong?' he asks, a tremor in his voice as if he senses what she's about to do.

'Nothing.' She laughs. *He thinks I'm weak, but in fact I'm strong.* 'It's just, I thought you were someone else.'

ACKNOWLEDGEMENTS

This book has been many years in the writing. In 2019 an early draft was shortlisted for the Lucy Cavendish Fiction Prize and I remain grateful for the support and friendship of the wonderful Lucy Cavendish community. Many thanks to the early readers and editors who gave me feedback during this time. Although I put the book to bed for several years after that, the tower on the remote Welsh mountain never truly left me. I returned to *Hear Him Calling* in November 2022, completely rewriting it, and exorcising a few ghosts of my own in the process.

This book is entirely fictional, but I have drawn on my own experience of living in Wales and my love of the Welsh countryside in writing it. A couple of names are drawn from real life: my lovely friend, Alison Seymour, who bears no resemblance to the Alison Seymour in this book but who asked to be named within it, and the Yorkshire Terrier, Pwtsyn or Pwtsin, who I knew in the 1990s, and who was the inspiration behind the fictional Pwtsyn, Eleri and Jon's dog (thank you, Clive).

I am very lucky to be supported in my writing by two amazing Welsh women. My heartfelt thanks goes to my agent,

Cathryn Summerhayes, who makes dreams come true for a living, and my editor, Rosanna Forte, who has such a brilliant editorial eye – this book is so much better because of it. Dioch yn fawr i chi.

Although I was born in Wales, and have lived in Wales for most of my life, my Welsh is sketchy at best. Many thanks to the legend that is Nina Cogger for correcting my attempts at the language. Who knew that North Walians and South Walians have a different name for milk? Many thanks also to Theo Wickenden who answered my questions about sculpting, and my physiotherapy colleagues at Cardiff University who talked to me about fractured fibulas.

This book wouldn't have been possible without the dedicated and hard-working teams at Curtis Brown and Sphere books. Thank you all! Also thanks to my copyeditor, Howard Watson, for fixing my commas and spotting inconsistencies.

My writing group continues to be a daily support for all things book- and life-related. Joanne Clague, Sarah Daniels, Asha Hick and Emma Clark Lam, where would I be without you and your wonderful stories? My sister, Heather Reagon, has read multiple drafts of this book – thank you so much and good luck with your own brilliant novels. My parents, Sue and Darrol, have always believed in me as a writer – thank you for all your love and encouragement over the years.

Finally, thanks to my husband, Steve, for diligently selecting the right mug for the right drink for the right occasion – it really is essential to the creative process. Thanks for all the other amazing non-mug-related things you do too. And thanks to my children, Wilf, Ebah and Taliesin, for your endless patience – first and foremost, I write for you, to prove it really is possible to follow your dreams.